THE SHADOWED
PATH

GAIL Z. MARTIN

A Jonmarc Vahanian
Collection

THE SHADOWED PATH

GAIL Z. MARTIN

A JONMARC VAHANIAN COLLECTION

WITHDRAWN

SOLARIS

First published 2016 by Solaris
an imprint of Rebellion Publishing Ltd,
Riverside House, Osney Mead,
Oxford, OX2 0ES, UK

www.solarisbooks.com

UK ISBN 978 1 78108 438 0
US ISBN 978 1 78108 439 7

Cover by Michael Komarck

10 9 8 7 6 5 4 3 2 1

A CIP catalogue record for this book is available from the
British Library.

Designed & typeset by Rebellion Publishing

Printed in Denmark

CONTENTS

INTRODUCTION

WE FIRST MEET Jonmarc Vahanian in *The Summoner*, the first book in my Chronicles of the Necromancer series. Jonmarc is the experienced, bitter mercenary who reluctantly agrees to guide an exiled prince and his companions to safety. Over the course of the four books in the Chronicles series and the two books in the Fallen Kings Cycle, Jonmarc grows into a very significant character, second only to Tris Drayke, the series' protagonist. Along the way, readers see glimpses of his past and get hints about his background, but never his whole story.

Jonmarc turned out to be a favorite character for readers, who wanted to know how he became the man we meet in *The Summoner*. I decided to write a series of sequential short stories—ultimately serialized novels—that tell Jonmarc's backstory. This anthology is the first ten of those short stories—plus a bonus, previously unpublished eleventh story—that reveal the first phase of Jonmarc's growth from a blacksmith's son to becoming one of the greatest warriors in the history of the Winter Kingdoms.

If you haven't read the novels, it's fine to start here. You'll see a lot of people and places again in the books, usually from a different perspective. Consider these stories to be a prequel to *The Summoner*.

Readers of the Chronicles series and the Fallen Kings books will recognize a number of familiar characters, met here ten years or more before we encounter them in *The Summoner*. Many things that were hinted at in the novels are fleshed out in these stories. Readers who paid close attention in the novels will recognize watershed moments in Jonmarc's life, and may have a sense of fate or déjà vu as he moves, step by step, along the Shadowed Path that takes him to his destiny.

Soldier. Fight slave. Smuggler. Warrior. Brigand lord. If you've met Jonmarc Vahanian in the Chronicles of the Necromancer and Fallen Kings Cycle books, you don't really know him until you walk in his footsteps. This is the first segment of his journey.

Raider's Curse

"Do you think it's true? About the raiders? Conrad said the fishermen spotted a strange ship, out beyond the bay." Jonmarc Vahanian set down the bucket of water he had drawn from the well. The small house was warm from the fire in the hearth, and the smells of mutton stew and freshly baked bread filled the air.

His mother, Dalia, sat at the table slicing vegetables. Along one wall sat a large loom, a spinning wheel, and skeins of the dyed yarn Dalia used in her craft. A half-carded heap of wool lay in a pile to be combed. The house was unusually quiet, since all three of Jonmarc's younger brothers had been sent to feed the chickens and tend the sheep.

Dalia repressed a shiver at his question. "Mother and Childe! Don't say such things. I hope not," she replied, and made the sign of the Lady in warding. "We haven't had raiders in these parts for years, not since King Bricen sent his ships after them."

"The king's ships moved on a long time ago," Jonmarc said. "If we know it, perhaps the raiders know it, too."

Dalia slipped a strand of her dark hair behind one ear, and her chopping sped up. "I don't want to speak of it. The fishermen watch the waters. The rest of the men watch the forest. And the women pray to the Lady. We'll be all right." She looked up and managed a smile at her eldest son.

"Go call your brothers and then go down to the forge and tell your father that dinner's almost ready so he has time to wash up." Her face was flushed from the heat of the fire, although the night outside was cool.

"I'm on my way," Jonmarc said and ducked out of the doorway.

Hens pecked at the bare ground near the house, and behind him, in the fenced yard, he could hear the sheep and goats. The night was cool and clear, but smoke from the forge's coal fire hung in the air.

His brothers, Neil, Piers, and Marty, were out in the small yard that separated the house from the barn and the forge. Neil, two years younger than Jonmarc and half a head shorter, was splitting wood. Piers, three years younger than Neil, was feeding the sheep, while four year-old Marty traipsed behind him.

"Finish up and get inside," Jonmarc called. "Dinner's nearly ready."

Neil stood up and stuck the blade of his axe on the chopping block. He wiped his brow with his sleeve. "Good thing. I'm hungry."

Piers and Marty were being mobbed by sheep eager for their own meal. "Did you hear me?" Jonmarc shouted.

Piers dumped the last of the feed into the trough and then lifted Marty onto his shoulder to get him away from the jostling herd. He glanced in Jonmarc's direction. "We heard you. We'll be there."

"Did mother know anything about raiders?" Neil asked in a voice pitched so the younger boys did not hear.

Jonmarc shook his head. "No—or at least nothing she'd say aloud. I think it spooked her when I mentioned it. Best not to bring it up at dinner."

Neil nodded. "What if it's true?"

Jonmarc let out a long breath. "Then we're in for a lot of trouble. Keep your axe sharpened, and hope we don't need it for anything except wood." He paused. "I'm going to get father. If I can, I'll see if he's heard anything from the fishermen."

Jonmarc took off running. At fifteen, he was tall, just a bit over six feet. Years of working alongside his father in the forge had given him a strong back and muscular arms. A mop of chestnut-brown hair hung in his brown eyes, and he pushed it out of the way as he ran.

A worn path led to the open shed that was his father's forge. Jonmarc could hear the steady pounding of his father's hammer on the anvil. The sound echoed from the hills, steady as a heartbeat. He skidded to a stop just outside the doors.

Anselm Vahanian swung a heavy hammer in his right hand while his gloved left hand turned the piece of metal on the anvil. Sparks flew around him, landing on the long sleeves of his rough-woven shirt, his gloves, and his leather apron. The forge smelled of coal, iron, and sweat. To one side lay two swords Anselm had completed for a client in the village. On a table lay a variety of farm tools—iron pots and pans, and hoops for the cooper's barrels. Jonmarc had helped to forge several of the pieces, though he longed to work on swords, like his father.

"Mother said to tell you to wash up for dinner," Jonmarc shouted above the clanging.

Anselm stopped and looked at him. "I'll eat supper later. You know I can't stop in the middle of something when the iron is hot."

Jonmarc nodded. "I know. I'll tell her to put a plate aside for you." He paused, and Anselm looked at him quizzically, waiting for the unspoken question.

"Have you talked to any of the fishermen lately?" Jonmarc tried to make the question sound off-handed, but Anselm frowned as if he caught the undercurrent of concern.

"You mean the talk about raiders," Anselm replied, and struck the iron he was working.

"Do you think it's more than just talk?"

Anselm didn't answer until he put the iron bar back into the furnace to heat up. He was Jonmarc's height, with a head of wiry dark hair and brown eyes that glinted with intelligence. A lifetime in the forge had given him broad shoulders and a powerful physique. His profession also showed in the small white burns that marked his hands and arms, scars too numerous to count. Jonmarc had gained a few of those burn scars too, but not nearly as many as his father. Not yet.

"Maybe," Anselm replied. "The real people to talk to are the traders. Their ships go up and down the Northern Sea coast, stopping at all the villages. I always get news when I trade iron with them."

"Have you heard anything?"

Anselm turned the iron rod in the furnace. "Some. One of the villages on the other side of the bay burned. Everyone was gone when the traders came. No way to know why or how. Eiderford, down the coast, did have a run-in with raiders a few months ago." He eyed the iron, and turned it one more time.

"So there *are* raiders," Jonmarc replied.

Anselm shrugged. "There are always raiders. But there's less to attract them here in Lunsbetter than in Eiderford. We're not a proper city, and we're as like to barter as deal in coin, so there's less to steal."

Unless they want food, livestock, or women, Jonmarc thought. *And there are enough people who trade with the ships that there's probably more coin here than anyone wants to admit.*

"There's a garrison of the king's soldiers beyond Ebbetshire," Jonmarc replied. "Can't they stop the raiders?"

Anselm shrugged. "They can't guard every village along the coast," he said. "And they'd have to know for certain when a raid was planned." He shook his head. "No, we're on our own." He paused.

"Don't worry yourself about it," Anselm said, drawing the rod out of the furnace and placing it on the anvil. "We've doubled the patrols, and the fishermen are on alert." He grinned. "And tomorrow, those swords are going down to the constable and the sheriff. We'll be fine. Pump the bellows for me. The fire's grown cold."

Anselm stood in front of a large open furnace filled with glowing coals. Jonmarc pumped the bellows that were attached to the back of the furnace, and the coals flared brighter, flames licking across their surface. Anselm lifted his hammer to strike the iron. "Now get back up to the house. Your mother's waiting. Just save some for me."

"I'll make sure of it," Jonmarc replied. The clatter of the hammer drowned out anything else he might have asked. He stepped out into the cool night, and started back up the path to the house. His stomach rumbled and he fancied that he could smell the stew. But the worry he felt when he went to the forge had not lifted; if anything, his father's comments increased Jonmarc's concern than the warnings about raiders were not mere tales.

If father says the men are keeping their eye out for trouble, then that's the end of it, he thought. *Naught I can do.* But he remembered his comment to Neil about keeping the axe sharpened, and on the way back to the house, he detoured into the barn. Thanks to his father's craft, they were well-stocked with farm implements.

He walked over to the space his father used to butcher meat. Butchering wasn't a pleasant job, but it was necessary, and a task with which Jonmarc was well acquainted. He had learned the craft from his father, practiced enough that it no longer made him lose his dinner to be awash in blood and entrails. His father had taught him to strike swiftly and cleanly, to block out the death cries of the terrified livestock, to go to a cold place inside himself until the job was done. He had even learned a few tricks of the trade, like how to hamstring a panicked animal that was likely to kick or buck. But nothing about how to fight men.

On the wall hung an impressive variety of knives. He selected a large butcher knife with a wicked blade as well as a smaller boning knife, and made his way around to the back door, hiding the knives among his mother's herbs before going in for supper. Tonight, when everyone was in bed, he would come back for them—one for him, and one for Neil. Just in case the men were wrong.

"Father said to save him a bowl of stew and some bread," Jonmarc answered his mother's unspoken question as he let the door close behind him. The others were already seated at the table, and his mother was ladling hot stew into bowls.

"I can't promise it'll be warm," his mother replied, but a smile tempered the crispness of her words. "I guess it can stay in the pot until he comes in."

"Did you see the people from the caravan?" Neil asked excitedly. "I heard they stopped in town to buy provisions."

"Were they dressed fancy? Did any of them sing?" Piers questioned.

Dalia laughed. "Yes, yes and no. Yes, there were caravan people in town, and yes, they were dressed fancier than anyone in these parts. But no, no one sang. Or danced, or juggled or paraded strange wild animals down the street." She smiled. "At least, not today."

"Tomorrow?" Piers asked, eyes wide. "Or the day after?"

Dalia chuckled and towseled his hair. "Perhaps. Today they came to trade for dried herbs, brined vegetables and some of my nice warm woolen cloaks," she said with a grin.

"Did they pay gold for the cloaks?" Neil asked.

"Not gold," their mother replied, "but silver. Look!" She put her hand into the pouch that hung at her waist and withdrew four silver pieces, each stamped with the likeness of King Bricen. "And I think I overheard one of the strangers saying that the caravan would set up out in the clearing beyond Dewson's farm. That's halfway between here and Ebbetshire, on the main road, so they probably figure on a good audience. No doubt they'll send a crier to let both towns and every tavern in the area know."

"Can we go?" Neil, Piers, and Marty begged in unison. "Please?"

"Sounds like smart business," Jonmarc said over a mouthful of stew. "Spend their coin in town, then get all the townspeople to give them the money back to come see the show."

Dalia shook her head and muttered, "Tsk, tsk. You have a head for business, just like your father and me. And you're right, of course, but where's the fun in that? The last time a caravan came by, it was quite an adventure, as I recall."

Jonmarc snorted. "Piers almost blundered into the knife-thrower's act, a stray goat ate Neil's lunch while he was watching the jugglers, and Marty wandered off and tried to tell people he was a prince."

"I was named for a prince!" Marty piped up. "Mama said so." Excitement over the birth of King Bricen's youngest son five years ago had reached even the far-off Borderlands, and the young prince's name, Martris, had instantly become so popular that it seemed to Jonmarc that it was impossible to meet a group of small boys without half of them being named for the prince.

"You and every other boy your age," Neil muttered. Dalia cuffed him gently.

"Hush," She commanded, and turned to Marty. "Yes, you were, sweetie." Marty stuck out his tongue at his older brother.

Dalia sighed and ate a few bites of her dinner before responding. "It depends on what your father gets for those swords he forged for the constable. If they fetch what they should, there might be a few coppers to go see the caravan." Piers and Marty cheered, but Jonmarc dug into his food, still thinking about the rumors of raiders. As the others talked about the curiosities that might be seen if they went out to the caravan, he finished his stew and then pushed away from the table.

"I'd better go help father," Jonmarc said.

Dalia gave him a questioning look. "It's not like you to skip seconds," she observed with an appraising glance Jonmarc knew was usually the precursor to her putting a hand to his forehead to check for fever or dosing him with one of her many medicinal teas to ward off ill humours.

"I'm fine," Jonmarc replied, ducking out of reach. "Father just looked like he could use a hand, and maybe if I go help out, he can eat before the pot boils dry."

Dalia nodded, though he saw skepticism in her eyes. "That's good of you," she replied. She turned to the others. "Neil, go fetch some firewood from what you cut, we're running low. Piers and Marty, I need you to card the rest of that wool. Be quick about it, all of you, and I could be persuaded to give you some of the sugared nuts I made," she added with a crafty smile. The three boys sprang to their chores as Jonmarc let himself out the kitchen door.

Outside, the air was crisp as late summer gave way to autumn. There was no moon to light his way, but he knew the path well enough. The night was filled with the chirps of crickets and the moans of frogs singing their final choruses. Soon the cold would silence them as the year wound toward winter. Jonmarc tried to bump himself out of his melancholy by thinking about the festivals to come in the fall, of bonfires and harvest feasts and the merrymaking that accompanied the solstice at Winterstide. Yet as he reached the warm, firelit haven of the forge, he was only partly successful.

Anselm looked up. "Done with dinner already?"

Jonmarc shrugged. "I ate. Figured you could use some help."

If Anselm could guess the cause of Jonmarc's moodiness, he said nothing about it. "That I can," he said. He plunged the hot bar of metal he had been working into a bucket of water, and a cloud of steam rose in a hiss. "I'm almost ready to put this by for the night. Give me a hand bringing in some coal for the morning and putting the tools on the table, and we can go up."

Jonmarc hurried to do as he was bid as Anselm banked the fire. The two swords caught Jonmarc's eye as he was setting tools back in their proper place, and he ran a finger down the smooth, cold flat of one of the blades.

"They're both beauties, if I say so myself," Anselm murmured, standing behind him. "Some of my best work, I think."

"I want to learn to forge swords like these," Jonmarc said.

"Keep at it, and you will," Anselm replied. "Go on, pick one up, but mind you don't swing it around. It's been sharpened."

Jonmarc grasped one of the broadswords and let his hand close around the grip. He lifted it, marveling at how well-balanced it felt. He turned it so that the firelight glinted off the blade, and he caught a glimpse of his own distorted reflection in the polished steel. He extended his arm, pointing the blade.

"No, no. Not like that." Anselm stepped closer. "Put your feet so," he said, kicking at Jonmarc's heels until he adjusted his stance, "and hold your arm thus," he added, reaching around Jonmarc's shoulder to position his arm. "There. That's how to hold a sword."

Jonmarc stared at the glittering steel. "You learned in the army, didn't you?"

Anselm gave a heavy sigh. "Aye. And I like forging swords more than fighting with them, to be damn sure. War's a business for fools and madmen."

Jonmarc let his arm fall and returned the sword to the table. "All I get to make are barrel hoops, shovels and bridles."

"They're good, honest pieces," Anselm said, and his large, heavy bear-paw of a hand clapped Jonmarc on the shoulder. "No shame in that. If we didn't need the money, I'd just as soon turn down orders for swords."

"Why?"

Anselm did not answer right away. His left hand rested on the grip of the nearest sword and his expression grew distant. There was a haunted look in his father's eyes that Jonmarc had rarely glimpsed before. "I wonder, sometimes, how the Lady sees it," he murmured. "All the blood that sword will spill, and mine the hand that forged it. Will it count against me, I wonder, when the Crone reckons my fate?" He shook himself, as if to change his mood.

"No more of that," he huffed, turning away. "We're done here for tonight. Let's go eat." He headed for the path, but Jonmarc cast a last glance at the swords, still thinking about his father's words.

LATE THAT NIGHT, screams broke the midnight silence. Jonmarc roused from his uneasy sleep to see Neil sitting up in bed, his hand closed around the boning knife.

"What was that?" Neil asked in a tight voice. "Please say it's cats fighting."

More screams, along with thumping and banging that echoed in the room. Piers and Marty woke with a start, and Marty began to sniffle. "Hush," Piers cautioned, handing a blanket to his brother to hold. "Get under the covers and don't come out until we say so."

By now, Jonmarc and Neil were on their feet, knives in hand. Piers looked from one to the other. "I heard you talking earlier, when you thought I wasn't listening," he said. He reached below his bed and brought out the axe Neil used to cut wood. He was pale and his eyes were wide with fear. He gripped the oversized axe with both hands, and Jonmarc could see that the blade was trembling.

"Put that down before you cut off your own leg," Jonmarc said. "You and Neil need to stay here, protect Marty and mother. Maybe you can hide down in the dugout where mother keeps the vegetables. I'll go help father."

He heard the door open and slam as more cries echoed on the night air. Jonmarc bounded for the door and took the steps at a run.

"Jonmarc! Where are you going! Oh goddess, why do you have a knife?" Dalia stood near the doorway clutching a woolen shawl around her, and Jonmarc thought his mother looked as if she had aged a decade just since supper.

Piers and Neil followed cautiously down the stairs, with Marty edging behind them, still holding tight to the blanket. Dalia gasped as she saw that the two older boys were armed. "By the Crone! Have you all gone mad? Put those knives down right now!"

Jonmarc stepped to the door and placed a hand on his mother's shoulder. "If it's raiders, it's wise to be able to protect ourselves," he said, marveling that his voice held steady when he was trembling. "Please, mama. Go to the vegetable cellar. Stay safe."

A fierce glint came into Dalia's eyes. "And let those sons of the Whore burn my house down around me? Your father and I worked too hard to build what we've got. They won't take it from me while I cower in a hole in the ground." She snatched up a butcher's knife from the kitchen.

"Go to your father, Jonmarc. He's often got more courage than good sense. See to it that he comes home safely, both of you." Delia gave a sidelong look at the other boys. "The rest of you, stay with me." She pulled Jonmarc close enough to kiss him on the cheek. "I'll pray to the Dark Lady for your safety."

The door slammed behind Jonmarc, and he strode off before his fear could stop him. After a few steps, he veered off toward the forge, only to find it deserted. One of the swords Anselm had forged was gone. Jonmarc shoved the knife he carried through his belt and grabbed the remaining sword, then took off at a run toward the commotion in the village center.

The shrill screams of women had woken him from sleep, but men's curses carried on the wind now, along with the clang of steel. Long after the night's fires should have been banked, the village glowed with firelight, and as Jonmarc grew closer, he realized that many of the buildings were ablaze.

He rounded a corner and skidded to a stop. The main street in the village of Lunsbetter held two taverns, an open market where farmers, butchers and traders gathered, and shops of tradesmen: cooper, chandler, and tailor. Flames rose from the thatched roofs of the shops, but no bucket brigades ran to fight the fires. Down the muddy main street, rough strangers fought an unequal battle against townsmen armed with kitchen knives and garden tools.

Jonmarc edged forward, and his boot kicked something solid. He looked down to see the body of the sheriff lying splayed on the ground, his gut split open from crotch to ribs, so freshly dead that his blood and spilled innards still steamed in the cold.

Jonmarc collapsed against the wall, heaving for breath, willing himself not to retch. *Pretend it's a just a goat,* he told himself as he gulped air. *Pretend you're butchering.* He found the cold place inside himself, the place he had learned to go when he helped his father slaughter livestock, where he did not feel and where the death shrieks did not make him tremble.

After a moment, he gathered his courage and moved forward again, avoiding the sheriff's corpse, until he could see the fighting in the street. He searched for any sign of his father. Bodies littered the rutted road. *Please don't let him be among the dead.*

"Looking for a fight, laddie?" A large man with a wild, dark beard lurched in front of him. The man's hard-used, mismatched clothing was splattered with blood and the long, wicked blade of his sword was crimson. His arms were covered in crude inked images, and around his neck on a piece of leather swung small talismans and charms. One of them was a star of bones, the symbol of the Formless One, the most feared of all the Aspects of the Lady.

Jonmarc backed up a pace, but he held his sword in front of him with both hands. "I'm looking for my father."

The raider's smile revealed broken, mottled teeth. "Then you'd best look among the dead. The men here are soft. Not a one of them knows how to fight."

The raider dove forward and on instinct, Jonmarc brought his blade up to block the blow. The force of it reverberated down his arm, jarring him to the bone, but he held onto the grip with all his strength. The man chuckled, then swung once more, and his time, the point of his sword opened a deep gash on Jonmarc's shoulder.

"I'm going to split you open like a pig, boy," the man said, chuckling. "Spill your guts out onto your shoes and let you drag them home with you," he laughed.

Once more, the raider swung at him. Jonmarc could smell whiskey on the man's breath, but it did not blunt the raider's aim. The sword slashed for his throat, but Jonmarc managed to get his blade up and parry the swing to the side so that it sliced open his other shoulder, but the force of the blow knocked the weapon from his hand.

All trace of humor was gone from the raider's face. "Next time, I won't miss, laddie."

Jonmarc saw the sword glint in the firelight. He ducked and dove, rolling. As the large man began to lumber around, Jonmarc yanked the butcher knife free from his belt and slashed it across the back of the raider's knees.

The man gave a hoarse cry of pain, then screamed curses as his useless legs buckled under him. Jonmarc darted forward and slammed his foot down on the man's hand, kicking his sword out of reach.

Never leave an animal in pain, his father had told him sternly. *If you begin a job, have the balls to finish it.* Jonmarc drew a ragged breath, steeling himself.

"A curse on you, boy!" the raider roared. "May you lose all you love to the flame and sword, and the Dark Lady take your soul!"

Jonmarc knew he was shaking with rage and adrenaline as he stepped closer, his knife raised. *I don't know how to fight with a sword, but I do know how to butcher a pig.* Before he could think about what he was going to do, he bent forward and grabbed the raider by his long, matted hair. The raider was still cursing him as Jonmarc jerked the man's head back. With one swift stroke, he drew his blade across the raider's throat. The man wheezed, blood gurgling and bubbling as he struggled for breath, and then with a spray of crimson, lay quiet in the mud.

Jonmarc did not have to look down to know that his hands were shaking. He was covered in blood, his own and that of the raider. He felt cold to the bone, though the night was mild for autumn. The sound of fighting behind him roused Jonmarc from shock. He bent to retrieve his sword, and turned back toward the carnage on the main street, willing himself not to look at the dead man at his feet.

He kept low, slinking in the shadows of the buildings that had not burned, trying to glimpse the faces of the few village men who were still fighting. He crawled over the bodies of men he had known all his life. Lars, the cooper, one of his father's best customers, lay sprawled on the ground, a gaping wound in his chest, his face frozen in pain. Dunn, the master of the Rattled Raven pub, was slumped and still against the wall, his body already growing cold, hands pressed against his belly in a vain attempt to force his entrails back into his open gut.

The burning buildings on the other side of the street gave the night an orange glow, casting the area in shifting light and shadow. With a sinking heart, Jonmarc realized that he could not spot his father among the men still fighting the raiders. Pushing away his grief, he began to search the faces of the dead and dying.

The light flickered, and Jonmarc caught a glimpse of a familiar scrap of clothing; the woolen cloak his mother had made for his father. His father was lying in the middle of the street near the bodies of two other men. Jonmarc took a step toward his father's corpse, and stepped into a puddle of blood. Blood darkened the mud and filled the wagon ruts. And in that moment, Jonmarc felt the coldness from the butchering take him completely even as rage animated his movements. He gave a roar and headed toward the nearest raider, a burly man who was about to best the constable.

He was too late to save the lawman. The raider sank his blade deep into the man's chest and jerked it back. The constable sagged to his knees, hands clutching his chest, as his shirt grew crimson. The burly raider wheeled, bringing his full attention to Jonmarc just in time to knock aside a blow that was made with more force than skill.

"Now that the men are dead, have they sent in the pups?" the raider chuckled.

Jonmarc wielded the sword two-handed, striking with all the strength he could muster. Work in the forge had made him strong, and the blows he rained down on the raider seemed to take the man by surprise in their ferocity. The leering grin gradually slipped from the man's face, replaced by dark anger.

"That your old man?" the raider asked, giving the body of Jonmarc's father a kick for good measure. "Is that it? Well hear this, pup. After I kill you like I killed him, I'll take your mother like a whore—and your sister, too if you've got one—before I slit their throats. Then we'll have your gold and silver, since you won't be needin' it no more." He chuckled, but his pale eyes were mirthless.

Jonmarc swung again. The raider parried, knocking his sword wide. Seemingly out of nowhere, a short sword was in the raider's left hand. Jonmarc only glimpsed the blade before the raider rammed forward, driving the point into Jonmarc's side.

Jonmarc stumbled backward a step, and the raider began to laugh. Blood was soaking down Jonmarc's shirt and trousers, and the wound hurt like a son of a bitch. But the sound of the laughter stoked his rage and he brought his sword up faster than the raider expected, jamming the blade into the man's belly just beneath his ribs. Vertigo tilted Jonmarc's world and he fell, holding onto the sword hilt with his full strength, slicing down through the raider's abdomen, so that the night air was filled with the smell of fresh offal as a pink cascade of warm entrails spilled from the burly man's belly.

"You damned cur!" the raider roared. He brought the pommel of his sword down on Jonmarc's skull, and his world went black.

CONSCIOUSNESS RETURNED SLOWLY, and Jonmarc struggled for breath. He opened his eyes and saw only darkness. Something heavy was on his chest, while whatever was beneath him was cold and oddly shaped. Pain flooded back with awareness, as if hot coals had been pressed to his side. Whatever lay atop him stank of sweat and shit and cheap liquor.

Gradually, memory sparked. *Sweet Chenne, I'm lying in a heap of dead men!* Panic tingled through him, warring with the pain. He gathered his remaining strength to try to hurl the body of the raider off of him when he heard voices nearby. It took all his will to force himself to lie still, breathing shallowly, listening.

"Is that everything?" The voice was whiskey-roughened and deep.

"Nearly. Loadin' it all onto the ship now, Cap'n." This voice was reedy and nasal. "Couple of the men wondered if we could bring a few of the wenches with us, shame to waste fresh meat," he said with a lecherous chuckle that turned Jonmarc's stomach.

"Poke 'em and choke 'em," Whiskey Voice replied in a bored tone. "Bad luck to have women on a ship, 'specially women who've seen you kill their men." His voice dropped conspiratorially. "They're like as not to slice off your nuts and branch when you're not lookin'."

"Aye." The reedy voiced speaker sounded disappointed. "This shithole of a town waren't good for much, if you ask me. Provisions are slim, women are ugly, not a man in the place worth the bother to slave, and hardly no gold nor silver."

"Patience," Whiskey Voice replied. "Think of it as practice. We'll take Ebbetshire next, when we need more provisions and a night on the town," he said with a chuckle. "Then Eiderford when I'm sure the new crew know their places." He paused. "Best we be gone before anyone comes to see about those flames."

Jonmarc felt a jolt as they threw another body on the pile. He heard boot steps recede, and let out a shuddering breath. It hurt to move; it ached to breathe. One leg had gone to sleep under the weight of the dead raider. His side was sticky and warm, seeping blood. He passed in and out of consciousness, then awoke once more to silence.

I don't care if there's anyone left to see. I've got to heave this big oaf off me before I suffocate, Jonmarc thought, taking strength from his foul mood. He shoved with all his might, rolling the body of the burly raider to the side and scraping the man's entrails off of himself. Jonmarc took a steadying breath, and struggled to his knees, looking around. He found his sword and picked it up, watching the shadows warily.

The main street was dark and silent. The shops had burned down to charred posts, and the flames that flickered inside the ruined buildings cast a dim glow across the carnage. Bodies lay everywhere. Some were dead raiders, but most were villagers. Jonmarc looked down at the body that had been beneath him. His father's corpse was cold and rigid, eyes staring. Next to the body lay the sword Anselm had made for the sheriff. Jonmarc sighed. He leaned over and closed his father's eyes, and he muttered the prayer for the dead that he had heard his mother say over the bodies of her stillborn babies. *I imagine every dead man here said a prayer before he fell,* Jonmarc thought. *Seems like the goddess isn't listening.*

He reached down and took the sword that lay beside his father's body, then climbed to his feet. The bleeding had slowed from the gash in his side, and it was hard to tell how much of the blood that covered him was his own, and how much belonged to the dead raider. The smell of smoke hung in the air. An odd scent of roasting meat wafted on the wind, puzzling Jonmarc until he turned. In the ruins of the chandler's shop he glimpsed two blackened forms.

By the Crone! The tradesmen lived above their shops with their families. When the raiders torched the stores... He did not need to put words to the thought. He fell to his knees retching into the blood-slick mud, every involuntary heave sending searing pain through his gashed side.

When Jonmarc finally caught his breath, his head was spinning. *I can't pass out again, he thought desperately. I might not wake up. I've got to get home, got to see—*

He trudged back up the road to the forge, making as good progress as his battered body would allow. He carried a make-shift torch he had lit from the ruins of the village shops, and it sufficed to light his way. He had no idea how long it had been since the raiders departed, but judging from the sky, dawn was still far off. He passed no one, heard no sounds to suggest that anyone else had survived the raid. Jonmarc struggled to hold on to the coldness that had carried him through the fight, but the best he could manage was numbness. Even his rage felt spent. Desperation carried him forward, along with the hope that by some luck their small home had been too far for the raiders to notice, too out of the way to be worth the bother.

Please, please, please, he begged silently, though to which of the eight faces of the Sacred Lady he prayed, he did not know.

He rounded a bend in the road. The house and the forge were both still standing. Nothing had been touched by fire. Jonmarc could smell the coal smoke from the furnace, its fires banked for morning. Yet everything was far too still, he realized as he approached. No lanterns burned inside the house. The barnyard was quiet, though the ruckus in town should have spooked the animals into a frenzy.

Jonmarc was so intent on reaching the door to the house that he nearly stumbled when his boot caught on something. He looked down and felt his breath leave him. Neil lay cold and still, his knife still clutched in his fist.

No, please no, please no...

Jonmarc ignored the pain and began to run. Piers lay a few feet closer to the house, with the axe he had used as a weapon turned against him, pinning his body to the ground. Jonmarc stumbled across the threshold, searching for signs of life. The fire had burned down to embers, casting the hearth in a warm glow, though most of the room was dark.

"Mother! Marty!" Silence answered him. Then he saw a bundle near the fireplace, and he took a step closer for a better look.

"Mama!" Jonmarc recognized the pattern on the dress his mother had worn that day, had been wearing just a few candlemarks ago, when she had served him dinner and the world had not gone spinning out of control.

Jonmarc rushed to kneel beside his mother. There was a smear of blood on the hearth, more blood on her forehead where she had struck the stones. He laid a hand against her skin. It was cold and waxy.

"Oh no," he moaned. He rolled her over, and felt his breath leave him. Beneath her body was Marty, and both of them were soaked with blood.

"No, no, no, no!" His moan became a howl, venting grief and rage. For a long time, he sat with the bodies across his lap, rocking back and forth, sobbing until he could no longer draw breath.

Gone, all gone. Jonmarc heaved for air, and drew a bloodied sleeve across his eyes. *I'm still bleeding. I could just lie down. If the cold doesn't take me, I'll bleed out. Fall asleep. So easy...*

The voices of the raiders came back to him. Ebbetshire was next, then maybe Eiderford. More nights of fire and blood and death, more people dead, and no one knew the plan except for him. No one else to warn them. No one else who might keep it from happening.

"Time to go," Jonmarc said softly. He leaned down to kiss his mother on the cheek, and he laid his hand gently on Marty's head. *Gone, all gone.*

He laid their bodies aside and dragged himself to his feet, pausing to take a last look around. His mother's loom looked as if she had been surprised in the middle of her work. The carding combs lay on the floor and a tangle of wool stained with blood had been kicked beneath the table. The wind whistled through the eaves, underscoring just how silent it was on the inside of a house that, with four boys, had never been quiet.

Jonmarc thought about going back to his room, but he eyed the stairs warily. It would take all his strength—perhaps more than he had—to make it to Ebbetshire. There was nothing in his room valuable enough to risk spending precious energy on climbing the stairs. He stopped and retrieved a few handfuls of wool from the pile on the floor, and packed it against the gash in his side, wrapping his belt against it to keep it tight.

He went out the back door. The sheep gate was open, and the chicken roost was empty. Looted, no doubt, by the raiders. Jonmarc turned and limped down toward the forge. He had both swords his father had made, as well as the butcher knife, so there was nothing he needed from the forge, but he could not leave without a last look.

The smell of coal smoke greeted him when he entered the shed. The furnace coals glowed brightly, banked for the next morning's work. But there was another smell, a strange one that put Jonmarc on alert. He drew his sword and advanced cautiously.

"Well, now. Lookit that. Guess there's one of ye left." The voice sounded from the corner as a dark, hulking shape rose from the shadows. "I thought I got all ye."

Jonmarc thought his rage was spent, but the raider's casual dismissal made his anger flare. "I'm going to kill you." His voice was utterly flat and not his own. It came from the cold place inside himself, the place that had expanded to fill his chest, the chill that drove out thought and fear, pain, and grief.

The drunken raider laughed. "Are ye now? Like those two pups in the yard? Came at me with a knife and an axe they did, and landed nary a scratch on me." He took a step out from the shadows, and Jonmarc saw a pockmarked face with a fresh, bloody slash down one cheek.

"That bitch in the kitchen had a knife hidden in her skirts," the raider growled. "I used it to stab the brat while she watched, and then used it on her. Pity. I might have had a bit of fun with her."

He's baiting me, the cold voice in Jonmarc's head warned. *I can't rush him. I've got to have a plan. He'll make ribbons of me if I fight him with the sword.* He looked past the raider to the tables littered with his father's tools, and a plan formed in his mind.

"I doubt you have the balls to screw a woman," Jonmarc said. "You're probably too clap-eaten to even get it up." He raised his sword, knowing the raider's eye would follow the movement.

"You mangy cur!" The drunken raider lumbered toward Jonmarc with a rolling gait as if he were forever aboard ship in a pitching sea.

Jonmarc ducked and dodged, coming up behind the man and grabbing for the workbench. He seized the pair of tongs his father used to pull hot iron from the fire and swung around, closing their jaws on the raider's full beard and yanking it with all his might.

It sent the raider stumbling toward him as Jonmarc backed away, deeper into the forge.

The raider reached for the tongs to grab them away from Jonmarc, and Jonmarc dropped his sword, taking up one of the iron bars that lay near the forge and using it to shove the raider, hard, so that he fell backwards, flailing for balance, against the furnace.

Jonmarc dove onto the bellows. He landed hard and bit his lip to keep from crying out in pain. The weight of his body on the bellows handles sent a blast of air beneath the furnace, and the fire roared to life. The raider's beard and clothing caught like tinder and the man screamed, his bleary eyes wide in panic. He lurched from the furnace and flailed toward the doorway, all of him aflame as the smell of scorching skin and burning wool rivaled the coal smoke.

A few more staggering steps and the raider collapsed to his knees then fell face-forward into the dirt. Painfully, Jonmarc lifted himself off the bellows, its handles stained with his blood, and stared at the dying raider. The flames receded, until the man's clothing and what remained of his hair still smoldered, but the raider did not move.

Jonmarc steadied himself and retrieved his sword, cautiously advancing toward the body. He could see the rise and fall of the man's breath, the limbs twitching involuntarily.

It could take the man hours to die, he knew from his father's tales of what could happen to hapless blacksmiths when no healer was nearby. He walked carefully toward the raider, alert for a trick.

He killed mama. He killed my brothers. He left them to die. I should let him lie.

He looked at the forge, still set as his father had left it just a few candlemarks earlier. Jonmarc glanced toward the looted barn and the slaughter floor. His father's admonishments rang in his ears as he looked back at the raider.

I could, but I won't. I won't... be... like... him.

He brought the sword down with both hands, point first, through the raider's back. The man jerked and arched and a gurgle escaped his throat. In a moment that seemed to last forever, the raider stiffened and then dropped forward to lie motionless.

Jonmarc withdrew the sword and wiped it clean on the dry grass. He looked toward the east, toward Ebbetshire. *It's only a few miles. It'll be dawn soon. I might make it. I could warn them.*

He paused long enough to take a lantern from the forge. Forcing himself not to dwell on what was behind him, Jonmarc trudged up the road. Although he had walked the distance before, and ridden it in the wagon many times when he took his mother's weaving to market, it now seemed as if the road stretched on forever, and the miles had become leagues. The adrenaline of the fight had faded, and with every step, the pain in his side worsened. By the time Ebbetshire's dark outline was visible against the rising dawn, Jonmarc had grown lightheaded and he knew he was much colder than he should have been for the night's mild temperatures.

What if I get there and they don't believe me? What if they think I had something to do with it? Goddess knows, I'm covered in blood.

Breathing hurt. Moving sent sharp pain through his side, down his leg. He focused on the narrow path in front of him. Take a step. Take another step. Again. Again.

His field of vision tilted, and he stumbled, nearly losing his footing. He staggered on several more steps, and fought to stay upright as his knees threatened to buckle. The sky had lightened first to indigo and then to shades of blue. He no longer needed his lantern to light the way, and in the distance, he could see lights in the windows of the village's homes and shops as the day began.

Jonmarc took a step, and his legs collapsed beneath him. He tried to rise, and his strength failed him. He got to his knees and managed a few more lengths before he fell hard against the dusty, rutted road.

No way to warn them, he thought before the blackness took him. *I failed.*

"DON'T STIR." The voice seemed to come from far away. It was a pleasant voice, though unfamiliar.

"He's a strong one." The second voice was rough but not unkind. "Surprised he's rousing so soon."

Jonmarc struggled to open his eyes. His vision swam for an instant, and then cleared. Two women bent over him. One was a girl close to his own age with blond hair and a shy, encouraging smile. The other was an older woman, perhaps the girl's mother, with worried eyes and careworn features.

Jonmarc opened his mouth to speak. His lips were dry, and his first sounds were desperate croaks.

"Lie still," the girl said, laying a hand on his shoulder. "You're safe. Mum's a healer."

"Warn you," Jonmarc managed to rasp. "Raiders. Coming. Ebbetshire—danger."

The two women exchanged a glance. "I'll go tell Kell," the older woman said. "Sit with him. Don't let him get up."

The girl gave a brisk nod and turned back to Jonmarc with a no-nonsense expression. "You nearly died, you know," she said when the older woman had gone. "Lucky I found you when I did."

"How?" Jonmarc managed. The girl helped him rise long enough to press a cup of water to his lips before gentling him down onto the mattress.

"I'd gone out at dawn to find bark and roots for mum's cures," she replied. "Those are best if you take them when it's cool out," she added. "There you were, face down on the road. I thought you were dead at first, then I saw you breathing. I dragged you to the wagon and managed to heave you in." She grimaced. "Might have bruised you some in the doing, but it was the best I could do."

She paused. "Mum said you were bad off, but she worked on you." She shook her head. "Someone sliced you up. Then the wound went sour, in spite of everything mum did, and you took fever for a few days."

"Raiders came," Jonmarc said in a hoarse voice just above a whisper. "Killed—"

The girl's expression sobered. "We know," she said, laying a finger to his lips. "Our men went to Lunsbetter first thing that day. We'd seen light in the sky from that way, like a great fire." She grew quiet. "When they got there, they saw." After a moment she went on. "They buried your dead, and burned the raiders. Naught else to do. They salvaged what little the raiders didn't take, since there was no one left." Her hand touched his shoulder. "I'm sorry."

She looked up as if she remembered something. "Here you are, waking up among strangers. I'm Shanna."

"Jonmarc Vahanian."

She frowned, thinking. "I've seen you at the market. You're the weaver's son."

Jonmarc turned his head to look away and did not answer. Shanna sighed as if she guessed the cause of his silence. "Your family—"

"Dead."

"Mum and I figured," she said quietly. "Mum also said that, from your hands, she thought you'd done some smithing."

He nodded, but could not bring himself to speak.

"Once you're better, mum said she'd take you to meet the smith in town. He might have known your father. Mum thought he might want an apprentice." She smiled encouragingly. "You'll be all right here, Jonmarc. You'll be safe."

Jonmarc met her gaze. She was not beautiful, but there was kindness in her brown eyes. "Thank you," he murmured.

She gave a worried smile and helped him take another sip of water. "You're probably starving. Mum got some broth into you, but not much more. Don't worry," she went on, "we'll make sure you don't go hungry now that you're awake."

Jonmarc moved to get up. "Tell the men—" he began.

"Mum's gone to warn them," Shanna said, and gently pushed him back down. "I figure Kell will be over as soon as she'll let him talk to you. Kell's the town mayor. You'll have time to tell your story," she assured him. "Probably more times than you'll want to. When the men came back with the news, everyone heard. They've been buzzing about it for days."

Overwhelming tiredness flooded through his body, and Jonmarc felt himself fading.

"Don't fight sleep, Jonmarc," Shanna said. "Mum laced the water with herbs. They'll make you sleepy, but they'll help you heal. You're safe here."

No one's safe, he thought, but he was too far gone to speak.

THE NEXT TIME he awoke, he was alone. Late afternoon light filtered through the window of a small room, and he could smell food cooking. For the first time since the night of the attack, nothing hurt. Gingerly, he touched his side where the raider had stabbed him. It was tender, but the skin was healed, leaving only a raised scar. *Shanna's mum must be quite a healer,* Jonmarc thought. *I thought for sure I was going to die.*

He pushed back the rough-woven blanket and sat up carefully. Someone had dressed him in a worn, homespun nightshirt, and he felt a flush of embarrassment, though he knew his own clothes had been damaged beyond repair. The small room held a lamp stand and the wooden bed with its straw-filled mattress on which he sat, plus a small trunk against the far wall. Atop the trunk, lay a shirt and trews. His boots stood next to the trunk, and he realized that someone had cleaned off the blood and mud that had caked them. He dressed as quickly as he could manage, fearing that Shanna or her mother might happen in before he was finished.

Drawing on more bravado than strength, Jonmarc managed to stand. Beyond the doorway, he could hear voices. Shanna, her mother, and a man Jonmarc thought looked vaguely familiar sat in the kitchen. Dried herbs and roots hung from the cottage's rafters, and along one wall were shelves filled with bottles and jars which he assumed held the herbs, potions, and mixtures Shanna's mother used to heal her patients.

Conversation halted as they saw him in the doorway, and all three people rose from their seats. Shanna and her mother rushed toward him, while the man drew up a fourth chair and made a gesture of welcome.

"You shouldn't be up yet," the healer fussed. Shanna said nothing, but gave Jonmarc a worried glance.

"I couldn't sleep," Jonmarc said.

"Have a seat," the man offered. They let Jonmarc hang onto his dignity by not insisting on helping him walk across the room, and he hoped he did not show just how happy he was to sit down.

"Elly here has been telling me about your recovery," the man said. "I'm Kell, the mayor, and Elly's cousin on her mother's side." He paused. "I'm glad you made it."

Elly bustled to the hearth and returned with a cup of tea for Jonmarc and a slice of bread with butter. "Eat. You need your strength," she said.

"Thank you," Jonmarc replied, feeling awkward under Kell's gaze.

"Shanna says your mother was the weaver who came to market. Is that right?"

Jonmarc paused as he chewed a bite of bread. "She's gone now. All of them are gone."

Kell nodded. "You're Anselm's boy, aren't you?"

"Yes, sir."

"I didn't know your father well, but I'd met him on occasion, and I knew of him," Kell replied. "People spoke well of him, and of the things he forged. Same with your mother and her work." He looked down at Jonmarc's scarred hands. "Looks like you've done a bit of iron work yourself."

"I helped in the forge since I could carry the tools," Jonmarc said, looking down so he did not have to see the pity in Kell's eyes.

"I thought so," Kell replied. "Elly's already talked to Tucker Erikson, our blacksmith. Once she says you're patched up, he's willing to give you a go in the forge as a helper, and he says he has a spare room in the back where you can live, if you want. Told me he can't pay much coin, but he has enough work to keep a roof over your head and food in your belly." He paused. "Tuck only had good things to say about your father," he added. "They fought together in the king's army. He wouldn't make an offer like that to just anyone."

Jonmarc stared into his tea, completely overwhelmed at both the reality of his loss and the unexpected kindness. "I don't know what to say," he murmured after a long pause.

Elly patted him on the arm. "Just say 'thank you' and then go back to bed and finish healing up so you can get on with things."

Jonmarc nodded and swallowed hard. He forced himself to look Kell in the eyes. "I heard the raiders say they'd come for Ebbetshire next. Are you ready?"

Kell gave a grim smile. "We're grateful for the warning. Elly told me straightaway, and I've had men doing what they can to protect the town." He shook his head. "Not so easy, since we're not a walled town and don't have a charter from the king to become one."

"You saw what they did," Jonmarc said, refusing to release Kell's gaze. "It only took a few candlemarks, and everyone was dead."

"Aye," Kell said, and his expression was resolute. "Not a man who helped bury your dead will ever forget that. We built watch towers, one on each corner of the town. We'll have a man in each one overnight every night," he said, his jaw set. "That puts two men watching the coast, and two watching the only roads in and out. The fishermen said they'd patrol the shoreline, and put a boat out each night with sentries."

Kell sighed. "We can't keep it up forever, but maybe long enough that the raiders decide to go somewhere else." He was silent for a moment. "One thing's for damn sure: we can give them an unpleasant surprise."

Jonmarc nodded, and forced down a lump in his throat. "We can hope."

THE RAIDERS CAME by the dark of the moon. The sentries in the boat raised the alarm before the raiders' ship angled their sails to ram the smaller craft and send its sailors to the bottom of the bay. The watchers in the tower rang bells in warning, and the town's crier ran through the streets beating on a tin pot to rouse Ebbetshire's citizens from their sleep.

Jonmarc stood shoulder to shoulder with the town's men on the shore road, between Kell and Tucker. A month of Elly's healing had put right his injuries, though he wondered if the nightmares would ever leave him. Working with Tucker in the forge had renewed his strength. Now, he waited, his hand clenched on the grip of his father's sword.

"They're taking their sweet time," Kell growled. "They don't seem to care that we know they're coming."

"They want us to be afraid," Jonmarc replied, feeling his heart pound. "They're certain we'll lose. It's a game to them."

"We'll see if the arrangements we've made will hold them off," Kell said grimly. "If not, it's been nice knowing you."

Five boats emerged in the faint glow the men's torches cast across the black water. Each boat, to Jonmarc's eye, held at least fifteen raiders, a number that could easily overpower the adult men of most small towns. One of the village's scouts ran up behind Kell and whispered in his ear. Kell nodded.

"Just as we thought—there's more of them coming in from the side. They mean to flank us." Kell reported quietly.

"We're as ready as we'll ever be," Tucker murmured. "Let's get the waiting over with."

Jonmarc scanned the shadowy shapes of the raiders looking for one man: Whiskey Voice. He shifted and let his left hand fall to the knife hilt in a sheath at his side. This time, he wouldn't be surprised. This time, he was ready.

The townsmen held their line at the edge of the shore where the ground gave them firm footing and the forest's edge forced the raiders up an open approach. Their torches gleamed in the darkness, lighting the way, making certain that the raiders knew they would not take this town without a fight.

There he is, Jonmarc thought. *Whiskey Voice*. The leader of the raiders strode up the beach as his men fanned out beside him, shouting to his men. The sea wind shifted, and Jonmarc caught the smell of unwashed bodies, sweat, and whiskey. He fought down flashes of memory from that other night, forcing himself to focus on the enemy that was nearly upon them. Down their line of volunteer defenders, Jonmarc heard men stirring as the tension became unbearable, but every man held his position and kept to his orders.

"Look at this," Whiskey Voice said to the raider beside him, loud enough for his words to carry. "They've made it easy for us. Now we don't have to drag them from their beds to put a knife through them."

Jonmarc could feel anger and adrenaline surging through his body, but he held his place, awaiting Kell's signal.

Whiskey Voice's taunts grew more graphic and obscene the closer he and his men got to the villagers. Yet their silence seemed to rattle him, Jonmarc thought. *Just wait...*

The raiders were almost upon them, and Jonmarc could hear murmurings among the men behind Whiskey Voice. Their stillness, their silence, and their suicidal stalwartness took the edge off the raiders' bravado.

They want us to fear them, Jonmarc thought. *They need to see our fear.*

"I'll give you something to make you move!" Whiskey Voice roared. He raised his sword and began to run toward the line.

Before the raiders could take two running steps, the twang of bows filled the still night air. A hail of arrows fell from both the right and the left, where archers waited hidden in the cover of the forest.

"Now!" Kell shouted.

With a feral cry, Jonmarc and the others broke their line, swords raised, rushing toward the attackers. At least a dozen raiders lay bleeding in the sand, arrows protruding from their bodies.

"With me!" Whiskey Voice rallied his surviving raiders. Rage reddened his features as he realized that he might lose both his profit and his sport.

Ebbetshire's men were not swordsmen, but they knew how to wield the tools of their trade. The long reach of the farmers' scythes made it possible to keep the raiders' swords at bay while sweeping a deadly arc at their ankles and knees.

Bertrand the butcher and his five stocky sons swung their cleavers with the certainty of men who knew how to cut up animals much larger than any of the raiders in their way. Beside Jonmarc, Tucker had forgone swords for the sheer brute force of a rod of iron and a sledgehammer.

In the distance, Jonmarc could hear more fighting, and he guessed that the men in the forest had intercepted Whiskey Voice's reinforcements. Whiskey Voice seemed to guess it, too, because his eyes narrowed with the look of a cornered animal.

"If we can't have what we came for, we'll take them all to the Crone with us!" Whiskey Voice shouted, laying about himself with his broadsword. His blade cleaved one of the townsmen from shoulder to hip, but three more villagers came at him with a ferocity that drove him back a few paces.

Much as Jonmarc hungered for a chance to settle the score with Whiskey Voice, he had his own problems. He had drawn the attention of one of the raiders who now circled him like a cat toying with a doomed mouse.

"I'll kill you quick, boy, if you don't struggle."

The voice sent a new surge of fury through Jonmarc as he recognized the thin raider as the reedy-toned man, Whiskey Voice's second-in-command.

"That's what you said the last time," Jonmarc said through clenched teeth.

The raider charged at him, but Jonmarc deflected the blade. He struggled to keep himself on solid ground, doing his best to drive the raider back into the sand. The raider laughed, drawing a second blade from behind him, coming at Jonmarc in a flurry of steel.

Jonmarc readied his sword, drawing his own knife. He caught the sword's stroke against his own long blade, feeling the jolt shudder down his whole body. Just in time, he struck back at the raider's second blow, missing the worst of it but taking a gash on his forearm.

The raider was stronger than his wiry frame suggested, and the next few strikes pounded him with such speed and rage that Jonmarc was certain he was about to die. It was all he could do to beat back the blows, forcing the blades clear of his chest and belly, accepting the bloody gashes that opened on his shoulders and arms.

Jonmarc slashed himself clear and fell back a pace, holding his sword level with his attacker's heart, unsure he could hold off another such salvo. The wiry raider chuckled and grinned, anticipating the kill. Then to Jonmarc's astonishment, there was a swish of air, a shadow there and gone, and the raider stiffened, eyes rolling back in his head. Before Jonmarc could move, the raider was hoisted into the air by a power yet unseen, and thrown with force against Jonmarc's outstretched sword.

Blood cascaded down the raider's head, which looked oddly angled. More blood seeped from his chest as he slid haltingly down Jonmarc's blade, sagging against the steel; a dead weight.

"That's one for you!" Tucker stood behind the raider, and raised his sledgehammer in salute.

Jonmarc dumped the body from his sword and stepped over the dead raider. "That's for father," he muttered.

Two more raiders came at them, and there was no more time to talk. Jonmarc and Tucker found themselves fighting back to back amid the bloody chaos. The sand at Jonmarc's feet was slick with blood and bodies littered the beach. Still, it looked as if more villagers were standing than raiders, and their allies in the forest appeared to have made good on their promise to keep any reinforcements from appearing.

Across the way, Jonmarc glimpsed Kell still on his feet, fighting off a raider who looked to be getting the worst of the match. The butcher and his sons, covered in blood, moved like a lethal wall down the beach. No new boats had come across the water from the sailing ship, and the fight had moved so that the townsmen blocked the raiders from reaching their boats had they been inclined to retreat.

The same coldness Jonmarc felt on the night of the attack in Lunsbetter settled over him once more. It quelled his fear, hardened his heart against the cries of dying men, and narrowed his focus. Without distractions, nothing existed except the sword in his hand. Jonmarc had no illusions about his skill with a sword. He fought on sheer instinct, fueled by rage and grief, hungry for vengeance. What he lacked in technique he made up for with an unpredictability that got him inside the guard of more than one raider. Blood soaked his shirt, his own blood and that of the raiders he killed.

"You should have stayed dead." Whiskey Voice seemed to rise out of nowhere from the torch smoke, his blade glinting in the firelight. "I've already killed you once."

Moving before Jonmarc could react, Whiskey Voice struck, stabbing deep into Tucker's side. Tucker gasped and swung his iron bar in a wide arc, connecting with Whiskey Voice's shoulder hard enough that Jonmarc could hear bones snap.

Jonmarc saw his chance in the instant before the raider could free his sword. He brought both his blades down in a 'V', striking with all his might, feeling his sword slice through bone and sinew and muscle. For a split second, Whiskey Voice stared at him in astonishment before his severed head toppled from his shoulders and his body landed with a wet thump at Jonmarc's feet.

When he looked up, the beach had cleared. Of the men still standing, none were raiders. The butcher and his sons moved among the dead, dispatching the fallen attackers with cold efficiency. Shadows moved at the edge of the forest and Jonmarc tensed, raising his bloodied swords for another onslaught before he recognized the uniforms of the soldiers from the garrison.

"There'll be no reinforcements coming this way," proclaimed a man wearing the insignia of a captain in the royal army as he strode toward Kell. His uniform was spattered with blood, but he appeared to be unharmed.

"The bulk of the raiders landed on either side, planning to cut behind you," the captain went on as he surveyed the bodies that littered the beach. "While this group kept you distracted, the others would have had the village in their hands before you could do anything about it."

Distracted, Jonmarc thought, eying the dead men on the ground. *That's one word for it.*

"Thanks for your assistance, Captain Duncan," Kell said as the soldiers gathered behind their commander. "I wasn't sure, when we sent the runner to the garrison, whether you'd be willing to bother with a village like Ebbetshire."

The captain spared him a weary grin. "I dare say the king will be happy to hear that at least one pack of raiders has been dealt with." He looked toward the water, where several teams of soldiers were rowing the raiders' landing boats back toward the sailing ship. "When my men are done with whoever's on board," he said, "we'll steer her into open water and burn her down to the waterline. That should give fair warning to anyone else who thinks to prey on the coast."

Kell and the captain moved away, concluding their business. Jonmarc looked down at the crimson-stained swords in his hands and the wide-eyed visage of Whiskey Voice's severed head. He had lost track of the raiders he had killed, and his father's voice rang in his memory.

Will it count against me, I wonder, when the Crone reckons my fate?

Tucker's heavy bear-paw of a hand landed on his shoulder. "You did well tonight, m'boy."

"I got lucky."

"Maybe the goddess likes you," Tucker replied. "We've had the favor of the Lady tonight, that's sure."

Jonmarc thought of the raider who had cursed him with his dying words, and of his father, who feared the judgment of the Crone. *I'm in too far to turn back now,* he thought, looking down at his bloody hands. He raised his face to meet Tucker's gaze.

"If the raiders come again, I want to be ready," he replied. "Teach me to fight."

CAVES OF THE DEAD

"I'M SORRY THAT you'll be moving on so soon. You're a good customer." Jonmarc Vahanian pocketed the silver coins for the load he had delivered. Forged iron and steel—bits and bridles, barrel hoops, rims for wagon wheels, and a variety of tools lay in bundles where the caravan workers had unloaded Jonmarc's wagon. Next to them lay a smaller pile of dried herbs, bottled potions, and powders that he delivered from the village hedge witch.

"Tucker's a fine blacksmith—and a smart man to have such a good apprentice." Maynard Linton, caravan master and traveling entertainer, put his velvet money bag inside his tunic. Linton eyed Jonmarc as if sizing him up. "You're Anselm's son, aren't you? Sorry to hear about your father."

Two years had passed since raiders destroyed Jonmarc's village, killing his family and the rest of the villagers. Jonmarc had been the sole survivor, and the thought of that awful night still put a lump in his throat. "Thanks," he said, more gruffly than he intended.

"I used to do business with your father when we passed this way," Linton continued. "It's a shame what happened. You're lucky to find a master like Tucker. And if you learned anything from your old man, Tucker's got himself a good deal."

'Lucky' wasn't the word Jonmarc would have normally chosen to describe himself, but he let it go. "What will you pay for the bits I brought you?" Jonmarc asked, nodding toward a canvas sack next to the forged items.

Linton opened the sack and poured out its contents onto the flat of the wagon. Old coins, copper jewelry tarnished with age, small carved statues, and other trinkets spilled onto the worn wood. Linton eyed them, then nodded and put them back in the sack.

"I'll give you twenty coppers for them," Linton said, withdrawing the coins from his pouch. "Things like these sell well in Principality. Soldiers are a suspicious lot. They hold with charms and talismans. These'll do just fine." He gave a sideways glance toward Jonmarc. "Does Tucker know you've been going into the caves?"

Jonmarc looked away. "Tuck's a businessman. He knows how hard it is to get by these days." A poor harvest for the last two seasons meant fewer travelers and fewer visits from merchant ships for the towns in Margolan's Borderlands. "We grow what we can and barter for what we can't, but the king wants coin for taxes." He paused. "How long will you be staying on in these parts?"

Linton shrugged. He was stout with broad shoulders and a restless energy about him that made people clear a path in front of him. His skin had darkened to a coppery leather tan from seasons spent out of doors. His waistcoat was brocade with velvet trim and his boots were of a sort favored by the gentry, but Jonmarc noticed both the waistcoat and boots had seen hard wear.

Linton's caravan was one of several that came through the Borderlands at odd intervals, setting up camp in a clearing on the outskirts of town. For the villagers, used to fisherman, tradesman and farmers, it was the most excitement to be had. The horses, brightly painted wagons, tents and flags, and dozens of oddly-dressed performers were quite a sight. Locals streamed in to see the acrobats and wild animals, sample unusual food, and buy trinkets from the artisans who traveled with the show. Linton's caravan was one of the more impressive ones Jonmarc had seen, looking more like a troupe of entertainers than a pack of vagrants.

"It all depends, m'boy," he replied. "We'll see how the farmers and town folk pay to see our shows and buy our wares."

Jonmarc grimaced. At seventeen, he was not a boy anymore, and Linton, who looked to be in his early thirties, was hardly of an age to set himself up as an elder. "And after this?"

Linton chuckled. "Wherever the road takes us," he said. "We had a good run in the palace city for the harvest festivals, but I'd like to be in Principality by Winterstide, if not before." He gave a conspiratorial wink. "Principality is where all the mercenaries make camp when they're not on campaign. And there's no one who's more like to spend gold on drink, women, and amusement than a bunch of holed-up mercs!"

Linton paused and gave Jonmarc a sidelong glance. "You know, if you're ever of a mind to see the world, I've got plenty of work for a good blacksmith. Takes one man just to keep the horses shod! My people get a tent to sleep in and food to eat, and enough coin to keep them in ale, that's for certain."

Jonmarc shook his head. "I don't think Tucker would be too pleased at that," he said. "And besides, my wife's due any day now with our first born. Her mother's a hedge witch and a healer—she'd like as not put boils on me if I tried a stunt like running off with a caravan."

Linton clapped him on the shoulder. "You wouldn't be the first to join under those circumstances," he said. "But I applaud your loyalty, though I'm not a family man myself. Get on then," he said, making a gesture with both hands meant to shoo Jonmarc back to his wagon. "I'll see you around, if the Dark Lady brings us back to these roads again."

Just then, shouts and loud cries rose from the center of the caravan, where cages held wild animals from all over the Winter Kingdoms. The center of the caravan's camp had bustled with people just moments before, but now the crowd parted to clear a path as the panicked shouts continued.

"By the Crone's tits!" Linton blustered, planting himself in the center of the opened space. "What's going on?"

Jonmarc spotted a dark form bounding toward them. Rippling with muscles under a sleek, dark coat of fur, the predator cat covered the ground as swiftly as a horse. The big cat growled, baring its sharp fangs, and ran straight for Linton.

The dark cat was on Linton almost before the caravan master could draw his sword. Linton let out a hoarse cry as he slashed at the cat. The crowd was backing away, and it was clear to Jonmarc that despite all the shouting, no help was on its way. Jonmarc looked around desperately, berating himself for leaving his swords in the wagon. He grabbed two of the heavy bridles he had delivered to Linton, and swung them with all his might at the cat that pinned Linton on the ground.

The steel in the first bridle slammed into the cat's head, knocking the big animal to the side. A cheer went up from the crowd, but they got no closer to the fight. The cat growled at Jonmarc, momentarily forgetting the prey beneath it. The second bridle hit, opening a bloody gash by the wild cat's ear. Jonmarc backed up, his heart racing, wondering if his damn fool plan would actually work.

The cat began to stalk him, and Jonmarc drew him off, giving Linton time to scramble to his feet. Jonmarc never took his eyes from the cat. The predator stepped up its pace, no longer walking but not yet at a full run. Jonmarc swung the bridle again, and the cat slowed warily.

The cat tensed to lunge just as a silver streak gleamed in the air, and the animal fell to the side, with the hilt of a dagger protruding from its fur. Jonmarc looked up to see Linton, his clothes torn and bloodied, ready with a second throwing knife.

When the cat lay still, Linton waved to several nearby caravan handlers who grudgingly responded. "Tie it up and get it to a healer. It's too damn hard to find cats like that to lose him now. And make sure he stays in his cage this time!" Linton growled.

Jonmarc had not moved. His heart was still pounding, and now that the fight was done, he felt his hands shaking. Linton strode up to him and clapped a hand on his shoulder.

"That was fast thinking," Linton said. Up close, Jonmarc could see where the big cat's claws had gashed Linton's shoulder,

"What was that thing?" Jonmarc asked, watching as the men tied up the wounded animal, which still had enough fight to snap at them until one of them looped a muzzle over its nose and chin.

"*Stawar*. You don't usually see one in these parts, but they're native to Eastmark," Linton replied. "They're the symbol of the Eastmark royal family, so it's highly illegal to remove one from the kingdom. I paid a pretty coin to smuggle that one out, and I'll not lose my investment! Thank you," Linton said, meeting Jonmarc's gaze. "That took balls—more than any of my whore-spawned performers had, that's for certain."

Jonmarc shrugged. "I'd hate to lose my best customer."

Linton guffawed. "Customer, indeed! You ever decide to see the world, I'll have a place for you, and that's a promise."

* * *

JONMARC DROVE THE empty wagon back to Ebbetshire alert for highwaymen. The trip had taken longer than he expected, and it was growing dark. Shanna would be worried about him. Shadows were already falling on the mountains just beyond town, and Jonmarc spared a glance for the high cliffs. In bright sunlight, you could just make out the dark places that marked the largest of the cave openings. But Jonmarc knew there were hundreds of others, many of them hidden or barely large enough for a man to enter. Places where long ago, the first people to settle this land had buried their dead.

It was their long-forgotten graves Jonmarc looted.

He hadn't set out to be a grave robber. It began with an off-handed remark from Linton about how much money one of his merchants had gotten for an old bit of jewelry. Intrigued, Jonmarc had stopped by the merchant's stall and recognized his wares were like the forgotten bits that littered the caves where he had gone exploring as a boy. Ever since then, Jonmarc had brought what he could find along with him he traded iron and herbs, and Linton was happy to pay him for the odd pieces. *The dead don't care, and the living need to eat*, Jonmarc thought.

His horse whinnied and stopped abruptly. Ahead on the road, Jonmarc saw a dark form in the shadows. He drew his knife. "Get out of my way, or I'll ride you down."

The figure took a few steps closer, moving out of the shadows and into the moonlight. Now, Jonmarc could see it was a man in a dark cloak with a hood that hid his face. "Who are you?" Jonmarc demanded.

"My name is Foor Arontala. I have a business offer for you, Jonmarc Vahanian."

Jonmarc's grip tightened on his knife. "How do you know my name?"

The figure chuckled. "You're the one who sells trinkets to the caravan. There's an item I'd like you to retrieve from the caves for me. I'll pay you well for it." The man lowered his hood. He had long, dark hair and a pale face with fine, aristocratic features.

"How well?"

"Three gold pieces. That should make it worth the effort."

Three gold pieces were more than most village men would see for years of work. Jonmarc nodded, but did not lower his knife. "Say on."

"I'm looking for a talisman," the man said. "Nothing most people would value, but it's of interest to me. It's very old. If you'll accept the job, I can tell you where to find it."

"If you know where it is, why don't you get it yourself?"

The man chuckled, and as his lips parted, Jonmarc could see the points of his long eye teeth. *Vayash moru*, Jonmarc thought, and a chill ran through him. "The lowest, oldest areas of the caves are spelled against my kind. But mortals may pass without harm."

"That's it? I go into the caves and bring back the talisman? Then what?" Common sense told Jonmarc he should snap the reins and ride on. Practicality made him stay. The last harvest had been poor, and the villagers had little coin to spend. Money had been too scarce over the last few years to turn down such a good prospect, and with a baby due any day and Shanna's mother also depending on their earnings, Jonmarc could not make himself turn away. Tucker was a good master and he paid Jonmarc his promised wage, but there had been weeks when business was bad enough that they had all gotten by on cabbage and leeks and a few rabbits poached from the king's forest.

"Then I pay you," the man replied. "Handsomely."

"You've got a deal," Jonmarc said. The stranger came closer, and Jonmarc's horse shied. The man held out a folded piece of parchment.

"These are the directions. Show them to no one else. They are spelled for your eyes alone."

Jonmarc's suspicion that the stranger was a mage deepened. "How will I find you?"

"I'll find you," the man said. "In three days, I'll come for the talisman at twelfth bells. Have it ready. I will be most unhappy if you do not have it for me when I arrive." He gave an unpleasant smile, and this time, Jonmarc was certain it was to make sure he saw the *vayash moru's* fangs.

"Understood," Jonmarc replied, but his gut clenched. *Sweet Mother and Childe! What have I gotten myself into?*

Jonmarc blinked, and the stranger was gone. He shivered, but it had nothing to do with the evening chill. He snapped the reins and sent the horse into a fast trot, and only his pride and the certainty that the dark stranger was watching from the shadows kept him from a full gallop.

SHANNA WAS WAITING for him when he came in from putting the wagon away and seeing to the horse. "I was beginning to worry," she said, smiling. "There's some stew left in the pot. I kept it warm for you." Her dark blonde hair was tied back with a bit of cloth, and her cheeks were pink from the warmth of the cooking fire. One hand fell to her swollen belly, and she smiled. "I felt the baby kick again. He's going to be a fine blacksmith, I wager!"

Jonmarc wrapped his arms around her and kissed her, and touched her belly gently. "Or a fine hedge witch like her mother and grandmother," he murmured.

Shanna chuckled and helped him out of his coat. "We'll have to wait and see now, won't we?" Her smile faded as she watched him. "Did something go wrong? Didn't you get the coin the caravan master promised?"

Jonmarc ladled some stew into a bowl and sat down at the table, ripping off a chunk of bread from the loaf that lay in the center. "Linton always keeps his word. He paid everything he said he would." He took out a pouch of coins and laid them on the table. "I'll take them to Tuck in the morning."

Shanna came to sit on the opposite side of the table. "What about the bits from the cave?"

Jonmarc withdrew a second pouch and dropped it onto the wood so that the coins jangled. "Twenty coppers. Not bad for odd rubbish just moldering in the cliffside."

Shanna made the sign of the Lady in warding. "You know how I feel about you going into the caves. There's a reason they're forbidden. They're haunted."

Jonmarc finished his bite of bread and stew before he answered. "I'm more afraid of the living than the dead," he said. "We'll have a new mouth to feed, and the caravan's moving on. No telling when we'll get more customers. I've got to make what I can while I can. I'd rather not eat cabbage for every meal."

Shanna reached out to touch his hand. "You have something else on your mind." Her brown eyes seemed to see right through him, and he sighed.

"I met a buyer on the road, coming home from Linton's," he said. "He wants something from the caves—and he'll pay gold."

Shanna's eyes narrowed. "Gold? For odd bits from old graves of people everyone's long forgotten?" She shook her head. "There's something wrong."

"Maybe you're right," he said, setting his empty bowl aside. "But I already agreed to the deal. A couple of gold coins will feed us all for a long time—Tuck's family, too, if need be."

"And how will you explain where you came by gold?" Shanna challenged. "Someone will say you stole it, and get the king's guard after you."

The same thought had occurred to Jonmarc. "The man's coming to pay me in three days. If Linton's not gone yet, I'll go to the caravan to change it to silver and coppers. Or I'll take a load of goods to Eiderford and exchange my gold for the silver they pay me. Tuck won't have a problem with getting his pay in gold, I wager."

"I wish you hadn't made the bargain," Shanna said. "We'd get by without it."

Jonmarc leaned over and kissed her. "I want to be a proper father, and a proper husband," he said. "I promised Elly I'd take good care of you."

Shanna smiled and twined her fingers with his. "You do right by mother and me, Jonmarc. I just wish times were easier."

"Nothing lasts forever, my father used to say," Jonmarc replied. "Bad times or good. Always a storm coming, or one just passed." He let out a long breath. "And I wager he knew what he was talking about."

THE NEXT EVENING, once his day at the forge was through, Jonmarc ate a hurried dinner and packed his gear. He left Shanna with a kiss and assurances of a quick return.

She pressed an amulet pouch of her mother's dried plants into his hand. "To ward off danger," she said, folding his fingers around the pouch.

Jonmarc forced a smile and tucked the amulet into his bag. "I'll be back before morning. You'll see. Nothing to worry about." He knew from the look in Shanna's eyes that she was unconvinced.

The moon was bright, and Jonmarc crossed the lowlands with relative ease, glad he did not have to light a lantern. So far, he had eluded notice, but he had no doubt that there would be some in the village who would look askance at his forays into the caves, although the ancient dead whose skeletons lay in the cliffside were none of their own. Tuck, Jonmarc was certain, would shrug and agree that the living had more need of the trinkets than the dead. Shanna's mother, Elly, would worry about the wardings and traps that might be set for tomb robbers, or the spirits of the restless dead. If any of them had seen the stranger, Jonmarc was quite certain they would have told him to forget the whole thing. *But there's no going back now.* He thought as he reached the cliffs and began his climb.

As a child, back in Lunsbetter, Jonmarc and his brothers had often climbed the cliffs and poked around the caves near their village. When Jonmarc had gotten settled into his new home in Ebbetshire, the allure of the nearby cliffs had proven irresistible. Climbing gave him a way to clear his mind, and in those quiet moments, he was alone with his grief for his murdered family. Investigating the caves had begun as a lark, and he had not considered selling the trinkets he found beside the old graves until money had gotten tight.

Jonmarc swore under his breath as he reached for a difficult handhold on the rough stone. He pulled himself up onto a narrow ledge, and inched his way along until he reached an outcropping in the rock. Ducking behind the outcropping, Jonmarc struck flint to steel to light his lantern, and held it aloft, alert for trouble. The stranger's knowledge of the caves made him wary, and Jonmarc half expected to find the man waiting for him. When nothing moved in the shadows, he let out a long breath, and started into the caves.

Shanna and her mother swore the caves were haunted, but Jonmarc rarely saw ghosts. Then again, few people without a touch of magic saw spirits except at Haunts, the Feast of the Departed. Jonmarc was just as glad to do without any special ability to see the dead. Even without magic, he saw enough ghosts in his dreams.

Jonmarc had memorized the stranger's map. Much of the route was already familiar; only the last portion was new. Once Jonmarc got past the first chamber, more rooms opened up into a warren of dark passages leading deep into the cliff. Over the last two years, he had explored most of them, but even he had only dared to go so deep. The stranger's map took him further down one of the remote tunnels than he had ever ventured, and Jonmarc felt a prickle of fear.

"At least the bats are gone," he muttered to himself. A benefit of coming after dark meant that the bats that clustered in the caves were out feeding, although the floor of the cave was slick with their droppings.

The deeper he got in the cave, the more aware he became of the faint green glow of the moss that clung to the walls of the tunnel. Most of the time, Jonmarc barely paid the moss any attention, but tonight, his nerves were enough on edge that the eerie glow just added to his feeling of foreboding.

This deal was a mistake. The thought repeated itself in his mind with every step, and Jonmarc pushed it aside. *I made a bargain. Not keeping it would be a real mistake—especially with a* vayash moru. It did no good to wish for his father's counsel or his mother's advice. They were two years dead and buried with the rest of his village. *Maybe I should have talked to Elly or Tuck, but what could they tell me? By the time I could have seen them, the deal was struck.*

The passage in front of him forked, and Jonmarc knew that the stranger's map led him to the left. Just in case, he marked the turn with a bit of coal he had brought for that purpose. *In case something down here doesn't want the talisman brought back up to the surface*, he thought.

Jonmarc's lantern cast a small circle of light, just enough for him to see a few steps in front of him. Darkness closed in behind him as he moved forward, and yielded temporarily to him as he advanced. But the further he went down this particular tunnel, the more the feeling grew that he was being watched. He stopped, wary of a trap. Nothing moved in the darkness, and the only sounds were the faint, distant dripping of water and his own rapid breath. Sometimes, he had surprised rats and other small creatures in the upper tunnels. All the same, he had the feeling that he was not alone, and not particularly welcome. Whispers hissed at the very edge of his hearing, and some of the shadows slipped away from his light as if they had a will of their own.

It feels like the realm of the dead, Jonmarc thought, and made the sign of the Lady in warding.

Enough foolishness, he berated himself. *I just need to grab the talisman and go.*

Two more turns took him much deeper into the cave, and for an instant, he imagined the weight of the cliff bearing down on him, stifling his breath. His heart raced, and he fought the urge to turn and run. He mustered his courage and went on, mindful of how much the candle in his lantern had burned down. *I've got no desire to be stuck down here in the dark*, he thought, though he had taken the precaution to bring an extra candle, just in case.

One more short tunnel led him to the end of the stranger's map. He had passed many old burial sites along the way, with yellowed bones wrapped in crumbling cloth. On a normal hunt, he would have looked in each one for saleable trinkets, but this night, he focused only on the stranger's errand. *They're not going anywhere*, he thought with a glance to the long-dead corpses. *I can always come back for them.*

At the end of the tunnel Jonmarc found a room carved into the stone. Unlike the other crypts which were natural recesses in the sides of the cave, this room had an arched doorway which still showed the faded remnants of ancient paint. Beyond the archway, a raised platform held the remains of a man. Jonmarc felt a tingle as he stepped through into the room, and he wondered what magics had been set in these tunnels, and by whom.

He had expected to find a skeleton, or even a jumble of bones. But the body that lay in repose appeared to be a fresh corpse, unsullied by time or decay. Jonmarc took a closer look. By the look of the dead man's clothing, he had been dead for a very long time, a century or more perhaps. But his outfit and personal items left no doubt about the dead man's vocation. A wicked sword lay atop the body, its pommel still clutched in his hands. Though the sword was of a more crude design than those Jonmarc forged, it was a lethal weapon for a man of war. The corpse wore a leather cuirass covered in metal rings over a finely-woven tunic with intricate embroidery along its hem. The dead man's boots and scabbard were of equally high quality. *A king?* Jonmarc wondered. *At the least, an important warrior.*

Jonmarc took a hesitant step toward the corpse, fearing it might rise from its slumber to defend itself. When nothing happened, he carefully made his way to stand beside the dead warrior, and looked at the body with amazement. *He said this tomb was spelled against* vayash moru, Jonmarc thought. *Perhaps the mages also cast a spell to preserve the dead.*

Along with the map, the stranger's parchment contained a sketch of the item Jonmarc was to retrieve. It was a flat silver medallion on a leather strap with several runes scratched into its surface. Jonmarc looked more closely at the warrior's corpse. Whoever he had been, the man had died wealthy. His cloak was held together by a silver clasp, and golden rings set with jewels glistened from several pale fingers. A chalice and ewer of gold lay beside him, and a large medal with a blood-red stone hung from his neck on a golden chain.

What could possibly be so valuable about a little silver disk compared to the fortune in gold he's wearing? Jonmarc wondered. He moved cautiously around the bier, still expecting the dead man to rise up and challenge him at any moment. *I don't want to touch him. And I really don't want to go riffling through his pockets.*

Almost hidden by the leather cuirass and the gold chain of the medallion, Jonmarc spied a thin leather strap around the dead man's neck. Gingerly, he reached out toward the body, fearing that any second the man's eyes would open and a hand would reach up to grab him by the wrist. His fingers touched the stiff old leather and he tugged, drawing it up from beneath the clothing. The silver medallion gleamed in the lantern light, untarnished by the years, preserved, Jonmarc guessed, by the same magic that sustained the appearance of the corpse.

He cringed as he drew the thin leather strap over the warrior's head, and sighed with relief when it was free in his grasp. Compared to the value of the dead man's medals and other belongings, the silver talisman looked roughly made and of insignificant value. *Why would anyone ask me to steal something that looks like a child could have etched it?* he wondered.

Jonmarc closed his fist around the talisman, then dropped the leather strap over his head and tucked the silver disk beneath his shirt. All around him, the shadows had grown darker, and a growing presence was impossible to ignore. Though Jonmarc could not see the spirits, he knew they were close, watching him. And though he possessed no magic, three words pushed into his consciousness.

Beware the beasts.

Jonmarc left the crypt as quickly as he could, banging his shoulder against the rough stone side of the doorway in his hurry. His boot steps echoed in the empty tunnels, and had he dared, he would have broken into a run. He imagined that the spirits in the darkness behind him laughed at his haste. The footing was too uncertain and the tunnels too narrow for him to run without risking a turned ankle or worse. Jonmarc could hear his heartbeat reverberating in the dark tunnel, and the sound of his own shallow breaths seemed deafening.

Twice he fell, rising with bloodied palms and scraped knees, protecting his lantern at the cost of his skin. The orb of light swung crazily, sending shadows flying back and forth across the tunnel walls. Jonmarc did not slow down until the cave entrance came into sight. The sky was already growing lighter, and Jonmarc realized that it was almost dawn.

Bruised and exhausted, he made his way back home.

He tumbled into bed next to Shanna, who was fast asleep, to catch a few candlemarks of precious rest before it would be time to go to the forge. As he drifted off, he wondered again about the stranger on the road, and the warning of the ghosts in the crypt. His sleep was restless, and his dreams were dark.

JONMARC WOKE WITH a start, troubled by bad dreams. He reached for the talisman on the strap around his neck, and touched the metal disk to assure himself that the night before had really happened. Although the disk lay against his skin, it was strangely cool to the touch.

He dressed quickly, chagrinned at the damage he had done to his pants and shirt getting out of the cave. One knee was out, the other pant leg was ripped, and a sleeve was nearly torn off. His boots were missing.

"Have you seen my boots?" he asked, glad he had taken a moment to wash up in the horse trough the night before.

Shanna was scooping hot gruel from a pan on the hearth. "Your boots stink. They're out on the step. I don't know what you trod in, but it's worse than horse shit."

"Sorry," Jonmarc mumbled.

"Were you in a fight?" Shanna set the bowl down in front of him and stood back, hands on her hips. Her stance accentuated her rounded belly, and reminded Jonmarc that it would only be a few days before she would likely go into labor.

"No fight," Jonmarc said, remembering the terror of the night before. "I was just in too much of a hurry to get out of those damned caves, and I made a mess of things."

"Humph." Shanna's expression was skeptical, as if she suspected he was omitting part of the story. She sighed and then smiled. "Well, it's nothing that a few patches and a little thread can't put right. You don't look much worse for the wear." She bent down to kiss him. "And you're home safe. That's all I care about."

Shanna ruffled his hair, and Jonmarc caught her hand and pressed it against his cheek. He felt a fierce stab of fear for her safety and that of their child. Before the journey into the cave, he might have dismissed it as new-father nerves, concern for the dangers of childbirth even with the help of an experienced hedge witch like Elly. Today, the fear felt far more real than nervousness over a new baby. Something deep inside screamed for him to pack Shanna and her mother into their wagon and drive until they reached the horizon, far from the caves and beyond the power of the dark stranger.

"Linton, the caravan master, offered me a job," Jonmarc blurted. "We could go with them—you, me, Elly. See the kingdom. It would be good money."

Shanna gave him a puzzled look. "And leave Ebbetshire? Our home is here. What about Tucker and the forge? And Kell and the rest of our friends? What's gotten into you?"

Jonmarc swallowed down his fear. "I told him no, but then I got to thinking. The pay is good. I wouldn't have to thieve out of the caves anymore. We could go far away, somewhere Foor Arontala could never find us."

Shanna met his gaze. "That's what this is all about, isn't it? That bloody strange man on the road and his gold." She lifted her chin. "I've got a mind to tell him what for, putting you through all that, gold or no gold!"

"I don't even want you here when he comes," Jonmarc said, knowing Shanna could see the fear in his eyes. "I don't want him to lay eyes on you or the baby. He's a mage, I'm sure of it, and not a good one, if there is such a thing. I should never have told him I'd do his bidding."

Shanna sat down next to him and took his hands in hers. "If he's as fearsome as you say, and if he really is a mage, you might not have been able to refuse him. Taking the talisman didn't harm anyone; it's not like he asked you to steal from the living." She met his eyes. "Just be done with him as quick as you can. He'll have no more need of you, and we can get on with our lives."

Jonmarc let out a long breath and gave a crooked smile. "I love how you always manage to think straight, no matter what's going on." He pulled her closer and kissed her, and laid a hand protectively on the bulge at her waist. "And after this, I promise to stay out of the caves unless it's the only way to keep body and soul together."

TUCKER WAS ALREADY at the forge when Jonmarc arrived, and the day passed quickly to the sound of the hammer on the anvil. The forge was a second home to Jonmarc, one of the places that reminded him most of his own family, especially since Tucker had retrieved the anvil and tools from Anselm's ruined workshop. Sometimes, Jonmarc shut his eyes, feeling the warmth of the coal fire, hearing the pounding, smelling the coal smoke, and for just a moment, it was as if the last two years had never happened. Just for a few heartbeats, he could make believe that his father was still at work in the forge, that his brothers were going about their chores outside, that his mother would be waiting for them with dinner. With a sigh, Jonmarc opened his eyes, resigned to the fact that the home he remembered was gone forever.

"I hate to see the caravan move on," Tucker said after a long silence. "You brought back a good price for the pieces you sold for me. With how bad the harvest's been and how tight everyone's been with their money, unless we get some ships in, or there are merchants on their way to the city, I don't know where we'll get the rest of the coin to pay our taxes."

If Arontala holds to his word, that gold will be enough to take care of Shanna, the baby and Elly plus pay our taxes— and Tuck's, too. Maybe I've let my imagination get the best of me, Jonmarc thought. *This could be a real stroke of luck.*

"I'm sure something will come along," Jonmarc said, hoping Tucker did not pick up on his unusual level of distraction.

Tucker laughed. "I can see you've got bigger things on your mind, lad. A baby on the way can cause anyone to lose their wits. Don't worry," he said, switching out the iron bar he was pounding. "It'll all go right. Fiona's had six babies— four what lived—and we've managed to make it through." He leaned toward Jonmarc conspiratorially. "Although with the racket one of them can put up, you may find it more restful here in the forge." Tucker laughed heartily and went back to his work.

The sun had long set by the time they finished for the day. Since orders were slim, Tucker had decided to make enough of their most popular pieces so that Jonmarc could take a wagonload to Eiderford, the large town further down the coast. They worked late into the night, trying to finish the pieces in time for market. Jonmarc and Tucker were finally banking the fire and putting away their tools when a strange sound made them both pause and exchange a wary glance.

"Did you hear something?" Tucker asked, cocking his head so that his good ear was toward the doorway.

"Yeah, but I'm not sure what it was," Jonmarc replied. Tucker reached for his hammer and a bar of iron, while Jonmarc drew his knife and grabbed a second iron bar. As he moved, for the first time that day he became aware of the amulet that hung on its strap around his neck. The metal disk had suddenly grown cold, icy against his skin.

The strange noise came again, reminding Jonmarc of a crab scuttling across rocks. *We're not close to the beach*, he argued with himself. *And it would have to be a very big crab to make a sound like that.*

This time, the sound seemed to come from more than one location, like claws on stone. The moon was bright and full, and Jonmarc did not pause to grab a lantern. Cautiously, Jonmarc and Tucker made their way out of the forge's doorway into the open space that separated the building from the road.

"Look there!" Jonmarc said, pointing to the right. "Did you see that?" Something skittered between the shadows of the trees.

"Saw it," Tucker said. "Don't know what it is."

"There's another one!" Jonmarc spotted movement to the left. The clicking and scratching grew louder, jumbled as if it came from many places at once.

"Dark Lady take my soul, what is that thing?" Tucker murmured as a figure stepped out of the shadows. Whatever it was, it wasn't human. The head was misshapen and bulbous, on a body with a stance all wrong to be a man. Wiry arms with long-fingered hands hung down from slim shoulders over a muscular torso and powerful, bowed legs. In the moonlight, its skin looked sickly gray, and Jonmarc was willing to bet that the thing's long fingers ended in claws. It sniffed the air, scenting them, and turned its burning yellow eyes toward them as it opened a maw filled with sharp teeth.

"It's heading our way!" Even before Jonmarc could voice his warning, Tucker stepped forward in a defensive stance.

Down the lane, toward the center of the village, Jonmarc heard shouts of alarm. A bell rang out, rousing the men of the village to arms. Ebbetshire's men and women poured from their homes brandishing whatever weapons were at hand as more of the gray-skinned beings stepped forward from the shadows, their talons scraping and clacking on the rocky ground.

The gray beasts began to move forward like wolves, crowding their prey together. Jonmarc could see Kell, the village mayor, running at one of the beasts with a broadsword, while the butcher and his four brawny sons set about themselves with cleavers. The good people of Ebbetshire had already proven their mettle driving off raiders, and they did not run from this new threat. Soon, the street was filled with villagers wielding kitchen knives and farm scythes, staves, and hoes, even the rope nets and sharp pikes of the fishermen.

The beasts were in no hurry, and their deliberate approach unnerved Jonmarc, as did the reptilian calculation in their glowing eyes. Three more of the things had emerged from the shadows near the forge, and Tucker was swearing fluently under his breath, waiting for the beasts to come into range.

Jonmarc swung at the nearest beast with his iron rod, wishing for the sword he had left under his bed at home. He struck the creature hard where the neck joined the shoulder, a blow that should have felled a man or slowed a wild animal. The creature hissed and swatted the rod away, fixing its cold gaze on Jonmarc.

"Watch those teeth!" Tucker warned. Jonmarc did not need to be cautioned. The beast's lantern jaw was filled with rows of sharp teeth, like the strange fish the nets sometimes brought up from the depths of the sea. Claws as long as a man's fingers clicked together on its hands and its taloned feet scratched against the cobblestones.

One of the creatures rushed forward with a speed Jonmarc had not expected. It slashed at Tucker with its claws, and staggered as Tucker slammed his sledgehammer against the thing's bloated head. Ichor streamed from where the hammer tore the beast's leathery skin, but the creature did not slow its advance.

Down the street, Jonmarc heard curses and cries to the Lady as the townspeople battled for their lives. He crouched, watching the beast that was watching him, ready for the attack. It came at him in a gray blur, and Jonmarc slammed his long knife into its chest, trying not to recoil from the cold touch of its leathery skin. Black ichor spurted from the wound, but the thing twisted, yanking the blade from Jonmarc's hand, and lumbered toward him.

Tucker had his hands full, fending off two of the beasts. The blacksmith was taller than most of the men in the village, brawny from his work, with strong arms and powerful shoulders. It was taking all of Tucker's skill to keep the beasts at bay as he swung the hammer and iron rod, knocking the creatures back. They shook themselves off and advanced once more, undaunted.

Out of the corner of his eye, Jonmarc saw a creature snatch one of the village men and hurl him across the road as effortlessly as a child might throw a ball. He spotted two of the fishermen using their staves and pikes to force one of the beasts into a fishing net, only to see the intruder shred the net with its claws as if it were parchment.

Jonmarc felt a coldness settle over him, driving out fear. It was the same cold distance his father had taught him in the slaughterhouse, and it had served him well in his fights against the raiders. No room for fear, no place for worry about Shanna and the baby, nothing except an icy cold in the center of his being strong enough to do what must be done.

The creature eying Jonmarc began to advance once more, then stopped and turned to watch as Tucker beat back the two beasts. Both of the beasts attacking the blacksmith were dripping with ichor, and it was clear that Tucker had done damage with the iron rod and sledgehammer. The face of one of the beasts looked sunken on one side where the hammer had smashed its bones, and the other beast's left arm hung uselessly at its side, with shards of bone protruding from the leathery skin.

Nothing natural could survive that pounding. Could a mage summon creatures like these? Jonmarc wondered, thinking of the dark stranger on the road. *And did he send them for me, or did the talisman draw them?*

Jonmarc seized the chance to launch himself at the beast nearest him, bringing his long knife down with both hands into its back, using his own weight to thrust the blade deep and drag it down through skin and bone. The creature hissed, and it turned faster than Jonmarc could get clear, raking the right side of his face and neck with its claws and opening up a gash from Jonmarc's ear down into his shoulder.

Jonmarc lunged out of the way as the creature swung its claws once more, barely missing a slash that would have caught him across the chest. Tucker was bleeding from a dozen gashes on his arms and face, and his heavy leather apron was no match against the creature's claws. Tucker swung again with his massive hammer, catching one of the beasts full in the chest. It stumbled, wheezing, and Tucker stepped toward it to finish it off with another blow. Before he could land his strike, the second creature moved with the speed of a coiled snake, lashing out its long arm and digging its clawed fingers into Tucker's face. Tucker screamed, and the beast jerked his arm back, snapping Tucker's head free from his body.

Jonmarc had no time for grief or horror. The creature he battled was backing him toward the doorway of the forge, intent on its prey. Jonmarc looked around, desperate for a better weapon than his knife and iron bar. His face and neck were sticky with blood, but the pain of the gash kept him going. The hot coals of the fire drew his eye. The forge's fire had not yet cooled, and Jonmarc thrust his iron bar into the coals, then backed up toward the bellow to blast air through the embers. Flames rose into the air, and the creature halted, eyeing the fire warily.

"Maybe fire isn't to your liking," Jonmarc said, carefully moving to where Tucker stored bundles of reed torches. Snatching up one of the torches, Jonmarc stuck it into the fire and it crackled to life. Jonmarc jabbed the burning torch toward the creature, moving slowly to keep the fire between him and the beast, until he reached the bucket of whale oil Tucker kept to prime the coals if they went cold.

Jonmarc grabbed the bucket and hurled its contents onto the creature, then lunged forward, igniting the oil with his torch. The creature screamed and flailed, backing away from Jonmarc, lumbering into the beast that hunkered over Tucker's bleeding corpse. In an instant, that beast and Tucker's clothing went up in flames, and the night air was filled with the smell of burning meat.

The forge was hot, but still the amulet that hung amid the tatters of Jonmarc's shirt was cold as ice. It glinted in the firelight, and for an instant, Jonmarc thought its runes glowed with an inner light. He looked around wildly for more oil, but found only an empty bucket. Jonmarc shoved his knife back into his belt. He slipped his hands into Tucker's heavy leather gloves. Snatching a coal shovel, Jonmarc loaded the bucket with hot coals and grabbed a basket full of torches, then picked up one of the iron rods whose tip had grown bright red in the fire.

"I'll get them, Tuck," Jonmarc muttered.

He walked around Tucker's smoking corpse and the cindered remains of the creatures and headed for the center of the village. Bodies littered the roadway. The creatures had scattered, and some tore at the fallen corpses or gnawed on the remains of the villagers, while others seemed intent on wrecking anything within reach. Twice, beasts lumbered in his direction only to veer away.

In the center of the village green, the butcher and his sons were still standing, but it was clear to Jonmarc that they were rapidly losing their battle. Jonmarc hurried his pace. He dropped the torches and set down the bucket of hot coal, then thrust one of the torches into the bucket where it caught fire quickly.

"Let's see how you like this!" he shouted, running toward the creatures. He swung the iron bar, landing its red-hot tip against the back of one of the beasts. The monster screamed, wheeling toward Jonmarc, who thrust the burning torch into its face. Jonmarc did not wait to watch as the beast burst into flame. He set about with the iron rod with all his strength, knowing he would tire long before he ran out of beasts. He jabbed at the creatures with the torch, and then hurled it into the midst of them, sending it wheeling through the darkness so that it rained bits of burning reed down on the shrieking beasts that scrambled to get away even as their skin began to sizzle and pop.

Jonmarc fell back to his bucket of coals and lit another torch. The creatures were gradually leaving the butcher and his sons and had turned their attention to Jonmarc. Cursing under his breath, he stood his ground. *Let's see how many of them I can take with me,* he thought grimly.

The dry grass blazed where the creatures Jonmarc set afire had stumbled and fallen, and the fire spread rapidly. "Get out of there before you burn!" Jonmarc shouted to the butcher, but in the firelight, he could see that three of the man's sons were on the ground and the butcher and his last son appeared too badly injured to flee. Smoke rose on the night air, smelling of burning grass and flesh.

Jonmarc grabbed the unlit torches and backed away from the creatures, waving his firebrand to keep them at bay. Much of the ground between him and the butcher was already on fire, trapping the creatures on the dwindling bit of unburned land. The creatures began to rush toward Jonmarc. Caught between a half dozen snarling beasts and the fire, Jonmarc ran toward the flames, closed his eyes, and leaped. He landed hard on the other side of the flames, scattering his torches and knocking the wind from his lungs. His hands and arms were covered with burns and his lungs protested at the scorching hot air, but he was still alive.

A nightmarish screaming rose from inside the flames, and Jonmarc could see the creatures writhing and curling like bits of paper tossed onto the hearth. Fearing for the butcher and his sons, Jonmarc ran as fast as he dared around the periphery of the flames, alert for any of the remaining beasts. He still had four of the torches, and he lit one from the curtain of fire.

When Jonmarc reached the butcher, the hulking man was kneeling, surrounded by the savaged bodies of his grown sons. Together, the butcher and his boys had been an unstoppable force against raiders, but even their brawn had proven no match for the beasts. Two of the bodies were headless. One son's arms had been ripped from his body. The fourth of the butcher's sons had been eviscerated, and as the butcher turned slowly toward Jonmarc, he could see that the man was as badly wounded as his boys.

"Go," he ordered, managing a nod of his head toward the center of the village. "Save anyone you can. We're done for."

For the second time in two years, Jonmarc found himself stumbling through the flame-lit darkness toward a burning village under siege. Emboldened by the flames, long past caring for his own survival, Jonmarc roared as he ran at the creatures, brandishing a torch in each hand. A year of drought had left the village lands and buildings tinder-dry, and the fire from the burning creatures had already spread down into the center of the town, catching on the thatch roofs and wooden beams, crackling through the tangle of dry grass and wilted hedgerows.

Jonmarc drove the beasts toward the flames, giving them no choice except to burn by his hand or to fall back into the fire. He blinked blood out of his eyes, felt his shirt clinging to his body with sweat as his skin reddened from the heat. Yet the metal talisman from the cave remained cold, sliding across his chest like dead fingers.

Exhausted and heart sick, bleeding from gashes and burns, Jonmarc shouted at the creatures like a drover. Two of the creatures lunged at him, but he jammed his torches into their open maws, choking as the gray flesh began to smolder and the screeching beasts staggered backwards, into the flames.

Finally, he could see no more of the beasts. Whether they had burned or fled, the gray-skinned monsters were gone.

Jonmarc took his remaining torches and began to search for survivors. For two years, in his nightmares he had relived the awful night the raiders burned his village and killed his family. Now, as he stumbled over bodies in the glow of burning buildings, he felt as if he were trapped in those dreams, or had awoken to relive that awful night once more. He found Kell's body, what remained of it, in the street. The merchants and tradesmen who had welcomed Jonmarc into their village now lay dead, their shops ablaze. Jonmarc checked the stables, hoping to find survivors hiding there, and discovered that the creatures had even savaged the horses and livestock. Save for the wind and the crackling of the flames, the night was silent.

Fear gave Jonmarc the energy to run through the ruined streets shouting for Shanna and Elly. No reply came save for the echo of his own voice. Smoke clouded the air and the smell of burning flesh threatened to make him retch. Jonmarc slowed when he came to the street where he and Shanna shared Elly's small house. The front of the building was Elly's shop of dried herbs and potions, where she provided her services as the village's hedge witch. It was badly damaged. The windows had been broken and the wooden door bore the slashes of the creatures' long claws.

"Shanna! Elly!" Jonmarc shouted, fearing the worst.

Elly lay in the doorway in a pool of blood. Her staff lay nearby, stained with the dark ichor of the monsters. Jonmarc swallowed hard, then bent down and closed her eyes, murmuring a prayer for the dead.

He straightened, and took a deep breath to steady himself. He felt as if he were moving through deep water, as if a seer's vision had already shown him what was to come. The memory of searching through his boyhood home only to find his mother and brothers dead at the raiders' hands was so real that he felt as if time had undone the past two years, dooming him to repeat his loss.

Jonmarc dodged the overturned bundles of herbs and broken jars of powders, heading for the living quarters in the back. The fires outside the building shone so brightly through the window Jonmarc did not need a lantern to see the wreckage the beasts made of the room. Shanna lay in the center of the room, one hand still gripping one of Jonmarc's swords. Her dress and the floor around her was stained with blood from where one of the beasts had slashed open her belly, leaving her stillborn child beside her.

Jonmarc wailed in grief and dropped to his knees. He gathered Shanna into his arms along with the child he would never know, and rocked back and forth, utterly lost.

May you lose all you love to the flame and sword, and the Dark Lady take your soul! The dying raider's curse echoed in Jonmarc's mind.

Sweet Mother and Childe, Jonmarc beseeched Margolan's patron aspects of the Lady, *You've taken everything from me. Why not take me, too?*

No reply was forthcoming, and Jonmarc felt the coldness saturate his being, numbing his fear, pain, and grief. He lifted Shanna and the baby in his arms and placed them on the bed, spreading the coverlet over them and closing their eyes. *I can't just leave them here for the scavengers*, he thought, swallowing down the lump that threatened to close his throat.

Jonmarc retrieved his swords and cloak, and laid them outside the shop, grabbing a lantern and fresh candles, and the small bag of coins Elly kept in a chest under the bed. He threw the coins into a sack along with his clothing, and then tucked a small scrimshaw comb, Shanna's prized possession, into the bag as well and put the sack with his sword. Then he moved around the hedge witch's shop, using herbs and powders and a bit of water for a salve to cleanse the gash on his face and neck. The wound had clotted, but it hurt like a hot poker, and Jonmarc wondered if the beasts' claws were poisoned. *If so, then I'll join Shanna and the others before long.*

He went to the front and returned with Elly's corpse, laying it on the floor beside the bed. Time and again he went into the street, bringing back as many of the bodies as he could until the back room and shop were stacked shoulder to shoulder with the bodies of his neighbors. Always, he was alert for a sign that the creatures had returned, but the night was utterly still.

When the small rooms would hold no more, Jonmarc took one of his remaining torches and lit it from the embers in the fireplace. He took a last look around himself, and once more murmured the prayer for the dead before he moved through the rooms, setting the building on fire.

Jonmarc stood in the street, watching the building burn as tears streamed down his cheeks. Despair urged him to hurl himself onto the pyre, but a shred of self-preservation held him back. His skin felt hot from the blaze, except for where the talisman hung on his chest. *Somehow, this damned amulet and Foor Arontala are responsible for this*, he thought. *He said he'd be back on the third night. Probably to finish me off if the creatures didn't do it for him.*

The sky lightened with the dawn, and Jonmarc turned to look at the cliffs. *I never should have taken the amulet from the caves. I'd best send it back to the pit where it belongs.*

Jonmarc gathered his meager belongings and headed toward the cliffs. His body ached and he was bone weary, but the conviction that he had to rid himself of the talisman grew with every painful step. He was reckless climbing the narrow ledges, no longer caring for his own safety, tempting the Formless One to take him. The rocks scraped and cut his hands, leaving a bloody trail. He felt nothing but cold, inside and out. Sheer resolve kept him moving. *If I survive, someday, somehow I will find that mage and make him pay,* Jonmarc thought.

He reached the mouth of the cave as the dawn brightened to full daylight. From the ledge, he could see the smoke still rising from the ruins of Ebbetshire. Jonmarc tore the amulet's strap over his head and flung the cold silver as deep into the cave as his rage gave him strength to hurl it. There was no way he was going to make the dangerous trek to the deep places; something warned him that this time, he would not escape the shadows. Ridding himself of the talisman would not bring back the dead, nor would it absolve him of his guilt over drawing the monsters to the village. But if it would cheat Arontala of his prize, it gave him a measure of cold consolation.

He sat for a few moments on the ledge. The same despair that had tempted him to the flames called to him to jump, but he was too weary for self-destruction. The smoke from the village would eventually draw attention. Jonmarc figured it was wise not to be found when that happened. One tragedy had won him sympathy. Two might gain him a hanging.

I've no home, no family, no village, no wife and child, he thought, staring out across the landscape. *I'm likely cursed, and I'll have a* vayash moru *mage after me.* He sighed. *But I've proven I'm good in a fight, I'm strong and I've got a trade. Maybe one of the mercenary companies in Principality will take me, no questions asked.*

He looked out to the horizon. Principality was on the other side of Margolan, a long way to travel. *Then again, I've nowhere else to be.*

By evening, he had put distance between himself and Ebbetshire. He washed the worst of the blood and dirt from his skin, dabbing at the painful gash along the side of his face. Jonmarc wondered if the shock that numbed him showed in his face.

The moon was high by the time Jonmarc reached his destination. Tents and wagons sprawled across a large clearing, and the smell of horses and other animals mingled with the smoke of cook fires. He eluded the guards and wound his way among the tents until he found what he was looking for.

Maynard Linton looked up, startled and alarmed when the tent flap opened suddenly. He was halfway out of his chair with his hand on the grip of his sword before he recognized Jonmarc. "By the Crone, Jonmarc! I nearly took you for a brigand!"

Linton stopped and looked closer, eyeing the bloody gash that ran from ear to collar, and the expression on his face, which Jonmarc guessed did not look altogether sane. "What in the name of the Dark Lady happened to you, m'boy?" He tilted his head to get a better look at the gash, and then gave Jonmarc a head-to-toe glance. Without another word, he went to a side table and poured Tordassian brandy into two cups, handing one to Jonmarc and taking the other for himself.

"Sit," he ordered. "Drink. You look like you've seen the Formless One."

"Near enough." Jonmarc let the brandy burn down his throat, but even it did not warm the coldness he felt.

"I'll get a healer for that gash," Linton said, knocking back his brandy in a gulp. "And I daresay the cook has food left." He gave Jonmarc a pointed glance. "But first, tell me why you're here in the dead of night without your wagon, looking like you've stumbled in from a fight."

Jonmarc took a deep breath and squared his shoulders. "I'm here to take you up on your offer. If you still need a blacksmith, I'm your man."

Storm Surge

"DON'T LET THE horses drown!"

Jonmarc Vahanian grasped the reins of the horse he was leading, fighting the panicked animal as he tried to move through surging waters that were proving far swifter than expected. "I'm trying not to drown myself!" he shot back. Thunder roared and lightning flashed.

All around him, the caravan maneuvered skittish horses, stubborn oxen, and heavily loaded carts through water that was flowing swiftly and rising steadily. They had been caught in the lowlands by a heavy rainstorm, and the sodden ground flooded far more quickly than anyone had expected.

Nearby, a man screamed and was swept off his feet and under the thigh-deep water.

"Hold this!" Jonmarc shouted to the man nearest him, handing off the reins. He grabbed a nearby sapling and thrust his arm down into the water, grasping at the coat that was barely visible beneath the surface. At seventeen, he was six feet tall, strong from years of working in the blacksmith's forge. It took all of his strength to keep his hold on the sapling and not lose his grip on the hapless man's coat.

"Help me out here," Jonmarc yelled, but his voice barely carried above the storm. His grip was waning, and the man in the current bobbed above the surface, sputtering for air, only to disappear once more. Jonmarc could feel the man scrabbling for a foothold, but he also knew his own position was growing more tenuous with each passing moment.

He gave a mighty pull with the last of his strength, and popped the man above the water once more, yanking him out of the worst of the current. They clung to the sapling, heaving for breath, as the rain pelted them and the wind plastered their wet clothing to their skin.

Jonmarc got a look at the man for the first time. It was Russ, a slender, bearded man who often worked with the caravan's exotic animals. "Thanks. I thought I was a goner," Russ said with an exhausted grin.

So did I, Jonmarc thought.

Shouting from the bedraggled procession of caravaners roused Jonmarc, and he looked up to see a human chain stretching across the treacherous stream to where the wagons sat on solid ground on the other side. Jonmarc made sure that Russ was secure, and then reclaimed his horse and took his position at the end of the chain.

Twice, his feet were nearly swept out from under him as he was pulled across the stream. After a few harrowing moments, he reached firm footing beside a wagon, and collapsed against it, breathing hard, adrenalin tingling through his body at the near miss.

"Yer lucky Jonmarc has a blacksmith's grip," the wagon driver said to Russ, who was pale and shaking. He turned to Jonmarc. "Nice catch."

"Keep moving, or we'll all be fishes!" Maynard Linton, the caravan master, shouted loudly enough to be heard over the storm.

Jonmarc hoisted Russ into the bed of a wagon, judging that he was too shaken and exhausted to fight the floodwaters. He took back the reins of the horse he had been leading.

Despite his cloak, he was soaked to the skin, and his long, chestnut-brown hair was plastered against his scalp, strands finding their way into his eyes.

It was early spring in the highlands of Margolan, and the snows in the mountains had been particularly heavy, making for swollen rivers and creeks. Maynard Linton's caravan—part traders and part traveling show—wound its way from the Borderlands in the far north across the kingdom. Whenever the caravan reached a populated area that looked prosperous enough to afford them a paying audience, they made camp for a few days to a few weeks, moving on when the novelty had worn off.

Only a month had passed since Jonmarc joined the caravan, fleeing the burning remains of his village and the monsters that had claimed the lives of his wife and child. Linton had taken him in when he had shown up in the middle of the night, bloodied from the fight and nearly incoherent with shock and loss. Since then, Jonmarc had lost himself in the caravan's never-ending need for a blacksmith's skills, staying busy to keep from thinking about what he'd left behind.

"Watch the wheels!" The wagon closest to Jonmarc bogged down in the mud, and he looped the reins of his horse over the wagon's side railing and joined a half-dozen other men who put their shoulders to the task of getting the heavily-loaded wagon moving again.

The swollen stream had overflowed its banks, turning the nearby land to mud. Water from the heavy rains formed swales where the water ran swiftly, growing deeper as the water carried away the dirt beneath it, eventually ending in the stream.

Ahead and to the right, shouts and curses erupted as a wagon broke an axle and overturned. One of the horses reared, flailing its hooves, striking down one of its would-be rescuers in wild-eyed fear. Boxes and sacks spilled onto the soaked ground, and some of them were carried away. There was nothing Jonmarc could do. It was taking all of his effort just to keep his own wagon moving. He glanced at the ruined items floating down the stream, and sincerely hoped the wagon had not been carrying the evening's dinner provisions.

Everywhere Jonmarc looked, the caravan's crew was struggling to save their livelihoods. The traders wrestled carts loaded with the Noorish carpets, boxes of jewelry and crates of trinkets and luxuries that attracted patrons and earned a tidy profit. The animal trainers labored to protect the exotic beasts which visitors paid to see. In their cages, the animals growled and twittered, protesting the storm. Even the powerful *stawar* looked wet and miserable.

Musicians and cooks, laborers and healers, acrobats and contortionists sloshed through the water carrying their possessions. Teams of horses pulled the large wagons that carried the caravan's folded tents and bundled equipment. Jonmarc spotted a group of tent riggers struggling with their own wagons in the thick mud. The oxen were balking, and one of the riggers, a tall, spare man with a pock-marked face, was muttering under his breath as he tugged on the unwilling beasts. There was a strong gust of wind, and a tree crashed to the ground, narrowly missing the wagon.

The spring wind was cold, and it was strong enough to lash the tops of the smallest trees from side to side. Jonmarc's hands were numb, and the cold stung his face. He glanced around at the soaked and weary caravan company. If they did not find shelter soon, a situation that was already dangerous would quickly become life-threatening.

"Over here!" Jonmarc could barely make out the shouts above the rain and wind. Ahead, he could see a man waving his arms, gesturing for the sodden travelers to take the right fork in the road. A few moments later, Jonmarc saw a large barn set on high ground, and breathed a sigh of relief.

It took at least another candlemark to get the caravan's people and animals inside and to secure the wagons on the sheltered side of the barn. Jonmarc helped tie down the cargo with oilcloth tarpaulins and rough rope, fastening the wagons themselves to anything that looked too heavy to float away.

Though the barn afforded shelter from the storm, enough rain had been driven in between the gaps in the planking or dripped in from the roof that it was still quite damp.

"What do you think the farmer will make of a group of motley performers squatting in his barn?" Jonmarc asked the sandy-haired man next to him as he set to seeing to the horses. Corbin, the farrier, spared him an exhausted grin.

"He won't say a blessed thing, because no sane man would be about on a day like this," Corbin answered, checking the nearest horse for injuries. Jonmarc followed him, holding a satchel with Corbin's liniments and ointments. Assisting the farrier was one of the many varied jobs to which Linton had put Jonmarc to work, and, grateful for a job and the promise of regular meals, he accepted the tasks without complaint.

"With luck, the storm will pass and we'll be on our way before there's any trouble," Jonmarc replied.

Maynard Linton strode back and forth, counting heads and taking stock of the situation. Linton was short and muscular, his skin coppery from seasons spent out of doors. Jonmarc guessed that Linton was in his early thirties, but while many members of the caravan were older than Linton, no one got in his way. Linton spoke rapidly as he moved among the caravan's members, switching easily from Common to Margolense and occasionally into other languages Jonmarc did not understand. The caravan's artisans, performers and crew were a varied lot, hailing from across the Winter Kingdoms, brought together by Linton's vision and energy.

"Do you think we're safe here?" Jonmarc asked as Corbin bound up a bad gash on one of the horses.

Corbin frowned. "Safer than we were in the storm. Why?"

Jonmarc shrugged. "That storm seemed to come up out of nowhere. Didn't seem natural. Too much lightning."

Corbin patted the horse and produced a carrot from his pocket as a treat. "You ever been this far East before? We're out of the Borderlands. Weather's different."

"Maybe."

Jonmarc searched the crowd for Trent, the caravan's chief blacksmith. Both Jonmarc and Corbin answered to Trent, along with two other apprentice smiths. The caravan's many horses kept two of them busy most of the time, while the others worked on the tools, barrel hoops, nails, fittings and weapons needed to keep the caravan moving. Finally, he spotted Trent among the healers' patients. The burly man was heading their way, and Jonmarc saw that Trent had one arm bandaged.

"What happened to you?" Corbin asked, eying the bandaged arm.

Trent grimaced. "I wasn't fast enough getting out of the way of the trees that came down. Damn that wind! I won't be sad if I never see another storm like that!"

"How many people got hurt?" Jonmarc asked, looking toward where the healers had set up a makeshift hospital over in a corner of the barn. It seemed to Jonmarc that more than a few of the caravan's guards were among the injured.

Then again, he thought, the guards had been clearing the roadway of debris, a dangerous job.

"At least a dozen that I saw, maybe more," Trent replied. He went to steady another horse so that Jonmarc could help Corbin apply a bandage. Around them, the stable boys did their best to rub down the sodden horses and get them as dry as possible and see to their food and water.

"I heard Linton say that three men are missing, and a horse had to be put down. Broke a leg when its wagon overturned," Trent added. "We've lost supplies, and we've gone several miles out of our way to get to higher ground."

"Where are we heading?" Corbin asked as he checked over another horse.

"There's not a lot between here and Huntwood," Trent replied. "Linton was planning for us to set up just beyond the manor's lands, near the town. We didn't stop there the last time we came north, and we can pick up the main road east from there."

He paused. "I wish we could have stayed on the original route. The forests are thick on this new route. I've heard tell of bandits."

Eventually, the caravan would reach the Nu River, crossing from Margolan into Principality, where the best mercenary troops in the kingdoms wintered. Linton had assured Jonmarc that the mercs had gold to spare and an appetite for food, drink and entertainment. Jonmarc had never been out of the Borderlands, making every day's travel a new adventure.

"We're within a week's ride of the palace city," Corbin said, frowning. "Surely King Bricen's soldiers would have the bandits well in hand."

Trent shrugged. "The king's men can't be everywhere. I hope Linton knows what he's doing."

"Did the forge tools make it through the storm?" Jonmarc asked.

Trent chuckled. "Oh yes. The anvils were heavy enough that the cart wasn't going to wash away or overturn, and I had oxen, not horses, so we didn't get stuck in the mud. We might be short a tent and some fancy rugs, but we've got what we need to shoe the horses and mend the tools."

"It's not the worst storm we've ever weathered." They looked up to see Maynard Linton standing behind them. Linton's broad face was creased with worry and anger. "Can't say I'm pleased about what we lost, but it could have been worse."

"Do we have any idea what the road looks like ahead?" Trent asked. Trent and Corbin had been with the caravan for several years, and had obviously earned Linton's trust.

Linton cursed. "What the road looks like right now doesn't matter. It's what the road looks like when the storm is done that counts." He shook his head. "I've taken this road across Margolan for years, never saw a storm like this come up without warning."

Jonmarc exchanged an 'I told you so' glance with Corbin, who shrugged.

"So what's the plan?" Trent asked.

Linton sighed. "We'll see how things look in the morning. If the road's washed out, we'll have to revise our route. If not, we find a way back to the main road, and stick to the plan. I think setting up for a few days outside Huntwood would bring us some extra coin. We'll need that on the next stretch; we won't have a chance to do another full show for a while, and we'd best have enough coin to buy provisions in the between places."

Linton withdrew a flask from his belt and took a swig of liquor. "I'm chilled to the bone," he muttered.

"If you're short on guards, Jonmarc and I can take a turn at watch," Trent said.

"So can I," Corbin volunteered. "I'd rather lose a few candlemarks' sleep and know we've got eyes open through the night."

Linton nodded. "I'll take you up on that," he said gruffly, his voice raspy from the weather. "The three men we've lost were guards, and the others took more than their share of injuries getting the animals and the wagons through the storm. I'll need to hire some men when we get to somewhere the people outnumber the sheep and cows."

Supper was a haphazard affair, since many of the provisions were still packed in crates and other supplies had gotten too wet to use. Hard biscuits, salt pork, and ale were the most readily available provisions, and Jonmarc was hungry and cold enough to eat his ration gratefully.

After supper, the barn grew quiet. People found their places for the night, and conversation dulled to a low hum. Several of the musicians began to play, partly for practice, Jonmarc guessed, and partly for solace. The music sent a hush over the exhausted crowd of caravaners, and even the animals seemed less restless. Jonmarc dug a dry blanket out of his pack and settled down to catch a few candlemarks' rest before his turn on watch.

"GET UP. IT'S TIME." Trent shook Jonmarc awake. Jonmarc blinked and yawned, trying to shake off drowsiness. He stuffed his blanket back in his bag and reluctantly followed Trent out to the barn doors, pulling his hat and gloves on as he went.

Most of the caravan's performers were sleeping. One of the animal trainers tended to his restless charges. A few of the riggers and crew were playing cards. The skinny man Jonmarc had spotted earlier was among them, and he seemed to regard Jonmarc and Trent with bored curiosity as they picked their way across the crowded barn floor. They stopped long enough to exchange a few words with the guards who were coming off watch, and to take two shuttered lanterns with them into the night.

Outside, the storm had waned. The ground was soaked and water dripped from the barn's roof, but the rain had stopped and the wind stilled. Out here, far from any town, there were no bells to mark the passage of time. Wherever the farmer who owned the barn lived, it was not so close that they could see a house, or that the farmer noticed lights and movement around his barn.

"How long have the riggers been with us?" Jonmarc asked.

Trent gave him a sideways look, as if wondering where that question had come from. "A few have been around for a while. Several came on at the last stop." He shrugged. "It's tough work, and dangerous business. Riggers always come and go, if they don't get killed in the meantime. Why?"

Jonmarc shrugged. "It's just, there's one of the riggers who just seems... odd."

Trent barked a laugh. "It would be stranger to find a rigger who wasn't odd. They have to be crazy to work the poles and the ropes, and it seems to draw a peculiar type. I mean, caravaners are a strange lot to begin with. Most of us took up with this to get away from something else. There's a reason a lot of folks make themselves scarce if the king's guard show up. I'd dare say more than a few are wanted by someone for something."

"Maybe," Jonmarc replied. "But something seems off." He paused. "Would someone want to harm the caravan, or Linton?"

Trent chuckled. "More than a few folks, I warrant. Linton runs a tight ship. He's had to get rid of people who caused problems—fights, stealing, that sort of thing. Made a few enemies that way, I'm sure."

Trent scanned the horizon. Nothing stirred. "There are always rivals. I've heard grumbling sometimes from the local merchants that when the caravan comes to town, local traders and shopkeepers lose business." He shook his head. "That might account for damage if we were camped near a village, but out here? Doesn't seem likely."

They fell silent, watching and listening. Jonmarc glanced behind them, into the barn. Most people were sleeping. A small group still played cards in the corner, including the skinny man, who appeared to be counting his earnings under his breath as he fingered the small pile of coins in front of him.

A low snarl carried on the night air. "Did you hear that?" Jonmarc said with a sudden glance toward Trent.

Trent drew a long, wicked-looking knife from his belt. Jonmarc drew his sword. Trent gestured in one direction, indicating with a nod for Jonmarc to head the opposite way. Cautiously, Jonmarc moved as silently as the wet ground would allow. He kept his lantern shuttered, using the faint glow that escaped to light his way, hoping it did not give him away.

Another growl sounded, closer than before. It sounded more like a wolf than like one of the large wild cats that roamed the lowlands. Jonmarc really did not want to meet either predator alone at night. Yet something in the low snarl seemed off, not quite right. Slowly, Jonmarc took another step.

He froze as he made out movement in the shadows ahead of him. The clouds parted overhead, allowing enough moonlight to stream down for Jonmarc to make out the form of whatever was watching him. It was big, too big for a dog, and too large even for a wolf. The shape was wrong for a big cat.

The shadow shifted, and a pair of glowing red eyes fixed their gaze on Jonmarc in the instant before the darkness moved.

Jonmarc's sword cut an arc through the night, but met only air. He heard the beast snarl, heard the snick of teeth, and felt claws tear through the sleeve of his coat. He dropped and rolled, coming up with his sword poised defensively, ready to gut the beast if it came at him.

The red eyes regarded him for a moment, then the beast sprang forward and a massive paw swiped for his throat. Jonmarc ducked, throwing up his left arm, and bit back a cry as claws raked across his skin. He could smell the beast's breath, a mixture of an old grave and a kill left too long in the sun. Footsteps sounded, and Jonmarc heard Trent calling his name.

"Over here! Watch yourself—there's a wild animal!" Jonmarc warned.

In the moonlight, Jonmarc could make out the beast clearly. It had the build of a wolf, but much larger than any wolf Jonmarc had ever seen. Baleful red eyes stared at him, and the snarl became a deep rumble.

The beast advanced, and Jonmarc swung again. To his horror, the blade sliced through the beast without meeting flesh or bone.

A howl echoed in the night air, more chilling than anything Jonmarc had ever heard. Jonmarc held his sword defiantly, knowing that if the blade couldn't slow the beast, there was nothing to keep it from attacking again. His arm throbbed from the gashes, pulsing with his heartbeat.

Trent rounded the corner of the barn, and the beast's huge

head swung to stare at him in the instant before Trent opened the shutters on his lantern, flooding the area with light.

The beast vanished.

Jonmarc did not move, staring into the darkness where the beast had been just an instant before, his wounded arm clutched close against his body.

"What in the name of the Crone was that?" Trent asked, shaken. He took in Jonmarc's bloody sleeve. "Sweet Chenne, are you hurt?"

"What's going on out here?" Linton stomped up, splashing mud with every footstep. Behind him were Corbin and two of the wagon drivers, each carrying sturdy wooden poles.

Jonmarc struggled to his feet, still breathing hard. "We heard a growl, and saw something moving in the shadows," he said, scanning the darkness. "Trent and I split up to circle the barn."

"Did you see anything?" Linton demanded.

"I saw movement, but I never got a look at whatever was out there," Trent said.

Jonmarc hesitated, wondering if they would believe him.

"Whatever it was came after a piece of you, m'boy," Linton said, eyeing Jonmarc's wounded arm. "You must have seen something."

"It was big, and dark," Jonmarc said. "Like a wolf, but more powerful. And it had red eyes."

"Red eyes?" Linton mused. He looked down at Jonmarc's sword. "It got close enough to do that to you, and you didn't get in a good strike?"

Jonmarc met Linton's gaze. "My blade went right through it, like shadow."

"He needs to see a healer," Trent said, stepping up beside Jonmarc. "Whatever it was is gone now."

Linton stared a moment longer at the bloody gashes on Jonmarc's arm, and nodded. "Aye. Let's get that treated before it goes bad." He turned to Corbin and the other men.

"I want four men out here until morning. Two teams of two. Each pair stays together. Open the shutters on your lanterns. I don't care who sees us here. I'll answer to an angry farmer, but I don't want whatever did that," he said with a nod toward Jonmarc, "coming around again and bringing its pack."

Trent steered Jonmarc into the barn and fended off the press of curious gawkers. It seemed as if everyone was awake now, and a buzz of nervous excitement hummed through the crowd.

They picked their way across the crowded floor toward where the healers had set up a place to treat the injured from their sodden trek through the storm.

"What do we have here?" The woman was in her middle years, young enough that most of her hair was still dark and old enough for it to be liberally flecked with gray. Her green robe meant she was a trained healer, not just a hedge witch with a talent for herbs and potions.

"Something attacked him while we were on watch," Trent said, nudging Jonmarc to have a seat on a large piece of firewood.

The healer bent over Jonmarc and tore his ripped sleeve open to expose four ragged cuts. "You're lucky whatever it was only got your arm," she said, frowning as he looked at his bloody sleeve.

"Can you help him, Ada?" Trent asked. "It's bad, but I've shown up looking worse."

Ada chuckled. "That you have, and we've put you right. Give me a moment to put an ointment together. That should keep it from going bad, and take away some of the pain."

The healer bustled off, rummaging in her packs. She withdrew several packs of dried herbs, a few seedpods, and a cruet of oil, as well as a mortar and pestle. "Go fetch me some water, Trent," she said in a tone that implied she was old friends with the blacksmith. "Something clean enough to drink, if you please. We'll not want the cuts to go sour."

Jonmarc felt flushed, and his heart pounded in his ears. Before he had taken his turn at watch, he would have said that the inside of the drafty barn was only somewhat warmer than outside, despite the press of bodies. Now, he was sweating as if it were summer. His throat was dry, and he felt lightheaded. The gashes in his arm sent stabbing pain up into his shoulder and chest, and it was getting harder to breathe.

He saw Ada turn toward him, and saw her lips move as if she were speaking, but he heard nothing. The world spun, and he toppled to the floor.

Nightmare images seized Jonmarc as he descended into unconsciousness. Flames surrounded him, and the stench of burning flesh filled the air. The memories took him, like they did most nights. He glimpsed faces in the smoke, the images of those he loved, and those who took them from him. His father, lying dead in the street with the other village men and the gloating raiders who had killed them. The first raider he killed—the first man he had ever killed—and the sound of the man's dying rasp: *May you lose everyone you love to the flames and the Dark Lady take your soul!*

The smoke shifted, and newer memories, fresher pain, replaced what had gone before. He saw the corpse-pale face of a *vayash moru* mage, heard his voice offering gold for a simple errand, and shivered, knowing what came next. Flames and death, streets littered with the bodies of his friends and neighbors, and glimpses of the gray-skinned monsters that killed them. He saw Shanna lying in a pool of blood, felt the dead weight as he turned her over in his arms, and in her unfocused eyes, he saw the acknowledgement of the raider's curse. Then the darkness and the monsters closed in around him, and he fought to free himself...

"Easy now!" Someone caught his wrists in a strong grip, keeping him from landing a punch. Jonmarc struggled to awaken, dragged back toward the nightmares from the potions that dulled the pain.

"Does he wake like this often?" A woman's voice sounded close at hand. Not his mother. Not Shanna. But someone familiar, maybe even safe.

"More times than you'd want to know," a man replied. "He's woken up fighting so many times that he's thrashed most of the other apprentices before he comes back to himself. That's why he's got a tent to himself, with the supplies. No one fancies getting a black eye or bruises just for sharing a tent." Jonmarc recognized Trent's voice, and focused on slowing his breathing, letting go of the panic that always remained after the dreams had gone.

"Do you know what he sees in his dreams?" the woman asked, a note of concern in her voice. Ada, Jonmarc thought, grasping the name from his feverish memories.

"I don't ask, and he won't say," Trent said. "Linton might know, but Linton keeps a lot of secrets. Whatever happened must have been pretty bad."

Ada sighed. "A mind-healer might help, but you won't find one of those—a real one—outside a palace or one of the big manors."

"He's still young," Trent said. "Time heals a lot of wounds."

"Unless they're poisoned," Ada said. "Poison lingers."

They might have said more, but the potions pulled Jonmarc back into the darkness. This time, the nightmares stayed at bay, though Jonmarc could sense the dreams were there, beyond the threshold, ready to overwhelm him.

"DON'T MOVE." TRENT'S voice cut through the fog in Jonmarc's mind. Jonmarc still felt feverish, but the stabbing pain was gone. It hurt to breathe, as if he had taken in great lungfuls of frigid air, and his whole body felt leaden.

"You're lucky that Linton hires good healers," Ada said. "If he didn't, you'd be dead."

"Cuts... weren't that deep," Jonmarc managed through parched lips.

"Don't have to be deep when they're poisoned," Ada replied.

"Why would they be poisoned?" Jonmarc paused as Trent lifted him up enough to sip water from a cup.

Ada came over to check on Jonmarc's bandages. He realized that he was lying on a cot, and that daylight glowed from between the boards in the barn's walls.

"Whatever got you wasn't natural," she said, spreading more ointment on his wounds. The mixture smelled like licorice and rotted fruit. Jonmarc caught a glimpse of his skin beneath the ointment, and saw that the gashes were closing into raised, pink scars.

"What do you mean, 'natural'?"

Ada met his gaze matter-of-factly. "That thing in the darkness, it was magic. A rather nasty piece of work."

Immediately, Jonmarc thought of the red-robed mage who had hired him to find a cursed talisman, a bargain he had failed to keep, but one that had cost him everything he held dear. That mage was out there somewhere, and likely to be quite unhappy with him.

"Magic?"

Ada nodded. "If it hadn't been for the poison, I would have accepted the idea that it was a wolf or a cat and that the darkness played a trick on your eyes. But the men have been over the land outside the barn since sunup, and there aren't any tracks, none at all."

Her eyes narrowed. "Something tore up your arm with poisoned claws. Linton said you told him that your sword went through it like a shadow. The beast didn't leave tracks." She shook her head. "Sounds like magic to me."

"Why would anyone send magic like that against the caravan?" Trent asked, sitting back on his heels.

Ada shrugged. "Might not be about us. Could be a curse on this barn, or on the farmer who owns it. We might have just blundered into it."

Jonmarc looked away, sure his guilt was clear in his face. *Or it could be an angry undead mage with a score to settle*, he thought. *By the Dark Lady! I don't want to put the rest of the caravan in danger for my mistake.*

"What kind of a mage would it take to summon a beast like that?" Trent asked.

Ada considered his question for a moment. "I don't think it would take someone with a lot of power, or even a lot of knowledge. With magic, often it's not the difficulty that stops a mage from doing a working. It's the mage's honor— or lack of it."

"Why send that kind of beast against the guards?"

Ada grimaced. "If the intention was to cause panic, maybe whoever it was didn't expect us to post a guard. I doubt either of you were the target." She looked out across the caravan workers who were gathering up their belongings from the night before so they could get back on the road.

"Can Jonmarc travel?" Trent asked with a worried glance.

"I've cleared a spot for him in one of the wagons," Ada replied. She interpreted the look on Jonmarc's face and smiled. "Just for a while, until I'm sure the poultice took care of the poison. By tomorrow, you'll be good as new."

BY LATE MORNING, Jonmarc insisted on walking. His arm was still sore, but nothing like the pain right after the attack. Within a candlemark of rejoining Trent, so many of his curious companions had asked Jonmarc to tell his story that Trent finally pulled him to a different part of the line and silenced inquiries with a dark glance.

A steady rain fell, though without the wind that had made the previous day's journey so treacherous. "We're coming to a fork in the road up ahead," Trent told Jonmarc. "Linton says we can get back on the road toward Huntwood, maybe even make up lost time if this damned rain lets up."

Abruptly, the procession stopped. Jonmarc and Trent were in the middle of the long line of caravan workers, too far from the front to see what had brought them to a halt. The wet and miserable travelers exchanged questioning glances, then began to speculate on the cause for their sudden stop.

"Stay here," Trent said, and began to slip up through the line. After a while, he returned with a worried look on his face.

"Trees are down across the route Linton wanted to take," Trent said. "We're going to have to go a different way. Linton sent scouts to take a look ahead."

"I don't like this," Jonmarc said quietly, with a glance over his shoulder to assure he would not be overheard. "First, unusually bad weather. Then what happened last night, and now this?"

"I don't like it either, but Linton's got to get us off the road, and if the route's blocked, we'll have to find another way," Trent said. He signaled for Jonmarc to stay where he was, and wove through the procession once more, but this time, Jonmarc saw Trent stop to talk with Corbin, Russ and several other men. They were too far away for Jonmarc to make out what they said, but the other men nodded, their expressions serious. Trent wound his way back, pausing to exchange a few words with Ada, who turned to make a comment to the other healers.

"What's going on?" Jonmarc asked.

"Nothing—yet. But we're all agreed that there are too many coincidences. We won't be the only ones keeping our eyes open."

They slogged on, eating a cold lunch from rations that had been distributed before they left the barn: dried sausage, a hunk of cheese, a piece of hard bread. Jonmarc forced himself to eat, finding that he had little appetite. He could not shake a sense of foreboding, and from the grim look on Trent's face and Corbin's terse manner, Jonmarc guessed that at least some of the others found cause for concern.

"There's a bridge up ahead, over the creek," Trent said as they hiked along the muddy, rutted road. The rain had stopped, but a cold dampness hung in the air, and the ground was slick and covered with puddles deep enough to challenge all but the highest boots.

"Then what?" Jonmarc asked. He had seen maps of Margolan once or twice, but he remembered few of the details, save that the Borderlands where he grew up was quite a distance from the palace, and even further from the border with Principality.

Trent looked around them, taking in the low rolling hills and the lengthening shadows. "On the other side of the creek, the land flattens out. There should be a town where we can resupply, and then Linton still means to make for Huntwood to set up the festival for the lord of the manor."

The group gathered along the banks of the creek, a swollen, rushing body of water Jonmarc would have called a small river. Given how badly their last attempt at fording a stream had gone, he was grateful for the security of a sturdy log bridge.

"If we're quick about crossing, we should reach Colshott before nightfall," Linton said. "We can replace what we lost in the flood, stock up on provisions, and get back on the road to Huntwood."

Jonmarc thought Linton looked ill at ease. The road they had traveled from the barn forked just ahead. One branch crossed the creek; the other headed into a stretch of forest. Many of the caravaners eyed the forest with suspicion. Thus far, the route Linton had chosen skirted the deep woods. While that meant they traveled in the open, it also made for wider roads, handy for the wagons and livestock. Open land also meant they could see if there were travelers or animals coming toward them. The forest might shelter them from the rain, but it also gave an advantage to wolves and other predators.

Linton called for the men who were not handling carts or livestock to go first across the bridge, and Jonmarc wondered if the caravan master was thinking of the attack the night before, hoping to secure the far bank before the wagons, women, and animals crossed. Out of the corner of his eye, Jonmarc saw that Trent and Corbin had drawn back their cloaks to make it easier to draw their knives, and he did the same.

The bridge was as wide as the road, made of thick planks. The wood was gray with time and the bed of the bridge was worn with the passage of many travelers. Jonmarc's sense of foreboding grew as he stepped onto the bridge. Beneath them, the creek swirled past the bridge supports, carrying with it flotsam from the headwaters.

He took one cautious step and then another, but the bridge held. He and Trent and Corbin were in the rear of the group of nearly a dozen men selected to go first. Jonmarc glanced over his shoulder at the rest of the caravan that were awaiting their signal from the other side.

The bridge looked sturdy enough, but the men fanned out, spreading their weight equally across the span. Jonmarc paused, then chided himself when the others did not seem to hesitate.

With every step, the bridge felt more unsteady. He was almost a third of the way across when a loud snap reverberated in the air. He heard the wood groan as the planks underfoot began to buckle. Nails popped from the planks, and the timber railing broke off and tumbled down into the creek. Two men, and then three more, ran across to safety.

"It's gonna go!" Corbin yelled. Jonmarc, Trent and Corbin were closer to the caravan than to the other side of the bridge, and Jonmarc could see Linton shouting at them, fear clear in his expression.

"Run!" Trent shouted.

Some of the remaining men ran forward, intent on reaching the other side of the creek. The bridge twisted in the middle, wrenching the planks loose, and as the center gave, men fell screaming into the water below.

Trent grabbed Jonmarc's shoulder and pushed him back toward the way they had come. Corbin was behind them, still shouting to rally the survivors and jar the panicked into movement. Another section collapsed, sending a sudden shock through the bridge that made Jonmarc stumble, nearly knocking him off his feet. Corbin grabbed his arm, propelling him toward shore.

Unteathered, the remaining structure began to wobble and sway as the current tore at the supports. Men crowded forward to stay clear of the ragged edge of the bridge platform. They neared the bank, as the horrified onlookers called for them to hurry.

With a rumble like thunder, the bridge dropped from under Jonmarc's boots. Corbin leaped to safety, with Trent an instant behind him. The bridge collapsed with a roar. Jonmarc hurled himself toward the bank, and his hands scrabbled for purchase on the splintered boards that had, moments before, been the edge of the bridge platform. Behind him, he heard Russ scream as he fell into the swift waters below.

Jonmarc caught himself, but a stab of pain through his wounded arm nearly made him lose his grip. He was dangling, and his boots scraped against the rocks, trying to get a toehold.

"Got you!" Trent grabbed one arm, while Corbin grabbed the other, hauling Jonmarc to safety. His palms were filled with splinters and he was covered with mud and dust, but he had never been so grateful to lie on the wet, solid ground.

"By the Crone's tits!" Linton roared. "How in the name of the Formless One did that happen?"

Jonmarc sat up and stared into the stream. Shattered timbers bobbed in the current, and broken planks littered the sides of the lower banks. A small portion of the far side of the bridge still remained standing, but the rest was gone. Out of the twelve who had started across the bridge, Jonmarc could see only eight remaining. Three were on the broken portion of the bridge, while five of their men were on the other side of the creek.

The crowd talked in nervous whispers, gathering close to the banks to see the damage. Ada and the healers pushed to the front, seeing to the survivors' injuries. Jonmarc glanced around and spotted the riggers on the fringe of the crowd, and with them the tall, thin man. He seemed to be staring right at Jonmarc, and glanced sharply away as Jonmarc returned the gaze.

"We've got no choice," Linton's voice carried over the noise. "We'll have to take the fork through the forest, at least until we reach another road."

"What about the men who got to the other side of the bridge?" Ada asked.

Linton sighed. "They'll have to meet up with us at the next crossing."

Linton bustled from one end of the caravan procession to the other, giving orders, fussing at wagon drivers and encouraging a few performers who looked too rattled to go on. Eventually, he found his way to where Ada and the healers were caring for those who had been injured. Jonmarc was too far away to hear their conversation, but Linton spoke in quiet tones to Ada, who nodded and then called over several of the other healers. At one point, Linton glanced toward Jonmarc and gave a nod, then turned back to finish his discussion before stalking away, hailing another member of the caravan.

Ada walked over and checked Jonmarc's palms. The splinters were gone, and between the healer's magic and the ointment she had used on his cuts, his hands were nearly healed.

"What's going on?" Jonmarc asked and Ada turned to head back to the others.

"What do you mean?"

Jonmarc met her gaze. "Linton looked pretty intent about something, and he glanced at me like I had something to do with it."

Ada chuckled. "Actually, he's a little worried with how dangerous the route has been so far. He asked me if we had enough herbs for potions, in case we have any more bad luck." She sighed. "I told him we'd gone through a lot of our stock, and he suggested we harvest whatever plants we can since we've got to go through the forest."

Ada gave him a sidelong glance. "Linton said I could ask you to help. Said something about you having worked for a hedge witch."

Jonmarc looked down. Few people in the caravan asked about a person's past, and fewer people gave true answers when asked. Linton knew Jonmarc's story, or at least most of it. If it were anyone else asking, he might not have answered, but Ada had been kind to him, and sometimes she reminded him of Elly, Shanna's mother. "My wife's mother was a hedge witch and healer. A good one," he said quietly, still not looking at Ada.

"I didn't know you were married," she said.

Jonmarc swallowed hard. "I'm not anymore. She died."

Ada knew him well enough to let the comment go without a fuss. "Right then," she said. "I could use your help. Trent can manage without you for a candlemark or two. I'm going to ask each of the healers to look for one or two medicinal plants, and hopefully we'll end up with a little bit of everything." She took two pouches from her belt.

"Do you recognize these?" she asked, pouring a little of the contents of each into her hand.

"Willow bark," Jonmarc said, pointing to one of the piles of dried material. "I'm not sure what the other is."

"Wormroot," Ada said. "I don't need it often, but it comes in handy sometimes." He listened as she described the plant to him. "When you find it, use your knife to remove the leaves and twigs. I just need the roots, stem and bark. Try not to lose the sap—I'll need that." She paused. "Oh, and keep your hands out of your mouth when you're handling it. It can give you a nasty upset stomach."

Usually, days when the caravan was on the move seemed light-hearted. Moving the wagons, animals, people and supplies was hard work, but a certain vagabond freedom infused the journey with goodwill. Often, performers would break into song as the group traveled, pranksters played tricks and the caravan's other members traded jokes and tales that became taller with the telling.

This day's journey had begun warily after the storms and the attack. The bridge collapse defeated even the most resolute optimists, and as the group moved into the forest, everyone seemed skittish and ill-humored. Jonmarc kept a watchful eye on the riggers, but had to admit he saw nothing to support his suspicions. Trent and Corbin had fallen back to talk in low tones with several of the other farriers and blacksmiths.

Jonmarc was just as glad to have a task to take his mind off the bad luck of the last few days. He was lucky enough to come upon a few willows before they had ventured far into the forest, and quickly gathered more than enough bark for Ada's needs. The wormroot was more difficult to find. It was a small, woody plant that grew knee-height at its tallest, and only its unusual, triangular leaves set it apart from the other scrub that grew beneath the trees.

After several frustrating candlemarks, Jonmarc came upon a small patch of wormroot and knelt to harvest it. He had often helped Shanna and Elly gather the leaves, bark and roots they used for their teas and poultices, and the work made him melancholy. The wormroot was tougher than he had expected, requiring him to scrape away the twigs from the stem with his knife and spreading some of the thin sap over his hands in the process. The caravan moved on, taking no notice that he had slipped away. For a moment, it crossed Jonmarc's mind to keep on going, leaving the caravan behind, and strike out on his own for Principality.

I've never been out of the Borderlands. I have no idea how to get to Principality, and only a week's wages in my pocket. And Trent and Corbin have been teaching me what they know about swords and fighting. He sighed. *Linton took me in when I had nowhere else to go. I'm not going to let him down.* He could not deny the lure of freedom and independence, but for now, he stuffed those thoughts away and hurried to catch up with the caravan.

The further they moved into the forest, the darker it became as the canopy blocked the late afternoon sun. After the previous evening, Jonmarc eyed the shadows warily. He had nearly caught up with the rest of the group when there was a loud noise ahead and the sound of men shouting.

Instinctively, Jonmarc flattened himself behind a tree and listened. He could hear Linton shouting, answered by a man's voice Jonmarc did not recognize. More angry voices carried through the trees. Jonmarc dared a glance, and realized that the caravan had come to a complete halt.

Jonmarc had done his share of hunting, back in his home village. He could move through the forest quietly, and he could track game reasonably well. Now, he circled the caravan, as an uneasy suspicion grew. He stayed low, taking advantage of the brush to keep out of sight. The view from a small rise revealed a company of rough-looking men blocking the caravan's way, and it appeared that several of the riggers had joined them, including the sharp-faced man who had caught Jonmarc's attention earlier.

Why aren't the caravaners fighting? They outnumber the bandits more than two to one.

Jonmarc gripped his knife and debated his next move. *If the others won't fight, what can I do?* They were far from any villages where help might be found, and he had heard no mention of passing near one of the king's garrisons. But the longer he thought about the riggers' treachery, the angrier he became.

I may not be able to fight them all, but maybe I can harry them, give the others a chance.

DUSK CAME EARLY under the spread of the large trees. The waning light filtered through the new spring leaves, enough for Jonmarc to pick his way toward the edge of the bandit camp. He crouched behind a large rock, watching, and looking for an opportunity to inflict damage. There were close to two dozen bandits, from what he could see. Freeing the others wouldn't be easy.

The crack of a stick underfoot made him turn sharply, knife raised. A man slipped from behind a tree, and it took a moment for Jonmarc to make out who it was. He let out a sigh of relief when he recognized Trent.

"What's going on?" he whispered.

"Bandits," Trent replied. "Linton suspected someone was using magic to herd us in a particular direction, and the bridge collapse sealed it."

"Then why isn't he fighting them? We've got plenty more men than they've got."

"Linton's a cagy one. He doesn't know how powerful their mage is, or whether they've got more than one. So he told several of us to fall behind as we moved through the forest, just like Ada had you do."

"She's in on it?"

Another figure slipped up behind Trent. "You bet I am," Ada replied.

Trent chuckled. "Ada had several of her healers slip away as well. All told, there should be a dozen of us."

"What's the plan?" Jonmarc asked. "Whatever it is, count me in."

"For now, we watch and look for an opening. If there's a way to do this without an all-out fight, Linton would prefer it. We've lost enough people and supplies without taking more casualties," Trent replied.

Jonmarc looked to Ada. "I understand having men who can fight. But healers?"

Ada gave a sly grin. "Watch and learn."

They waited, watching the encampment. The bandits were well-armed, and had posted sentries at the corners of the encampment. Jonmarc watched, taking note of their movements.

"I'm willing to bet that tall one, the blond, is a mage, or at least a strong hedge witch," Ada murmured, and Jonmarc followed her nod toward a slender man with greasy hair who looked too slightly built to be a fighter, but stalked through the camp as if he owned it.

"If it comes to fighting, I want a chance at those riggers," Jonmarc muttered.

"You'll have to beat Corbin to it," Trent replied.

Jonmarc remembered the willow bark and wormroot he had collected. "Here," he said, giving Ada the pouches that held the plants.

"This will do nicely," Ada said, smiling. She looked to Trent. "Do you have your knives on you?"

Trent grinned. "Never without them." He took a set of five throwing knives from beneath his coat. Ada carefully coated each blade with the sap of the wormroot Jonmarc had collected, taking care to get none of it on her hands

"You're going to make them throw up?" Jonmarc asked, looking askance at the preparations.

Ada's eyes held a mischievous glint. "Oh, that's part of it, but I've got their mages in mind. If you're not a mage, wormroot will rile your stomach. But if you're a mage—or even a hedge witch—even a small amount will drop you in your tracks. Get enough of it, and a mage can go mad—or die."

"I'll go after the mage," Trent said. "And by now, the others should be in position. It's up to your people, Ada."

Ada sighed. "I should probably feel guilty about this. Healers aren't supposed to do harm. Then again, the bandits are likely to survive what my folks throw their way. That's more than I can say if it went to an all-out fight."

Jonmarc watched, curious, as the healer worked her way closer to the encampment. He could see her lips moving, though he could not hear her words. Suddenly, the guard nearest them doubled over, clutching his gut. He moaned, and ran behind a tree with a panicked expression on his face. A moment later, the area was filled with a decidedly foul smell. Ada grinned triumphantly, and motioned for Jonmarc and Trent to come closer.

From where they hid, Jonmarc could see the other guards collapse, some retching and others soiling themselves. Ada's healers had begun the assault.

"Can you do that to all of them?" Jonmarc asked.

Ada shook her head. "It takes energy to call on the magic,

and we tire quickly, especially after all we've been through. But we can cut down on the number of men the rest of you have to fight."

The bandit leader, realizing his guards were down, sent men to investigate, and launched into a shouting match with another man, whom Jonmarc presumed to be the group's cook.

"Here we go," muttered Trent.

The bandits had relieved the caravan members of their weapons and valuables, and bound their wrists. Jonmarc had no idea what plans the bandits had for the caravan, but he did not intend to wait long enough to find out. Ada hung back, promising to watch for opportunities to help. Jonmarc and Trent moved forward, staying low. There was barely enough light to allow them to maneuver, but the growing darkness hid them from the bandits and the moon would not rise for several hours.

Trent threw a rock at the nearest bandit, clipping him on the side of the head. Jonmarc followed with a second rock, striking another brigand in the temple and dropping him to the ground. The man Trent hit growled a curse and wheeled around, blood dripping from his scalp. Trent lobbed a knife. The bandit fell to his knees, his hands clutching his chest.

"Go!" Trent hissed, stopping long enough to retrieve his blade. Jonmarc was already on his feet, sprinting toward the next brigand, as the camp burst into action. Linton had been waiting for the attack, and had worked his wrists free. He kicked the man guarding him, then grabbed a stout fallen branch and began swinging it like a cudgel.

"Get the mage!" Jonmarc replied as the blond man Ada had pointed out began to chant.

Trent let his knife fly, catching the mage in the back. As the wormroot-tainted blade sank in hilt-deep, the mage gave a strangled cry. His legs gave out beneath him, and he fell, convulsing, into the dirt.

Linton grabbed a knife off the bandit he bludgeoned, and paused long enough to free one of the other captives, who began to move down the line, cutting the prisoners' ropes. Having accomplished that, Linton snatched up a sword from one of the fallen bandits and began laying into the robbers with a ferocity Jonmarc had not imagined the stout caravan master was capable of mustering.

Across the way, Jonmarc saw Corbin emerge from the trees with a few more men. One of the bandits headed for the caravan wagons, and Jonmarc tackled him from behind, landing several hard punches before the man could react. The bandit twisted in his grip and his fist shot out, catching Jonmarc on the temple so hard that lights flashed before his eyes.

He was too angry to give up. Jonmarc came at the bandit again, this time getting the man in a chokehold. The bandit was wiry, but Jonmarc's arms were strong from work in the forge. The bandit sputtered and gasped for air, unable to buck Jonmarc loose. His hands tore at Jonmarc's clothing, and dug at the dirt as Jonmarc kept up the pressure. With a gurgle, the bandit slumped forward, and Jonmarc let him fall, pivoting as he heard footsteps behind him.

Out of the corner of his eye, he saw two more of the robbers fall to the ground retching, and smiled, knowing the healers were at work. Trent and Corbin were both busy fighting back the brigands who had gone for the horses, and from the look of it, the robbers were losing badly. Someone had reclaimed the caravan's weapons, and the men and women of Linton's caravan were giving the robbers a thorough thrashing.

Jonmarc spotted movement toward the wagons, and went to investigate. He glimpsed the thin tent rigger, and scrambled up and over the wagon between them, taking a flying leap onto the rigger and knocking the breath out of the man.

"You led us into a trap! You sold out the caravan!" Jonmarc had the rigger by his hair, and the man's pox-marked face was flushed with the struggle.

"It would have been better money than I've seen with this whore-spawned caravan," the rigger snarled, gasping for breath.

The rigger was taller than Jonmarc, and strong. He broke free of his grip, and got to his feet. Jonmarc grabbed a fistful of the man's shirt with one hand, and landed a roundhouse punch with the other, solidly connecting with the rigger's chin.

The rigger fell back a pace. "You've done me out of my share of the take, boy," he said, and flashed a malevolent smile. "I'm going to enjoy taking you down a peg."

Jonmarc braced for the rigger to come at him with a knife. Before Jonmarc could launch another attack, the rigger spoke a few strange words, and he found himself gasping for breath as if iron bands crushed his chest. The rigger's lips moved once more, and Jonmarc fell hard onto the ground as the pressure moved to his throat, cutting off his air.

He's a witch too, Jonmarc thought, struggling to breathe. *And he means to run out on the fight and save his own skin.*

His ears were ringing painfully, and his lungs burned. His body spasmed, and he began to tremble violently. He could hear the rigger laughing.

The fight from the main camp was moving past the ring of wagons. Two brawling men fell hard against the wagon nearest Jonmarc, rocking it up on two wheels and causing it to dump several casks, which shattered on the ground. For an instant, the rigger's concentration broke, loosening his hold.

Jonmarc sucked in a great gasp of air and threw his knife with all his remaining strength. It dug into the rigger's shoulder.

"Is that the best you've got?" the rigger mocked.

"Just wait," Jonmarc gasped.

The rigger's expression took on a look of horror and his face twisted in pain. "What did you do? By the Crone, what did you do?" His last words came out as a strangled cry as he went down in a heap, convulsing.

Trent came around the wagons and ran toward Jonmarc, who was struggling to his feet, still breathing hard. "What happened?"

"Wormroot. On my knife. From before. Mage." Jonmarc answered, his voice raspy from the near-strangulation.

Trent took one look at the downed rigger, then crossed the distance in two strides. He bent down, and brought his blade across the traitor's throat in one clean movement. Trent straightened, his expression both resolved and regretful. "That's done," he said. He turned back to Jonmarc.

"We've won," he said. "There's just a little mopping up left, but it's all over for the bandits." He managed a wan smile. "Good job taking down the hedge witch. He could have caused some problems."

"He was running away," Jonmarc managed. "I didn't realize, until just before he went down, that he was a hedge witch."

Trent regarded the rigger's corpse with contempt. "He was a thief and a traitor, probably sent by the bandits to steer us here. Don't lose sleep over it. I suspect the bandits meant to kill us all, or sell us as slaves." He bent down and retrieved Jonmarc's knife, wiping it clean on the rigger's tunic, and offering it, hilt first.

Jonmarc took the knife and sheathed it. He looked at the dead rigger, and thought of the other times he had killed raiders. *Does the Crone count their blood against my soul?*

"There you are!" Linton's voice boomed as he strode past the wagons. He took in Jonmarc's torn shirt and bloodied arm and the dead rigger.

"Jonmarc took him down," Trent said before Linton could ask. "I just happened along at the end."

Linton clapped Jonmarc on the shoulder. "Nicely done, m'boy. Nicely done." He frowned at the blood on Jonmarc's forearm. "Go see Ada and have her patch you up. We're going to put as much distance between ourselves and this accursed spot as we can, night be damned, just as soon as the wagon masters can pull everything together. Goddess! I'll be glad to see Huntwood."

Linton turned and bustled back to the bandit's camp, already shouting orders. Trent's expression made Jonmarc sure the other could guess his thoughts. "There's no shame in defending yourself," Trent said quietly. "And if he was one of their hedge witches, then he shares the blame for the deaths of everyone who died at the bridge, maybe even the ones who went missing in the floodwater. No one will fault you for doing what needed to be done."

Goddess help me, Jonmarc thought. *If I mean to sell my sword as a mercenary in Principality, I'd best get accustomed to killing the enemy. But when it becomes too easy, have they killed me as well?*

"Let's get you patched up," Trent said, interrupting his thoughts. "It's time to go." He grinned. "You see the healer, and I'll see to getting you some brandy for the pain. We've got a long road ahead of us."

A long road ahead, and no road that leads home, Jonmarc thought. Then he turned his back on the corpse and headed back to the caravan.

Bounty Hunter

"I DON'T THINK I've ever met a blacksmith who doesn't like horses." Jonmarc Vahanian dipped a piece of hammered iron into the cooling bucket. He glanced up at Conall, the journeyman blacksmith, who was withdrawing another rod from the furnace.

"Huh," Conall grunted. "You haven't met every blacksmith in Margolan, have you? So that doesn't say much." He began to hammer the iron, and for a few moments they were silent, since the din was too loud to do more than shout. Conall stood a couple of inches shorter than Jonmarc, but he was a few years older. He had a lithe, muscular build, with shoulders and arms strong from his work. His black hair was tied back in a queue, but it still accentuated eyes that were more violet than blue. Conall wasn't a big man, but he could put a level of power behind his strikes that Jonmarc hoped he could someday rival.

"I guess I just figured shoeing horses was most blacksmith's steady work," Jonmarc replied when Conall was done with that piece. Today, Jonmarc was on loan to help Conall finish up an odd assortment of tools and barrel hoops. A traveling caravan needed plenty of horseshoes, but it also required tools, weapons, and utilitarian items like barrel hoops to keep nearly one hundred performers, artisans, cooks, riggers, and laborers in business as they made their way across the kingdom.

Conall shrugged. "It's kind of a mutual thing with me and horses," he said, eying the iron bars in the furnace as if debating which one to take. "I don't much care for them, and they aren't that happy to see me, either."

"You have a horse for your wagon," Jonmarc pointed out, throwing another log on the fire and giving the bellows a pump. "You seem to like her just fine."

Conall grinned. "Lizzie and I have an understanding. She's different." He shook his head. "You're still new in the business. Tell me again how wonderful horses are after you've been kicked in the balls, stepped on, had a finger nipped off and nearly had your head taken off with their hooves."

Jonmarc grimaced, acknowledging the truth in Conall's words. Blacksmithing was dangerous work, and adding very large, very heavy and sometimes cantankerous animals to the mix made it that much more perilous. Jonmarc had heard plenty of stories, from the smiths with the caravan and from his late father, about blacksmiths that had been maimed or killed by balky horses.

"Give me a hand with this," Conall said, bringing Jonmarc back to the present. At seventeen, Jonmarc was just over six feet tall and strong from working in the forge. A shock of chestnut brown hair fell in his eyes as he bent to retrieve one of his leather gloves, hiding a ragged scar that ran from his left ear down below his collar. His dark eyes glinted with intelligence, and more recently, fresh grief. Every day the caravan traveled took him one step further from the loved ones who lay buried in graves back home in the Borderlands.

For a while, they worked without speaking, a companionable silence. Jonmarc had been with the caravan now for three months, long enough for the group to meander its way across part of Margolan, stopping near towns and manors for a few days at a time to perform and earn enough money for the next leg of the trip. Jonmarc had hired on as an apprentice blacksmith, and he often worked with Corbin, the head farrier, shoeing horses. But it was just as likely for him to be loaned out to the caravan's other blacksmiths if there was work to be done, and Jonmarc did not mind the change of routine.

"The next time you forge blades, can I help?" Jonmarc tried not to sound too eager, but Conall's grin let him know he had not succeeded.

"Blades," Conall repeated. "You know, very few smiths have made more than a handful of real weapons in their lifetime, and some make none at all." He gestured toward the iron clamps, bridle bits, wagon axles, and sundry tools that lay in various stages of completion around the forge. "This is what keeps food on the table for most smiths."

Jonmarc sighed and turned away. "I know that." His father had been known for his craft back in the Borderlands, and Jonmarc had been helping around a forge since he was just a boy.

Conall swore under his breath. "Sorry. I forgot. Of course you know that. It's just that few smiths who aren't with an army or a mercenary company spend all their time forging swords. And to tell you the truth, I wouldn't envy them their work."

Jonmarc's father had once said something similar, though he could craft a fine sword, and Jonmarc had the last two swords his father had ever forged back beneath his cot in his tent. "Never mind," he mumbled.

Conall's expression softened. "You know, once we get the barrel hoops done and a few of the tools finished up, I don't imagine Maynard would mind if we made a few knives for sale at the next market." He shrugged. "Maybe when we get closer to Principality, we could do some swords—the mercs up there will buy."

"Thanks, Conall," Jonmarc said, kicking at the dirt. "That sounds good."

Conall grinned. "Tell you what. After dinner, Trent and Corbin and a couple of the others are going to get together to play cards, maybe some contre dice. It's not like any of us have more than a few skrivven to wager, but there'll be ale, and maybe some of Lissa's jerked meat if I ask nicely."

Conall was one of the caravaners who traveled with his family, a wife—Lissa—and a young daughter named Brietta. When the caravan was camped for a show, some of the crew hunted small game for extra meat. Maynard Linton, the caravan master, didn't mind so long as no one poached on the king's land. Lissa and Conall were usually lucky in their hunts, and Lissa's jerked meats were in demand among their fellow travelers.

"You sure Lissa won't mind?"

Conall clapped him on the shoulder. "Someday, when you settle down, you'll learn the rules to a happy marriage. I've already gotten her blessing on it," he said with a hearty laugh. He did not seem to notice the shadow that passed across Jonmarc's features.

"I'll be over after supper," Jonmarc promised, trying not to dwell on Conall's comment. Few in the caravan other than Linton and Trent, the head blacksmith, knew about his murdered family, the wife and child he had commited to the flames just before he had joined the traveling show. Still, the words seemed to conjure a mood, and Jonmarc knew it would take a while to shake it off, or at least, he thought ruefully, to push back the dark memories that never actually left him.

"Then let's get the rest of the work out of the way so we can at least start on one of those knives," Conall said with a conspiratorial grin.

Jonmarc's dark mood had mostly lifted by the time he and Conall banked the fire and closed up work for the day. The sound of the bells from a village down the road carried on the evening air, ringing the eighth hour. The caravan had chosen a place to pitch its camp and unfurl its banner in between two middling towns, not far from a grand manor house. Business was good, and if the weather held, it would be a profitable week or two.

Though the spring days had grown longer, it was already dark, and small fires dotted the caravan's camp. The evening was cool, and Jonmarc pulled his cloak around him as he headed toward the cook's wagon for supper. Linton's camp was set up with the public areas toward the front, with the tables of artisan's wares, the tents where the acrobats and contortionists performed, and the cages filled with exotic beasts from across the Winter Kingdoms and other oddities for which visitors paid a coin or two to see.

Behind the line of exhibits and tents, the caravan crew pitched their tents and parked their wagons, making their home for however long the caravan stopped. Horses grazed in a hastily assembled corral, and Jonmarc spotted the dogs, goats, and chickens that were kept by some of the workers and performers. The cook's wagon was in the center of the camp, and a crowd had gathered, eating and trading stories. By the smell of it, there would be rabbit and bean stew tonight, and maybe if he were lucky, some of the hard biscuits if they hadn't all been eaten.

"Jonmarc! You're eating late tonight." Kegan, a healer-in-training, hailed Jonmarc from where he sat with several other apprentices. Like Jonmarc, Kegan was in his late teens. Why he was traveling with the caravan, Jonmarc never asked. Most of the people in the band of musicians, performers, and workers were as interested in leaving the past behind them as they were concerned about where the future led them. And since Jonmarc had only the vaguest of plans himself, it made for comfortable companionship, as if it were an unspoken agreement.

"If the riggers and the hired hands didn't break so many tools, Conall and I would have been done long ago," Jonmarc said, settling in after he had gotten a portion of stew and a biscuit, along with a tankard of ale to wash it down. Linton's pay was fair but not overly generous, but employment included food and the promise of some kind of shelter for the night, as well as the chance to see the kingdom. Jonmarc considered it a good bargain, especially when it came with decent traveling companions like Kegan.

Kegan rolled his eyes in response. "You only have to fix their tools. Ada and the rest of us have to put their bodies back together after they get torn up in a drunken brawl or they get themselves kicked by one of the mules."

In the distance, a wolf howled, and another answered its cry. The moon overhead was waning, and the shadows were deeper than usual across the camp. "Damn wolves." Sayer, one of the assistant carpenters, frowned at the noise and shivered. "I hope they'll keep their distance."

"How was the crowd today?" Jonmarc asked with a mouthful of food. "I didn't get out of the forge. Good enough Linton will stay on a while?"

Dugan, a rigger, nodded. "Aye, it looked good from where I was. Plenty of people buying from the traders, and carrying off food and ale. The tents were full of folks watching the jugglers and the acrobats. I thought Zane would likely get a swelled head from all the applause for his knife-throwing act."

Jonmarc was in no particular hurry to move on. He had considered looking into signing on with a merc group in Principality when they reached the neighboring kingdom, but that still seemed distant and unreal. For now, the caravan was home, and it boded well for all of them if the crowds were heavy and inclined to part with their coin. "That's good to hear," he said. "We've still got some wagons to patch."

Jonmarc lingered a while, finishing his food and listening to the day's gossip. As usual, it was talk of trysts revealed and confidences betrayed, petty fights, and overheard arguments. Dugan's comment roused him from his woolgathering.

"Who's the bloke wandering around asking questions?" Dugan asked. "Squat, ugly little man, oily blond hair—did you see him?"

Sayer frowned. "Toady little runt? Yeah, I saw him. At first, I thought he was with some friends and got separated, since he seemed to be looking for someone. Now, I'm not so sure."

"Do you think he was with the king's guards?" Kegan asked, and for once, the young healer looked nervous. Whatever Kegan's reason for not wanting to come under the guards' scrutiny, Jonmarc was sure his friend was not alone in his concerns. Everyone here seemed to be trying to forget who they had been before they signed on.

Dugan barked a laugh. "Not unless the king's let down his standards! I can't imagine him passing muster in any army."

"Maybe he's a tax collector," Sayer leaned forward, and dropped his voice. "I've heard that sometimes, they've been known to wander around poking their noses into things."

"And I'll bet Linton makes short work of them if they do," Kegan replied.

"If you're talking about the shifty little troll I saw, he didn't look smart enough to be a danger to anyone," Dugan said.

The group bantered for a little while longer, then went their separate ways. Jonmarc meandered back toward Conall's wagon. The night was cool but not cold, pleasant enough if there was a fire. Perfect for a card game with friends. His mind was on what he would do with any winnings when he caught a glimpse of a shadow moving furtively from wagon to wagon. That was unusual, because the area where the caravaners made their camp was regularly patrolled to keep out intruders.

Jonmarc frowned and drew his knife from its scabbard. He moved quietly to close the gap between himself and where he had last seen the shadow. The figure moved again, and now he realized it was a short man in a hooded cloak. The man seemed to be observing the caravaners around their campfires, but made no move to come closer.

Is he a thief? Jonmarc wondered. *If so, he's a stupid one. Linton and the merchants are the ones with the money. The rest of us don't have enough coin to buy a round of ale for our mates at the nearest pub.*

The figure darted to another wagon, and as Jonmarc followed, he began to wonder whether the man intended to circle the entire camp area. *Maybe he's not looking to steal something, Jonmarc thought. Maybe he's looking for someone. But why?*

Had the man been tall and thin, Jonmarc would have been certain it was the *vayash moru* mage with whom he had broken a bargain. But the man's build would be right for the stranger Dugan and Sayer had seen, and Jonmarc began to suspect that the newcomer's appearance here, after questioning workers that day, could only mean trouble.

The more he thought about it, the angrier he got, and he picked up his pace, closing the gap between him and the short man. The stranger must have sensed he was being watched, because he turned suddenly and spotted Jonmarc.

"Stop right there!" Jonmarc ordered, beginning to run.

The squat man took off running, and he was fast for his size. Jonmarc caught up and grabbed the man by the shoulder, but the newcomer swung at him with the small club he had in his other hand. He caught Jonmarc on the temple, and Jonmarc staggered back, fighting to remain conscious.

"Thief!" Jonmarc managed to shout. The squat man was at the outskirts of the camp, heading into the forest by the time two of the caravan guards arrived in answer to Jonmarc's shout.

"A thief was prowling the camp. He went toward the woods." The guards took off after the stranger, but Jonmarc guessed the man was long gone by now. He raised hand to his temple and his fingers came away bloody.

"What happened?" Conall, Trent, and Corbin appeared, followed by several other men from around the camp who had heard his shout.

Jonmarc told them about the stranger, and his suspicions that it was the same man Dugan and Sayer had seen. Trent and Corbin looked angry, but for an instant, before he regained control, Jonmarc thought he saw a flash of fear in Conall's eyes.

"We'll go out with the guards," Trent said, and Corbin nodded. Trent looked at Conall. "Do you think Lissa would have a rag to put on Jonmarc's face before his eye swells shut? We're closer to your wagon than to the healers' tent. Neither of us will get much work out of him if that happens," Trent added with a grin and a wink.

Conall's concern for Jonmarc seemed to war with something else, making him hesitate. "Sure," he said. "Come with me."

"Sorry to bother Lissa," Jonmarc said as he followed Conall back to the wagon. "I could go rouse a healer."

"It's already swelling shut. They're on the other side of camp, and by that time, your eye will be a mess," Conall replied. "We'll get you a cold rag and a glass of ale, and then I'll go find someone to fix it for you."

Conall led Jonmarc to an enclosed wagon, the kind many of the caravaners used both to live in and to carry their supplies, instruments or merchandise. It was nondescript and a little shabby, a snug fit for Conall and his wife and daughter. Jonmarc would have felt more embarrassed about inconveniencing them, but his head had begun to throb so badly he was having difficulty seeing straight.

Jonmarc had only been with the caravan for a few months, but even in that short time, he knew that the evenings playing cards and dice at Conall's wagon were quite popular among the group's tradesmen. Some nights, the wives and girlfriends came as well, gathering with Lissa as they sewed or knitted, watching as the children played in the firelight. Brietta, Conall's daughter, was quite fond of Jonmarc, no doubt in part because he often brought her small figures of animals he had carved from bits of wood. It was an old habit, something he had done to amuse his younger brothers, and making the figures for Brietta made him feel a little closer to the memory of his brothers.

Brietta peeked out of the wagon. She was four years old, with dark ringlet hair and the same violet eyes as her parents. Brietta also had a clear resemblance to her mother. "Daddy?" she called. Then she saw Jonmarc and smiled. "Hello, Jonmarc. Do you have an animal for me?"

Jonmarc chuckled, and reached into his pocket. He had

finished carving a small dog that morning. "Just for you," he said, presenting her with the gift.

Brietta squealed and jumped up and down. Lissa stepped up behind her and took Brietta in her arms, admiring the small wooden dog. "Jonmarc spoils you," Lissa admonished, but her tone indicated that she didn't mind at all. Lissa glanced at Jonmarc, and gasped at his injuries.

"What happened?"

"Go into the wagon and keep Brietta quiet," Conall said before Jonmarc could reply. "I'll be there in a moment to get that rag." To Jonmarc's ear, Conall's voice had an odd urgency.

"Wait here," Conall said, indicating that Jonmarc should take a seat near the fire on a log. He brought Jonmarc some ale. "I'll be right back."

Conall disappeared into the wagon, and Jonmarc could hear him conversing in low tones with Lissa. Jonmarc concentrated on staying upright, since the pounding in his head made him feel as if he were swaying back and forth. Although he was not trying to eavesdrop, he could not help overhearing a few words of their conversation.

"—leave now," Lissa urged.

"Wait," Conall replied. Jonmarc lost the next few words. "—reach family."

"What if he knows?" Lissa's voice was a bit louder, and Conall hushed her. Jonmarc heard Conall speaking in soothing tones, while Brietta had begun to wail.

"Soon. I promise. Linton will—" Again, Conall's words were lost.

"Can he?" Lissa challenged. "What if—" Brietta's crying drowned out the rest of her words.

"—take care of it," Conall promised. A few minutes later, he emerged from the wagon holding a wet rag.

"Sorry," he said. "Brietta has been having nightmares. She doesn't want to go to sleep." He managed a smile. "Here's your rag. Trent's probably gone to fetch a healer."

He's frightened, and he's hiding something, Jonmarc thought, pressing the cold, wet rag against his swollen eye. *But what could possibly scare Conall like that? And what could someone know that would get him into that much trouble?*

It was common knowledge that most of the caravaners were running away from something—or someone. Jonmarc counted himself among the refugees, since he was trying to stay out of sight of the mage he had disappointed. If he believed the gossip, his fellow travelers had left behind quarrelsome spouses, family obligations, broken indentures, and not a few arrest warrants. He had heard tell that their group included accused thieves and pickpockets, trollops, and smugglers, disgraced former soldiers, brawlers, drunkards, and debtors. Jonmarc did not have trouble believing the tales. Even if they were true, Linton kept a firm hand on those permitted to be among his entertainers and crew. Those who could not or would not change their ways did not remain long.

No one here seems to care what anyone did before, or what they're running from, Jonmarc thought. He shifted the rag to get the last coolness before his skin warmed the cloth. *What could be so bad? Murder? If so, I've killed raiders and bandits, and my foolish bargain cost my family their lives. If Conall killed someone, there was probably good reason. Treason? Conall doesn't seem the type. What's left that could be so bad someone would hunt him down for it?*

"He's right over here." Trent led Ada, one of the caravan healers, to where Jonmarc sat.

She pulled the rag away from Jonmarc's eye and shook her head. "Tsk, tsk. How did you do that?"

"I saw a thief watching the camp and I chased him," Jonmarc replied. "Unfortunately, he did better at catching me than I did catching him."

"I should say so," Ada said in a reproving voice. "Next time, call for the guards."

"I did. But by the time they came, he was gone."

Ada sent Conall for some water, and mixed up a poultice, which she applied to the rag and had Jonmarc hold it against where the swelling was the worst. Then she placed her hand on the torn skin where the club had hit his temple and murmured a few words under her breath. Her hand grew warm, and his skin began to tingle. A moment later, when she removed her hand, the skin was closed and the swelling had almost completely vanished.

"Keep the poultice on it tonight, just to be sure," she ordered. "With the healing I did, it should be safe for you to sleep, just be careful for the next few days not to get too much of a jolt or you'll undo some of what I mended." Her tone was stern, but her eyes were kind.

After he promised to check in with Ada the next morning, Jonmarc thanked both her and Trent and Conall and made his way back to his tent. Tired as he was, too many questions buzzed in his mind for him to sleep for quite a while, and when he finally did drift off, his sleep was fitful and his dreams were dark.

THE NEXT MORNING at the forge, Conall was more quiet than usual. Gone was the cheery conversation that Jonmarc usually enjoyed. Conall seemed distracted, and he often looked up from his work and scanned the crowd, frowning.

"Is there something I can do to help?" Jonmarc offered.

He did not expect Conall to confide in him, but something had made a dramatic change in the blacksmith just since the previous day.

"No," Conall said, and struck the iron particularly hard. He seemed to reconsider his abruptness. "There's nothing wrong."

Jonmarc raised an eyebrow, but said nothing. He tried to be particularly good at anticipating Conall's requests, hoping to do what he could to ease the other's stress. Without their usual banter, the day dragged on. Conall seemed to be channeling his concerns into his work, and it taxed Jonmarc's stamina to keep up with him.

"Did you hear anything about the stranger from last night?" Jonmarc asked.

"He's none of your concern," Conall snapped.

"He tried to split my skull open! I'd say that makes it my concern."

"It's bad business," Conall said without taking his eyes from his work. "Stay out of it."

"So you know something? Did Linton find something out?"

"Drop it." Conall fixed Jonmarc with a stare that silenced anything else he might have thought to say. Jonmarc took a deep breath to avoid making a sharp reply, and turned away. He grabbed a bucket.

"We're almost out of water for the cooling trough. I'll get some more." Before Conall could reply, Jonmarc walked out, hoping to cool his anger and temper the hurt from Conall's rebuff.

He took a roundabout route to the well. On a hunch, Jonmarc dodged behind the main performance tent, and found Dugan sitting on one of the wooden crates, smoking his pipe.

"Jonmarc! I heard you caught a fist to the face last night," Dugan greeted him.

Jonmarc smiled ruefully. "Actually, it was a club, not a fist, and I'm lucky it didn't put a hole in my skull," he replied.

"Your head's too thick for that," Dugan laughed. "So who did you manage to annoy this time?"

Jonmarc frowned. "That's just it—I didn't know the man. It was the squat, toady fellow you were talking about yesterday."

Dugan leaned forward, interested. "Now that's interesting. Why did he hit you?"

"I caught him sneaking around the camp. He's not with the caravan; there was no reason for him to be in the sleeping quarters. I got the feeling he was looking for someone."

Dugan took a draw on his pipe and looked thoughtful. "That's real interesting. Especially since I spotted him early this morning, at the edge of the public area, talking with a tall, thin pox-faced man and a rough-looking bloke who seemed dodgy."

"Do you think they're robbers?"

Dugan pondered the idea. "If so, they're scraping the bottom of the barrel robbing caravan folk. Linton's got money, and the merchants, but the rest of us don't have a pot to pee in."

"That was my thought," Jonmarc replied. "So if he was a thief, why skulk around the crew area? Linton's tent is easy enough to find."

"And pretty well guarded," Dugan said. "Same for the merchants. Maybe he's a lazy thief."

"So he came back, with two friends? That means whatever he's planning, he hasn't given up on it."

Dugan shrugged. "Maybe he's just the scout. He didn't look like he'd be smart enough to dream up a robbery. The other two, they looked smart—and dangerous."

"I'd better get back before Conall has my hide," Jonmarc said. "I've still got to get water."

"I knew I was forgetting something," Dugan said. "Kegan told me the new strangers were asking more questions than the stout man did. And from what he heard, they were looking for someone who sounds a lot like Conall."

"Thanks for the warning," Jonmarc said. "I'll pass it on."

Conall's mood had not improved by the time Jonmarc returned. "Took you long enough."

"There's a good crowd at the performances. I had to go the long way round." Jonmarc put the bucket back in the corner, and paused, debating what to say.

"The man who hit me, he was back again today. Dugan saw him."

"Where?"

"He didn't come into the caravan area. You know Dugan— he's up on the tent poles, and he's got quite a view up there. But the guy who clipped me brought two friends this time, and they were asking more questions. Dugan thought they might be looking for you."

Conall's eyes widened, just a bit, but enough for Jonmarc to see the reaction. "I've got to warn Lissa."

Jonmarc stepped to block Conall from the door. "Think about it. If someone's watching you, you don't want to lead them to your wagon. Last night, the man who hit me didn't seem to know where to look. Why not send me? No one looks twice at an apprentice."

Conall seemed to debate the question in his mind for a moment, then nodded. "All right. Tell her to keep Brietta in the wagon and to gather up our things. Tell her we'll leave tonight."

"Won't you be safer here, with Linton's guards?" Jonmarc

knew he was overstepping his boundaries, but he hated to think of Conall leaving the caravan.

"We were only going to be with the caravan for a little while, until we could meet up with my family," Conall replied. "We're nearly to where they're waiting."

It had not occurred to Jonmarc that Conall might not be a permanent fixture with the caravan, since he had been with the group since before Jonmarc joined up. He felt a stab of disappointment. Conall had been a good master, and a friend.

Conall seemed to read his thoughts from his expression. "Sorry to tell you like this. I meant to tell you before, but we just kept so busy, there wasn't time." He cast a nervous glance toward the caravan crowd. "Please, go now and find Lissa. I'll stay here in the forge, and if they come this way, I'll hide in the supply tent. We'll leave after dark."

"She's gone!" Lissa burst into the forge. Her violet eyes were red-rimmed from crying, and she looked terrified. "Brietta's missing!"

Conall took Lissa by the shoulders. "Tell me what happened."

Lissa was so upset she was barely coherent. "I was doing what you told me, getting us ready to go. I told Brietta to stay in the wagon. I went to get our pay from Linton, and when I came back, she was gone. I wasn't gone long."

Conall's jaw set. "Someone was watching the wagon," he said. "Waiting for the chance to take her—or you—to get to me."

"What's this about you leaving?" Maynard Linton strode into the forge. Behind him were Trent and Corbin, looking grim.

Conall looked up, surprised. "How did you know?"

"Kegan saw Lissa making preparations like you planned to leave without the rest of us. He told Ada, and Ada told me," Linton replied.

Conall slipped a protective arm around Lissa, who was trying to gather her composure. "Someone's taken Brietta. There were three men, poking around the camp, asking questions, looking for me."

"Bounty hunters." It was a statement, not a question, and by the anger in Linton's face, Jonmarc guessed that the caravan master had already figured out who was responsible.

Conall reddened and looked down. "Yes. I'm sorry. I didn't mean to put the caravan at risk. I only hoped to hide us for a little bit, until we could reach my family. We almost made it."

"I don't understand—" Jonmarc began.

Conall met Jonmarc's gaze. "They don't want me for what I did. They want me for what I am. What Lissa and I are."

"We know what you are," Trent said. "We've known since the first month. Corbin saw you change."

Conall looked at Corbin in astonishment. "You knew, and you didn't say anything?"

Corbin shrugged. "I mentioned it to Linton, who had already figured it out. Trent got it on his own, too."

"The point is, you and your family are part of this caravan. We don't care that you're *vyrkin*." Linton said.

Jonmarc felt as if the conversation was rapidly spiraling away from him. "*Vyrkin?*"

As he looked at Lissa and Conall, Lissa's form took on a faint glow. The outline of her body seemed to blur, changing its contours. A moment later, a large she-wolf sat in the middle of the clothing Lissa had been wearing. Conall reached down to lay a hand on the wolf's head possessively.

"Shapeshifters," Linton said. "There are small clans in the mountains, and more in Principality."

"We don't hunt humans," Conall said defensively. "We keep to ourselves. But when we're hunted, we protect ourselves."

"There are people who fear what they don't understand," Trent said, trying to help Jonmarc come to terms with what he was seeing. "Some of them think getting rid of all *vyrkin* will make them safer. They place bounties on the *vyrkin*, and unscrupulous hunters go after the payoff."

"Can't Brietta just shift and get away from them?" Jonmarc asked, still trying to make sense of what his eyes had just seen. *That's why Conall 'doesn't like' horses. They sense what he is unless they're used to him.*

"She's too young," Conall said, his voice rough. "Young ones can't shift until puberty." Jonmarc could hear the worry in his voice, and the anger.

The she-wolf had gathered Lissa's clothing in its mouth and trotted off behind the stack of firewood. In a few moments, Lissa returned, looking as she had when she entered the forge. Concern for her daughter was clear in her face, and she stood close to Conall, who took her hand.

"This was pinned to the door of the wagon with a knife," Lissa said, withdrawing a piece of parchment from a pocket in her skirt. On it, a crudely-scrawled message read, '9 bells. Forest edge. Both.'

"The bounty is just on me," Conall said. "I'll go. But please, make sure Lissa and Brietta get to my people safely."

Lissa's grip tightened on his hand. "Do you think they'll really let Brietta go? Or me, now that they know I exist? The bounty may just be on you, but they'll want all of us to get a bonus." She shook her head. "They'll kill you if you go."

"Who issued the bounties?" Trent said. "That's what I want to know."

Linton shrugged. "No way of knowing unless we saw the warrant. But from the descriptions Dugan and Kegan gave me, I think I've run into these three before. The squat fellow is Chessis. Nasty, and not too smart—perfect for his job. Vakkis is the tall thin man. He's nasty and smart—a dangerous combination. But Tarren, the pox-faced man, is the one to worry about. He's the one who seems to have the connections with the money. They're well-known in these parts, and much disliked. None of them have qualms about killing anyone who gets in their way," he added. "Remember that, all of you."

"So how do we get Brietta back?" Lissa asked. Her voice was cold, and her eyes made it clear that fear had become anger.

"I've got no qualms about killing bounty hunters," Linton said. "Scum of the world. So I suggest that we make a plan to get Brietta back and get rid of the bounty hunters— permanently. And I have a couple of ideas about how to make that happen," he said with a malicious gleam in his eye.

CONALL INSISTED ON holding to the kidnapper's demand, and Lissa could not be dissuaded from accompanying him. The forest's edge was about a hundred yards from the edge of the camp, with a wide, open section between the ring of wagons and the tree line. Linton, Trent, and Corbin worked out the plan at the table in Linton's tent, and Jonmarc returned with the people Linton had told him to fetch.

"Archers, stay behind the wagons until you can get a clear shot," Linton ordered his six best bowmen "The edge of the forest should be well within range." They nodded, and slipped away to their vantage points.

"Ada and Kegan, I know you don't like to do harm with your healer's magic, but if there's a chance to incapacitate these sons of the Bitch and spare us a fight, it might save you the trouble of patching up the wounded later," Linton said.

"We're forbidden to use our magic to kill," Ada said, fixing Linton with a meaningful look.

Linton held up his hands to placate her. "I didn't ask you to kill. But if you can... I don't know... give them a horrible headache, make them throw up or shit their pants... something that turns the tables on them."

Ada nodded. "We can do that—assuming they don't have wardings in place. It's not unknown for bounty hunters to have protective charms. They're in a dangerous business."

Linton turned to look at Jonmarc, Trent, Corbin, and Zane, one of the performers whose knife-throwing act was a marvel of aim and accuracy. "Jonmarc and Trent, You've been with the hunters when they've gone into the forest. That means you're at least passing familiar with the area. I want you to put on your darkest clothing and do your best to get around behind these bastards, take them from the rear."

He looked at Zane. "If you can get them in the back with a blade from a distance, do it. Just have a care for the girl. They'll likely have her with them to force Conall's hand, or tied up nearby."

"If we have a choice between getting the girl and launching an attack—" Trent began.

"Save Brietta," Conall said, his voice a low growl. He looked to Linton. "I've got to show up, like the bastards want. I'll keep Lissa behind me, but they've got to see both of us, or they'll hurt Brietta." His eyes took on a hard glint. "My people have run into their kind before. They won't hesitate to hurt her if they think I've broken the bargain."

"So you're the bait?" It was clear Trent didn't like the arrangement.

Conall glared at him. "If it were your daughter, would you do anything different?"

Linton shrugged his acquiescence. "You've got your orders. Get into place early, so you're not spotted." He met the gaze of each person in the room. "We've got three lives at stake here. There's no room for error."

It took only a few minutes for Jonmarc and the others to change clothing. "I really hope Linton knows what he's doing," Jonmarc muttered as he and Trent moved into position. Zane and Corbin went in the opposite direction. It was nearly ninth bells.

"I'm just hoping the bounty hunters don't have any surprises for us," Trent muttered. "Ready?"

Jonmarc nodded. He had his two largest knives, after deciding that his swords would be of little use amid the undergrowth. Trent had a nasty-looking long blade, the kind of knife used for clearing brush. He also had an assortment of throwing knives in a bandolier across his chest. On better days, Trent won many a round of drinks with his ability to put a knife in the center of a playing card that had been pinned to a wall or fencepost. Once before, Jonmarc had seen his friend use the knives to take down a bandit. He hoped Trent's aim was true tonight.

Linton had a place on the front line as well. He was dressed from head to toe in black, and while he had several knives on his belt, a slingshot was his weapon of choice. "I've used this to drive off plenty of wolves when I herded goats as a child," he mused. "Never thought I'd be protecting the wolves." He looked to Trent and Jonmarc. "Time to move."

Jonmarc, Trent, and Linton entered the forest about a mile from the caravan and around a bend from where the bounty hunters had specified their meeting place. They split up, keeping low and moving with all the stealth they could muster. Since both Linton and Trent had weapons that could strike at a distance, Jonmarc's task was to go after Brietta while the others handled the bounty hunters. He was just fine with that.

The bells from the nearby village clanged nine times. Jonmarc had circled around, and now he was almost to the meeting point. To his left, in the direction of the tree line, he heard a man's voice call out, and the muffled cry of a child.

"I'm here." Conall's voice carried on the night air. "So's my wife. Now show us my daughter."

Jonmarc edged closer, until he was able to see the three bounty hunters. One of them, the tall, thin man Linton had called Vakkis, held Brietta. Tarren, the leader, was the spokesman. Chessis, the muscle, hung back, looking around nervously.

"Daddy!" Brietta's shriek was filled with terror and hope.

"I did what you told me to do," Conall said. "Now give me my daughter."

Tarren chuckled. "Why would I do that? Three monsters are certainly worth more than just one."

None of the bounty hunters seemed the least inconvenienced by what the healer's might have sent their way. Jonmarc caught the glimmer of something at Tarren's throat. *Amulets,* he thought with a shiver. *Just as Ada feared. No help can come from the healers. We're on our own.*

Everything that happened next seemed to occur all at once, and when Jonmarc thought about it later, it seemed as if time had slowed. A knife flashed, biting into Vakkis's hand, scarcely an inch from Brietta's chest. *That's got to be Zane,* Jonmarc thought. *No one else would be so bold—or utterly insane.*

Vakkis cursed and released his grip, allowing Brietta to drop to the ground.

"Brietta! Over here!" Jonmarc dove forward, and Brietta shrieked and ran to him, hurling herself into his arms. He caught her with his left arm, brandishing his knife with his right hand.

Vakkis snarled a curse and came after them. Jonmarc slashed with his knife, cutting a deep gouge into Vakkis' cheek. Jonmarc heard the twang of bows and ducked as a hail of arrows descended. He ran for cover, shielding Brietta with his body, and looked back at the bounty hunters, hoping to see them lying on the ground, arrows protruding from their bodies. To his horror, the arrows bounced harmlessly against their cloaks. With a sinking heart, Jonmarc realized that the glint he had seen at Tarren's throat might have been more than an amulet. Without a doubt, they had worn chain mail beneath their cloaks.

Conall's form took on a faint glow, and then a huge wolf lunged, snarling, toward Tarren, bounding across the short area of open land between them. Vakkis and Chessis threw blades that sank deep into the man-wolf, but the wolf shook them off, and the gashes closed before their eyes.

Tarren's response was a quick twitch of his wrist. A glowing knife sank hilt deep into the wolf's chest. On the wolf came, relentless, in spite of the blood that caked its fur. But this time, the wolf stumbled, and collapsed, still trying to drag itself toward Tarren until it fell on its side and gave a final heaving breath. The light from the knife glowed brightly and spread over the wolf's body, then dimmed until it was barely visible. The wolf's form melted to become a man, covered in blood, with the glowing knife between his ribs. Lissa's scream echoed in the night.

He used a spelled blade, Jonmarc thought. He had heard legends of such things, tales that held such a weapon was required to fell a *vyrkin*, because the shifters could heal quickly from wounds that would kill a human. *Conall never had a chance.*

Brietta shrieked. Vakkis, blood streaming down his gaunt face, regarded Jonmarc with a feral look and came at him at a dead run. There was a swish of air, a loud clang, and Vakkis staggered as a stone from Linton's slingshot caught him in the head. Chain mail kept it from being a killing blow, but it was hard enough, Jonmarc wagered, to make the bounty hunter see stars. Seizing the opportunity, Jonmarc tightened his grip on Brietta and ran for camp.

Conall lay where he had fallen, in a pool of blood. Jonmarc turned Brietta into his chest, trying to shield her from the sight, as Lissa's form began to shimmer and a large she-wolf bounded from where a grieving woman had knelt seconds before.

"Lissa, don't!" Ada shouted from the line of wagons behind them.

Trent, Corbin, and Zane had emerged from cover, as had Linton. The four men, enraged by Conall's murder, circled the bounty hunters, knives at the ready to end the fight. The she-wolf launched herself at Tarren, knocking him to the ground, and pinned him, howling her grief to the night. It would all be over in a few moments, and Conall would be avenged.

"Halt! By the authority of Lord Guarov, I command you to lay down your weapons!"

Two dozen men wearing livery emerged from further back in the forest, crossbows nocked and ready. The speaker wore a captain's insignia, and he looked angry.

The she-wolf growled, then relented, taking a step back and allowing Tarren to scramble to his feet. Tarren strode over to the captain. "Take the wolf—and the child," he said with a glare directed at Jonmarc. "My quarry is dead, but the woman and child are monsters, just like he was."

The captain regarded Tarren with contempt. "Your warrant was for the man, dead or alive. You'll receive coin for his body, though less of it because of your clumsiness. I have no orders regarding the woman and child."

"No orders! They're monsters just like him!" Tarren ranted. "When I see your master—"

"Lord Guarov has gone on a hunt," the captain said in a flat voice. His face gave no indication of his feelings, but his eyes gave Jonmarc to think that the soldier disliked Tarren and was disinclined to interpret his orders more broadly than absolutely necessary. "He won't be back at the manor for several weeks—longer, if the hunt is good. The exchequer will have your bounty. The rest is none of my concern."

"I'll have you flogged!" Tarren shouted. "I'll have you stripped of your commission."

The captain looked unfazed by the threats. "My men and I were under orders to make sure you collected the quarry. We're leaving now. I would advise you to take the body and leave with us. If you remain behind, I will not be responsible for your safety."

"Do something," Trent urged Linton.

Anger stirred in Linton's eyes, but he shook his head. "If he's got a warrant from the local lord, there's naught I can do. I'm sorry."

Corbin wrapped his cloak around Lissa. She shimmered, and stood in human form. Her face was streaked with tears. She watched Vakkis and Chessis retrieve Conall's body, and her hands clenched at her side in rage, but she would not give his murderers the satisfaction of seeing her surrender to her grief. Vakkis removed the still glowing knife and returned it to Tarren.

Brietta cried out for her father, and Lissa took her from Jonmarc, holding her possessively while Brietta sobbed. Jonmarc looked at the faces of the caravan crew, and he did not doubt that they all longed to avenge Conall.

Tarren turned to Lissa with a smirk and held up the knife. "Still plenty of magic left. I'll get a warrant for you, and the brat. I'll find you."

Lissa stood tall and met his gaze. "Go to the Crone."

"Soldiers, with me!" the captain called. The troop began to move off, Vakkis and Chessis with them, and Tarren joined them, but not without a backward scowl at Lissa and the others.

Trent and Linton spoke in low tones to Zane and the archers. Ada and Kegan moved to where Lissa stood with Brietta in her arms. Ada put an arm around Lissa, and together, the four of them moved back toward the caravan camp. Corbin walked over to Jonmarc, who found himself torn between grief and rage.

"We're going to keep a watch in teams of two all night and through the day on Lissa's wagon, until she can meet up with Conall's family," he said. "I figured you'd want to be part of that."

Jonmarc nodded. Lissa's loss opened up his own wounds over the loss of his wife and child, engulfing him in sorrow. "I'm in."

Jonmarc saw Linton and Trent moving from group to group around the fires. "What's going on?" Jonmarc asked.

"We're leaving tomorrow," Corbin said. "Linton wants to be gone before Tarren manages to come back with another warrant."

Jonmarc looked toward the bloodstained grass where Conall had died, and then toward the camp. Without a word, he walked over to a large rock and carried it back, setting it down in the middle of the blood. Corbin watched him for a moment, then lent a hand, working together until a small cairn was raised over the site.

"I know they took the body," Jonmarc said, wiping sweat from his brow with his forearm and pushing back a lock of hair. "But it seemed wrong not to leave something behind." Corbin nodded, and they stood in silence for a moment, then made their way back to the camp.

Fires were burning outside many of the tents and wagons, but not next to Conall's wagon. Jonmarc swallowed hard, knowing first-hand the grief Lissa was dealing with, and knowing also that there was nothing he could do to help.

"Let's get out of this goddess-cursed place," Jonmarc muttered. "The further we get from here, the better."

The next day, the caravan moved out, in spite of the fact that the crowds might have made it profitable to stay another week. They avoided the roads that led close to Lord Guarov's manor, making an effort to avoid the bounty hunters and the lord's soldiers. Jonmarc and the others kept a constant watch day and night, fearful that Tarren might return to snatch Lissa and Brietta with or without a warrant, but to Jonmarc's relief, there was no further sign of the bounty hunters.

A WEEK LATER, Linton brought the caravan to a halt. They had reached a crossroads, where the main highway intersected with a smaller road that looked like it saw few travelers. Trees bordered the road on both sides. Jonmarc had watched the forest, unable to shake the feeling that they were being observed, but he had seen no one. Part of him feared that the bounty hunters might have followed them. Or perhaps

Conall's family was watching them from the cover of the trees, deciding whether they were friend or foe. While he had not feared Conall or Lissa, the idea that an entire pack of *vyrkin* were stalking them made a chill run down his spine.

Linton rode back to where Jonmarc, Corbin, and Trent were riding behind Lissa's wagon. Linton dismounted, and knocked on the wagon door. "Lissa," he called gently. "We're here."

Lissa opened the wagon door, with Brietta on her hip. She had been thin before Conall's death, but her grief made her gaunt despite the healers' best efforts. "So soon?"

Linton nodded. "We'll wait until you've made contact," he said. "We can't just leave you here to wait for Conall's family."

Lissa took a deep breath. "Thank you." She climbed down from the wagon and walked around to the front, where Zane had been handling the reins. "I'll take the horse from here," she said.

Zane glanced from Lissa to Linton, but Linton nodded. "Do as she says," the caravan master instructed.

"Has she ever met Conall's family? Does she know these people?" Jonmarc asked Trent in a quiet aside.

Trent shook his head. "I don't think so, although she said they would know her by her scent, that they could tell that she was Conall's mate, and that she was part of their pack because of it."

Pack. Family. Something Jonmarc no longer had. A stab of loneliness made it difficult for Jonmarc to breathe for a moment. Lissa was talking to Corbin, Trent, and Zane, thanking them for guarding her, and thanking Linton for sheltering them on their journey. She came finally to Jonmarc, and Brietta reached out to him for a hug. Jonmarc took the child in his arms for a moment and kissed her dark hair, giving her a gentle squeeze before handing her back to Lissa.

"I never had a chance to thank you for going after her in the forest that night," Lissa said.

"I'm glad I was able to get her back for you," Jonmarc replied.

Lissa nodded. "I can barely stand it, having lost Conall. I couldn't have borne it if—" She could not finish the sentence. It was a grief Jonmarc knew all too well.

"I think Conall's pack is here," Jonmarc said, nodding toward the trees. A few moments ago, the woods had seemed deserted. Now, he could see at least ten men standing at the forest's edge, and he wondered if there were more hidden in the shadows.

One man stepped forward. Though he was a good bit older than Conall, the resemblance was unmistakable. Lissa drew a deep breath and stood straight, squaring her shoulders.

"Let's go meet daddy's family," she whispered to Brietta. She walked toward the edge of the road, then turned again to look at Linton and the others. "Thank you, for everything."

The man walked closer, and even the way he carried himself reminded Jonmarc of Conall. When the man was just a few paces away from Lissa he stopped, and seemed to sniff the air. Then he nodded.

"My son's mate, and his child," the man said. "You smell of tears. The shaman saw in a vision that Conall is dead. Is that true?"

Lissa nodded. "He is dead," she replied. "Am I still welcome among your people?"

Conall's father was watching Brietta, cradled in Lissa's arms, playing with the ties to the cloak her mother wore, and a sad half-smile reached his lips. "You are blood. You are pack. You are welcome." He paused, and looked behind Lissa to where Linton and the others stood.

"These people fought for Conall. They saved Brietta's life, and protected me. Please, assure them that the pack will cause them no harm as they travel through its lands," Lissa said.

Conall's father nodded. He looked toward Linton, recognizing him as the leader. "Thank you for bringing me my new daughter, and my son's child. Be assured that they are welcome with my people. You will be safe traveling through our territory. We will not harm you, and insofar as it is in our power to do so, we will protect you. Go in peace."

Lissa gave one final look backward with a sad smile of farewell. Conall's father took the reins of the wagon horse, and led him along the side road. No one said anything for a moment, until the two had disappeared into the forest.

"Mount up," Linton said, turning back to the others. "There's an audience waiting for us on the other side of the woods. Let's get going. We've got a show to do."

BLOOD'S COST

"IF YOU WANT something done right, get a dead man to do it." Trent said as he and Jonmarc loaded a heavy box into the wagon.

"Does Renden make all of the items you're going to buy tonight?" Jonmarc asked.

Trent shrugged. "No, but he or his brother make most of what we're after. They're both *vayash moru*. Which means they've each had a couple of hundred years to get very good at what they do."

Trent secured the heavy box while Jonmarc went around to untie the cart horse from where he was tethered. Shifting the box to ride better might have posed a problem for other men, but Trent was strong from years spent as the head blacksmith for Maynard Linton's traveling caravan, and he was used to moving heavy loads.

Jonmarc calmed the wary horse, speaking in low, reassuring tones. At nearly eighteen years old, he had not put as many years in working the forge as Trent, who was almost ten years older. Yet Jonmarc was strong for his age, having worked in his father's forge from the time he could carry the tools. Going out on an errand late at night normally would not have worried Jonmarc. He and Trent could handle just about anything that came their way. But tonight, he was nervous. This was different.

Tonight, they were going to meet a man who had been dead for two hundred years.

Trent swung up into the driver's seat and Jonmarc climbed into the seat next to him. They set off, moving slowly through the dark caravan camp to avoid attracting attention. Most of the camp was asleep: the performers, tent riggers, cooks, artisans, healers, wild animal trainers, farriers, laborers, and acrobats who made up Linton's marvelous caravan. Part traveling fair, part merchant road show, the caravan meandered its way across the kingdom of Margolan, into a few friendly neighboring kingdoms, and back again under the watchful eye of its owner and impresario, Maynard Linton.

At this hour, only a few of the caravan's company were still awake. Some were guards, patrolling the camp to ward away robbers, vagabonds, and wild animals. Others were bakers and cooks, preparing for the next day's task of feeding the caravan's crew and preparing treats to sell to their customers. Most of those working the night shift were regular folks doing a hard job. A couple of them, to Jonmarc's knowledge, were also *vayash moru*. Until now, he had done a good job avoiding the caravan's few undead members. But tonight, there was no getting around spending time in the company of *vayash moru*. That had Jonmarc worried.

Trent and Jonmarc did not speak until they were on the road beyond the outskirts of the camp. The box in the back, filled with bars of pig iron, made the cart heavy. Trent kept the horse at a steady pace. The load on the return trip would be lighter, allowing the horse to rest. For a candlemark neither man said anything, though both watched the road and the hedgerows for signs of highwaymen. Nothing stirred.

"You ever meet a *vayash moru*?" Trent finally asked.

Jonmarc nodded. "I've avoided the ones with the caravan,

but I did once. On the road in Ebbetshire, back when I used to sell tools and herbs to Linton."

Trent raised an eyebrow. "Alone on the road? And you're still alive?"

Again, Jonmarc nodded. He had expected this conversation, and dreaded it. "I only saw him the once. I guess he wasn't hungry."

The pale, robed man he had met on that dark road had not made any attempt to drain Jonmarc of his blood. Instead, he had offered a bargain Jonmarc could not refuse, one that had cost him everything he held dear. Somewhere in the night that *vayash moru* was still out there, likely to be unhappy because Jonmarc had not kept his part of their deal. The thought made him shudder.

"They're not all monsters," Trent replied. "I know most people are afraid of them, and there's cause to be, but some of them, like Renden and his brother, just want to be left alone to go about their business."

"If you say so," Jonmarc replied. "I try to keep my distance."

Trent gave the reins a snap to move the horse along a little faster. "Not a bad idea, though the couple of *vayash moru* who work for the caravan have never given me any cause to fear them."

It seemed that everyone in the caravan's company was running away from something, pretending to be someone else, or trying desperately to avoid being found. For Jonmarc, it was a desire to put as much distance as possible between himself and his memories. From what little Jonmarc knew of Trent, his friend was trying to outrun some bad debts. In the six months Jonmarc had been with the caravan, he had heard stories about what nearly everyone in the company was trying to leave behind: jilted lovers, cuckolded husbands, vengeful masters, broken promises. Linton didn't tell tales, but that didn't stop others from speculating.

"Why would a *vayash moru* want a job with the caravan— or work as a smith, like Renden?" Jonmarc asked, curiosity overcoming his reluctance to discuss the subject.

Trent never took his eyes off the road ahead of them. "Immortality lasts a long time, I guess," he said. "Gotta do something to fill the nights. For Renden and his brother, it's the love of their craft. Wait until you see the swords Renden forges, and his brother Eli's silver work. They might have been master craftsmen before they were turned, but a few hundred years of practice have made their work more beautiful than anything you've seen before."

"The other people—mortals—don't bother them?" Jonmarc asked, frowning.

Trent chuckled. "For one thing, Renden and Eli aren't the only *vayash moru* in the farm country where we're heading. They're a little off the main road, and folks out here mind their own business. Plus, family counts for a lot in farming areas like these. Renden and his brother have been the neighbors of these farmers, and their fathers, and their grandfathers and so on. It wouldn't be neighborly for Renden and Eli to drain them, and it wouldn't be right for the neighbors to try to kill the brothers."

Jonmarc came from a small village where the eccentricities of long-time neighbors were overlooked so long as no one got hurt, so Trent's comment made sense in a strange sort of way. "You said that Renden and Eli aren't the only *vayash moru*. Are the others smiths, too?"

Trent shook his head. "You'll see. We're expecting a few of them to bring goods to trade." he said. "Several are farmers, working the land they lived on back before they were turned. They lend a hand during the night to help out their great-great-grandchildren, who are old men themselves now."

"What about the ones who work with the caravan?" Jonmarc had wondered about their *vayash moru* workers, and he had heard plenty of rumors, but Trent seemed to know what he was talking about, and Jonmarc found curiosity getting the best of him. That, and the fact that carrying on a conversation kept him from wondering whether any wolves were lurking in the shadows along the roadside.

"Linton likes them because they're stronger and faster than the rest of us," Trent replied. "A *vayash moru* can do more work in one night than a mortal man can do in two days, and he's not going to miss work like mortals who get drunk and sick and injured." Trent shrugged. "They're dead—I guess undead is more the truth of it—and so they don't take fever from the night air. If they get hurt, short of being stabbed in the heart or having their head cut off, they heal up quick, practically fast enough to see. Makes them good workers to have around."

"How does Linton know one of them won't get hungry one night and kill one of us?"

Trent gave him a sideways glance. "How does Linton know that any of us won't up and kill someone? More than a few of the folks in the caravan have killed in the past, I wager, self-defense or not, you and me included."

Jonmarc grimaced. He and Trent had been in a few tight spots when raiders and bandits had attacked the caravan, and both of them had defended themselves and the company to the death. "All right. But does it work the same way for *vayash moru*? After all, we didn't want to kill anyone. We don't kill because we're hungry."

Trent's expression grew somber. "No? We didn't kill because we wanted anyone's blood for food, but I've known men who've stolen food they couldn't pay for and killed the guards who caught them."

"That's not what I meant," Jonmarc said. "If *vayash moru* like Renden and the ones at the caravan don't drink human blood, how do they survive?"

Trent shrugged again. "Cows, sheep, goats, horses, even rats, I hear. They don't have to kill when they drink. Linton lets our *vayash moru* workers keep a flock of goats to feed on."

That was a relief. Although Jonmarc had not wanted to back out of helping Trent on his errand, he had also not been comfortable with the thought of meeting several *vayash moru* who might decide he looked like a good meal. "People talk about them," he said quietly. "The *vayash moru* with the caravan, I mean."

Trent nodded. "Aye. Just like they talk about everyone. Talk is cheap. But Linton runs a tight camp, and you know he won't stand for anyone making the caravan unfriendly for good workers." He chuckled. "Truth be told, I think most folks in the caravan are more afraid of Linton than any *vayash moru*."

Jonmarc was silent for a few moments. "Is there anything I need to know before I meet them?" he asked. "Anything that will keep them from eating me?"

Trent frowned. "You don't have to worry about being eaten, but there are some courtesies, and a few safety measures. Renden and the others will make sure they feed before we arrive, which decreases the risk to us. Still, it's best to avoid anything that makes your heart pound." He gave a wry chuckle. "I'm told it's a bit like waving food in front of a dog. They can't really read your mind, no matter what the rumors say, but they are very good at reading your expression and body, so don't do anything that might look... aggressive." He paused. "Oh, and try not to meet their gaze."

"Why?"

Trent shrugged. "One of their abilities is compulsion. If they capture your gaze, they can compel you to do what they want. Most *vayash moru* won't use their ability except to protect themselves, but it's best to avoid the situation."

Trent turned the cart up a dirt path, and not long after, a couple of modest wooden houses came into view. Behind the houses was a barn and a fenced yard for sheep and goats, along with a large plowed field. Off to one side was a blacksmith's forge. The smell of charcoal wafted on the night air, and the glow from the furnace made Jonmarc think of home. He swallowed hard, and tried to focus on the task at hand.

"We're here," Trent said.

The night was quiet as Trent stopped the wagon. They were in a clearing in the center of a small group of homes. The windows in several of the homes were dark, while a few glowed with lamplight, and the forge's glow kept the area from being too dark to navigate. No one was in sight. Yet Jonmarc knew they were not alone. The hair on the back of his neck stood up with the clear sense that they were being watched, and on a primal level, he knew the watchers were predators.

Trent seemed to sense his nervousness. "Do what I do," he murmured. Trent swung down from the driver's seat and walked around to the front of the cart, holding the reins loosely in one hand, his other hand open and slightly away from the sword at his side. Jonmarc did the same.

"It's Trent," he told the darkness. "I've brought a helper. We're here to see Renden and Eli."

For a moment, nothing stirred. There was a movement of air, a rustling noise, and suddenly a man stood in front of them. Jonmarc jumped, and the man smiled, showing just the tips of his elongated eye teeth.

"Good to see you, Trent," the man said. He was lanky and loose-limbed like a farm boy, with dark, short-cropped hair that stood out in a cowlick on top. In face and manner, Jonmarc guessed his age to be early twenties, but then he met the man's eyes and revised that number to be significantly higher. The man was very pale, making his dark eyes even more prominent. He wore a leather shirt with sleeves that fell to below the elbow, and had leather riding chaps over his trews and high boots. The stranger returned his gaze directly, with an intent look as if he meant to ask a question. Jonmarc felt his skin prickle, and looked away.

"Interesting," the man murmured. He turned his attention back to Trent. "Who did you bring us?"

His phrasing sent a chill down Jonmarc's spine, but Trent did not react as if the comment posed a threat. "This is Jonmarc," he said. "He came to help me load." Trent turned back to Jonmarc. "This is Renden. You've never met a blacksmith who can do the kinds of forging he can."

Renden chuckled. "Comes with lots of practice," he said. "Follow me. My men will unload the wagon."

They headed toward the forge. Jonmarc still had the sense that they were being watched, though no one else stepped out of the night. But he thought the tension had lifted, feeling on a gut level that he and Trent had passed some kind of test.

They stepped inside the forge building and Jonmarc let out a breath he did not realize he had been holding. Just being near the furnace and anvil, smelling the charcoal smoke, hearing the rustle of the flames soothed him and made him think of his own lost home. The forge was a three-sided building, protected by the roof and walls from wind and rain, but open on one side to vent the heat. And though every blacksmith arranged the tools and set up to his own liking, Jonmarc knew that he could walk into a forge anywhere in the kingdom and it would feel familiar.

"Take a look at these swords, Jonmarc." Trent's voice called him back to the present. He walked over to where Trent and Renden stood next to a table. A dozen swords lay displayed, and Jonmarc caught his breath. He had seen well-crafted blades before. His father had been a skilled blacksmith who made swords for prosperous men near their village. Jonmarc's two swords were the last his father had made, and were nicely forged and balanced perfectly.

Yet as he looked at the swords Renden set out, he could not help feeling sheer awe at the man's craftsmanship. From the design of the grip to the perfectly forged edge, to the runes etched along the flat of the blade, each sword was a deadly work of art. One of the blades in particular caught Jonmarc's eye. The steel looked as if it had been folded many times upon itself, forming a pattern of swirling lines.

He looked up at Renden. "That's a *damashqi* blade," he said, a hint of wonder coloring his words. "I've heard of them, but I've never seen one before."

Once again, Renden met his gaze for an instant longer than normal, and Jonmarc felt... something. He looked away, back to the knife. "They're all beautiful," Jonmarc said, "but the *damashqi* is amazing."

Renden smiled, though he looked puzzled by something. "Thank you," the *vayash moru* replied. He looked to Trent. "The *damashqi* is a gift, for you, to thank you for the trade you do with our village. Use it in good health."

Trent handled the blade respectfully, admiring the workmanship. "That's quite a gift. Thank you."

Renden turned his attention to Jonmarc. "I see you've done work in a forge yourself," he added with a nod toward the tell-tale white scars on Jonmarc's hands and arms.

"My father was a smith," Jonmarc replied. "I worked with him until I apprenticed in the next village over." It was the truth, as far as it went. He didn't need to mention the circumstances that had caused the untimely deaths of his father and his new master, as well as the rest of his family, his wife, and their village.

Renden nodded. "I worked for my father as well, though I suspect that was a while longer ago." He gestured toward the blades. "Go ahead. Handle them." He chuckled. "You look like you know your way around a sword. I doubt you'll lose a finger."

Jonmarc picked up one of the swords and weighed it in his hands. As he expected, it was expertly forged and perfectly balanced. "What do the markings mean?" he asked.

Renden's smile faded. "Just a bit of magic I put into all my swords," he replied. "A prayer to Istra that the blade never be used on the innocent." His gaze rose toward one wall of the forge, and Jonmarc turned to look in that direction.

The metal sculpture of a woman sat in a small shrine constructed against one of the forge walls. The woman was tall and beautiful, yet the expression on her face was grief-stricken and fierce. Her cloak billowed around her, and behind it crouched desperate figures who clung to the woman and her cloak.

"Did you make that?" Jonmarc asked, his voice hushed. Part of him was in awe of the skill required to forge the sculpture, but another part, to his surprise, reacted on a visceral level to the image. It was the first time he had ever seen that Aspect of the goddess portrayed, yet it seemed as if, somehow, he had always known her.

"You're familiar with the Dark Lady?" Renden asked.

"A little," Jonmarc replied, unable to tear his gaze away from the expression on the statue's face. "Everyone knows the faces of the Lady." The Sacred Lady of the Winter Kingdoms was a goddess with eight Aspects: Mother, Childe, Lover, Whore, Crone, Warrior, and two more forbidding presences: Nameless, the Formless One, and Istra, the Dark Lady, patron of the outcast, the damned... and the *vayash moru*.

"Beautiful work, Renden," Trent said, breaking the mood. "Linton will be happy with the swords. Where's Eli?"

Renden turned back toward Trent. "Eli went to fetch the silver pieces he made for you, and to bring the others. They've got the supplies you wanted."

Jonmarc managed to look away from the shrine and glanced around the forge. His attention was caught by a pile of leather gear set to one side. Every blacksmith wore a leather apron and protective leather gloves that covered the wrist and part of the forearm. These gloves were longer, and Jonmarc realized they would meet the long sleeves of Renden's leather shirt.

"It must get hot, if you wear all that to work the forge," he said, thinking of how often he had stripped off his shirt when he had helped his father with tasks other than striking the hot iron.

"Heat and cold don't bother me," Renden replied. "But I don't want to catch fire."

Jonmarc's face reddened. He'd heard the stories about how *vayash moru* could be destroyed with flame. "I'm sorry. I didn't think." He looked up. "If it's so dangerous, why do you still work the forge?"

Renden's eyes grew sad. "The forge and the flame never change," he replied. "If you're like me, people come and go too quickly. The forge remains."

His answer chilled Jonmarc despite the warmth of the nearby furnace. In the months since his family was murdered and he had fled his home, he had taken consolation in the simple constants of the forge, the glow of the flames, the rhythm of the hammer on iron, the smell of the coals and the hiss of steam. It was a sentiment he understood all too well.

"Would you like to see the silver now that my brother has bored you with his iron?" The voice made Trent and Jonmarc jump, as the speaker seemed to appear out of nowhere. *Vayash moru* speed and stealth would take some getting used to, Jonmarc thought as his heart pounded.

The man Jonmarc guessed to be Eli sauntered into the forge, looking pleased with himself for startling them. Eli had Renden's dark hair and angular features, but he was younger in appearance, looking little older than Jonmarc.

Trent shook Eli's hand. "Good to see you. Eli. Silver treating you well?"

Eli smiled. "Always."

Jonmarc looked confused. "I didn't think *vayash moru* could work silver, or even touch it," he said.

Eli looked his way, and met his gaze. The same odd prickle tingled at the back of Jonmarc's neck, and the same strange feeling of pressure in his temples. He blinked, and forced himself to return the stare levelly. "Interesting," Eli replied, looking away from Jonmarc and giving Renden a meaningful glance Jonmarc could not decode.

"One of many legends about our kind that aren't true," Eli replied. "Fortunately for me. I think the Nargi priests started that rumor, because they wanted to make their people think we couldn't touch the objects sacred to the Crone." He gave a derisive snort. "The only things dangerous to us were the priests themselves."

Unlike in Margolan, where King Bricen was tolerant, even protective of the *vayash moru*, Nargi's Crone priests were known to hunt and kill *vayash moru*—and mages, or so Jonmarc had heard. He and Trent followed Eli out of the forge while Renden began packing up the swords.

The previously empty open space in the middle of the small gathering of houses now bustled with activity by moonlight. One man was unloading the box of pig iron, handling the heavy weight single-handedly without apparent strain. Jonmarc had helped to lift that box, and knew just how heavy it was. Two other men hoisted large boxes of produce onto their shoulders, balancing them as if they were empty, and carrying them to Trent's wagon to replace the pig iron. Over to one side, two women were unwrapping a cloth bundle that revealed delicate jewelry, while a woman and a man set out beautifully-crafted pottery for Trent's examination.

"Is everyone in the village *vayash moru*?" Jonmarc asked Trent in a low voice.

Renden heard him, and laughed. "No. Eli and I live here with our great-grandchildren, and other relatives. The craftspeople you see here come from all around. They are *vayash moru*, but they don't live here." He gestured toward the horizon. "We're scattered all through these parts, and up into the mountains. It's safer that way."

"You've been busy," Trent remarked, eyeing the wares. "Linton's going to be very happy."

Eli shrugged. "We don't see a lot of caravans, and even fewer like to trade with us. Tell Linton we appreciate his partnership."

Trent chuckled. "Linton appreciates the extra coin your workmanship brings to the caravan," he replied. "You know that to Maynard, gold is the most sincere compliment."

"We're grateful for the pig iron," Eli said. "The nearest miners don't like to trade with us, and the next nearest mine is several days away, which makes it difficult to move the iron by night."

While Eli and Trent talked, Jonmarc began to move around the small green, eyeing the wares. The *vayash moru* craftsmen watched him with curiosity, saying nothing but giving him a nod in greeting. After the strange reaction from Eli and Renden, Jonmarc avoided making eye contact.

He paused at the jewelry-maker's display. "I've seen these designs before," he murmured, looking at the delicate pieces.

The woman snorted. "I doubt it," she replied. "Not unless you're a whole lot older than you look."

"I've seen these in the old tombs," Jonmarc said, fascinated by the workmanship. "Up in the mountain caves."

The woman eyed him. "What's a mortal doing in the caves of the dead?"

Jonmarc realized that his comment might have given offense. "I used to go exploring when I was a boy. I swear, I meant no disrespect." He felt it wise to leave it unmentioned that in hard times, to feed his family, he had stolen some of those grave goods and sold them for a small profit to Linton. And he remembered the *vayash moru* he had met on the road, who had wanted a very specific old piece of jewelry from the caves, a talisman that had brought Jonmarc nothing but grief.

"Dangerous places for the living," she replied. "I'd stay away from there if I were you. Some of the old pieces had magic."

Indeed they did. Deadly magic. Jonmarc thought. "Your jewelry is beautiful," he said, deciding a change of subject was best. "Did you copy the old styles?"

The woman laughed, rocking back on her heels. "No, sonny. I didn't copy them. I made them then, just like I make them now. Might even have made some of the pieces you saw in those tombs. Sooner or later, everything goes to the grave."

Shaken by her answer, Jonmarc was just starting to turn back to Trent when he heard his friend talking with Renden.

"... is he a mage?" Renden asked.

"Jonmarc? Not to my knowledge," Trent replied. "Why?"

Out of the corner of his eye, Jonmarc could see Renden shrug. "He has an unusual resistance to compulsion," the *vayash moru* said. "Very unusual."

Trent chuckled. "So you can't bargain him down on price the way you do with me?"

Renden rolled his eyes. "You and I have an agreement. I don't compel you, or Linton. But it's best to know about someone new, especially when you bring them among us. I had to try. The result was... interesting."

They moved off then, and Jonmarc could not hear them, though he wondered whether the other *vayash moru* could catch every word of the hushed conversation. He was full of questions, but knew they would have to wait until the night's business was concluded.

After a few moments, Trent left Renden and motioned for Jonmarc to join him as they slowly circled past the wares of the artisans. True to his promise, Eli's silverwork rivaled his brother's for sheer skill. Rings, necklaces, earrings, belt buckles, pins, and chalices glimmered in the light of Trent's lantern, necessary for mortal vision to inspect the intricacies of design.

"I can't take everything this trip," Trent said apologetically, "and I still need to buy from the others, but I can take these pieces," he said, gesturing toward the items he wanted. "We'll be back through here in a while—I'll stop in and see if you've got anything left for me."

As Eli began to wrap up the chosen items, Trent continued around the circle, occasionally asking Jonmarc's advice as he selected jewelry, pottery, and produce. Along the way, he chatted with the artists, complimented them on their work, and jokingly flirted with the old women. One of the *vayash moru* came behind them, carefully wrapping the items for shipment and placing them in wooden crates. Jonmarc hoped that he and Trent could move the crates when it came time to unload.

"A good night's work, don't you agree?" Trent said as he withdrew his coin purse from inside his shirt and counted out a tidy sum of gold and silver to cover what the pig iron didn't bring in trade. He placed the coins in Renden's hand. "I'll leave it to you to divide it up among everyone."

Renden nodded. "A very good night," he agreed. "We're rather self-sufficient, but we do have some need to trade with the villagers, and coin comes in handy for what we can't make ourselves."

Within a few minutes, the other *vayash moru* had packed up their goods and vanished from the village green. Renden walked back with them to the cart. With the box of pig iron gone, there was plenty of room for their purchases. "Give Linton my thanks," he said, shaking Trent's hand, and then extending his hand to Jonmarc. For a moment, Jonmarc met Renden's gaze, and he waited to feel whatever the 'compulsion' was that Renden had spoken of, but nothing happened. Renden gave a languid blink and a nod.

"Safe travels," Renden said. "And may the Dark Lady bless your path," he added, making the sign of the Lady in warding.

Neither Jonmarc nor Trent spoke until they were well away from the village. Finally, Jonmarc got up the nerve to ask his question.

"I know you said not to meet their gaze," Jonmarc said. "I'm sorry—I forgot and did it anyway, and both Renden and Eli seemed to react... oddly. I hope I didn't give offense."

Trent frowned, never taking his eyes from the road. "I didn't warn you to keep you from offending them; it was for your own protection. Making eye contact can give a *vayash moru* who's so inclined some measure of power over you."

"Is that what Renden meant by 'compulsion'?"

Trent nodded. "I've heard it varies by individual, both for the mortal and for the *vayash moru*."

"Have you ever felt the compulsion yourself?" Jonmarc asked. He was thinking about the pale stranger he had met on the road, the man whose bargain had changed his life.

"Yes. Before I knew better, I fell under the compulsion of a *vayash moru* trader in another village, and nearly ended up giving him all my money." Trent grimaced. "One of the other *vayash moru* stepped in and ended it, so I got my money back, with a warning and advice on how to keep it from happening again."

"What did it feel like?" Jonmarc pressed.

Trent thought for a moment. "Do you know how it is when you've had some ale and one of your friends suggests you go do something and, at the time, it seems like a good idea, but when you sober up you realize it really wasn't too smart?"

Jonmarc nodded.

"It's a little like that. Not that someone forces you to do something, but more like it's a suggestion that at the time seems like what you ought to do, until your head clears."

"I didn't feel anything like that, either time I met their gaze," Jonmarc said. *Or before, when I met the stranger on the road.*

"Did you feel anything that seemed odd?" Trent asked.

It was Jonmarc's turn to pause. "There was a strange buzzing, like someone humming a long way off," he said, searching for the right words. "And pressure in my temples, the way it feels when you're about to get a headache on a rainy day. But I didn't have the urge to hand over my coin purse, or anything unusual."

"I'd have noticed," Trent replied with a chuckle. "And don't take it badly that both Renden and Eli tried their compulsion on you. It's sort of a test. They've never really said, but I don't think they like to deal with humans who are very easy to compel. My guess is, that kind of person wakes up angry when they realize what's happened and comes back looking for trouble."

"I heard Renden mention something to you about me," Jonmarc replied. "Something about compulsion."

Trent spared a glance to the side to look at him. "He said you were very unusual. Neither he nor Eli could compel you at all."

Jonmarc frowned. "He's lived a long time. I'm sure he's met others like me."

Trent shrugged. "He says not. And he said that he doesn't mind, but that other *vayash moru* might take you for a mage of some sort and not be as welcoming."

Jonmarc laughed. "Me? I don't have a magic bone in my body. And while I'm fine with healers and hedge witches, I don't much fancy mages."

"Well, magic or not, you've got an unusual talent. I'll have to remember to bring you along if I ever have cause to trade with *vayash moru* I don't know. You might help me hang on to my money," Trent said with a laugh.

They were nearly back to the caravan's camp, and the moon was low in the sky. Jonmarc's attention was on the road ahead of them, and he saw something dark lying across the path.

"Watch out," he said, pointing. "There's something in the roadway."

Trent slowed the cart, and both men drew their swords, alert for robbers. It was common for brigands to block the road in order to ambush their victims. He gave a nod to indicate that Jonmarc should climb down and investigate, and gestured with his sword that he stay alert for a trap.

Warily, Jonmarc moved around the horse toward the two dark shapes that lay on the road. He kept his sword at the ready. They appeared to be men, one lying on his side and one splayed across the lane. There were tales of robbers who pretended to be injured, only to spring up and surprise would-be rescuers. But as Jonmarc grew closer, he saw no movement, not even the rise and fall of breath.

He moved forward quickly, hoping to gain the edge of surprise if the figures suddenly attacked. He poked at the nearest body with the point of his sword, not enough to do harm, but with enough force to be uncomfortable if the man on the ground were faking injury. There was no response.

Jonmarc toed the body over onto its back, sword leveled, and stared down at the man. He was unnaturally pale with a strange ashiness to his features Jonmarc had never seen, even in a corpse. Still alert for trouble, he knelt next to the man and checked for a pulse, then assured himself that the stranger was not breathing.

"He's dead," Jonmarc called to Trent.

"Check the other one," Trent replied.

Jonmarc crossed to the other body, the one that lay spread-eagle in the roadway. He knelt down and made the same examination, then frowned as something caught his eye. Turning the corpse's head to one side, Jonmarc stared at the raw puncture wounds and the two bloody trails that ran down the dead man's neck.

"What did you find?" Trent asked impatiently.

Jonmarc waited to answer until he checked the first body again, and found the same wounds. He looked up. "We've got a very big problem."

"WHAT IN THE name of the Crone is so important that you had to wake me up at this forsaken hour?" Maynard Linton grumbled. Still wearing his nightshirt over a pair of hastily-pulled on trews, Linton stalked across the darkened camp toward the forge. He was a short, stocky man, tanned copper from a life lived outdoors, with a round face and shrewd dark eyes.

"Trent and I found two dead men on the road—" Jonmarc began.

"So? Leave them there. You didn't kill them, did you?" Linton seemed determined not to let go of his pique over being awakened before dawn.

"We didn't kill them, but someone did."

"Obviously. Why is that costing me my sleep?"

Trent stepped out of the shadows of the darkened forge. "Because whoever killed them was *vayash moru*."

Linton quickly sobered. "Are you sure? Maybe wolves, or a wild cat?"

Trent shook his head and led Linton to the back of the forge where he and Jonmarc had laid the two bodies. Trent opened the shutters on his lantern enough to give Linton sufficient light to examine the corpses. Muttering to himself under his breath, Linton squatted next to the dead men and looked at the marks on their necks, going over their bodies to assure there were no other wounds. Finally, he turned out their pockets, and found a handsome carved pipe, flint and steel, a shell comb, and a small pack of bronze and copper coins.

"Looting the dead, Maynard?" Trent questioned, only partly joking.

Linton scowled. "Well, they certainly don't need more than a coin for the Crone," he replied. "Thought there might have been something to tell us who these blighters are." He sighed. "Whoever killed them didn't rob them, or took something valuable enough that he didn't want the small stuff in the pockets." He stood and stretched.

"Do you agree it's a *vayash moru* kill?"

Linton nodded. "Seems to be." He glanced over his shoulder to assure himself it was still full dark outside. "Who knows about this?"

Trent nodded toward Jonmarc. "Just Jonmarc and me. We came here straightaway."

"Good. Stay here. I'm going to find our *vayash moru* folks and see what they make of it."

"How do you know that one of them—" Jonmarc began.

"I don't, but we've got to start somewhere." Linton shook his head. "I'd hoped things wouldn't come to this."

"Things?" Trent asked.

Linton's scowl deepened. "There've been some incidents in the last couple of days," he replied. "That's why I was eager to have you meet with Renden, so we could be on our way."

"What kind of things?" Trent pressed.

"Livestock gone missing," Linton replied. "Some of the sheep and goats from the main herd, and a horse. At first, we thought a wolf or a wild cat might have gotten into the pens, but we would have found the bodies nearby, or some trace of the animal being dragged off. Nothing."

Linton looked over his shoulder once more. "I've heard talk that the same sort of thing happened at one of the villages nearby. Some of the customers were talking about it yesterday when they walked past me. Whether or not it's true, the *vayash moru* are being blamed."

"Did you ask our workers if they'd seen anything?" Trent asked. "After all, they handle a lot of night duty."

Linton nodded. "I did, and I asked the *vyrkin*, too." *Vyrkin* were shapeshifters who could take the form of animals, often wolves. It was news to Jonmarc that the caravan had picked up some *vyrkin* workers since an incident with local bounty hunters had ended badly not long ago.

"And?"

Linton shook his head. "Nothing. So I went to the hedge witches. And I asked them to spell the barns and livestock pens. The attacks stopped." He grimaced. "Then one of the woodcutters came to me with a tale of finding some of the carcasses in the woods a ways off. 'Course by then, it was too late to figure out what killed them, but I thought it was strange that they didn't look chewed on. Wouldn't be, if they were drained of blood."

Linton walked off to find the *vayash moru* workers, leaving Trent and Jonmarc guarding the dead men. They were silent for a while, then Jonmarc glanced back toward the bodies. "Should we worry about them turning into *vayash moru*?" he asked, eyeing the corpses warily.

"You're asking me?" Trent replied. "I'm no expert."

"You know more about it than I do."

"They won't be rising." The voice came from behind them, and both Trent and Jonmarc startled. They turned, swords raised, to see three men standing in the entrance to the forge, with Linton a few steps behind them. It was hard to make out their faces clearly in the dim light from the lantern, but Jonmarc thought he had seen them around the caravan at night.

"How do you know?" Trent challenged.

The tallest of the three men stepped closer. He had dirty blond hair that hung to his shoulders, and carried himself as if he had once been a soldier. The other men were shorter and dark haired, one slender and one stocky. All gave the appearance of men in their late twenties or early thirties, but like Renden, looks were deceiving, and Jonmarc guessed they were at least a generation or two older than they appeared.

Remembering what Trent had told him about compulsion, Jonmarc met the *vayash moru's* gaze, and smiled as his directness seemed to startle the man. For a moment, their gaze locked. The *vayash moru* looked away first. Whether he did not try to compel Jonmarc or was not able to do so, Jonmarc did not know, but he felt nothing.

"Trent, Jonmarc," Maynard said, bustling up to stand near the corpses, "these are Hans, Jessup, and Clark," he introduced, with a nod toward each of the men in turn. "They've come to see if they can help us figure out who's doing the killing."

"How do you know the dead won't rise?" Trent repeated.

Hans, the blond man, knelt next to the corpses and turned the dead men's heads to get a better look at the wounds on their throats. Then he looked at their faces and pulled back their lips, studying their mouths before answering.

Hans looked up from where he knelt. "These men were drained, not turned," he replied. "For one thing, if someone meant to turn them, they would have taken more care with the bite." He turned the dead man's head so that they could see the torn flesh on the neck. "This is savage, intentional or driven by hunger. A bite can be clean, almost painless."

He turned the head back to show the man's mouth. "Just being bitten doesn't turn a person. It requires intent. The *vayash moru* has to drain the mortal nearly to death, then feed some of his own blood to the mortal, who has to drink it—willingly or not. Neither of these men have taken blood."

Hans stood and faced them, his expression a mix of uneasiness and defiance. "We didn't do this," he said, hands on hip. "I can vouch for the others, and they for me. These kills were made earlier tonight. Since we rose at sundown, Jessup, Clark, and I have been busy with our chores. Tonight, we went to help the riggers. You can ask them. We were never gone."

"I didn't call you here to accuse you," Linton said. "If I didn't think I could trust you, I wouldn't have hired you on. The question is, do you know anything that could help us find out who did the killing?" He glowered at the *vayash moru*, but Jonmarc noticed that even Linton avoided meeting their eyes. "If word gets out, you know how it'll be."

Hans nodded soberly. "We will have to leave." From his expression, Jonmarc guessed it was not the first time such killings had caused dangerous repercussions for other *vayash moru*.

"Have you heard anything that would help us?" Linton asked. "I don't know how much contact you've had with others of your kind."

"Very little, by design," Jessup replied. Both Jessup and Clark also moved like soldiers, and Jonmarc wondered if the three men were, if not brothers by blood, then brothers at arms. *Were they turned willingly, or against their will?* he wondered. *What have they—and Renden and Eli and the others—seen in their long lives?*

Hans, Jessup, and Clark exchanged glances, and Hans cleared his throat. "We try to stay clear of *vayash moru* broods because we haven't ever quite gotten over feeling more mortal than not," Hans said, uncomfortably. "As *vayash moru* go, we're fairly young. We were captured and turned during the Mage War, by one of the *vayash moru* loyal to the Obsidian King."

"That war ended fifty years ago," Linton said quietly.

"And so did our lives," Hans replied. "Some *vayash moru* are fortunate. Their families will take them back, so happy to see them that no one cares if they're undead. Others stay close to their maker and create a family of their own. Our maker was killed when the Obsidian King fell, and we escaped leaving us with no one but each other. We feel more comfortable around mortals."

"Tell him about the sheep," Clark said.

Hans looked down. "Last night, we went out to where the animal carcasses were found. We were soldiers, prisoners... and now, *vayash moru*. We're not as squeamish as mortals. We examined the carcasses. They were *vayash moru* kills."

"Why wasn't I told?" Linton demanded.

Hans raised his head. Linton and Trent avoided his gaze, but Jonmarc looked straight into his blue eyes. "We were afraid," Hans said. "We like it here, and we didn't want to have to leave because of someone else's deeds. After the animals were taken, we started guarding the livestock when we weren't required to be somewhere else. And we have looked for evidence to find the guilty one." He returned Jonmarc's direct gaze, and

Jonmarc felt no attempt at compulsion.

"And?" Trent asked.

"We think there are rogues, trailing the caravan," Jessup replied. "Either we just happened into their territory, or more likely, they blundered across the caravan and decided it made for some easy hunting."

"Rogues?" Linton pressed.

"Most *vayash moru* in Margolan want to exist in peace. We want to go back to our old lives if we can, or go about our business without problems," Hans replied. "But sometimes, the turning doesn't go well, or the person turned is not of good character."

He looked from Trent to Linton to Jonmarc as if pleading his case. "Just as there are bad mortals, some see the speed and strength and stealth of being undead as an unfair advantage. They go rogue."

"If they're trailing us, just packing up the caravan and moving on won't help, will it?" Trent asked. "The rogues could just follow us."

Hans nodded. "And they will, if they believe they can prey on our workers or customers."

Linton cursed under his breath. "Can we trap them?"

Hans, Jessup, and Clark exchanged a glance among themselves. "Possibly. We'll help you, because we don't want to have to leave the caravan. But it's going to cost you some sheep."

Linton nodded. "Try to cost me as few as you can—they're not cheap. But it's better than losing my workers, or my customers."

"Corbin would help us," Trent said, volunteering the head farrier who was a good friend and, as Jonmarc knew first-hand, also knew how to handle himself in a fight. "He can keep his mouth shut, and we can trust him."

"Let's keep this small," Linton replied. "I don't want people to panic, and the more people who know about the killings, the more likely it is for there to be problems."

They spent the next candlemark planning the trap, until the horizon began to lighten and Trent and Jonmarc covered the *vayash moru* in freshly dug graves in preparation for the night.

"It's too bad we don't know where the rogues go to ground," he said. "We'd have the advantage if we could take them in the light."

"And stand a good chance of destroying innocent dead men," Linton replied. He swore, shook his head as if to clear it, and rubbed his eyes. "I can't believe I just said that. I'm going back to bed. I'll be with you tonight—if no one bothers me with any foolishness."

Trent and Jonmarc stood alone in the forge. "What are we going to do with the bodies?" Jonmarc asked.

Trent sighed. "I hate to do it, but we don't have much time to make them disappear. Let's carry them to the ravine behind the camp and pitch them down the side."

Jonmarc hesitated for a moment, then nodded. "It doesn't seem quite right, but there's no time to bury them, and we don't want to explain why there are two dead men behind the forge."

Trent turned to pick up the first man, and began to chuckle, shaking his head.

"What?"

Trent pointed to where a small pile of objects lay next to the corpse. The comb, flint, steel and pipe were set out neatly. "Linton took the damn coins," he said with a sigh as he hefted the body over his shoulder.

"Then again," Jonmarc replied, lifting the other man, "this is going to cost him a couple of sheep."

BY THE TIME the sun set, the trap was in place. Jonmarc and Trent had recruited a few trusted friends, men who had proven themselves in a fight and who could be counted on even when those at risk were not mortal.

Dugan, one of the young riggers, was strong, fast on his feet, and quick-witted. Zane, an entertainer, was a professional knife-thrower, a talent that was likely to come in handy. Corbin, the head farrier, was level-headed and could hold his own in a brawl, and Sayer, an apprentice carpenter, came armed with a hastily made wooden bat and enough sharpened stakes for all of the defenders.

Linton was with them, dressed for a fight in a simple dark tunic and trews, and armed with a sword and a long knife. Trent had an iron bar and a wicked-looking machete. Jonmarc wore both his swords and had a short knife in his belt, just in case.

"I hope this works," Jonmarc muttered quietly from where he hid.

"I suspect it will work just fine," Trent replied. "I'm worried about whether or not we can kill them."

The trap was simple, but Hans assured them it would appeal to a hungry *vayash moru* looking for an easy meal. After the men who tended the caravan's livestock had gone for the night, Linton, Trent, and Jonmarc had returned to the barns. They selected four doomed sheep and took them outside the enclosure, securing a long, slim cord to one of their hind legs. The other ends of the cords were attached to stakes pounded flat in the ground, giving the sheep the appearance of having wandered away while still keeping them—and hopefully their attackers—in a set area.

Hans, Jessup, and Clark lay buried in shallow graves in the pasture where the sheep grazed. Hans had insisted that the three *vayash moru* workers be the first to confront the rogues, and warned the others to stay back so that their warm blood and beating hearts did not give them away.

Jonmarc and the others were scattered in teams of two in nearby hiding places, obscured by brush, empty wagons, and debris. Jonmarc fingered a small amulet that hung from a leather cord around his neck.

"Do you think the amulet will work?" he asked, watching as the sun sank lower in the sky.

"Ada said it would," Trent assured him. "At least, until the rogues get real close."

At which point, the fight is on, Jonmarc thought.

Ada, the caravan's lead healer, had puzzled over how to mask the vital signs of the defenders. While a number of herbs and potions could actually mimic death, they also left the user in a motionless sleep, hardly ideal for springing a surprise attack. In the end, Ada had settled for creating amulets for each of the fighters.

"She said it would make us difficult to notice, but not invisible," Jonmarc quibbled. "And she wasn't entirely sure the magic would work on *vayash moru*."

"Hans said it worked on him," Trent replied.

"I hate amulets," Jonmarc muttered.

The sun disappeared below the horizon, and Trent gestured for silence.

For several candlemarks, the area behind the caravan camp was silent except for the sounds from the sheep. Behind Jonmarc and the other watchers, the camp went about its nightly routine, serving supper, making repairs, feeding the livestock, and socializing among themselves. Jonmarc had eaten an early supper, but still the smells of fresh stew and roasting pig made his stomach grumble.

"No one is going to try to steal the sheep while there's so much going on," Jonmarc whispered to Trent.

"We knew we'd have to wait for things to quiet down," Trent replied in a barely audible voice. "But Hans believes the rogues will be watching, sizing up their chance. That's why we had to be out here before they rose for the night."

Time crawled by. The camp slowly settled down for the night, until only a few rowdy souls remained awake. From their off-key, bawdy singing, those still awake were also quite drunk. Gradually, as the night wore on, even the drunkards' songs began to wane, and as the sliver of a moon began to rise in the sky, the camp grew quiet.

By now, Hans, Jessup, and Clark would be awake in their shallow graves. They had insisted on being buried beneath a foot of topsoil, far enough below the ground to be shielded from the sun but close enough to rise in an instant if the rogues took the bait. *What would it be like, lying there, buried alive?* Jonmarc wondered, and shuddered.

Trent jabbed Jonmarc in the ribs, indicating with a nod that something was up. There was a rush of air, the frightened cry of a sheep as it was plucked off its feet, and a blur of motion in the moonlight.

We're on, Jonmarc thought, gripping his sword.

Hans had also heard the commotion, rising in a spray of freshly-turned dirt. Jessup and Clark broke loose of their hiding places, one on each side and in the rear of the area where the 'loose' sheep grazed.

"That's our signal," Trent murmured, as he and Jonmarc

burst from cover. The other mortal fighters revealed themselves, blocking the way toward the camp.

Trapped in the center were three young *vayash moru*. They were overdressed for a night of sheep poaching, looking like the wastrel sons of errant nobility with their velvet frock coats, high riding boots, and brocade vests. But there was no refinement in their angry expressions. Two of the intruders held tight to bleating, panicked sheep that were struggling to get loose.

Do our amulets still make it difficult for them to sense us, or was that only when we were hidden? Jonmarc wondered. Ada had been unsure about the limits of protection, and now that they were about to put her magic to the test, Jonmarc would have felt better with a little more certainty.

Hans, Jessup, and Clark made the first move, attacking with supernatural speed. One of the thieves dropped his sheep and pulled his sword, managing to parry Hans's angry assault. A second thief tried to keep hold of the sheep and run, only to have the animal reach the end of its tether and bring him up short. The third thief growled in anger and launched himself at Clark, waging a full-out attack that was a blur of motion and a clatter of steel on steel as Clark fought back.

Per their plan, Trent ran forward, sword at the ready, while Jonmarc zigzagged to the side, slicing the sheeps' tethers from the stake in the ground to set them free. Panicked by the fight unfolding around them, the animals ran off, veering crazily between the running men.

Trent went to back up Hans. Corbin and Linton joined Jessup, and Zane maneuvered himself into position to put a dagger into the back of the *vayash moru* fighting Clark. Jonmarc, Dugan, and Sayer hung back, swords drawn, forming a line of defense between the battle and the camp.

The fight moved almost too quickly to follow. By pre-arrangement, Hans and his friends were supposed to get their opponents into position so that the mortal fighters could attack from the rear. From where Jonmarc stood, what ensued was chaos. The *vayash moru* fighters moved in a blur, so swiftly that it was nearly impossible to tell who was whom, or for the mortals to get off a clean strike.

Engrossed in the action unfolding in front of them, Jonmarc almost didn't hear the whoosh of air nearby.

"Watch out!" he shouted hoarsely, barely able to get the words out before three new *vayash moru* rogues came at them.

The new rogues were also dressed in finery like the other vampires. Gems glittered from rings on their fingers, and gold chains sparkled in the moonlight at their throats and wrists. Yet for all the speed the sheep thieves used against Hans, Jessup, and Clark, these new *vayash moru* slowed their attack to mortal speed, with a languid, deadly grace.

They intend to toy with us before they kill us, Jonmarc thought, feeling a cold wave of fear clench his belly.

Dugan's attacker made the first move, with a lunge that nearly got inside the rigger's guard. Dugan was fast on his feet, narrowly avoiding the strike, and returning a wild series of jabs that gained the advantage of confusion, since they followed no normal mode of attack.

Sayer set about himself with the wooden bat, bellowing like a bull, made strong and unpredictable by his fear. He came nowhere close to hitting the *vayash moru* who danced away from his strikes, but his unorthodox style kept his attacker from getting close enough to do any damage.

They're going to tire us out, then strike, Jonmarc thought as he and his opponent circled. *All they have to do is outlast us, which won't take long.*

Jonmarc could not spare a glance for Hans and the others. The leer on his own opponent's face made it clear that the *vayash moru* was enjoying the game, and most likely, looking forward to feasting on his blood.

The *vayash moru* lunged, and Jonmarc narrowly escaped the worst of his sword strike, taking a cut on his thigh. His opponent gave a throaty, hungry chuckle and made a show of licking his lips as blood colored the fabric of Jonmarc's trews. His opponent advanced once more, this time at almost mortal speed and Jonmarc parried, feeling the shock of the strike reverberate through his bones.

That's his game. Speed or strength. He's got me either way, all he has to do is get me to make a mistake.

Out of the corner of his eye, he saw Sayer's swing slow, then stop as the carpenter stood transfixed, staring into the eyes of his opponent.

"Don't look in his eyes!" Jonmarc shouted, pivoting aside at the last second as his own attacker struck again.

Sayer remained motionless, and then the wooden bat dropped from his hand. His attacker sauntered up to him with an exaggerated swagger until he stood nearly toe to toe, an ugly, taunting grin on his face. Sayer did not move, and his features were slack, as if he was completely unaware of the danger he faced.

"Sayer!" Dugan shouted.

"Sayer, move!" Jonmarc yelled.

Jonmarc's attacker drew back a step, as did Dugan's, and it was clear that they were supposed to watch what happened next. Jonmarc dove to the right, trying to go to Sayer's aid, but his opponent blocked him. Dugan tried to do the same, only to be hemmed in.

Sayer's opponent reached out and tousled the young man's

hair, then brushed a fleck of dirt from his shoulder, making a show of his power. Sheathing his sword, the *vayash moru* reached forward to embrace Sayer like a lover. He shot a gloating grin to his fellow attackers, and then with a snarl, bared his teeth and sank his fangs into Sayer's neck.

Jonmarc and Dugan tried to rush forward, and once more, their attackers blocked their way.

Sayer's opponent must have dropped the compulsion, because Sayer began to thrash against the iron grip that held him, and a strangled scream tore from his savaged throat. Hans had told them that a *vayash moru* could feed without killing, that the bite could be clean and painless, but it was clear Sayer's assailant relished his victim's struggle, fear, and pain.

The *vayash moru's* pallor lessened as he gulped down the blood and Sayer's face grew ashen as he slumped in his killer's arms. The draining took only minutes, but when it was done, the *vayash moru* tossed Sayer's limp form aside like an empty husk and made a show of wiping the blood from his mouth with his lace cuff.

Dugan's attacker used the moment of shock to strike, lunging forward with a savage attack that he barely evaded. Jonmarc, still stunned by Sayer's death, felt himself go cold with killing rage. He knew this coldness. It was a skill that had served him well when raiders and monsters had attacked his village. In the coldness, there was no grief, no fear, no anger, just pure, deadly clarity.

"Your blood is high," his attacker whispered. "I can hear your heart. The ones who fight the hardest taste the best. Come at me. You know you want to." The *vayash moru* met Jonmarc's gaze, and Jonmarc did not look away. "Fight me," the *vayash moru* goaded. "Show me what you've got."

Jonmarc gripped his sword in one hand. One of Sayer's stakes protruded from the top of his boot in easy reach. A desperate plan formed in his mind, and he hoped Trent was right about *vayash moru* not being able to read minds.

He thinks he can compel me, Jonmarc thought. *Let's see how he likes getting what he asked for.*

Jonmarc's face twisted in rage, and he dove forward with a powerful series of strikes. His attacker grinned, baring his fangs, gleefully deflecting the blows. Certain that he had Jonmarc well within his power, he kept up the barbs, baiting him, seeking to stoke his anger. But within the cold place, Jonmarc seemed to watch the battle as an emotionless observer, waiting for his chance to strike.

"That's it! Come at me, strike at me. Strike me down, make me pay," the *vayash moru* baited.

Jonmarc's sword skills were cobbled together from whatever lessons he had been able to beg from Trent, Corbin, and the few itinerant soldiers who made their way through the caravan. His practice had been sporadic, but his erstwhile teachers had praised what they called 'native talent.'

Now, Jonmarc's seemingly random strikes tested his opponent, gauging his skill and mastery. He fought back a smile as he realized that the *vayash moru* had little training, no doubt relying on his undead speed, strength, and compulsion rather than his swordsmanship.

"It's time to finish this," the *vayash moru* said, lashing out with a strike that knocked Jonmarc's sword from his hand with its sheer force. The tip of the blade scored a gash in Jonmarc's forearm, and blood soaked his sleeve.

"Hot blood is the sweetest," the *vayash moru* hissed, meeting Jonmarc's gaze with hungry intensity. Jonmarc heard a distant buzzing noise, and felt the familiar pressure in his temples. The coldness deadened his fear, though his heart was thudding and adrenaline tingled through his body.

Jonmarc willed himself to take a step toward the *vayash moru*, then another, his hands open and empty at his sides. The *vayash moru* lowered his sword, but it was clear from his leering, hungry smile that he was confident of his prey. Dugan was screaming Jonmarc's name, shouting for him to fight, but Jonmarc forced himself to move forward, until he stood arm's length from the *vayash moru*.

"This will be a banquet," the *vayash moru* gloated.

Now! Jonmarc thought as the *vayash moru* reached for him. Jonmarc dropped down, yanking the stake from his boot, turning it point up in his hand. He used his upward momentum to drive the stake between the *vayash moru's* ribs, throwing his body weight against it so that they tumbled to the ground, pinning his would-be murderer.

The rogue's eyes widened in shock and black ichor fountained from his ravaged chest, spilling from the corner of his mouth, soaking them both. His body bucked and writhed, but Jonmarc kept him pinned, forcing the stake deeper with one hand while his other ripped the sword from the *vayash moru's* fingers. Rearing back, Jonmarc brought the blade down hard across the vampire's throat.

The first blow cut through skin and tendon, sending ichor in a bloody spray. The second blow severed bone, sending the head rolling. Beneath him, the body fell still.

Soaked with gore, breathing hard and trembling from head to toe, Jonmarc yanked the stake free and stood, gripping his sword white-knuckled. While he had been embroiled in his death match, the battlefield had changed.

More *vayash moru* had joined the fight, but on the side of the caravan, tilting the odds against the attackers. Renden was making short work of Dugan's attacker, while Eli battled Sayer's murderer to his knees. Across the way, one of Zane's throwing knives protruded from the chest of a rogue, while Hans held a downed thief at sword's point on the ground. Jessup and Clark stood over another captive, the man Corbin and Linton had been fighting.

Two more *vayash moru* Jonmarc recognized from the village were patrolling the tree line, alert should more rogues appear, but after a few moments, satisfied that there were no more attackers lying in wait, they returned to guard the captives.

Linton's clothes were torn and streaked with blood. A cut on his cheek oozed. His eyes held a killing gleam as he strode to stand in front of one of the bandits.

"Are there more of you?" he demanded.

Jessup held the thief in a bone-crushing grip with one hand, holding a knife against his throat with the other. "Answer him, and you exist for a few more minutes," Jessup growled.

"No," the rogue replied, glaring at Linton. "All we wanted were your sheep."

"And the men you killed on the road last night, you wanted their sheep, too?" Linton snapped.

The *vayash moru* glowered at the thief Eli had subdued. "It wasn't my idea," he muttered. "I told him it was going to cause trouble."

Linton's gaze traveled to where Sayer lay still on the grass. "Crone take your soul," he said.

Eli looked down on his captive. "They've brought trouble on the village," he said. "Those men they killed were from the town up the road. A couple of people found the bodies in the ravine. Someone remembered that there were *vayash moru* among the farmers. Today, during daylight, townsfolk came and threatened our kin."

Linton looked from Eli to Renden. "What will you do?"

Renden grimaced. "We'll deliver these troublemakers to the authorities, and see that they confess." He shrugged. "Whether or not they will accept that, and keep the truce with my people, I don't know." He grew sad. "My family has farmed that land for four generations. I don't welcome the thought of leaving, but I won't allow my kin to come to harm."

"Take the other three," Linton said, his voice growing hard. He pointed at Sayer's killer. "But I want that man dead."

Jessup had come up behind Sayer's killer as Linton spoke. Moving swiftly, he drove his sword through the rogue *vayash moru's* back, piercing the heart, and protruding from his chest. Black ichor spread down the thief's stolen finery, and gurgled from his lips. The body began to tremble, until it was spasming uncontrollably.

Jonmarc and the other mortals stood back, while the *vayash moru* from the village watched dispassionately. Smoke began to rise, and then the skin grew dry and papery. In another breath, the thief gave a final death rattle, and the body collapsed in a pile of ash. Jonmarc glanced back toward the *vayash moru* he had killed and the one that Zane had felled with his blade. Both were no more than cinders.

"Take them," Linton said in a cold voice. "Thank you for coming to help. I hope no harm comes to you and yours because of this."

Renden nodded. "It would be best if you moved on as soon as the sun rises. It's unlucky for you here."

Linton nodded. "My thought, too. Dark Lady willing, we'll pass this way again, and when we do, I'll have more iron and coin to spend with you."

Renden clasped Linton's arm. "Istra watch and keep you," he said. Something in his dark gaze chilled Jonmarc. *He doesn't think things are going to go well,* Jonmarc thought. *He's afraid.*

In the blink of an eye, Rendon, Eli, and the other *vayash moru* from the village were gone, along with the three surviving thieves. Hans, Jessup, and Clark hung back, as if unsure of their place. Linton looked at them sharply. "What are you staring at? There's work to be done. Strike the tents. Ready the wagons. And for the love of the Mother and Childe, figure out where you'll spend the day so you can catch up with us," he barked.

Hans looked up, surprised. "You want us to stay?"

Linton rolled his eyes. "Didn't I just say as much? Stop lollygagging and get to work!"

Reprieved, the three *vayash moru* vanished in a blur. Linton turned back to Jonmarc and the others. He looked down at Sayer's bloody body. "Come on," he said, his voice suddenly tired. "He deserves better, but we need to get him buried in the woods before we have to explain it to anyone."

Jonmarc hefted Sayer's shoulders, while Dugan carried his feet. Zane and Trent ran back to the camp for shovels, returning a few moments later with grim expressions. Linton led them to a clear place not far from the camp's perimeter, and they worked in silence to lay Sayer to rest in a grave deep enough to keep his body from the animals.

"Let the sword be sheathed, and the helm shuttered. Prepare a feast in the hall of your fallen heroes. Sayer died with valor. Make his passage swift and his journey easy, until his soul rests in the arms of the Lady," Trent murmured, and Jonmarc suspected it was a soldier's prayer.

And may the Dark Lady take his soul, Jonmarc added silently, thinking of the shrine in Renden's forge.

They filed back to the camp, which had come alive in the darkness as the news of their sudden departure spread.

"We've got a few pieces to finish before we can take the forge apart," Trent said.

"I'll handle it," Jonmarc offered, glad for something to do. "Go ahead and start packing things up. I'll finish the pieces."

A few pumps of the bellows revived the embers and made the coals glow brightly. Jonmarc fastened on his leather apron and pulled on his gloves. He heated the iron, placed it on the anvil, and struck it with his hammer. The pounding formed a rhythm as familiar and comforting as his own heartbeat.

Everything goes to the grave. People come and go too quickly. The forge remains.

STORMGARD

"KEEP YOUR WITS about you," Maynard Linton warned. "There will be pickpockets at the market."

The two wagons bumped and rattled their way toward Kerrton, the nearest town that might offer fresh supplies for Linton's traveling caravan of wonders. Their wheels sent clouds of dust into the air on the dry, rutted road, leaving grit on everything. In a futile effort, Linton brushed the dirt from the sleeves of his shirt

"Just remember: strength counts in fistfights, but thieves use knives," Linton said, glancing at his companions.

Maynard Linton was a short, stocky man in his early thirties, his skin turned a coppery tan from a life lived outdoors. He had shrewd eyes and a quick wit, and while he was ferociously protective of the caravan's crew, his ethics in other areas could be rather flexible. Linton was the shortest of the four men who had set off for Kerrton, and while he could hold his own in a fight, he had neither the height nor the brawn of the three men who accompanied him.

From his seat in the second wagon, Jonmarc Vahanian glanced at his companions. Trent, the caravan's head blacksmith, had broad shoulders and powerful arms from a lifetime in the forge. Corbin, the fourth member of their group, was the lead farrier, and the daily work of wrestling uncooperative draft horses into being shod had given him both strength and speed.

Although Jonmarc was not yet eighteen, he was on his way to a similar build, having worked in the forge for several smiths from the time he could carry the iron bars. Jonmarc was Trent's apprentice, and on this outing, was quite sure he'd been brought along for extra hands and a sturdy back. There was likely to be a lot of loading involved.

"We should be done loading supplies by the noon bells. By the time we get back to the caravan, things should be pretty well set up," Trent said. He flicked the reins, directing the wagon horse to turn left.

"I've got a bit of business to transact. While you, Corbin, and Jonmarc load the supplies, I'll go see to that and meet you at the brewery," Linton replied.

Usually, Linton preferred flamboyant colors and elaborate fabrics that suited his role as grand master of one of the largest caravans in the Winter Kingdoms. Today, he had chosen muted colors in brown and black; for Linton it was a fairly somber outfit. On the other hand, the dust didn't show as badly with Linton's outfit as it might on his usual choice of silks or brocade.

"You and Jonmarc can get started," Corbin directed as the wagons drew up to the Pheasant and Quail, the only brewery within a league of Kerrton. "I'll see to loading the barrels of ale." He grinned. "And if you take too long, I may see to drinking some of it, too."

Jonmarc and Trent stayed in the driver's bench of the second wagon. "We'll head over to the market," Trent said, twitching the reins once more to move their horse along, farther down the road toward the heart of the village. "The head cook gave me a list of provisions he'll need to keep the caravan fed for the next week, and Maynard told me to be on the lookout for any good pottery, wood carving or jewelry the artisans might be able to resell."

Maynard Linton ran one of Margolan's many traveling caravans. The motley assemblage of acrobats, dancers, artisans, craftspeople, workers, musicians, and roustabouts was part freak show, part entertainment, and part merchant faire. With Linton as caravan master and impresario extraordinaire, the caravan had made a name for itself as it traveled the length and breadth of Margolan and its neighboring kingdoms.

"What's up there?" Jonmarc asked, nodding his head toward the hillside above Kerrton. Thick walls of white stone ran across the crest of the hill, with rounded turrets at intervals along the wall, and crenellations along the length. The walls flared out at the bottom, the better to keep potential invaders from easily scaling them with ladders. Whoever had built that fort had obviously expected trouble.

"That's Stormgard," Trent replied with barely a glance. "It was built as an outpost back when this part of Margolan was considered to be the wilderness. There are tales about the battles fought there and the marauders turned away, but it's been decades since there's been any fighting in these parts. King Bricen tries to keep it that way."

Stormgard seemed to loom over the small farming town. The massive walls and tall towers might make the townsfolk feel protected, but something about its hulking size silhouetted against the sky made Jonmarc feel watched.

"Keep your eyes open," Trent said to Jonmarc as they jostled along the rutted road.

"You expect trouble?"

Trent shrugged. "No reason to, but Maynard seems a little jumpy. He said a messenger came to the caravan last night when we made camp and invited him to meet the head of the merchants' guild." He grimaced.

"Those kinds of meetings can go sour pretty quickly," he added. "On occasion, the merchants want to sell their wares to the caravan. But more likely than not, they don't like having competition, even if it's only for a week or two, and they'll do their best to get the caravan run out of town."

"My money's on Maynard," Jonmarc said.

The market bustled with activity as they rode up. Trent pulled the wagon up to a hitching rail, and Jonmarc jumped down to tie the horse's reins to the post. Stalls and carts lined the village square, filled with fresh vegetables and fruits. Under the shade of a portable awning, a butcher had set up his wagon. Freshly slaughtered geese, sheep, calves, and pigs hung from the side of his cart.

Across the way, a spice merchant offered her wares. Dozens of baskets overflowed with fragrant seasonings from every corner of the Winter Kingdoms. Flower vendors set out cut blooms in a patchwork of colors, while further down the row, a fishmonger spilled out a basket of his fresh catch onto a table for shoppers to examine.

Jonmarc was a few inches taller than Trent, and about ten to fifteen years younger. The wind picked up, and Jonmarc pushed a lock of shoulder-length chestnut brown hair out of his brown eyes. Often, he wore his hair tied back in a queue, but today, among strangers, he let it fall loose, the better to hide the scar that ran from his left ear down below his collar, the reminder of a battle that had cost him his family.

"Keep a hand on your money. Maynard's right: the market's the best spot for thieves," Trent warned in a low voice. "And that includes the vendors. Make sure you count your change."

So many people jostled through the crowded, narrow walkways that it would be impossible to tell whether any collision was intentional or accidental. Jonmarc wasn't too worried. Trent carried the bag of silver for the provisions. Jonmarc's small stash of silver from his wages was hidden at the forge. He had brought a few coppers to buy some candied fruit, a bit of bread, meat, and cheese for lunch, and some ale at the end of the day.

Jonmarc drew a deep breath, taking in the jumble of colors, the mix of aromas and the babble of accents. The caravan had traveled halfway across Margolan from his home in the Borderlands and the forsaken remains of the village where he had buried his loved ones. Every stop on the caravan's journey was a new set of smells, tastes, and sights—and, far too often, dangers.

Trent had begun bargaining with one of the wood-carvers in the marketplace. "Two pieces of silver for these items," he said, gesturing to the majority of what the carver had laid out on a blanket for sale.

"You wound me!" the wood-carver cried, dramatically clutching at his heart. "Two silver coins for my life's work? I've poured my blood and sweat into these pieces!"

Trent leveled his gaze at the man. "Oh? Then how is it I saw four more bags of the same pieces behind the fishmonger's stall?"

"You do not appreciate what it takes to create these pieces," the carver protested. "Two silver coins! My family would starve if I took your offer."

Trent rolled his eyes. Jonmarc had seen him negotiate these bargains before, and the blacksmith usually came out ahead, although the process could be lengthy.

"Three coins, but I get the rest of what's displayed," Trent said, his eyes narrowing shrewdly.

"I should report you to the constable! What you want is theft!" The woodcarver was giving quite an impassioned performance, but it seemed to Jonmarc that both he and Trent were actually enjoying the process of coming to an agreement.

Knowing from experience that the bargaining could last for half a candlemark or more, Jonmarc wandered a few steps away to the next stalls. One vendor offered skeins of yarn died in a variety of hues. The next called out to passers-by to look at her selection of woven shawls and scarves.

Jonmarc paused at the spice trader's stall. His late wife's mother had been a hedge witch and a healer, and her home had smelled of dried flowers and medicinal herbs. Jonmarc let himself take a deep breath, savoring the familiar scents, as the old sadness coursed over him.

A glimpse of someone familiar in the crowd roused Jonmarc from his thoughts. He caught sight of the top of a head of greasy blond hair, and while he could not see the man's face, the gait reminded him of someone he had no desire to see.

"Trent—"

Trent flicked his hand from his side to indicate that he did not want to be bothered. Jonmarc frowned, and turned to see if he could catch another look at the man he had seen.

The crowd around him ebbed and flowed like the tide. Market-goers bunched together in a knot, then spread apart, offering a better view of the square further down the aisle between vendors.

Jonmarc spotted the blond man again. This time, he got a look at the squat figure and rounded shoulders, the pock-marked face and the flattened nose. There was no mistaking it. That had to be Chessis. And if so, then Jonmarc knew they had a big problem.

Chessis was a bounty hunter.

Jonmarc retraced his steps to where Trent was still arguing with the wood carver. Although their conversation had gained volume, it appeared that Trent was winning concessions, though the carver had gotten the price raised by another coin.

We could be here all day, Jonmarc thought. He shot another glance in Chessis's direction.

"Trent, I'm going to walk down the row," Jonmarc said.

"Don't go far. We need to load the wagon," Trent replied, distracted, and returned immediately to his bargaining.

It was clear that Jonmarc was not going to pry Trent loose when he was so close to achieving victory, but by then, Chessis would be lost in the market day crowds. Jonmarc worked his way through the press of people, glad he stood taller than many of the market-goers so that he could glimpse Chessis through the crowd.

The last time Jonmarc had seen Chessis, the circumstances had cost a good friend his life. Jonmarc had not forgotten that, nor had he—or Trent—forgiven Chessis and his partners Vakkis and Tarren for Conall's murder.

Chessis was just ahead in the crowd. Jonmarc had no desire to confront the bounty hunter, but he itched to see what the greasy little man was up to. By now, Chessis, Tarren, and Vakkis were probably tracking down another quarry, on their way to creating someone else's tragedy. It was likely none of Jonmarc's business, he knew. But still, he couldn't shake the feeling that it would be prudent to know just what Chessis was doing.

A hand came down heavy on his shoulder. Jonmarc jumped and pivoted, expecting to have somehow drawn the eye of the local guard. Instead, Trent gave him a questioning look.

"Where are you going? I'm going to need you to help me load what I buy at the market."

"I saw Chessis," Jonmarc said, trying to pitch his voice so that no one else would hear. At Trent's momentary confusion, Jonmarc added, "The bounty hunter. One of the men who killed Conall."

The look in Trent's eyes grew hard. "Where?"

Jonmarc nodded toward the lower end of the market. "I caught a glimpse of him a few moments ago, but you were busy. I didn't think I should let him out of my sight until we're sure he isn't looking for someone in the caravan."

Trent seemed to debate the idea for a moment, then nodded. "Agreed. Follow him for a little bit, but don't go too far, and don't let him see you. Come right back and let me know what you find out. I've got a few more vendors to haggle with."

Jonmarc nodded and was about to set off when Trent's hand caught his shoulder once more.

"Be careful, Jonmarc. Chessis and his friends are killers. They won't have forgotten that you, Corbin, and I tried to keep Conall from them. And Vakkis will be sure to remember the crease your knife blade put in his face." Trent's expression was somber. "If they catch you unawares, they'll kill you."

"The feeling is mutual," Jonmarc replied. He headed off down the crowded aisle, dodging between shoppers, anxious to catch sight once more of Chessis.

It had been a few months since the bounty hunters had come to the caravan, pursuing a man who had done them no harm. Memories of that night still haunted Jonmarc's dreams, which were already disquieted. He could still remember the look on Conall's face as he fell, still remember the blood pooling under his friend's body, and the triumphant—gloating—looks on the faces of the bounty hunters as the dead man's widow wailed and his child screamed.

Jonmarc shook off the memories. Trent was right: Chessis was dangerous, and if Jonmarc was going to shadow him, then he needed to approach it the way he would if he were hunting a wild animal. He would need all the skill he had gained from his recent sword training with Trent and the other military men in the caravan who had an inclination to teach him what they knew. It was more training than he had before, but still far less than what he would likely need to hold his own against professional killers.

All around Jonmarc, shoppers talked with friends and familiar vendors, jostled for position to buy the best and freshest items, and browsed the market's treasures, oblivious to the danger. But Jonmarc doubted that Chessis had come for provisions. The furtive way the man moved through the throng proved that he had more on his mind than finding some fresh fish or a good-luck talisman from the seer hawking her amulets on the thoroughfare.

No, Jonmarc thought. Chessis was looking for someone. And the odds were good that if Chessis was seeking a specific person, that man had a bounty on his head—whether he knew it or not.

Jonmarc had lost sight of Chessis for a few moments as the crowd surged. Chessis was short, making it easy for him to disappear in the press of bodies. But Jonmarc was tall, and his height gave him the advantage, enabling him to catch another glimpse of the bounty hunter's greasy yellow hair.

Unwilling to lose his quarry, Jonmarc jostled and pushed

his way clear of the crowd, paying no attention to the annoyed comments and curses that greeted his progress.

Chessis had reached the far end of the market square. On one side of the courtyard, a trio of minstrels played for the crowd with a hat set out to collect a coin or two from grateful listeners. On the other side, a man had set up a cook fire in a large iron cauldron mounted on a metal wagon and was simmering a kettle of soup over the coals. Patrons were lined up, cups at the ready. The soup smelled of cabbage and pork, with an undertone of something that reminded Jonmarc of the odor of wash water.

Just as Chessis dodged around a corner into a narrow lane between buildings, Jonmarc caught a glimpse of him. He sprinted through an open space to get closer, but not so close that the bounty hunter might realize that for once, he was the pursued instead of the pursuer.

Jonmarc cast a backward glance toward the bustle of the marketplace. Here in the crowd, he was relatively safe. He might lose his wallet to a cutpurse, but it was unlikely that Chessis would murder him in front of so many people. Jonmarc had lost track of which lord ruled the area in which he found himself, but few if any of the lords of Margolan permitted murder to go unpunished—at least, when committed with a crowd of witnesses.

In the winding streets of Kerrton, however, the rules were likely to be different. Jonmarc moved forward into the alley, making sure to stay far enough behind Chessis that the bounty hunter would not hear his steps and turn around.

Even the alleys thronged with people. Jonmarc smiled grimly. It was in his favor that the market crowds hustled through the narrow alleys. Most were laden with packages, either taking their purchases back home or bringing wares to sell. Here and there, food vendors hawked their offerings from small tables that further constricted the passageway. Men and women stood in the shallow recesses of doorways, offering jewelry, perfumes, and in some cases, more 'personal' services for sale.

Jonmarc bustled past the vendors, paying no heed to their offers. He sidestepped puddles and tried not to gag on the smell from the press of unwashed bodies, or the gutter that stank of emptied chamber pots. Chessis seemed to know where he was going, but Jonmarc made mental note of the names of the streets and the turns he took so he could find his way back to the marketplace. The bounty hunter was likely to lead him to an unsavory part of town, and Jonmarc wanted to be able to make a quick escape.

The sheath that held his long knife slapped comfortingly against his leg as he moved through the crowd. It might have drawn attention to wear a sword, and neither Jonmarc nor the other men had any desire to raise suspicion among the town guards. But most freemen carried knives, and while Jonmarc's was well-forged, nothing about the sheath or the grip looked remarkable. A small dirk in his boot was strapped to his calf. Now, on the track of a killer, having the knives close at hand gave Jonmarc a measure of reassurance.

Chessis stopped to speak to a man on the corner at the next plaza. Jonmarc was too far away to hear what was said. From what he could see, it was difficult to tell whether Chessis asked a question of a stranger or checked with a lookout for information. Chessis was on his way after a short exchange of words, and Jonmarc made sure as he passed the stranger to keep his head turned so that he would not be recognizable.

As Jonmarc suspected, their path led them away from the nicer streets. Kerrton's better blocks had glittering marble shrines to the goddess in her aspect of Mother and Childe. The plazas in those parts of town had elaborate public fountains and wells, and were ringed by nicely-maintained homes.

Now he crossed over into areas that looked hard used and questionable in character. Pawnbrokers set up their rickety tables in the run-down plazas, calling out to anyone who passed by to shop their wares. Next to a dirty and defaced alcove that was a shrine to Athira, the Whore, one of the Aspects of the Sacred Lady, four men hunched over a game of chance. Jonmarc had seen enough from the caravan vendors to know that the man running the game always won.

Chessis did not seem to suspect he was being followed, but he did stop now and again to glance over his shoulder. Jonmarc dodged behind any cover that was handy, or ducked his head to be unrecognizable in the crowd. It was difficult to tell whether Chessis was really checking for a tail or whether he was looking for someone he expected to meet and so far, no sign of his partners Vakkis or Tarren.

It had only been about ten minutes since they left the market, but this part of Kerrton did not seem to share in the market vendors' bounty. Dirty children and mangy curs clustered in the shadows of side streets. Ragged old women begged for coins, while provocatively clad young girls made explicit suggestions of what they were willing to do for pay. Scrawny, worn-looking mothers hung washing out to dry from the balconies and window sills of upper floor tenements, while haggard men sat on the steps of a burned out building, smoking their pipes and watching the street. Over to one side, a hunched woman wrapped in a black shawl called out, offering to read the future and tell the fortune of any who cared to part with a few skrivven.

"Looking for company?" one of the strumpets asked as

Jonmarc dodged around the body of a drunk that lay in the middle of the narrow street. Jonmarc glanced up. The girl looked a few years younger than he was, too young even for an arranged marriage, but her leer suggested she was not new at her trade. Her torn shirt and shredded skirt left little to the imagination. She was pretty in a worn way, although her skin was dirty and her hair was matted. From the bleary look in her eyes and her unsteady gait, Jonmarc bet that she dulled her senses with dreamweed or raw whiskey; maybe both.

"Not tonight," he replied brusquely, shaking off her hand as she reached to touch his sleeve. He heard her muttered curses as he walked away. If the area was this unsavory while it was still early in the morning, Jonmarc had no desire to see what it became after dark.

Some of the shops in this area looked permanently closed, with boarded-up windows scrawled with crude markings scratched with coal or rocks. Several more appeared to be in business but closed at the moment, and Jonmarc wondered if their proprietors expected patrons to come out at night. Two pubs faced each other across the square, and to Jonmarc's eye, they were equally decrepit.

The Baited Bear, on his right, had a broken sign that might once have depicted a bear fight but now was barely legible and hung by its rusted chain on only one side. The smell of burnt toast, roasting meat, and pipe smoke covered up, for a moment, the scent of decay that clung to the back streets.

The Hind and Hound's sign was faded with age, depicting a deer and a hunting dog, and Jonmarc wondered if the place had been respectable at some time in its past. If so, its social status had fallen badly. The front window was cracked and dirty enough that it was difficult to see inside. Whether that was by design or accident, Jonmarc wasn't sure.

Enough foot traffic bustled through the streets that Jonmarc hoped he was not immediately noticed as an outsider by the locals. Chessis paused in the street outside the Hind and Hound and once again looked both ways, but this time Jonmarc was close enough to see the look of confusion on the bounty hunter's face, as if he had expected to meet someone and was concerned about their whereabouts.

From the concealment of a shadowed alcove, Jonmarc eyed Chessis, trying to determine how well-armed he was. Few men besides nobles and guards could carry a sword within the boundaries of most towns without being challenged by the constabulary as potential brigands. Jonmarc saw a sheath for a long knife, and bet that Chessis had several more such blades secreted within the loose folds of his clothing, and a shiv or two in his high boots as well.

I don't plan to fight him. Odds are, what he's doing is none of my business, Jonmarc told himself. *I just want to make sure whatever he's doing doesn't concern us or the caravan. Then I'll be on my way.*

Chessis entered the Hind and Hound and several patrons seemed in a hurry to get out of his way. Jonmarc sidled up to the cracked window, straining for a look inside. Too many bodies blocked the view, and he stared at the open doorway, debating what to do.

Three men shouldered past Jonmarc and pushed into the pub's doorway. The opportunity gave Jonmarc cover, and he trailed along behind them, staying to the back of the crowd. He found a place in the furthest corner and paid the bar maid a copper for a questionable looking tankard of ale that he did not intend to drink. He was just about to turn away and head back to the market when a familiar voice carried over the noise.

"You're wasting my time." Maynard Linton stood up from a table near the bar. From where Jonmarc was standing, he could not see Linton's companion. Obviously, the other person said something Jonmarc could not hear, because Linton did not stride away, although his expression made his displeasure clear.

After a moment, Linton sat back down. Someone must have signaled the bar maid, because she brought two more drinks over to the table. Linton had angled his chair so that his back was to the wall, and he sat so that he had a view of the door. Jonmarc hoped the shadows and the crowd concealed him. He did not want to explain what he was doing at the Hind and Hound when he was supposed to be helping to load the wagon.

Linton can certainly handle himself, and he looks at home here, which is more than I can say for myself, Jonmarc thought. *But does he know Chessis is in town? And is it really just an accident that Chessis shows up at a pub when Linton is here?*

Jonmarc strained to catch a glimpse of Chessis among the crowded pub patrons, and he thought he saw the top of his greasy head at the far end of the bar. From that vantage point, there was no way Chessis wouldn't notice Linton, or recognize his voice. But Jonmarc could also see that Chessis had positioned himself to be difficult for Linton to spot. It seemed hard to believe that the bounty hunter's choice of location was coincidental.

There's no way to warn Linton without tipping my hand to Chessis, Jonmarc thought, sizing up the room and considering his options. *Chessis may know Linton's here, but he doesn't seem to have spotted me. That's an advantage. Maybe I can be some use.*

Jonmarc did not recognize the man seated at Linton's table, but if he had to guess, he would have said the stranger was a minor city bureaucrat, a lesser noble, or even a fairly prosperous merchant, although what any of those types of people would be doing in a pub like the Hind and the Hound was unlikely to be legal. He remembered Linton's comment about meeting with the head of the merchants' guild, and wondered whether the tall, nervous-looking man was Linton's contact.

Hard to believe that fellow is much good selling to customers, Jonmarc thought. *He's as twitchy as a squirrel.*

Linton and the stranger resumed their conversation, and the outcome this time must have been satisfactory, because they toasted each other and knocked their tankards together before downing the contents in one draught. The thin stranger thumped his chest as if to prompt a burp, and then got up and headed for the back door.

Linton looked pleased, and sat back in his chair. But as Jonmarc watched, Linton's expression grew concerned, then uneasy. He struggled to stand, and wobbled unsteadily before collapsing across the table with a crash, sending the tankards flying. Patrons at the next table cursed in surprise and skidded their chairs out of the way with barely a glance toward Linton, who lay sprawled and unmoving.

"I'll take care of him." Chessis's nasal voice was barely audible over the noise of the tavern.

"Get him out of here before he pukes on my floor," the tavern master shouted, and there was scattered laughter from those who weren't working hard on their own inebriation.

Jonmarc tried to move forward, but the pub's patrons were pressed too tightly together for him to do more than take a few steps. Vakkis appeared from somewhere, and together he and Chessis half-carried, half-dragged Linton's limp body out the back door of the tavern.

Jonmarc struggled toward the door, trying to make haste without resulting to actually fighting his way clear. He had no idea of what he could do single-handedly to get Linton away from Chessis and Vakkis, and he doubted Linton's sudden collapse was due to the ale alone. Linton's capacity to drink without getting drunk was legendary among the caravan folk.

Poison, most likely, he thought. *But did they kill him or just knock him out?*

Jonmarc managed to push his way back out to the street and looked for a way to get to the other side of the building. The Hind and Hound was part of a block-long façade, and Jonmarc ran as fast as he dared to the nearest alley between buildings, hoping he was not too late.

He arrived in time to see a wagon pull away from the back of the pub with Vakkis and Chessis in the drivers' seat. Burlap covered the crates in the back of the wagon, and Jonmarc was certain Linton was hidden under there as well.

What now? He thought, and cast a glance over his shoulder as if by some miracle Trent and Corbin might appear. They did not, although the wagon was moving as quickly as it could given the crowds in the streets.

Even if I catch up to them, I can hardly fight off both Vakkis and Chessis by myself, Jonmarc thought. *And if I drag Linton off the wagon, what then? I'm not going to get far hauling his dead weight.* He looked around once more, but constables were scarce in this part of Kerrton, assuming they bothered to venture to these streets at all.

Why would a constable believe me? For all I know, Chessis and Vakkis could be paying the guards to look the other way, or even be working for the aldermen. I'm likely to end up in irons if I ask for help, and Linton will be gone.

Still unsure of what to do, Jonmarc stayed to the shadows and followed the wagon. In the bustling streets, the wagon's wheels barely rolled a full turn before the vehicle was obliged to stop in order to avoid running down pedestrians. Once outside the town's gates, however, Jonmarc knew he would be unable to keep up on foot for long, certainly not without being spotted.

If I can't stop them from taking Linton, maybe I can find out where they're going so I can get Trent and Corbin to help, Jonmarc thought. *Trent knows I went after Chessis. At least he won't think I've just run off.*

Jonmarc watched the burlap tarpaulin, hoping to see movement that might indicate whether Linton was dead or alive, but between the distance and the crowds, he got barely a glimpse. Nothing to give a clue one way or the other. The alley was barely wide enough for the wagon to drive through the center and have enough room on either side for pedestrians to flatten themselves along the wall to get out of the way. Shouts and curses filled the air as passers-by let the wagon's drivers know what they thought of the inconvenience.

All the while, Jonmarc tried to come up with ways to keep the wagon from leaving the town, but nothing workable came to mind. After rolling at a walking pace for several blocks, the crowds cleared as the wagon neared the edge of town, and Chessis urged the horse to pick up speed. Jonmarc jogged a distance behind, fearing at every moment that one of the bounty hunters might think to turn around. To his relief, neither man bothered looking round.

Once outside the village gate, the horse began to trot, jostling the wagon behind it on the rutted road. But instead of turning to the left, toward where the caravan made its camp not far outside the town, Chessis headed up the hill, toward Stormgard. A steady stream of foot traffic stymied any attempt to move at full speed. Men and women toting baskets and burlap bags full of goods to sell trudged down the hill toward Kerrton, while buyers laden with their purchases hiked back toward the walled enclave. Brown-robed suppliants made the journey in silent groups of two and three, headed, Jonmarc guessed, for whatever shrine within Stormgard's walls was the object of their devotion.

Chessis and Vakkis are bounty hunters. They might have a grudge against Linton, but I doubt they go around poisoning and kidnapping people unless they're being paid for their trouble, Jonmarc thought as he kept the wagon in sight. *So who are they working for? The thin man in the tavern? And where's Tarren? Can't afford for him to sneak up on me.*

Some of the towns near where the caravan made its camp had made their displeasure clear at the threat to the income of local merchants, but those incidents had never escalated beyond shouts and vague threats. Murder—or at least, attempted murder—seemed extreme.

Stormgard's walls seemed even more massive the closer Jonmarc got to the stronghold. Huge stone blocks rose from the bedrock of the hillside, rising to a height taller than a four-story building, and the corner towers scowled down on the land outside the wall like dour sentries. Hidden in the crowd, Jonmarc filed past the uniformed guards, across the drawbridge over the dry moat that surrounded the keep, and through the entrance archway with its heavy iron portcullis.

Without a plan more solid than to keep the wagon in sight, Jonmarc fell into step behind any groups of pedestrians that were headed in the same direction as the bounty hunters.

Foot traffic was sparser in Stormgard than in Kerrton, making it difficult to stay out of sight. The wagon rolled across the cobblestones, and with every jolt, Jonmarc willed Linton to rouse beneath the tarp and break free.

A line of silent supplicants, all robed and cowled in brown, filed along the city's main thoroughfare, toward the center plaza and whichever shrine they chose to make their offerings to the Lady and her eight Aspects. As Jonmarc dodged down another alley, a ragged man dragging a wheeled cart came around the corner. The other pedestrians scrambled to get out of his way, and the stench as the man passed nearly made Jonmarc retch. Stacked in the crude cart like logs wrapped in burlap were the bodies of the dead, enroute to Stormgard's burial ground.

What if Linton is dead? I'm looking for a chance to rescue him. What if he's beyond rescue? What then?

Jonmarc had heard tales about bounty hunters who earned their pay whether the quarry was dead or alive upon delivery to the buyer. It was already clear that Linton had run afoul of someone angry—and wealthy—enough to put a bounty on his head.

If I can just find out where they're going, maybe Trent can think of something, Jonmarc thought miserably.

Inside the walls of the city, Stormgard's buildings of white stone gleamed in the mid-morning sun. Whoever had overseen the city's construction had obviously feared the use of fire as a weapon, because Jonmarc saw few wooden houses or little else near the walls that might go up in fire. The fortifications might no longer be needed during the peacetime of King Bricen's reign, but the stronghold's military past gave Stormgard a cramped, oppressive feel.

The wagon rattled through the streets, and no one seemed to give it or the two men driving it a second glance. Jonmarc took care to provide no reason for anyone to notice him, either, making sure to avoid the gaze of those he passed and to move fast enough to keep the wagon in sight without making anyone wonder about his pace.

Stormgard was smaller than Kerrton, not surprising since the walled city was built to be defendable under siege. Jonmarc fell back as the foot traffic thinned, doing his best to avoid the notice of the two bounty hunters. The wagon slowed, then pulled into a narrow alley behind a hard-used stable and storehouse. Jonmarc waited in the shadows, watching. He stepped back into an alcove where a rickety wooden gate blocked off a ginnel between two buildings that was so narrow a broad-shouldered man would have to turn sideways to fit down the footpath. The gate looked as if a strong wind would blow it down, and Jonmarc took care not to lean his weight against it.

If both Vakkis and Chessis left the wagon unattended, he resolved to see if he could somehow get to Linton to at least find out if he was still alive. He had no desire to risk a rescue only to bring home a corpse.

Trent will want details, Jonmarc thought. *What does the storehouse tell me?* Just two floors, the stone building was modest compared to some of the taller and more ornate structures. By the look of the stone, the building was not new, the wooden roof could use some repairs and some pockmarks near the top suggested that it might have withstood a bombardment or two, many years ago.

Vakkis climbed down from the drivers' bench and walked around the corner, likely to the front of the storehouse. Jonmarc weighed his options. *If we were on the open road, I might be able to take Chessis, if I got him by surprise,* he thought, slipping his long knife from its sheath. Common sense made him reconsider.

Even if I could kill Chessis without alerting Vakkis, I'd never get the wagon and Linton out of the keep before the guards were on me, Jonmarc thought.

A servant came out of the building and spoke to Chessis, but Jonmarc could not hear what was being said. Chessis got down from his perch and went to the back of the wagon, where he and the footman struggled to lift down a large man-shaped bundle. Jonmarc had no doubt that Linton was inside.

"Looking for Linton?" Vakkis asked from behind him. Jonmarc wheeled, knife already in hand.

Vakkis looked even thinner than Jonmarc remembered, but his eyes were just as cold and remorseless as the last time they met. Vakkis noticed Jonmarc's gaze on the scar that left a jagged valley across one gaunt cheek, and he gave a hideous smile.

"Like it? You're the one who gave it to me." The smile twitched into a snarl, and Vakkis advanced.

Jonmarc stepped away from the rickety gate, but that put him squarely between Vakkis and the wagon—and Chessis, when he returned from dumping Linton's body in the building.

"Why Linton?"

"Because someone wants him," Vakkis replied. "Once again, you've got your nose where it doesn't belong, and I'm going to cut it off for you. We have a score to settle…"

In a moment, Chessis would be back and the odds of fighting his way past both bounty hunters was slim. Jonmarc rushed at Vakkis, knife upraised and roaring like a lunatic, a suicide move. At the last second, Jonmarc dodged to the side and slammed Vakkis hard, sending him sprawling against the ramshackle gate, which collapsed under his weight.

Jonmarc had no intention of sticking around to fight. He ran, and behind him, Vakkis's voice echoed in the narrow walled streets.

"Stop that thief!"

Vakkis's shouts brought two guards running, and they pounded after Jonmarc, their boot steps like thunder in the warren of winding alleys and ginnels. Jonmarc dodged around corners and switched directions, hoping he could throw off his pursuers and still find his way out. His improvised route brought him to Stormgard's main plaza and a crowd of robed supplicants awaiting the chance to enter an ornate building Jonmarc guessed to be the shrine to the Sacred Lady.

Before the guards and Vakkis could clear the corner, Jonmarc plunged into the crowd, ducking his head, making straight for the entrance to the shrine. The supplicants' faces may have been shadowed by their cowls, but more than one pilgrim muttered unholy sentiments as Jonmarc shoved toward the front and nearly dove into the darkness of the shrine.

It took a moment for his eyes to adjust from the bright morning light to the torchlight of the shrine. Whoever had erected this place of worship had obviously been funded by a wealthy patron. The flickering torches reflected off mosaics inlaid with gold. Water, sacred to the Mother, filled a long reflecting pool that ran from just inside the doorway to the statue of the Sacred Lady at the rear of the shrine, her hand lifted in blessing. Beside her was a statue of the preternaturally wise Childe, whose arms were upraised toward the sky.

Doves, the symbol of the Aspect of the Childe, cooed overhead in their cotes. In the mosaics on the floors and on the walls, Jonmarc saw the symbol of the Lady. Along the side walls, statues honored the other six Aspects: Sinha the Crone, Athira the Whore, Chenne the Warrior, Istra the Dark Lady, the voluptuous Lover, and the fearsome and nameless Formless One.

Jonmarc's mother had been scrupulous in making the family's offerings to the Lady; and Shanna, his wife, had likewise kept the feastdays with care. But since their deaths, and the silence that had answered his prayers when he had begged the goddess in vain for their lives, he had made no offerings and offered no more prayers.

You weren't listening the last time I asked for something, and you probably don't exist, but if you do, now would be a good time to be paying attention, Jonmarc pleaded silently.

He did not know whether the guards would dare pursue him into the shrine, but Jonmarc was certain Vakkis would not be constrained by propriety. Few of the supplicants had looked up when he entered, and no shouts intruded yet on the quiet of this holy place. He eyed the room, assessing his options. Quite a few of the supplicants knelt at the front, and he figured his odds of slipping among them unnoticed and unreported were poor.

Jonmarc worked his way along the darkened wall to where he saw a slight figure kneeling in reverence by the shrine to Istra. The Dark Lady's statue was life size, her gaze sorrowful, and her wide cloak billowing around her to reveal the wretches that clutched at her ankles for protection. Istra was the goddess of the lost and damned, of the outcast and misfit, and the patron of the undead *vayash moru*. Jonmarc saw his opportunity and made his move.

He brought the metal pommel of his knife down hard on the back of a supplicant's head. "Sorry," he murmured, and in two steps had dragged the man's body into the deep shadows behind the statue.

Hidden in the darkness behind Istra's cloak, Jonmarc stripped the supplicant of his robe and bound the man's wrists with a belt, shoving a wad of cloth into his mouth to muffle any shouts should he regain consciousness too soon. Jonmarc slipped into the robe, flipped the hood up to hide his face, and forced himself to relax into the slightly hunched, deferent posture of the seekers. He had no sooner knelt before the statue of the Dark Lady than he heard the pounding of boot steps and terse directions to the guards.

Jonmarc forced himself to remain still, head bowed, hunching to hide his height, hoping he did not look tense. He heard Vakkis move behind him and expected to feel the bite of a knife against his throat at any moment, but the steps passed by without incident. He waited until his feet began to go numb from kneeling and his shoulders ached from bending forward. Jonmarc raised his face to look at the statue of Istra, and the glow of the firelight gave the smooth marble an almost-living warmth.

"If you had anything to do with that, thank you," Jonmarc murmured as he cautiously rose to his feet. Alert for a trap, he moved as he had seen the other supplicants do, folding their hands in front of them beneath the loose sleeves of their robes. Jonmarc followed their example, but he palmed his small knife, just in case.

The robed seekers filed silently out of the shrine, heads bowed, murmuring a quiet chant of thanksgiving. Jonmarc jockeyed for position so that he was in the middle of the procession. He wished he dared glance around the square to see if Vakkis and the guards had gone, but knew that would give him away if anyone were watching, so he took a deep breath and kept walking, fighting the urge to run.

Jonmarc remained with the supplicants as they wound their way through the narrow streets, down toward the city gate. He breathed a quiet sigh of relief as he passed beneath the portcullis and began to make his way down the road toward Kerrton. By now, the sun was overhead, and several candlemarks had passed since he had left Trent in the marketplace. *Trent and Corbin will be worried—or angry. Maybe both.*

Once the supplicants had fulfilled their pilgrimage, they dispersed to their individual journeys, and Jonmarc slipped inside the Kerrton stockade, then veered down a shadowed ginnel to pull the robe over his head and roll it up under his arm. Watching for Vakkis, he strode toward the Pheasant and Quail, figuring that if Trent and Corbin had not given up or gone searching for him, they were likely to wait for him there.

The brewery and pub had grown more crowded since their morning arrival, but the wagons were nowhere to be seen. Jonmarc headed for the barn, wondering if Trent had grown frustrated enough to leave him behind. At the entrance to the barn, he stopped, waiting for his eyes to adjust. One of the wagons they had brought from the caravan was there, its horse already in the harness. The other wagon was missing.

"Where in the name of the Crone have you been?" Trent grabbed Jonmarc by the arm and yanked him so hard into the shadows that he nearly pitched headfirst into the hay.

"They've got Maynard," Jonmarc said, trying to tamp down on his panic.

"Who?" Trent demanded, looming over him.

"Chessis and Vakkis. I followed Chessis to a tavern called the Hind and Hound—"

"I know the place," Corbin replied. "Not one of the better sort."

Jonmarc shook his head. "No, it isn't. Linton was meeting with a man there I didn't recognize. The man got up and left the tavern, and Linton finished his ale, then collapsed.

It had to be poison. Chessis and Vakkis were waiting, and they swooped in and grabbed him, then whisked him out the back into a wagon."

"It can't have taken that long to come back from Hind and the Hound," Trent said, his voice clipped with anger.

"I followed the wagon," Jonmarc said. Now that he had made it back safely, his heart was pounding. "They took him to Stormgard."

Trent and Corbin exchanged glances. "Going to be hard to find him in there."

"I know where they took him. There's a storehouse in the center of Stormgard—"

"Oh sweet Mother and Childe, don't tell me you followed them into Stormgard?" Trent's face was a mixture of anger and horror, which might have been funny if Jonmarc were not on the receiving end of his temper.

"Someone had to," Jonmarc snapped. "Then Vakkis left the wagon and I thought about jumping Chessis and stealing the wagon with Maynard still in the back."

"Please tell me you didn't," Corbin replied, his tone dangerously flat.

Once again, Jonmarc shook his head. "Too many people around. Then Vakkis came after me, and I shoved him down a ginnel and ran." He recounted the rest of the escape, including the foray into the shrine, as Trent and Corbin looked on, incredulous. During the telling of the tale, several more of the caravan's regular members came out of the shadows to hear Jonmarc's story. Dugan, one of the junior riggers, and Zane, a knife-thrower with deadly aim, along with Kegan, a healer-in-training.

"That's a tale you'll be telling when you're old and gray, assuming you live that long," Corbin said with a sigh when

Jonmarc finished. He eyed the rolled up supplicant's robe. "Still, it was quick thinking on your part, and you made it back in one piece. That's more than most men can say who've come toe-to-toe with Vakkis."

"How did the rest of you get here?" Jonmarc asked, looking at Zane and the others.

Trent glared at him, apparently still not ready to forgive his disappearance. "When you didn't come back, I sent Corbin back to the caravan with orders for them to strike camp and move to our next location. Just in case Vakkis and Chessis were planning some trouble. He came back with volunteers to find you and then beat the shit out of the bounty hunters for what they did to Conall."

"Do you know if Linton was still alive?" Corbin asked.

Jonmarc shook his head. "I couldn't get close enough to tell. But something about the way Vakkis responded made me think whoever paid for Linton's capture wanted him alive."

Trent muttered a few creative curses. "I don't know how we'll get back in there without bringing the guards down on us."

Corbin nodded toward the supplicant robe. "We could waylay a few more seekers."

Trent shook his head. "Vakkis may not have found Jonmarc, but the fact that he went looking in the shrine meant he had a good idea how he disappeared. He'll be watching."

"We could wait for night, get a couple of the *vayash moru* who work for the caravan and tear the place apart," Zane suggested.

Corbin gave him a withering look. "That just sends the bounty hunters after our *vayash moru*, and every other *vayash moru* within a dozen leagues. Bad idea."

"I have an idea," Jonmarc said, looking up. "But you'd have to be barking mad to make it work."

Trent gave a mirthless laugh. "Then you've come to the right place, lad. Tell us what you've got in mind."

AFTER DARK, NO one paid any attention to the two men in ragged clothing pulling a cart full of corpses.

"Damn, they're heavy," Jonmarc muttered to Trent as they hauled the ramshackle wagon through the shadowed streets of Stormgard. They had cobbled together a makeshift wagon from parts Trent and Zane stole from the brewery's barn, and helped themselves to clothing on a wash line within easy reach. Jonmarc and Trent had smudged their faces with dirt and soot, patting liberal amounts on their clothes for good measure. Corbin, Kegan, and Dugan were rolled up in burlap like corpses, and Zane followed mournfully in the supplicant's robe, chanting for the souls of the dead. Corbin had brought their weapons from the caravan, so the cart with the 'corpses' also carried their swords and throwing knives.

"You'd just better hope no one pays any attention to what Zane's chanting," Trent hissed. "He's gone through every tavern song I know, and moved on to some I doubt you'll hear outside a whorehouse."

"I hope we're not too late," Jonmarc said. Worry had knotted his stomach all afternoon. Not only might they find Linton already dead, but their rescue attempt could easily cost the lives of his friends. Despite that, none of the men had questioned the need to go after their boss.

"How much further?" Trent asked. "And why are we still going uphill? Isn't anything in this city level? I may not be able to swing a hammer for a week after this."

"Not far," Jonmarc said, lifting his head to have a look around. Stormgard was even more intimidating after dark, when the fortified walls loomed, dark and menacing, casting the interior of the city in shadows that even the torchlight did not fully dispel.

They turned a corner and Jonmarc signaled for them to stop. "That's it," he said, pointing toward the two-story building. "And the wagon is still over by the stable." He looked to Trent. "Any idea who the building belongs to?"

Trent gave a cold smile. "Actually, yes. While you and I gathered our disguises, Corbin made a few inquiries around town. It seems that the head of the merchant guild fits your description of the man Maynard met at the pub. And even more damning—he's said to own a fine barn and warehouse in Stormgard that he won from a noble in a card game."

Jonmarc and Trent pushed the cart into the shadows. Corbin, Kegan, and Dugan cast off the burlap to ready themselves for the work at hand. Trent had a set to his jaw that told Jonmarc the blacksmith was ready for a fight. "Dugan—go get Vakkis's wagon ready. Hitch up the horse and wait around the corner, out of sight but close enough to hear me whistle," Trent directed. "Kegan—go with him and lend a hand. We won't need you until the fighting is over." Dugan gave a sharp nod and ran off with Kegan close behind.

Unlike that morning, the area was quiet, and nearly empty of foot traffic. The storehouse had few windows, so it was impossible to tell if anyone was inside. The rest of the street was dark. Jonmarc heard Dugan in the stable and froze, awaiting discovery, but when no one appeared to check on the noise, Jonmarc breathed a sigh of relief.

"Think it's a trap?" Jonmarc murmured.

"Probably." Trent replied. He signaled for Zane and Corbin to go around to the back. "Don't see a choice, do you?"

Jonmarc shook his head, and Trent grinned. "Let's make it expensive for them," Trent said, drawing his sword.

The wooden door splintered under their weight as Jonmarc and Trent shouldered their way in. A crash at the other end of the building signaled that Corbin and Zane had the same idea.

Barrels, crates, and bales filled most of the storehouse's large, open interior. Sawdust covered the hard dirt floor, and stout wooden pillars and roof beams indicated that more goods were likely housed above. A single oil lantern hung from a rusted nail below a roof support, and its light cast a dim circle. From the footprints and scuffs in the sawdust, the storehouse had seen plenty of recent traffic.

Stacked wooden boxes and bales made it impossible to see beyond the center of the building. Here and there, piles of barrels lay on their side, stacked one atop the other taller than a man's head. Linton lay in a heap on the floor to one side, bound hand and foot, and he did not stir at the noise as they entered.

"You go for Linton. We'll circle around," Trent whispered. A shake of his head confirmed Jonmarc's suspicion that Vakkis and Chessis were likely to be waiting for them in the darkness.

"I wish we knew whether or not Tarren is with them," Jonmarc said.

Trent shrugged. "I've heard he works on his own sometimes. Maybe we'll get lucky and he's off making someone else's life miserable. We'll find out soon enough."

Jonmarc's sword was in his hand as he approached Linton. Out of the corner of his eye, he glimpsed Trent moving behind the boxes on one side while Zane headed into the shadows on the other. Corbin removed the ladder to the top floor, and stood ready with his sword in one hand and an iron rod in the other.

Linton groaned as Jonmarc turned him over. The caravan master's skin was ashen and clammy, and his breathing was shallow. From his torn clothing and the bruises on his face, it appeared his captors had vented their anger with a beating. Blood flecked Linton's lips, and one eye was swollen shut.

The clang of swords and the scuffle of footsteps sounded in the darkness behind the crates and barrels. One set of crates wobbled dangerously, and the top crate tumbled to the floor, sending splinters and shards of pottery flying.

Jonmarc hoisted Linton over his left shoulder, leaving his right hand free for his sword. Shouts and curses rang out from the shadows, and Jonmarc heard the familiar thud of Zane's throwing knives. A loud crack echoed as Corbin's iron rod collided with force against something hard. He could not see the battle, but it was easy to guess that Vakkis and Chessis had brought reinforcements.

Halfway to the door, Chessis stepped out from behind a pile of barrels. The squat bounty hunter shook a lock of oily blond hair out of his eyes and gave a predatory grin. "Figured you'd be dumb enough to come after him," Chessis said, his voice a nasal whine.

"Get out of my way."

"And let you walk out with our prize catch?" Chessis gave a wheezing laugh. "Not when we could get good silver from the slavers for the likes of you."

Chessis was plump and slackjawed, but it would be a mistake to underestimate his skill with a sword. Jonmarc had seen Chessis in action the night Conall died, and the bounty hunter was faster than he looked. He was also not encumbered by the dead weight of a grown man, which Jonmarc knew would slow his own reactions. Chessis looked like he was relishing the chance for revenge.

"Your friend's not quite dead yet," Chessis said. "But soon. The Guild Master wanted a slow death, as a warning for others."

"Go to the Crone," Jonmarc muttered.

Chessis lunged, and Jonmarc parried, but Linton's weight made him slow and blocked his field of view. Chessis laughed and came at him from the left, forcing Jonmarc to wheel, slamming Linton's legs against the stack of barrels, which tottered but did not fall.

"Vakkis saw you at the Hind and Hound," Chessis gloated. "He figured you'd follow us. He wanted to catch you for the slavers then, but you got away and we figured you'd be back."

Jonmarc did not waste his breath with a reply. He remembered Chessis's fighting style from the last time, and recalled that the bounty hunter relied on strength rather than style, bashing his way through an enemy's defense.

Chessis came at him again, driving Jonmarc back a step. Linton's weight threw him off balance, and he caught himself against the center pole, jarring it hard enough to send the oil lantern crashing to the floor. Flames spread rapidly in the loose sawdust, but Chessis did not run.

"Burn or bleed," Chessis taunted. "Your choice."

Jonmarc had no desire to do either. He charged at Chessis, sword angled for a blow to the chest. Chessis parried, and Jonmarc swung suddenly to the right, using Linton's dangling legs as a weapon and catching Chessis hard enough to send the bounty hunter onto his back and into the growing fire.

Smoke was rapidly filling the storehouse, and Jonmarc gasped for air. Across the way, he caught a glimpse of Vakkis and Trent still locked in combat. Corbin was fighting two-handed, using his iron bar to block the swings of a man in the uniform of a private guard.

Chessis rolled away from the fire to extinguish his burning shirt, and scrambled to his feet, coming after Jonmarc with a roar of obscenities. Chessis's blade was angled to skewer Linton through the back, and Jonmarc dodged to the side, just as a streak of silver glinted in the firelight and one of Zane's throwing knives lodged in Chessis's shoulder.

Chessis howled in pain, but there was determination and hatred in his eyes and he slashed with his left hand, wielding a blade Jonmarc did not see until it was too late. The knife cut deep into his side, and Jonmarc bit back a cry of pain as he managed to land a solid kick to the bounty hunter's chest that sent him sprawling.

"Come on!" Zane emerged from the smoke, and half pushed, half dragged Jonmarc and Linton out to the street.

"Trent, Corbin—" Jonmarc gasped, trying to breathe. The wound in his side staggered him, and he focused on keeping his feet.

Two figures crashed through what remained of the wooden door, wrestling for control of a single sword. Vakkis and Trent rolled into the rutted road, both bleeding from multiple gashes. Zane went running toward them, and Vakkis bucked beneath Trent's weight, landing a solid kick before wresting out of Trent's grip and running into the night.

Corbin came around the side of the storehouse as Zane helped Trent up. "Better hope Dugan got that wagon," he grunted as he joined them. "Those flames are going to draw a crowd soon."

Thick smoke poured from the upper windows of the storehouse and the broken doors. It looked to Jonmarc as if the entire first floor was engulfed in flames, and he wondered if Chessis had managed to get out, or if the bounty hunter had died in the flames.

Chessis is like a cockroach. He's probably still alive, and madder than ever, Jonmarc thought. He could feel warm blood soaking his tunic and the waist of his trews, and he took deep, slow breaths, willing himself not to pass out.

From the direction of the plaza, Jonmarc heard the sound of boot steps and half a dozen guardsmen burst into the roadway, taking in the sight of the burning storehouse and the five wounded men who had obviously just come from a fight.

"I don't think I'll make it if we've got to fight our way out," Jonmarc said, staggering a step under Linton's weight and his own injury.

Trent let out an ear-piercing whistle and from behind them, Jonmarc heard the snap of reins and a drover's cry. The wagon careened toward them with Dugan in the drivers' seat, a crazed smile on his face and a hard glint in his eyes. Behind the wagon came a half dozen panicked horses, being driven from the stable by Kegan who was shouting and waving his arms to send the horses into a frenzied gallop.

Dugan angled the wagon for the guards, who had no choice but to throw themselves out of the way or be ridden down. "Get in!" he shouted as he reined in the horses.

Zane grabbed Linton from Jonmarc and tossed the caravan master into the bed of the wagon like a cord of firewood. Corbin climbed in over the side and Trent swung up beside Dugan as the wagon began to roll. Jonmarc had not realized Zane knew he had been wounded, but without a word, Zane hefted him and threw him into the back of the wagon, climbing on and reaching a hand back to grab Kegan's outstretched arm and haul the healer up as the wagon sped up.

"Linton's in bad shape," Jonmarc said, holding tightly to the side slats of the wagon as it bumped over the cobblestones and ruts.

"You're bleeding," Zane said, eyeing the growing stain on Jonmarc's shirt.

"Linton's worse," Jonmarc said, trying not to lose consciousness as every jostle sent pain lancing through his side.

If the guards had thought to give chase, the loss of their horses ended that option, and after the soldiers picked themselves up off the ground, they left off with shouted curses before turning back to the storehouse. Flames shot from the roof and had leapt to the stable next door.

"Whatever was stored in there went up like a torch," Corbin commented. "With a little wind, that fire could take out the center of the city."

"I suspect the Guild Master's fortunes have taken a turn for the worse," Zane chuckled.

Dugan shouted to the horses to keep up the pace and snapped the reins. The wagon rumbled at top speed, barely clearing the walls of the narrow alleys, and threatening to spill out its passengers or break a wheel as it jolted through the streets.

Stormgard's massive entrance loomed ahead of them, and Jonmarc feared the guards might have lowered the portcullis, but the fire and fight were too far toward the center of the city to have attracted the attention of the soldiers. The night guard saw them coming, and looked as if, for a split second, he weighed his duty to try to stop them against the certainty of being run down. He and the other guard dove out of the way as Dugan sped through the gate with a cry of triumph.

Jonmarc managed to lash himself to the side of the wagon. He was fading in and out of consciousness, and the night seemed much colder than he remembered it. Dimly, he heard the buzz of voices around him, but it took too much effort to focus on what was being said. Exhausted and in pain, he let the darkness take him as the wagon hurtled into the night.

WHEN THE DARKNESS lifted, Jonmarc realized two important things. The pain was gone, and he was warm. *Maybe I'm dead,* he thought, but if so, 'dead' felt a lot like lying on his cot back at the caravan.

"He's awake." The voice was nearby, and Jonmarc recognized it as Ada, the lead healer with the caravan.

Jonmarc opened his eyes slowly, feeling as if every muscle fought his will to move. Ada was sitting next to him, and Trent walked over, taking in Jonmarc's condition with a shake of his head.

"You're luckier than you deserve," Trent said. "Chessis and Vakkis didn't get their reputations as bounty hunters by missing their targets." He managed a smile. "Good to have you back with us."

"Linton?" Jonmarc's mouth was dry and the word came out as more of a croak, but Ada seemed to understand.

"He's fine. Just sleeping off a dose of Mussa poison. He'll have a foul headache and not be able to keep any food down for a day or so, but he'll survive," she said with a half-smile.

"I thought... Mussa poison was... deadly."

Trent leaned closer. "It is if you haven't built up a tolerance. This isn't the first time someone's tried to poison Maynard. Since then, he's taken a tiny dose every day, which means it would take a whopping amount to kill him." He gave a conspiratorial grin. "But don't tell anyone, or they might change what poison they use."

Jonmarc felt for the place on his side where Chessis's blade had cut him. The skin was unbroken, and the area was tender but no longer agonizing to touch. He looked to Ada. "Thank you."

She nodded. "Glad to do it. Can't help that you'll have a scar."

Jonmarc sank back into the cot and closed his eyes. "It probably won't be the last."

"Chessis didn't die in the fire." Trent's voice made Jonmarc open his eyes again. "Vakkis is gone—no idea where and I don't care. But we heard from one of Linton's informants that Chessis's body wasn't found in the ashes, so he may be injured, but he's still alive—and he's going to be out for your blood for sure."

"Not the first," Jonmarc replied, still groggy from the healing.

"If there's a bright side, the man who hired Vakkis and Chessis not only lost his storehouse and stable, but word has it he is no longer head of the Merchant Guild," Trent said, sounding rather pleased. "In fact, it seems that some powerful men in Stormgard have let him know he is no longer welcome inside the city walls."

"Good to hear," Jonmarc murmured. He wasn't sure what Ada had done, but he felt cocooned in honeyed warmth. He didn't feel like fighting sleep, and he suspected Ada had a hand in that, too.

"I'll expect you at the forge tomorrow, bright and early," Trent said brusquely. "No malingering."

Jonmarc let the voices drift out of reach. He was alive, which was more than he expected, and so was Linton. He let that knowledge sustain him as he sank into a deep, healing sleep. The caravan had taken care of its own.

Monstrosities

"I'M GOING TO take you down." Jonmarc Vahanian muttered between gritted teeth as he swung his sword. Steel clanged against steel as their blades hit, with a jolt that shuddered down Jonmarc's arm.

His attacker disengaged and lunged, forcing Jonmarc into a series of desperate parries. One of the blows got inside his guard, slicing down his forearm.

He gave an angry roar and took the offensive, delivering blow after blow that rang out as their swords clashed. He scored a hit on his attacker's shoulder, only to be driven back with strikes that nearly took him off his feet.

His attacker wheeled into a high kick, and his boot connected hard with Jonmarc's sword arm, sending his blade flying and numbing his hand beyond use. In the next instant, a sword's point nicked the underside of Jonmarc's chin.

"I win."

Jonmarc's attacker lowered his sword and let it swing away, laughing. "That was a good run, Jonmarc. You're getting better."

Jonmarc swore and shook his numb hand. "Thanks, but I'd be dead by now if you'd meant any of that."

Karl Steen pushed a lock of dark red hair out of his eyes. "Maybe, maybe not. After all, you weren't going for the kill, either. It makes a difference, when you know it really matters." He met Jonmarc's gaze. "I think you know that."

Jonmarc looked away. At nearly eighteen years old, he was as tall as Karl, who was ten years his senior. Years of working with blacksmith's tools had made Jonmarc strong, and the tragedies of the last few years had given him reason to sharpen his sword skills. So far, he had been lucky enough to survive the fights that had come looking for him. But the closer the caravan got to the border with Principality, the less Jonmarc was willing to rely on luck.

"Can you show me how to do that kick?" Jonmarc asked.

Karl chuckled. "It's called an Eastmark kick for a reason. Eastmark's got one of the best armies in the Winter Kingdoms. They fight like *dimonns*, and I think they start training from the time they can walk."

"I heard they hire a lot of Principality mercs," Jonmarc said, following Karl over to a stump where a bucket of water and a tin cup awaited them. All around them, the regular bustle of the caravan continued, as the small group of onlookers to their sparring match drifted away.

Karl's expression darkened. "Oh, they hire plenty of Principality mercs. But never forget—if you're not of Eastmark, you're good enough to die for them, but never good enough to promote."

"Were you a merc?"

Karl looked away. "Yeah. For a while. Not anymore." His eyes narrowed as he looked back at Jonmarc. "That's what you're planning? Joining up once the caravan gets to the Principality border?"

Jonmarc shrugged. "If they'll take me. I heard it pays better than signing up for King Bricen's army."

Karl finished his water and handed the cup to Jonmarc. "Maybe. 'Course you've gotta live long enough to spend it. And your odds of that are much better serving the king."

"There's nothing to fight in Margolan except some highwaymen and the raiders near the coast."

"Exactly," Karl said, stabbing a finger into Jonmarc's chest to make his point. "So you get paid to march from here to there and there to here without being attacked. You draw your pay and spend it on ale and wenches in taverns where you're not likely to be killed before morning."

"Is that what you're planning to do?" Jonmarc asked, watching his sparring partner closely. Karl had joined up with the caravan a few weeks before, since the traveling show always needed guards. Jonmarc had been with the show for nearly a year as an apprentice blacksmith, ever since the night everything he loved went up in flames.

Maynard Linton's caravan journeyed from one side of Margolan to the other and back again, entertaining audiences with performers, musicians, acrobats, artisans, and soothsayers, exotic wild animals and unusual trinkets. People like Karl came and went. Most of the caravan crew were running away from something or someone, glad to be anywhere except where they'd been.

"Sounds like the good life to me," Karl said. "Adventure isn't what it's made out to be. What's the use of gold if you're dead?"

Jonmarc didn't answer. He retrieved his sword and cleaned it carefully before sheathing it. *I'm not chasing adventure. I just want to get lost.*

"If you do go—and I'm telling you it's a bad idea—stay well away from Nargi." Karl shook his head. "They're trouble."

"Isn't Nargi on the other side of Dhasson?" Jonmarc said, brushing the dirt from his trousers. "That's nowhere near Principality."

Karl nodded. "No, but the Nu River runs along the borders, and on past Trevath. Many a man's gotten off course and made landfall where he ought not be. If you're unlucky enough to blunder into Nargi, you don't leave."

"They don't take prisoners?"

Karl gave him a sidelong glance. "That's the problem. They do." He laced up the opening of his shirt. "The strongest ones, the best fighters, they take for their games. Make them fight each other to the death, wager on which one dies." He shook his head. "Horrible thing, being entertained by someone's suffering."

"How do you know about the games?" Jonmarc asked.

Karl looked away. "They took a friend of mine. He got lost on the river, and the Nargi got him. I heard from traders that they took him for the games. The better you are, the longer you suffer. He was good."

It was late spring, and the day was warm even in northern Margolan. Jonmarc grabbed his shirt from where it lay across a log and slipped into it. "I'll stay out of Nargi," he replied. "But right now, if I don't get over to the forge, Trent will have my head and I'll never make it to Principality." He gave Karl a mock salute. "Thanks for the lesson. Do it again tomorrow?"

Karl pulled his shirt over his head. "Sure. You know where to find me."

Jonmarc whistled as he walked the distance to the forge. Tomorrow, his body would be sore from the exertion of the sparring match, and he would have cuts and bruises to show for his effort. Still, he found it exhilarating when his sword and body moved together perfectly. He had fought for his life enough times that battle held no romance. But there was something about the way a fight narrowed his concentration, sharpened his senses and made time stand still that called to him. It didn't hurt that he was good at it.

"There you are!" Trent hailed him as he worked the bellows. "I'm glad Karl left you in one piece," he said, chuckling.

Jonmarc tied his chestnut brown hair back in a queue to keep it back from the fire. The jagged scar that ran from one ear down below his collar, a reminder of the night his family died, would not bother Trent. "Did you see us?"

"Just in passing. You seemed to be holding your own." Trent gave the furnace one more blast, and then rolled an iron bar into the heat.

Jonmarc used a scrap of fabric to daub at the fresh cut on his arm. It was a testimony to Karl's skill that the wound was shallow, enough to mark but barely deep enough to bleed. "Not as well as I'd like," he replied.

"You do all right for yourself in a real fight, which is all that matters," Trent said, turning the bar to heat it evenly.

Trent raised his hammer and began pounding the hot iron. Jonmarc bustled around the forge, bringing water for the cooling bucket, pumping the bellows and lining up more iron rods for Trent to work. When he had finished that, he tied on his own leather apron, pulled on his heavy gloves and started work on a fresh rod of iron. The pounding of hammer on anvil was like a heartbeat to Jonmarc, a comforting sound he had heard all his life.

Blacksmithing in the caravan was different from the work Jonmarc's father had done in their Borderlands village. There, the blacksmith took on jobs for everyone in town, and commission work if the smith's skill was good enough. Most of the work was functional: hoes and ploughs for the farmers, barrel hoops for the cooper, nails and tools for the joiner. Jonmarc's father forged swords commissioned by the constable and the captain of guards. Most of his items were made to sell.

In the caravan, almost none of their items were for sale. The caravan blacksmith kept the show on the road, forging horseshoes and wagon parts, pulleys for the tent riggers and pots for the cook. The entertainers and merchants brought in the crowds and earned the caravan's living. But behind the tents, it was the blacksmith, the farrier, and the cooks who kept the troupe in business.

"Do you have those horseshoes I ordered?" Corbin's voice thundered above the clatter.

Trent paused and pushed the sweat from his forehead with his arm. "Got a box of them in the corner," he said. "I'll have more for you soon."

"Don't forget," Corbin warned. "Or there'll be the Crone to pay." Corbin was as broad shouldered and strong as Trent, a good thing for a farrier who had to strong-arm stubborn horses. Jonmarc was officially apprenticed to Trent, but often found himself loaned out to give Corbin a hand. He did not mind the change of scenery.

A young man waited outside the forge for Corbin. He looked to be a year or so younger than Jonmarc, tall and gangly, with a badly pock-marked face. "This is my nephew, Pol," Corbin said as he hefted the heavy box of horseshoes. "He'll be with us for a while. I went into one of the towns we stopped at last week to see my sister, and found out that everyone in the family but Pol died of the pox. So he's with us for a bit, until he figures something out."

Pol did not look up as Corbin told his story. He kicked at the dirt and looked as if he wished to disappear from view. *It wasn't pox that took my family, but I wager I know a bit about how he feels,* Jonmarc thought. *At least he's got Corbin to look after him.*

Corbin had no sooner left than Maynard Linton bustled into the forge. "Trent! Jonmarc! I need to know when you'll have new *stawar* cages? Damn big cats. Their trainer is after me for bigger cages. Says the cats need more room to prowl, makes more people come to watch them."

Maynard Linton was a short, stocky man in his early thirties, the mastermind and impresario behind the caravan. He worried like a dyspeptic bookkeeper, and fought like a bee-stung bear. And while Linton's ethics were flexible on most matters, when it came to the caravan, he would face down the Formless One.

"Working on it now, Maynard," Trent replied, giving the iron another strike. "Be another day or two, like I told you the last time you asked."

Linton muttered a curse and glowered. "Hurry it up. I'm tired of hearing from the cat trainer. I've got other things to worry about."

"Anything that should worry us?" Trent asked. His hammer fell in a deafening clatter.

"Actually, yes. That's the other reason I walked over here." Linton stepped in closer to the furnace. Though it was late spring, they were far enough north that the days still held a nip in the air, especially when the wind blew. "I want Jonmarc to do a job for me."

Trent looked up. Linton was technically the master of everyone in the caravan, but Trent took his responsibility as Jonmarc's patron quite seriously. When Jonmarc sought refuge with the caravan with nowhere else to go, Trent took him in without question. And while everyone in the traveling show looked to Linton to watch out for their best interests, Trent and Corbin knew that Linton's schemes sometimes borrowed trouble.

"What kind of job?" Trent asked, setting down his heavy hammer.

"A bit of spying. Seems we have some competition."

Trent frowned. "What kind of competition?"

Linton leaned against one of the upright poles that held the lean-to roof over the forge. The whole set-up could be struck and packed onto a wagon, then rebuilt at the next stop. "I've heard tell there's a monstrosities show over on the other side of Dunleigh, near the cairns. Word has it their collection of oddities is quite impressive—enough so I'm afraid they're costing us business."

"If you already know that, why send Jonmarc?" Trent asked suspiciously.

Linton waved his hand as if to dispel the question. "Oh, I wasn't going to send him alone. I've already gotten Kegan and Dugan for the job, but I thought safety in numbers and all."

Kegan was a healer-in-training, and Dugan was a junior rigger. Both were close to Jonmarc's age, and the three were good friends. "There's also Pol," Jonmarc said. "Corbin's nephew."

Linton nodded. "Excellent. Four young men, out to see what they can see, wandering through the traveling show. I'll even give you the coppers for the fare, and all I want is a full story when you return."

Trent's eyes narrowed. "Spill it, Maynard. I've never known you to pay good money for someone's entertainment. What's really going on?"

Linton huffed in rebuttal, and then shrugged. "There are rumors, and it's hurting our attendance."

"What kind of rumors?" Trent had been with the caravan for years, and he was Linton's right-hand man. He had a sixth sense for when Linton was prevaricating, and the patience to wait him out. "Are they thieves? Smugglers?"

Linton shook his head. "No more than the rest of us," he replied. The caravan had been known to smuggle contraband from time to time when crowds were thin or times were hard. "But there are whispers about people going missing from the villages where the monstrosities show has been. It's said that the show just seems to appear out of nowhere one night, and that no one has ever seen it travel, save near a crossroads at midnight."

Trent snorted. "You're just jealous. Whoever's running that show might just be more of an impresario than you are."

Linton glowered and hiked his thumbs in the waistband of his trousers. "Huh. So you say. But if people believe what they're hearing, and they're frightened, they stay home. Which means no money to buy food at our next stop."

"So you want us to go in and look around, and then come back and tell you what we've seen?' Jonmarc asked.

Linton grinned. "That's all. Four young men out for the evening won't attract attention. Just have a good time and see what you see."

Trent folded his arms across his chest. "On one condition," he said. "Zane and Corbin and I follow them, as reinforcements." He held up a hand. "We won't go in unless there's a problem. But if any part of what you've heard is true, then I'm not going to send four boys in there by themselves."

"Fine, fine. Do what you want. But go tonight. Word has it the show arrives and leaves without warning. I want to know what we're up against." With that, Linton bustled out of the forge.

Jonmarc and Trent looked at each other for a moment. "Linton never ceases to amaze me," Trent said, shaking his head. "Pump the bellows," he ordered, and Jonmarc went to fan the flames. "Of all the nonsense—"

"What's a monstrosities show?" Jonmarc asked.

Trent shoved the iron rods back into the fire. "Just what it sounds like. A traveling show of monsters."

"Monsters?"

Trent shrugged. "Depends on your definition. Oddities. People and animals that aren't what you'd expect. Calves with two heads. A cat with a paw where its tail should be, or a dog with no ears, or a monkey with a third arm. Someone who can put a nail through his flesh without bleeding, or swallow fire. I heard tell of a man with an axe blade in his skull. Didn't kill him, and he couldn't take it out, so he charged people a skrivven apiece to look at him."

"Better than begging, I guess," Jonmarc said.

"Maybe," Trent replied. "Not many other places folks that different could get work, or much use for animals like that. But there are dark stories that maybe some of them weren't born like that." He struck the iron, ending the conversation, but his comments made Jonmarc all the more curious.

Across the caravan grounds, Jonmarc heard the bell clang the seventh hour. He and Trent were just banking the fires and closing up the forge for the night. "Go ahead and get dinner," Trent instructed. "Then meet up with Kegan and the others. I'll roust up Corbin and Zane and we'll follow you." He paused. "Jonmarc—"

"Yes?"

"It won't do for you to wear your swords, but take a knife. I don't like the feel of this."

Jonmarc felt a thrill of excitement as he left the forge. He had become used to the attractions of the caravan, and knew nearly all of the performers. It had been quite a while since he had watched a show with the kind of keen interest he saw in the face of the caravan's patrons. The monstrosities show sounded like fun.

"Over here!" Dugan hailed him. Dugan and Kegan sat on a log near the cook fire, each with a trencher of stew.

Jonmarc lined up to get his dinner and a tankard of ale. A hunched woman got into line behind him. She wore a long gray robe with a cowl, and her gray hair was matted like a bird's nest.

"Watch yourself," the old woman muttered.

Jonmarc turned, frowning. "Did you say something?" He glanced around, thinking that he had stepped on her hem.

"In the shadow place," she murmured. "Things are not what they seem."

"You want your stew or not?" the cook grunted, and Jonmarc turned around, reaching for his trencher.

"The taken ones are watching you," the old woman muttered. "Beware."

"Show's over for the day. Keep your predictions to yourself," the cook snapped, shoving a trencher toward the old woman.

Jonmarc went back to join his friends, and cast a glance over his shoulder. "Do you know who what is?" he asked.

Dugan frowned, following his gaze. "The old woman?"

"She's new. Just came on a few towns back," Kegan said. "She's a seer and a hedge witch. Says her name's Alyzza." He gave Jonmarc a look. "Why?"

Jonmarc shook his head. "No reason. Just hadn't seen her around. Strange duck." He took a drink of ale. "You talked to Linton?"

Dugan nodded. "He must be plenty worried to give us each a copper to check this place out." Dugan was one of the most fearless people Jonmarc knew. As an apprentice rigger,

Dugan scaled the high poles inside the caravan's tents and ran lines to keep the canvas in place. It was dangerous work, but Dugan seemed to relish the risk.

"Is Pol coming?" Jonmarc asked.

"You mean Corbin's nephew?" Kegan asked. "The one with the pox scars?"

Jonmarc nodded. "Have you met him?"

Kegan shrugged. "Only once. Keeps to himself, like you did when you first joined up. If he just lost his family, I don't imagine he feels much like talking." Kegan lacked Dugan's daring, and did not share Jonmarc's love of sparring, but he always knew interesting gossip, thanks to spending his days among the healers.

"Here he comes," Dugan said.

Pol ambled toward them, head down. By torchlight, the scars on Pol's face were not as noticeable as in daylight. From the way the young man hunched his shoulders and let his hair fall, Jonmarc guessed that Pol felt the weight of his disfigurement. Seeing him, Jonmarc was conscious of the long scar that ran from his ear down under his collar, a permanent memento of all he had lost.

Pol shuffled through the food line and stood just outside the circle where Jonmarc and the others ate. "Room for one more?" he asked in a tone that said he would not have been surprised to be turned away.

"Plenty," Kegan said, sliding down to make a space on the log. "You in for the adventure tonight?"

Pol nodded, still not making eye contact. "Should be interesting," he said without looking up.

"I'm thinking it'll be pretty tame," Jonmarc said. "After all, we've had *vyrkin* and *vayash moru* here in the caravan. Most people think they're monsters, but they're not. After that, what could still be strange?"

"My grandfather told stories about a show like that," Dugan said. "Said there were creatures who were cursed by the Lady, maybe even some that crawled out of the underworld."

Kegan rolled his eyes. "I heard the master healers talking about it. They said such things happen when the body's humours are shifted. Things get off center, odd, like when a wagon's wheel isn't on the axle right."

"Guess we'll see for ourselves," Jonmarc said. "You ready to go?"

Linton had loaned them a wagon for the occasion, more proof that the caravan master was seriously worried. When Jonmarc and the others reached the wagon, they found Trent, Corbin, and Zane the knife-thrower waiting for them, along with Karl. The men were dressed all in black, astride black horses so that they blended into the night.

"We'll follow you," Trent said. "And we'll wait outside the show. If all goes well, no one will know we're there."

Jonmarc had seen battle with Trent and the other men. Left unspoken was just how much trouble they could cause if things did not go well. Jonmarc's hand fell to the hilt of the large knife in its sheath on his belt. Wearing his swords would have been conspicuous, but Jonmarc would have felt better with a bigger blade at hand. He noticed that Dugan and Pol also wore knives. Kegan carried a stout walking stick.

"Tell me again why healers can bash someone over the head with a stick, but using a knife is forbidden?" Jonmarc asked, raising an eyebrow.

"I could, but you still wouldn't understand," Kegan replied. It was an old debate between them, mostly in jest.

Dugan already sat in the driver's seat of the wagon.

"Come on!" he urged. Jonmarc swung up beside him, while the others piled into the back. It was already dark, and Jonmarc watched the sides of the road for wolves. The ride to Dunleigh took less than half a candlemark, but Jonmarc found himself on edge, unable to get Alyzza's warnings out of his mind.

"There it is," Dugan said, pointing.

Pitched at the crossroads was a large tent, larger than the biggest of the caravan's enclosures. Torches burned on posts along a pathway leading to the tent, and the tent glowed with fire from within. As they drew closer, Jonmarc saw a large banner hung across the entrance. 'Monstrosities', he read. Beneath it was another banner in red, 'Come and see'. Outside the door stood a man collecting coins. A small line waited to enter.

Dugan pulled the horse and wagon off the road and threw the reins over the branch of a tree. Jonmarc knew that Trent and the others would keep an eye out for thieves. He glanced toward the shadows of the tree line, and spotted the men, although with their dark clothing and black horses, he would not have seen them if he had not known where to look. Reassured, he jangled the coin in his pocket. "Let's go," he said to the others.

Jonmarc and Dugan walked in front, with Kegan and Pol behind them. An unusually short, fat man held a chubby hand out for their coins. "One copper each," he said in a voice that sounded like it belonged to a roustabout.

The man watched them as they entered as if he thought they might set the tent afire. They walked past the tent flap, and stopped.

"Well now, that's not quite what I expected," Dugan murmured.

Stages were set up all along the tent's walls, each with a stranger exhibit than the last. In the center of the tent, several performances were underway. A small cluster of visitors milled about, tittering and pointing.

"Let's see what there is to see," Jonmarc said, heading toward the nearest stage. A man led a slow parade of animals across the platform, each more hideously deformed than the last. A two-headed calf balked at the lead, its second head hanging blackened and shrunken from its neck. Behind it was a sheep with three extra legs protruding from its body and hobbling its gait. A dog with a badly misshapen head followed, and a pig with two snouts.

Some of the onlookers jeered and laughed. Jonmarc felt a cold dread settle in his stomach. "There's something very wrong here," he said quietly.

"Agreed," Dugan replied.

On the next stage, an unnaturally muscular man held a huge snake. When Jonmarc and his friends drew closer, they realized that the snake was covered with large growths that rippled as it moved.

"Do you see the face?" Kegan whispered over Jonmarc's shoulder.

Jonmarc could not take his eyes from the snake. Beneath the scales and despite the elongated snout, the eyes that looked back at him were human.

"Just keep going," Jonmarc murmured. He glanced behind them and saw Pol straggling behind. "Keep up," he whispered. "We don't want to get separated."

The next stage had a large banner that read, 'See the Spider Girl'. A thin girl was on her hands and knees on the stage, with four sets of arms and legs. As Jonmarc and the others watched in horrified amazement, she reared back on two limbs, then moved through a series of contortions that defied even the skills of the acrobats Jonmarc had seen with Linton's caravan. Her body twisted and bent in places Jonmarc was certain there were no natural joints, and beneath the torch light, her skin had a gloss to it that looked like a carapace.

'The Human Bull' the next banner proclaimed. Kegan caught his breath as they came into view. The creature on stage was neither man nor beast. The head was broad like a bull but with human features, although a thick brass ring pierced the creature's nose. Massive shoulders ended in hooves, like the forequarters of a bull, while the bottom torso and legs were those of a man. The creature's skin was mottled with patchy bits of ox hide. The eyes in the distorted face were human, and as the beast was prodded to turn and parade for the jeering crowd, those eyes fixed Jonmarc's gaze with an anguished stare.

Every stage held a new transmogrification, each more hideous than the last. The '*Stawar*-Man' had the heavy head and shoulders of the big predatory cat and the spindly legs and scrawny body of a half-grown boy. It seemed to Jonmarc that whatever power had made the combinations took the weakest and ugliest portions of both.

Some of the wretches on the stages appeared to have been twisted and tangled by an angry god. Arms or legs were elongated far beyond their normal lengths, jointed backwards like a dog, or bent in unnatural ways. Under the banner of 'The Boneless Wonder', a gelatinous mass flopped on the stage like one of the creatures fished out of the deep sea, save for the desperate, all-too-human eyes.

"Let's get out of here," Jonmarc muttered.

But before they could turn, a ring of torch light flared in the center of the tent. The aimless crowd turned to stare at the figures moving into the flaming ring. One was an impossibly tall man dressed in a black frock coat and trousers, with high black boots. In front of him scuttled a half dozen pathetic creatures, grossly twisted and altered. Each was an unholy combination of human and animal parts, cobbled together by nightmares. The master snapped a white whip and the cursed beings limped and hobbled through their paces.

"Is that whip what I think it is?" Dugan wondered in horror. Pol edged closer for a better look.

"It looks like a spine," Kegan murmured, and his face had gone pale.

The audience cheered and clapped, catcalling and pointing. As the man with the frock coat took his bow, the torches flared again, and the next stage in the middle of the tent became the center of attention.

"Look at that," Dugan whispered as a man made his way on stage. His gait was hitched and his shoulders stooped, but all the audience cared about was the slender iron shaft that appeared to impale his skull, its ends obvious on either side of his hairless head. A woman shambled behind him. Hundreds of needles protruded from her skin everywhere on her body, as her scandalously brief scrap of clothing made clear. Behind her staggered a man with a lance through his belly, its point clearly evident poking through his shirtless back, its broken shaft penetrating his belly.

"I really think we need to go," Jonmarc hissed urgently. Kegan and Dugan seemed to share his uneasiness, but Pol was staring at the center stage with rapt attention. "Come on," he said, tugging at Pol's arm. "We're leaving."

The tent had grown more crowded since they had entered. Jonmarc had to shoulder his way through the press of people.

He glanced behind him, catching a glimpse of the others, only to be cut off again by the mob. It felt as if he were swimming upstream, caught in a current, and the tent's doorway looked much farther away than he remembered walking. Odd thoughts flitted through his mind, images best forgotten, random impulses that did not feel like his own. Impatiently, Jonmarc brushed them aside, focused on the door.

"You don't want to leave now," the fare man chided. "Things are just starting to get interesting."

Jonmarc pushed past him. "I've seen enough," he growled, striding toward the door. Everything he had seen disgusted him, yet as he stepped toward the darkness outside the tent, out of the warmth of the torches within, it felt as if something tugged at his sleeves and caught at his ankles to make him stop.

Fear welled up in him, deep in his gut. Jonmarc hurled himself across the threshold, bursting into the cold darkness of the spring night. Kegan stumbled out behind him, and Dugan nearly plunged face first into the dirt.

"Where's Pol?" Jonmarc said, wheeling to look behind them. The tent and everything in it vanished.

Jonmarc and the others stood staring, dumbfounded, at the empty space where the huge tent had been. Trent, Corbin, Karl, and Zane galloped up.

"Where's Pol?" Corbin demanded.

"He was a step behind us," Jonmarc said, staring aghast at the open field. "There was a crowd, and we had to push our way through. We got separated, but I saw him just behind Dugan, right before I made it through the door."

"I got the feeling that something didn't want us to leave," Kegan said. "Like it was pulling us back. Maybe Pol couldn't get loose."

Jonmarc and the others tramped across the field, assuring themselves that the traveling show was actually gone, and not just somehow hidden from view. Nothing remained, not even footpaths trodden over the dry grasses. Trent swore loudly, while Corbin looked near panic. Zane looked like he wanted to kill someone. Karl's mouth was a tight, angry line.

"We've got to find him. By the Crone! I'm responsible for that boy!" Corbin groaned.

"Let's get back to the caravan, and sort things out there. Nothing to be done here tonight," Trent said. He held up a hand to forestall Corbin's protest. "I'm not giving up on Pol. But standing in an empty field won't help him. I don't think they're going to reappear—at least, not here."

"I'll stay, to make sure," Corbin said, crossing his arms over his massive chest. "Until daylight. Just in case."

"I'll stay with him," Zane said. "The rest of you, go back." Jonmarc suspected that Zane did not expect the caravan to show up, but he would not allow Corbin to keep his vigil alone.

Jonmarc and the others rode in silence back to the caravan. Trent and Karl followed them, their cloaks thrown back and their swords visible. They saw no one on the return journey, but Jonmarc could not shake the feeling of being watched. Linton was waiting for them when they arrived.

"Well?" He asked expectantly, and then his face fell. "Wait—where are the others?"

"Pol disappeared, along with the entire tent and everything in it," Trent snapped. "Corbin and Zane are keeping watch where things were."

"Disappeared?" Linton repeated incredulously. "Come in and tell me all about it." They followed the caravan master to his tent, and he waved them to be seated. "Start from the beginning," he said.

Linton listened in silence as Jonmarc told the story, then peppered Dugan and Kegan with questions. Finally, he sat back and let out a long breath. "Well," he said, "I didn't expect that."

"The real question is: what do we do now? Corbin's beside himself." Trent said. "He won't leave without Pol."

"And there's no reason to think the monstrosities show will come back," Jonmarc replied. He looked from Trent to Linton. "I don't think the creatures we saw in there were accidents of birth. Magic did that—bad magic. And I think it took Pol."

Trent frowned. "Why do you think it wanted Pol and not any of the rest of you?"

Jonmarc searched for the words to express himself. "It seemed to speak to Pol," he said finally. "Kegan and Dugan and I didn't like what we saw. Most of the people around us were laughing, not taking it very seriously. But Pol seemed to be drawn to what was going on. And I think whatever it was called to him."

"Listen to the boy." They startled at the sound of the hoarse voice. Alyzza stood in the doorway, wrapped in a stained and torn gray cloak.

"What do you know of this?" Linton demanded.

"I know blood magic when I feel it," Alyzza rasped. "I heard the tale the boy told," she said with a nod toward Jonmarc. "That's not a mage you face; it's a *dimonn*."

"I don't care if it's the Formless One herself, how to we get Pol back?" Linton replied.

Alyzza made the sign of the Lady in warding. "Don't speak of such things, even in jest," she said, shaking her head. "Words have power."

"Those creatures you described, the ones in the tent," Karl said. "They sound like *ashtenerath*."

"That's foul magic you speak of," Linton said, fingering an amulet on a strap around his throat. "I pray you're mistaken."

"What are *ashtenerath*?" Dugan asked.

Karl met his gaze. "Men, twisted by blood magic and potions—and pain—until they're broken and mad, used to do the bidding of their maker. I've fought them on the battlefield."

"Can they be saved?" Kegan had gone pale at Karl's description.

"Not that I ever heard," Karl replied. "Just put out of their misery."

"I will not believe that of Pol, not until I see it myself," Trent's anger was clear.

"If it's magic that strong, what can we do?" Linton asked. "And what can a hedge witch do against a *dimonn*?"

Alyzza chuckled, a wheezing sound. "You might be surprised. Yes, you might," she replied, wagging a finger at Linton. "First, we call the *dimonn*, and then we trap him. Then, we get Corbin's boy back."

Trent sighed in exasperation. "She's mad," he said, beginning to pace. "Call a *dimonn*?"

Alyzza stood up to him and drew herself up to her full height. She was tiny compared to Trent's huge form, her head barely reaching his ribs, but her eyes sparked fire. "How else do you think you'll find him, huh? Ride every crossroads in the kingdom at midnight?" She shook her head. "You won't find him unless you call him."

"No one sane calls a *dimonn*!" Trent argued.

Alyzza laughed. "No," she agreed. "They don't. Do you want the boy back, or not?"

* * *

"Do you think the *dimonn* will come?" Dugan asked nervously as they crouched in the darkness. Only one night had passed since the ill-fated journey to the monstrosities show, but preparations for the evening's foray had taken nearly every candlemark.

"Alyzza thinks it will," Jonmarc replied.

"Maybe she's crazy," Kegan whispered.

Jonmarc watched the old woman as she unpacked her things from a satchel. "Maybe she is. Doesn't mean she's not right about this."

After picking up Corbin and Zane, they traveled half a candlemark from where the monstrosities show had appeared, to a crossroads Alyzza judged just right for the type of magic to be worked. Alyzza had insisted that each of them fill their pockets with iron nails, and she had made them all necklaces of iron nails to wear against their skin. She also prevailed upon Linton to give each of them a gold coin to hold for the night.

"This type of *dimonn* hates iron and gold," she told them. "That's why he didn't take a smithy like you," she said, thrusting a gnarled finger at Jonmarc. "It wouldn't want a healer," she said with a look at Kegan, "and you weren't going to feed it the way Pol would have," she added, glancing at Dugan.

"What do you mean by that?" Dugan challenged.

Alyzza chuckled. "Challenge the witch who's going to tangle with a *dimonn*, will you?" she said slyly. "*That's* what I mean. You're a fighter. *Dimonns* like the weak."

Jonmarc remembered Pol's hesitant stance, and the way he hung back from the conversation. Perhaps it was his nature, or the effect of the scars the pox left him with, but of the four of them, Pol had been the weakest. "It's my fault he came along," Jonmarc said. "I suggested it."

Alyzza gave him a glance that seemed to see down to his bones. "You meant no harm," she grated.

I never do, Jonmarc thought bitterly. *But in the end, someone dies.*

"There are different types of *dimonns*?" Trent asked.

Alyzza nodded. "Aye. And each with its own weaknesses and hungers. I've heard tell of this kind, the ones they call *gwyndullhan*, the 'form twister'." She made a sign of warding. "Not as many about as there used to be, thank the Lady. They served the Old Ones, like Konost and Shanthadura."

Jonmarc repressed a shiver. He knew the names of those beings from the bogey stories told to keep children close to the fires at night. As legends, they had frightened him as a child. Finding out they were true was terrifying.

"You have the other things I told you to bring?" she asked the others. One by one, they nodded. "Good," she said. "We'll need them—and the luck of the Lady."

This crossroads suited, Alyzza said, because there was a burying ground in sight, further down the valley. One of the roads led into the forest, and the other crossed a stream. Both augured well for the magic to be worked. Alyzza gathered her things, and turned to look at the small group that had come with her. Linton rode up to join them.

Alyzza led them to the center of the crossroads. She instructed them to step back, giving her room to pace off the circumference of a huge circle, which she drew with a line of salt. Then she walked widdershins around the circle, burning a bundle of sage as she muttered to herself.

"Stand just outside the circle," Alyzza ordered. "Leave an equal distance between each of you. The circle will contain the *dimonn*, if we're lucky. When it comes, do as I told you, but don't cross the circle. If the circle is broken, the *dimonn* is loosed."

And we all die, Jonmarc silently finished her sentence. Tonight he wore both swords, the last his father had forged. They remained sheathed. In each hand he held a length of iron rod, as did all the others. Trent and Corbin set up torches on iron poles to ring the circle and lit them.

Jonmarc looked to each side. Dugan and Kegan stood with him, and each looked terrified. He guessed that they saw the same fear in his face.

Alyzza carried a burlap sack with her into the center of the circle. She drew a knife and cut the burlap, seizing the frantic chicken inside. Alyzza held the bird aloft by its legs, paying no attention as its beak opened bloody tears on her arm.

Alyzza was muttering, but Jonmarc could not hear her words. She lifted the screeching bird once to each of the four quarters, and Jonmarc knew she called on the light Aspects of the Lady: Mother and Childe, Warrior and Lover. Walking widdershins once more, Alyzza offered the bird again, this time for the dark Aspects: Crone, Whore, Formless One, and the Dark Lady.

Abruptly, Alyzza raised her knife and plunged it into the squawking bird, then swung its carcass back and forth to sprinkle the dry ground with warm, fresh blood. Her chanting grew faster and louder, and Alyzza's footsteps grew quicker, until she was dancing within the warded circle, spattered with blood, her stained hands raised to the moon.

The night sky was clear, but a crack like thunder broke the stillness. Darkness obliterated the stars like a rift in the heavens. Out of the darkness a shadow descended, and became the form of a man dressed in black, holding a spine like a whip.

"We've come for what is ours," Alyzza demanded. "You are bound here, without power. Return Pol to us, unharmed, and be gone."

In the torchlight, the man's face was the color of a drowned corpse. His black eyes darted from side to side like flies on carrion, and his mouth was a bloody slash that ran from ear to ear. When he spoke, his voice was a low growl that raised the hair on the back of Jonmarc's neck, a voice from nightmares.

"You have no power over me, witch."

"Give us back Pol, and our business is finished," Alyzza said, raising her face defiantly to the *dimonn*.

"Take him from me," the *dimonn* challenged, throwing his right arm open and spreading his fingers wide. Pol appeared in the circle with him, but the night had worked a horrible change. Pol's pox scars were swollen into oozing pustules, covering his body in sores, twisting his features and nearly closing both eyes. His hands were crabbed into claws, and patches of his hair had fallen out.

Alyzza raised one hand, and a flash of light burst from her palm, driving the *dimonn* back.

The *dimonn* dissolved into dark mist and swept out of the way of the light, solidifying a few steps away. "You'll have to do better than that."

From the folds of her skirts, Alyzza withdrew a length of iron in one hand, and a gold piece in the other. "Fie," she muttered. "You are bound by iron and gold, sage and salt, blood and fire. Give me Pol—as he was."

At Alyzza's cue, each of the watchers held up their iron rods and gold coins. The *dimonn* turned to look at them, and the slash of a smile widened. "But what of those bound to me?" the voice grated.

Jonmarc heard footfalls behind him and spun around. Shadowy shapes approached from all sides. Even before he could make out their features, he knew them by their movement. The spider girl skittered with unnerving speed across the dry grass. The *stawar*-man prowled toward them with all the power of the legendary big cat. A dark, hulking shape lumbered toward them like a bull, and a thick shadow, low to the ground, undulated like a massive snake.

"They're all *ashtenerath*," Karl said. "Even the boy. He's past helping."

"Don't you dare say that!" Corbin challenged.

Karl dropped the gold piece into his pocket, then grabbed one of the torches from its sconce, holding the iron bar in his other hand. "Doesn't matter whether you believe me or not. It's the truth."

Jonmarc had barely gotten a torch in hand when the *stawar*-creature lunged for him. Powerful jaws with long fangs snapped just short of his arm as Jonmarc dodged aside. He thrust the torch at his attacker, then brought the iron bar down hard on its thick skull. The *stawar*-man let out a howl of rage and attacked again, barely missing him with its claws.

"Fire!" Karl shouted. "You've got to burn them!"

Jonmarc swung the bar again, slamming the creature on the side of the head. He heard bones break, and ichor oozed from the wide gash. Jonmarc jabbed again with the torch, going for the tattered clothing that hung from the creature's frame. The cloth caught fire, spreading to the fur, and the monster screamed as the flames engulfed it, a howl both animal and human.

Trent and Dugan together battled the spider-thing, hacking at its many legs, frustrated by its unnatural speed. Trent's sword sliced down with a stroke that should have snapped bone, only to skid along the hard carapace of the creature's skin. To Jonmarc's left, Corbin and Linton were hard-pressed to hold their own against the bull-monster. Linton jabbed with the torch, dancing around it like a drunken boxer, while Corbin rained down blow after blow that should have felled anything mortal. More of the things loomed in the shadows, shuffling their way toward the fight. Some moved faster than others, but it would not take many to overrun the rescue party.

Inside the warded circle, the *dimonn* and Alyzza were warily circling each other. Alyzza brandished her gold like a shield, while the *dimonn* flicked his bone whip, waiting for an opening.

A streak of blue-white lightning sizzled from Alyzza's outstretched hand, and at the same instant, the spine-whip snapped out. The lightning grazed the *dimonn*, sending him reeling, but the whip struck Alyzza on the shoulder and she stumbled.

"Not tonight!" Karl shouted, running toward the circle.

"Karl, no!" Jonmarc yelled, sprinting to intercept him. "You can't break the warding."

"There won't be a warding if that thing gets in another blow," Karl snapped, and with one leap, cleared the salt line without breaking it. Muttering a curse, Jonmarc followed an instant later.

Karl managed to land next to Alyzza, and he thrust the torch between her and the *dimonn*. "Go back to the depths where you came from, monster!" he shouted.

Jonmarc eyed the spine-whip as it flicked, and glanced toward Pol, who had inched his way closer to the fight. Jonmarc almost moved to intercept, but there was a flicker of something human enough in Pol's eyes to make him pause.

Alyzza had regained her footing, and she straightened, paying no heed to where the whip had laid open a gash on her shoulder. She raised her hands to chest level and opened them. With a word of power, iron nails flew like darts into the *dimonn's* body. Jonmarc struck at the arm with the whip, bringing his iron rod down on the *dimonn's* hand as he held his torch aloft. The whip flailed, knocking the burning brand from Jonmarc's hand and throwing it across the circle.

With a battle cry, Karl dove toward the *dimonn*, holding his torch like a lance. The *dimonn* shrieked an ear-splitting howl, opening its toothed maw wide. Alyzza seized a fistful of gold coins from her skirt and leapt forward, pouring the golden treasure into the *dimonn's* mouth. The *dimonn* began to smoke and shriek, falling to the ground though one hand scrabbled for its whip.

"Go." The voice sounded behind Jonmarc, drawn out like the shuddering breath of a dying man. Pol had grabbed Jonmarc's fallen torch, and his twisted hands held it in a tight grip.

"Pol!" Jonmarc shouted as the *dimonn* snatched back its whip and cracked it toward Jonmarc.

Pol fell toward the *dimonn*, impaling it with the torch, and blocking the whip's strike. The spine-whip cut Pol's flesh deep enough to show his ribs, but Pol held tight to the torch. Alyzza leveled another blast of blindingly bright light, and Jonmarc was struck by something heavy, taken off his feet, and thrown into the air. He landed hard on the dirt, still blinking from the flare, scrabbling to get to his feet before one of the *ashtenerath* attacked.

"You're safe," Trent said.

Jonmarc blinked again, and as his eyes adjusted, he saw the circle completely engulfed in flames. "Alyzza... Karl—"

"Right here," Karl assured him, sitting on the ground not far from Jonmarc. He spotted Alyzza near the circle but outside the warding, watching to assure herself that nothing escaped.

Flames lit the empty field bright as a bonfire. The misshapen creatures of the monstrosity show lay dead, cut down by the sword or burned by torches. Thick black smoke rose from the conflagration inside the circle, smelling of old blood and putrefying flesh.

Corbin was on his knees near the circle, head in his hands, grieving. Jonmarc stared into the fire, but nothing stirred.

"He was already dead, or near enough," Karl said quietly, coming up behind Jonmarc. "Too far gone to help."

"You don't know that," Jonmarc snapped.

"You can tell yourself that," Karl said. "But it was too late. Pol used the last bit of himself to save us. Honor that, and move on." He turned and walked away, toward the horses, and Jonmarc saw that Karl was limping.

Trent's heavy hand came down on Jonmarc's shoulder. "You're bleeding," he said, with a glance toward where the bone whip had knocked the torch from Jonmarc's hand. "Best get you back to a healer soon. A wound like that can go bad."

Jonmarc never took his eyes from the fire. "They were people once," he said. "All those *things*. Before they were monsters, they were people."

Trent nodded. "They always are."

BAD PLACES

"You're going to get him killed." Trent's voice carried in the cool air. The smoke from the blacksmith's forge hung on the wind as the coal fire grew hot enough to work.

"No, I'm trying to keep him from getting killed," Karl Steen argued. "He's going to go, prepared or not, and if he isn't prepared, he won't make it."

Jonmarc Vahanian slowed down, trying to listen without being seen. He was certain the conversation was about him, and his plans to leave Maynard Linton's caravan once they reached the border in order to sign on with one of the many mercenary troops in Principality.

"He doesn't need to leave," Trent snapped. "He's got a steady job with the caravan. Linton favors him. He's good at the forge—Corbin and I depend on him." Corbin, the caravan farrier, often borrowed Jonmarc from his apprenticeship with Trent. Blacksmiths and farriers went together like coal and iron.

"He's not ready to settle down," Karl replied. "This caravan is a last resort, a place people gravitate to when they've lost everything else."

"Which is why he came here in the first place," Trent said, banging the iron rods around more than necessary. "The kid's been through a lot. Being a soldier won't help." Trent knew most of Jonmarc's story, at least that he had lost his family to raiders and his wife and relatives to wild, magicked beasts. Some things he didn't know, like the part about the red-robed *vayash moru* mage whose bargain had led to the tragedy, a powerful enemy who was somewhere in Margolan still nursing a grudge against Vahanian.

"He's a natural fighter," Karl countered. "He's better with a sword at eighteen than most men are after several years in the army. Jonmarc picked up the Eastmark kick quickly— and that's a move few soldiers ever master."

"He's safe here." Trent's voice was a growl. Although the blacksmith was only ten years older than Jonmarc, in the year Jonmarc had traveled with the caravan, Trent had become not just his master but his friend, and he was as protective as an older brother.

"Men become mercs when they've got nothing left. They're a rough bunch, and the mercs who make it aren't the kind of people you want to know." From where Jonmarc stood, he could hear the squeak and blast as Trent pumped the bellows. "He doesn't have to end up like that."

"No one could have told me that at his age," Karl said. Karl, who had signed on a few months prior as one of the caravan's many hired guards. From what little he had shared with Jonmarc, Karl had done his time both as one of King Bricen's soldiers and as a merc. So had Trent. "How well would you have listened, at eighteen?"

Trent barked a harsh laugh. "Me? I didn't listen to anyone. Got me where I am today." There was a note of bitterness in his voice. Jonmarc knew almost nothing about Trent's life before the caravan, but here within the tight-knit group of the traveling company, Trent had a wife and children, a respected position, and the trust of the caravan's owner and impresario, Maynard Linton.

"The caravan isn't big enough for him, Trent," Karl said. There was a note of sadness in his voice that Jonmarc had never heard before, a jaded disappointment and a certainty that nothing ever went as planned. "He might come back to it someday, but he's got to strike out on his own, leave his ghosts behind. Most of us sign on with a troupe like this after we've spent all our dreams and come up a few coins short."

Jonmarc decided that he had eavesdropped long enough, so he made a noisy approach before he rounded the side of the blacksmith's lean-to and came into view.

"Hello Trent, Karl."

"You're late," Trent grumbled. The conversation had put Trent in a dark mood, and Jonmarc also guessed that Trent surmised the discussion had been overheard.

"Still trying to get the tents set up," Jonmarc said, although from the look on both men's faces, his excuse didn't fool anyone. "I got waylaid to help people on the way over."

"I'll see you when you're done with your work," Karl said, taking his leave. Jonmarc and Karl sparred nearly every night after he finished up in the forge and the supper fires were banked. In the months since Karl had signed on with the caravan, Jonmarc knew he had improved as a swordsman, and his natural skill only deepened his resolve to seek his fortune in Principality.

Maynard Linton's caravan traveled the breadth of the kingdom of Margolan, and occasionally into the neighboring kingdoms of Principality and Dhasson. Linton's marvelous troupe included acrobats, jugglers, musicians, and wild animal trainers, artisans and merchants, healers, tent riggers, hedge witches, and the assembly of wagon masters, cooks, farriers, blacksmiths, and guards that it took to keep such an entourage on the road. The individual members changed along the route as people came and went, but the caravan's ability to amaze and mystify never waned.

Linton had taken Jonmarc in when there had been nowhere else for him to go, and for that, Jonmarc would be forever grateful. But Karl had summed up Jonmarc's restlessness exactly, and as much as Jonmarc had come to care for his friends with the caravan, he was increasingly ready to strike out on his own and see what he could do. He suspected that Trent understood, even if he didn't like it.

"How long do you think we'll camp here?" Jonmarc said, tying on his leather apron and getting to work. "We're not going to draw any crowds in the middle of nowhere."

Trent shrugged and took out his frustrations on the hot bar of iron he worked on the anvil. "Not too long. Give everyone a rest after how busy it's been, fix the wagons and the tents, and pasture the horses."

"Linton decide yet which way we're going after this?" Jonmarc hurried to bring more coal for the fire and ready more iron bars in the forge, since he figured he was partially responsible for Trent's sullen mood.

"Not that I've heard," Trent muttered. "Linton keeps his own counsel—too much, if you ask me, and he doesn't." He struck the iron a few more times. "I've already told him what I think. Too damn dangerous trying to take everyone across on barges down by the floating city. I'd much rather go across the North Bridge—soldiers be damned."

Jonmarc had heard Trent's thoughts on the matter before. If they went north, a large bridge connected Margolan and Principality across the wide Nu River. That bridge, however, was guarded by King Bricen's troops and those who crossed not only paid a toll, their goods were subject to inspection.

Since the caravan made some of its money by smuggling,

Jonmarc understood why Linton was loathe to subject his wagons to the inquiries of the king's guards. The alternate route involved going south to a less formal arrangement of river traders who would take groups across for a fee, no questions asked. Trent and Corbin had already expressed their opinions about the traders, but Jonmarc expected Linton would take the southern route. He was also curious about what everyone called a 'floating city', an arrangement of houseboats, barges, rafts, and other boats that tied up to each other when the mood struck them and went their separate way when necessity required.

"How did Linton pick this forsaken spot to camp?" Jonmarc asked. Usually, the caravan chose an open meadow large enough for the performance tents and trader's stalls, with room in the back for the tents, wagons and lean-tos of the crew, plus their horses, cook fires, and the moveable blacksmith's forge. When they were performing, the meadow also had to be close to well-traveled routes and several towns or villages in order to bring in plenty of customers.

Trent shrugged. "Nice and flat, out of the way, not likely to get us into trouble with anyone. And there's a village not too far up the road where we can buy provisions. We've camped worse places." He paused. "Not much traffic on this part of the road. I saw a single rider earlier today, nothing since then."

Northeastern Margolan was not as thickly populated as the southern half of the kingdom. The ground was rockier, the grazing lands sparser, and the weather colder. Since they had left the Midlands, towns and villages had been smaller and farther between. Farms looked poorer here, and even the taverns and inns they passed along the road seemed down on their luck.

Maybe Jonmarc shouldn't have been surprised, given all that, when the caravan found a large flat open space dotted by small hills. There was a clear stream nearby for water, a stand of trees for wood, and good pasture for the horses. They had arrived that morning and the camp was still busy setting up. But something about the place made Jonmarc uncomfortable. He felt on edge, as if they were being watched, yet no one else was around. That bothered him too, the isolation of the place. He kept his thoughts to himself, since his opinion of the caravan's camping spot was of no importance to anyone.

After a morning in the forge, Jonmarc headed toward the cook wagons to bring back lunch. The caravan sprawled out across the grassy meadow. Without the need to put up the big performance tents and the avenue of food vendors and merchant's stalls, the group pitched camp quickly, gathering their tents and wagons around the central area where the small team of cooks set out their fires and cauldrons.

Jonmarc could smell roasting meat and vegetables. Lunch was likely stew, since it made the most of whatever meat was cheap and whatever vegetables were at hand. Most of the time, the caravan's cooks served up food that was edible and warm, which was all Jonmarc cared about.

"We shouldn't be here!" The raspy voice turned heads and brought frowns. "We're all in danger! This is a bad place. A very bad place."

Jonmarc turned as Alyzza, one of the caravan's hedge witches, stalked past with the zeal of a prophet. Her gray hair fell long and tangled, and she was stoop-shouldered, with a lined face and stained clothing. She leaned on a gnarled walking stick, but her step was quick and sure and her eyes flashed with anger. Many in the caravan thought her crazy, and perhaps she was, but Jonmarc had seen her power and knew it to be real.

"Danger!" Alyzza shouted to any who would listen. "We must leave before nightfall. We are not meant to be here. This is a bad, bad place."

The others turned away, shaking their heads, but Jonmarc paused. "Why is it bad?" he asked.

Alyzza looked at him for a moment as if trying to place him, and then she smiled in recognition and nodded. "You were there," she said in a wheezy rasp. "The night the monsters came. You saw the *dimonn*."

Jonmarc nodded. "I was there. And I saw what you did."

Alyzza gave a breathy chuckle. "Crumbs. That's what left of my power now. Just crumbs. I lost my power when I lost my mind." She tapped her forehead with two broken-nailed fingers. "But not completely," she said, her eyes alight. "I've got enough left to know we should not be here."

"Why not?" Jonmarc asked, intrigued enough to fish for the answer from her crowded, cluttered mind. When the caravan had been threatened by a hungry spirit that yearned for blood and pain, Alyzza's power helped defeat the *dimonn*. He had an inkling of what she could do, and her warning worried him.

"Do you see those hills?" she asked, pointing at the rolling slopes that bounded the valley.

"Yes," he answered uncertainly.

"Those aren't hills!" she snapped. "They're barrows. Cairns. Ancient burying places. Restless spirits dwell inside, and worse things. Much, much worse things," she replied, her eyes wide. "Don't you wonder why no one else lives in this pretty meadow? Because they know better, that's why. They stay away, because this is a place of the dead. And if we don't leave before sunset, the dead will have their due!"

Karl and one of the other guards ambled up. "Come on, Alyzza. Stop scaring the folks," Karl said with a friendly grin. The other guard looked at Alyzza warily.

Alyzza tossed her head and stood, one hand grasping her walking stick, and the other hand on her hip. "If you were doing your job to guard these people, you'd insist Linton move the camp right now!" she said defiantly.

Karl's grin slipped just a bit. "Look, Alyzza, you've made your case to Linton and you've already given the rest of the caravan your opinion. We'll have the usual night watch plus our *vayash moru* guards. There's not going to be trouble, way out here."

Alyzza's eyes blazed. "Not from the living. But can you protect these people from the barrow wights?"

The second guard guffawed. "Them's just tales told to keep children in at night," he countered. "You don't believe them, do you?"

Alyzza's glare stopped his laughter. "I don't have to believe in them," she said, jabbing her walking stick against his chest for emphasis. "I've seen what they can do. And mark my words—someone will die if we don't leave here by nightfall."

"That's enough," Karl said, all humor gone from his face. "Come along. You're causing a scene."

"I meant to cause a scene!" Alyzza shrieked. "We need to leave this place!"

Karl moved toward Alyzza as if he meant to take her by the shoulder. Alyzza raised one gnarled hand, and Karl stumbled backwards as if thrown. She gestured toward the second guard, and he fell flat on his ass in the dirt. Jonmarc saw the anger on the guards' faces, and stepped up before either man got back on his feet.

"Come on, Alyzza," he said in the voice that had always won over his mother in an argument. "I'll walk you back to your tent, and I promise to take your warning to Trent. You know he and Corbin have Maynard's ear."

"Thank you, young man," Alyzza said, accepting his offer to take her arm. With a warning look at Karl and the guard to stay back, Jonmarc escorted Alyzza around the thickest part of the crowd, back to the tattered tent she called home.

A ring of salt circled the tent. Bunches of feathers and the bones of small animals tufted the ridge of the tent. A weathered post with a bleached rabbit skull guarded the entrance, festooned with garlands of dried herbs and seed pods and stone disks etched with runes. He stopped outside the salt circle.

Alyzza turned to look at him, and her eyes were clear of madness. She took hold of his arm with her bony hand. "The barrow wights lie," she hissed. "They show faces that aren't their own. Shake off the lie, and free the others."

Her eyes clouded again and she turned abruptly, making her way carefully over the salt boundary and back into the tent. Jonmarc stared after her for a moment, then turned, remembering that he had not yet retrieved the lunches for which he had been sent.

He walked back to the cook circle, deep in thought. He'd had some experience with old graves and the ghosts that haunted them, and it had cost him everything he loved. He had heard stories of barrow wights, evil spirits that haunted the dead places, showing themselves to lure the unsuspecting to their deaths. Most people believed in the stories enough to steer clear of known barrows, but laughed about the legends in the light of day.

"Jonmarc! You're late for lunch. Better get there before Dugan eats it all!" Kegan, one of the apprentice healers, called out to Jonmarc as he approached the cook fires. Dugan was a junior rigger, and both young men were close to Jonmarc's age.

"You look like you've been in a fight," Jonmarc said, taking in Dugan's appearance. He had a black eye and scratches on one cheek.

Dugan grimaced. "It's one of those days," he said. "I swear, just because we aren't setting up for a show, people are letting their tempers get the best of them. I helped Corbin break up a fight between two men over a bet gone bad, then one of the horses Corbin was shoeing broke loose and damn near trampled one of the handlers. Took five of us to get the horse back under control."

Kegan swallowed his bite of food and nodded. "Aye, it's the same thing over in the healers' tents. We've patched up the oddest assortment of stupid injuries just since the caravan pitched tent. One fellow smashed his foot with a sledge hammer putting up his tent, and other almost lost a finger chopping wood. One of the other woodcutters brained himself when a tree fell badly, and we've treated about a dozen bites—horses, dogs, even the goats."

"Folks are tired," Dugan said, grabbing another piece of bread from the hearth before the cook swatted his hand. "We've done twenty shows in as many days, with no time off. Makes people testy—animals, too."

"Tell him about the rider we saw," Kegan prompted.

Dugan rolled his eyes. "You've got too much imagination."

"Do not!" Kegan replied. Since Dugan wouldn't oblige him, Kegan took up the tale himself. "I saw a lone rider on a strong horse ride by—the only traveler on the road past us all day, mind you." He dropped his voice. "I think he was a highwayman. All in dark clothes, with a studded leather cuirass and a baldric, and a wicked-looking sword. He didn't look like he was from around these parts."

"Probably a soldier," Dugan said with a wry expression.

Kegan drew himself up. "I know what King Bricen's soldiers look like and they don't look like him."

"One of the local noble's men then," Jonmarc suggested.

Kegan looked unconvinced. "So you say now. But if there's trouble, mind my words! I tried to warn you."

Dugan gave him a friendly slug in the shoulder. "Enough of that! Folks are tired and grouchy without talk of brigands. Keep your tales to yourself, and we won't have any trouble."

Jonmarc wasn't so sure about that, but he said nothing. He waited for the cook to ladle stew into the two tin bowls and hand him several of the thin hearth cakes to go with them. "I'd better get back to the forge or Trent will have an earful for me," he said, and then paused. "Be careful tonight."

Dugan and Kegan grinned. "You know us. We're always careful!"

"No, I mean it. Old Alyzza says there are ghosts in those hills."

Dugan and Kegan had seen Alyzza's power as well, and they sobered quickly. "You sure?" Dugan asked.

"Does Linton know?" Kegan glanced around, as if he might see spirits rising from the barrows in the light of day.

"Yes to both," Jonmarc said, dropping his voice. "Maybe there's nothing to it. Half the time, I think she's crazy," he added. "But the other half—"

They nodded. "Aye, we'll keep an eye out," Kegan said.

Satisfied that he had done all he could, Jonmarc hiked back to the forge with the lunches. Trent glanced up when he walked in.

"Did they move the cook fires to Principality?" he asked, looking askance at Jonmarc.

"It's a little crazy out there," Jonmarc said, holding out the tin bowl of stew as a peace offering.

He and Trent walked away from the forge's smoke to stand outside, looking out over the camp. "Have you heard about anything unusual going on?" he asked.

Trent frowned. "Unusual, how?"

Jonmarc shrugged. "Just... not right." He paused and took a few bites of his stew, tearing off some of the chewy hearth cake to go with it.

Trent looked at him oddly, then nodded. "Aye. Corbin stopped by to see if I could spare you for a couple of candlemarks to help with the horse shoeing. Seems all the horses are a mite skittish today," he said.

"Dugan said as much," Jonmarc replied. "Had a black eye to show for it, when one of the horses got loose."

Trent nodded. "Linton wandered in, complaining more than usual. Said it felt like a full moon, with the way people are acting. Didn't go into details, but I figured tempers were shorter than usual."

Jonmarc hesitated, then worked up the courage to ask his question. "Do you think it's true? That those are barrows, not hills?"

Trent glanced at him sharply. "Who said that?"

Jonmarc recounted his run-in with Alyzza and her dire predictions. Trent said nothing as he finished his stew, then set the bowl aside and rocked back and forth on his heels as if debating how to answer.

"Hard to tell, just by looking at them," Trent said finally. "If they're barrows and cairns, they're very old." He shrugged. "Thing is, down through the ages, lots of people have died and been buried. Probably bodies under our feet no matter where we go. They don't all get up and walk."

True enough, Jonmarc thought. Then again, he'd heard the warnings about barrows ever since he was a young boy. No doubt, in part, they warned children not to wander off. But his own experiences made him believe that at least sometimes, there was more to it.

"Do you think they're real? The ghosts, I mean," Jonmarc asked, finishing the last of his stew.

Trent shrugged. "What do I know about such things? I'm just a blacksmith." He poured some water from the bucket to rinse out his empty bowl, and Jonmarc did the same, then he handed the nearly empty bucket to Jonmarc.

"What I do know is that iron won't bend itself," he said. "And that we need more water from the creek. Let's go. Work to be done. Time's a-wastin'."

"TURN OUT! TURN out!" The crier ran through the caravan camp, banging on a tin pot with a spoon. The sound of eight bells had just rung from the village down the road, and the supper fires were banked for the night.

In minutes, the entire caravan crew had gathered, leaving their tents, wagons, and campfires. Linton rarely sounded the general alarm, so people came with weapons and buckets, expecting either attack or fire.

"Listen up!" Maynard Linton shouted. He was a stout, sturdily built man in his early thirties, the indefatigable impresario behind the most successful traveling caravan in Margolan. Linton had no qualms about bending the law when it suited him, but he was uncompromising in his protection of his nomadic crew of performers. "We've got a missing child."

Jonmarc, Kegan, and Dugan had been playing cards and drinking ale around one of the large campfires. They shouldered up to the crowd, listening intently.

"Shouldn't be too hard to find her," Linton yelled, his voice carrying clearly on the cool night air. "But the meadow's pretty big. And of course, there're the trees, we need to look there as well."

"Who're we looking for?" one of the men in the back asked.

"Kettie, the tinker's daughter," Linton replied. "She's four-years old, dark hair, wearing a pink dress." He paused. "Everyone grab a torch or a lantern, and let's get going. It's chilly out tonight."

Heading into late summer, the caravan's crew numbered around seventy-five people, although that changed frequently as performers joined up or went on to other things. One group of men went to search the stand of trees, while two more groups headed down the road in both directions, calling for Kettie. That left a large party to search the meadow, lining up in long rows to make sure no bit of grass or gully was missed.

"Did you see that?" Kegan whispered.

"See what?" Jonmarc asked.

"The bright balls, in the sky," Kegan said, pointing. Jonmarc was about to make a snide remark about stars when he saw what Kegan was talking about. Scattered around the meadow, pulsing orbs of blue-white light flew and floated, streaking high into the sky and then dropping to just above the tall grass, bobbing and weaving.

"I don't know, and I'm not sure I want to know," Jonmarc replied, remembering Alyzza's warning. "Best to stay out of their way."

Jonmarc looked out over the meadow. While the group made its way in a fairly orderly fashion across the flat land, searchers were avoiding the hills. Now that it was dark, they seemed to be wreathed in shadows that were darker than elsewhere.

"What's that noise?" Dugan asked.

Jonmarc frowned. "What?" Then he heard it, a low moan that seemed to rise from everywhere and nowhere. "Just an owl," he replied. But the moan came again, too human to be a bird.

"That's not an owl," Dugan said, eyes widening. "Maybe Alyzza was right."

"None of that," Jonmarc snapped, though his own nerves were on edge. "Keep a watch out for the girl."

The farther into the meadow they walked, the darker the night seemed, despite their torches. Where the caravan was camped, the barrows formed a line on either side of the clearing, leaving a large flat space in the middle. But as they got deeper into the meadow, the land under their feet rose and fell in shallow hills, making Jonmarc wonder if the entire area had been a burial ground, and the low undulations were old barrows time had worn away.

The meadow was broad, and by the time the search party reached the center, Jonmarc noticed that their lines had broken down, and searchers were wandering freely without any organization. The night seemed too quiet, and when Jonmarc concentrated, he heard none of the usual night noises of owls, crickets, and the distant howl of wolves. The silence was eerie and unnatural, as if someone had lowered a clear dome over the area, cutting it off from the rest of the world while allowing the stars to shine through.

The stars. Jonmarc had looked up at the night sky at the beginning of the search, confirming the time from the bell tower with the position of the constellations. Yet now, looking into the black canopy, the stars were wrong.

Jonmarc shook his head and blinked, sure he was just tired, but when he looked once more, the constellations were not as they should be.

"Kegan! Dugan!" Jonmarc shouted to his friends, who were each a stone's throw away from him, but they did not turn, or even flinch as if they had heard.

The orbs glowed brighter as the stars receded. The moon was bright, and the meadow should have been awash in moonlight as well as the glow of the torches carried by the searchers. And yet, shadows pooled around the barrows, so dark that the torchlight did not dispel them.

A chill ran down Jonmarc's back. The night had grown unseasonably cold. It had been a cool late summer evening when they had set out for the search. Jonmarc's breath misted in the air. He shivered, but not from the cold. The longer they stayed in the meadow, the more certain he grew that Alyzza's warning was correct.

A cool wind raised the hair on the back of Jonmarc's neck as it slipped by. Mist was rising from the tall grass, faint tendrils of fog at first, then mingling with the torch smoke in a haze that blanketed the meadow and made it difficult to see more than a few steps ahead.

Jonmarc. The voice was faint, but it stopped him in his tracks, eyes wide and heart pounding.

Jonmarc. Louder now, and unmistakable. His heart caught in his throat. It was a voice he heard in his dreams, his memories, but would never hear again this side of the Gray Sea. Shanna, his wife, dead and buried almost a year. Jonmarc peered into the fog. He could make out Shanna's image, recognizable but distorted, like a reflection on water.

You left us. The voice was his mother's. Jonmarc wheeled, catching just a glimpse of her before the fog shifted. *Your brothers and I died because you left us.*

"Not true," Jonmarc murmured. "I went with father to fight the raiders. You were supposed to be safe at home."

You called the beasts that killed me. Shanna's voice, echoing Jonmarc's deepest shame and fear. He had gone into the burial caves to bring back a talisman for a mage who offered him enough gold to provision his family for a year, and that night, monsters had descended on his village, killing everyone but him. He'd thrown the talisman back into the caves, sure it had brought the beasts.

"I didn't know," he murmured. "You've got to believe me. I didn't know."

One by one, the images coalesced in the fog. His three younger brothers, killed by the same raiders that slaughtered his father and most of their village and left Jonmarc for dead. Shanna and her mother, who had found him and taken him in. Friends and neighbors in their village who had given the orphaned young man refuge, until the beasts destroyed everything. All because of a raider's curse.

The ghosts surrounded him, eyes accusing, demanding atonement. Tears streaked down Jonmarc's face as the old grief welled up anew. His intentions didn't matter. He had failed them. Failed them all.

"I'm sorry," he said raggedly. "I'm so sorry."

The ghosts crowded closer, faces contorting in anger, bent on revenge. And as they grew nearer, Jonmarc remembered what Alyzza had said.

The barrow wights lie. The faces they show aren't their own.

Jonmarc closed his eyes, concentrating on Alyzza's words, repeating them under his breath. "You're not real," he muttered. "Shanna, mother, the rest of you, you're not here. I buried you. I mourned you. You are dead."

He opened his eyes, and though the fog remained, the ghosts had vanished.

Voices carried across the meadow. Some wailed in fear, others keened in grief, and some shouted in anger. Free of the illusion, Jonmarc saw the mist roiling like a storm at sea, covering the meadow like a shroud, separating each searcher into a private well of despair.

"Alyzza!" he shouted. "Where are you?"

Jonmarc began to run through the thick fog. Kegan was the first person he came to, huddled on the ground in a ball with his arms thrown over his head, shaking with fear.

"Kegan! It's not real. There's nothing out there." Jonmarc coaxed, but Kegan flailed at him when he tried to raise his friend to stand, fighting with a wide-eyed terror that told Jonmarc Kegan could see nothing but the visions of the barrow wights.

Trent stood a short distance off, sobbing in grief. "Come on, Trent," Jonmarc begged, reaching for the blacksmith's shoulder. "It's a trick. It's magic. They're not real."

Trent shook off his hand, weeping so hard that he gasped for breath. "I was wrong," he groaned, talking to ghosts only he could see. "I was wrong. Forgive me. Please, please forgive me."

Then Jonmarc spotted three shapes moving toward him through the fog. At first, they were silhouettes, but more solid than the apparitions. They grew closer, and he stood ready, sword raised. The three shapes stepped through the curtain of mist, and Jonmarc recognized Hans, Jessup, and Clark, three of the caravan's *vayash moru*.

"Did you see visions?" Jonmarc asked, lowering his sword once he had assured himself of their reality.

Hans nodded. "Aye. But we're undead. Ghosts don't have the same hold over us that they do with the rest of you.

"Where's Alyzza?" Jonmarc asked. "If there's anyone who can send those spirits back where they came from, it's her."

"We'll find her," Hans promised. Jessup and Clark nodded their agreement. "And if there's aught we can do, just name it. The caravan is our home, too."

The three *vayash moru* split up, and Jonmarc took off again, searching for the hedge witch, making his way through the fog around the paralyzed forms of his friends and fellow caravaners. "Alyzza!" He shouted again. "Alyzza!"

Jonmarc had seen Alyzza hold her own against a *dimonn* and its *ashtenerath* minions. Getting free of the *dimonn's* power had nearly killed them all. That was one *dimonn*. But the wraith-like wights that rose from the barrows and ghosted along the fog numbered in the hundreds.

He had run the length of the meadow, searching for Alyzza, hoping to find someone else who was not under the sway of the barrow wights' magic. The largest mound loomed at the meadow's edge near the line of oak and elm trees. The fog swirled heaviest around this ancient barrow. Spirits circled the barrow, and a dark opening gashed the side of the mound. The body of the missing child, pale and still lay sprawled at its threshold. He ran to her, hoping to get her to safety, only to find that she was already dead.

"Alyzza!" Jonmarc shouted, searching the mist. Then he spotted her, standing between three of the largest barrows, and ran to catch up with her, fearing that at any moment, something worse than the wights might escape and doom them all.

Bundles of dried herbs hung from twine like a mantle around Alyzza's shoulders. Jonmarc recognized agrimony, boneset, and hyssop among the herbs, all powerful against evil and restless spirits. Bits of gemstone—amber, citrine, and chalcedony—were strung together on a lanyard around her neck, and the twine of the lanyard was knotted in a complicated pattern that increased its magic.

Alyzza carried her staff with the rabbit skull, and with her tattered robes and wild gray hair, she looked like something out of legend. At her feet was a squirming burlap bag and a branch from a fir tree.

"What do we do?" Jonmarc asked. He had drawn his sword, but it was of no use against the legions of restless spirits. He spotted Corbin and Karl, transfixed by the wights, their strength and fighting skill of no use against this disembodied enemy.

"I'll break their hold," Alyzza said. "My power is a shadow of what it used to be, but it'll suffice for this, I think. You wake them up. The wights are draining them. That's how the spirits get their power. They took the child to summon the power to leave their barrow. The big mound, the elder barrow, is the hub."

She took Jonmarc's hand and pressed a lump of salt and a silver coin into his palm. "Keep that on you," she said. "It will help clear your head and protect you from the wights." He poured the mixture into a pouch on his belt.

Alyzza grasped the staff in her left hand and stretched out her right hand, palm out toward the gaping hole in the side of the barrow. She spoke a word of power, and energy crackled from her outstretched hand, burning across the mist, striking deep in the darkness of the open hole. "Go!" she shouted.

Jonmarc, Hans, Clark, and Jessup ran through the fog, shouting and waving their arms in an attempt to rouse their comrades from the wights' visions. Jonmarc shook Kegan by the shoulders, leaning so close he was shouting in Kegan's face. Kegan continued to sob and mutter, bound by the nightmare vision, completely oblivious to anything Jonmarc did.

The three *vayash moru* had no better luck with the caravaners they tried to rouse. Desperate, Jonmarc ran to Dugan, then to Karl and Trent, and finally to Linton, shouting until he was hoarse. He backhanded Linton across the face, but the caravan master regarded him with a blank stare, murmuring a heartbroken confession to whomever he had wronged.

"It's not working!" Jonmarc shouted.

"Then get back here and help me hold off what's in there," Alyzza countered, with a jerk of her head toward the elder barrow.

"Hold out your sword," Alyzza commanded when he reached where she was standing. He did so, and she laid her hand on the flat of the blade, muttering words Jonmarc could not catch. The blade glowed with a faint greenish light.

"Guard the tomb," she said. "For as long as I can hold the magic, your sword will keep the worst from passing."

Jonmarc stood facing the dark hole that gaped into the ancient barrow. He planted his feet wide, holding the sword with both hands, trusting in Alyzza's power since he was certain that steel alone posed no threat to whatever dwelled in the darkness.

Standing in the center of the clearing surrounded by the three largest barrows, Alyzza cast a warded circle of salt and silver coins and walked widdershins to seal it. With a guttural cry, she raised her willow rod high above her head and then plunged it down into the ground.

Chanting loudly, Alyzza walked widdershins around the circle two more times. She drew a boline knife from her belt, and reached down for the squawking burlap bag. Grasping it by the tied-off mouth, she held it up, invoked the words of power, and plunged her knife into the squirming mass, drawing her knife down in one swift stroke.

Her knife ripped open the bag and dug deep into the body of a black chicken, sending its bloodied feathers flying. She made a circle around her staff, pouring out the chicken's blood onto the ground and tore bits of dried leaves from the bundles of herbs she wore on the mantle around her shoulders.

When she had circled the staff again, Alyzza raised her voice chanting in a strange language. She grasped the willow staff and raised it, and a loud cry tore from her throat.

"Akanathani!"

A blinding, pure white light streamed from the upraised staff. It rolled out from where Alyzza stood, like ripples in a pond, waves of glowing power that blasted across the meadow, making it bright as day.

The light swept the fog and the malicious spirits back like a gale. For a moment, the crew of the caravan, frozen in their places by their nightmare visions, staggered.

The light faded as fast as it flared, and the fog and the ghosts rolled in like a storm surge, taking back their captives. Even without magic, Jonmarc could sense a shift in the energy. Before, the barrow wights had merely been hungry for the energy of the living. Now, after Alyzza had challenged their power, the spirits were angry.

He blinked, and saw that Hans, Jessup, and Clark had joined him. The three *vayash moru* took up places so that, together, they and Jonmarc made a semi-circle around the dark gash in the barrow's side.

"Alyzza!" Jonmarc shouted, still standing guard at the mouth of the entrance to the barrow. "Something's coming!"

Deep within the shadows of the barrow, Jonmarc could see movement. The maw of the barrow smelled dank and cold, stinking of moldering cloth and rotted flesh. He had no time to grieve the dead child. He feared they would all join her soon if worse things than the wights emerged from within the ancient tomb.

Whatever was coming from deep inside the barrow dragged heavily across the ground, its labored steps growing louder by the moment. The thing inside the mound hissed and growled, guttural noises that sounded to Jonmarc like a predator sniffing out its prey.

A large black shape like a massive, elongated wild cat sprang from the darkness, bounding toward Jonmarc. Red eyes glowed like coals and long fangs snapped. Jonmarc stood his ground, hoping that whatever enchantment Alyzza had placed on his sword was sufficient to hold the beast at bay.

The greenish glow of the ensorcelled sword reflected off the mist like foxfire. Jonmarc's hands trembled as he swung the sword to block the ghostly beast's path. It dodged one way and then another, taunting him, yet wary of the luminescent blade that barred its path. *It won't tire, but I will,* he thought grimly.

Alyzza was chanting again within her circle of salt and silver. Jonmarc could hear tiredness and desperation in her voice.

The wight-cat sprang at Jonmarc faster than he could react. Hans moved with *vayash moru* speed, knocking Jonmarc to the ground and coming up under the beast with his own sword. Han's sword was not spelled, but he had the advantage of undead strength and speed. Jessup jumped into the fray an instant later, and the two of them stabbed at the spectral cat with their swords, but every time, their blades found nothing but mist.

The cat-thing howled again, and reared back. Its massive paw struck Jessup across the head and chest, and its long claws dug so deeply into his flesh that it severed his head. Jessup's body crumbled into ash.

Hans and Clark let out a battle cry and lunged toward the creature again. Jonmarc regained his feet, and circled, looking for an opening. He had neither the speed nor the strength of the *vayash moru*, nor their centuries of experience. But Jessup had been a good man, and Jonmarc was angry at his death and that of the tinker's daughter. *If we can't kill this thing, we're all going to die anyhow*, he thought as he struck at the monster.

His sword connected with the thing's haunches, and its blade flared as Jonmarc sank it deep into the cat-thing's shape. To his amazement, his sword found purchase, and it felt as if the blade was ripping into cold corpse-flesh, not the dark mist that met the weapons of the *vayash moru*.

The creature shrieked in anger, but Jonmarc sank the blade hilt-deep. The monster gave a shake, and Jonmarc went flying, his sword still firmly in his grip. Black droplets sprayed the air, not blood but something like it, as the cat-thing yowled in rage.

"We'll distract—you attack!" Hans shouted. Jonmarc could see in Hans's face that the *vayash moru* wanted vengeance for the death of his friend. Hans and Clark began to dodge and weave around the cat-creature as Jonmarc got to his feet. When the thing's attention was on the two *vayash moru*, Jonmarc made his move, running at full speed for the monster's rib cage. He leapt into the air, using his momentum to help him drive his glowing blade between the cat-thing's ribs, into the place where a heart should be.

His sword sank deeply into the corpse-flesh of the creature. Black ichor gushed over Jonmarc's hands, splashing his face and chest, covering him to the elbows. The cat-thing snapped at him with its fangs, grabbing at his cloak and tearing him away from the wound, sending him and his sword sprawling.

Jonmarc dug his hand into his pouch and grabbed a fistful of the salt and silver, hurling it into the creature's face. It reared back, just for an instant, then lunged forward again, intent on its prey.

The wight-cat raised its paw to rake Jonmarc with its claws. Just as the paw descended, a wide-bladed sword swung between the creature and Jonmarc, blocking its strike. A dark-clad stranger stood between Jonmarc and the monster, holding his *stelian* sword in a two-handed grip. The newcomer ran at the cat-thing with a cry, fighting it back to give Jonmarc time to regain his feet.

"Who in the name of the Crone are you?" Jonmarc rasped. He was grateful for the help, but wary.

"My name is Madeg, from among the Sworn." Madeg and the creature regarded each other warily, each waiting for an opening to strike.

Madeg wore a dark tunic and trews, with a cloak of mottled brown. In his hand was a wicked-looking *stelian* sword, neither broadsword nor scimitar, but a deadly, jagged flat blade of *damashqi* steel. Jonmarc had heard of those fabled swords, crafted with magic as the metal was folded again and again on itself. Such blades were rare, priceless, and powerful.

Across Madeg's chest was a leather baldric that held a large number of knives, and around his throat, on leather cords, hung amulets and charms. The stranger had black hair, tawny skin and amber eyes, the same color as the eyes of the Sacred Lady, the goddess. He wore studded leather armor under his cloak. On his baldric were dozens of *damashqi* daggers.

"I hope you're up for a fight," Jonmarc replied.

The wight-cat's retreat was short. Enraged, the creature stalked him, intent on exacting revenge for its injuries.

Hans and Clark ran at the monster, slashing at it with their swords and launching themselves onto its back where they stabbed their blades down again and again until the creature dissolved beneath them, only to emerge a few feet past them.

"Your blades are the only ones that hurt that thing!" Hans shouted to Madeg and Jonmarc.

Jonmarc looked up just as the cat-thing suddenly changed direction, making a lightning-quick turn and lunging toward Hans. The creature snapped its sharp teeth shut over Hans' body, and its fangs sank deep into his flesh, snapping him in two. Hans's body disintegrated.

The thing is solid when it wants to be, mist when it doesn't for everything except my sword and Madeg's, Jonmarc thought.

Clark gave a howl of fury and made a headlong run at the creature. It swung its huge paw at him, pinning him to the ground with its full weight. The cat swiveled its head, fixing its red eyes on Jonmarc, issuing a challenge. It dug its sharp claws into Clark. The *vayash moru* screamed in pain. The blow would have killed a mortal; Clark would remain in agony until the creature clawed him through the heart or tore off his head.

Madeg gave a roar and ran at the cat-thing, chanting as he swung his long *stelian* blade. The magic in his sword and the skill of his swordsmanship inflicted more damage than Jonmarc's strikes, but Jonmarc remained ready, fearing that even one of the Sworn might be outmatched alone.

The cat-creature snapped at Madeg with its fangs and slashed with its claws. Madeg pivoted out of the way, though one of the claws caught him on the shoulder, cutting a gash on his left side.

"Alyzza! Do something!" Jonmarc shouted. He feinted to one side and then the other, sizing up his opportunities. The mist had rolled back over the meadow, and their fellow caravaners remained motionless, trapped in their separate nightmare visions.

Jonmarc was bleeding from gashes on his arms and back where he had fallen when the beast threw him. His left ankle had bent badly under him in the last fall, and he suspected it might be broken. He was tiring fast, and with the *vayash moru* down, it was up to him and Madeg—and Alyzza.

Alyzza leveled her willow staff at the cat-creature and a blast of brilliant light struck it in the chest. The creature shrieked and fell back, dragging Clark along with it, impaled on its hideous claws. It gave a low, deep-throated growl, as if daring Jonmarc to come at it again.

Madeg's sword took the beast full in its chest. Jonmarc mustered his courage for another strike, fearing that Clark might not survive. Ignoring the pain in his damaged ankle, Jonmarc ran at the monster's front leg, holding the sword two-handed, swinging with all his might. The sword still glowed with Alyzza's enchantment, a dim phosphorescent green that reflected eerily from the clouds of mist. All around them, the glowing blue orbs bobbed and wove through the clouds of fog

Just as Jonmarc's sword ripped into the dead flesh of the monster, Alyzza sent a different swell of magic streaming from her staff. This time, the magic flowed out in a cone, amber-colored, holding the monster in its place. Madeg raised his voice, adding his magic to Alyzza's spells, and Jonmarc saw the light grow brighter. The creature shrieked and snapped, frozen in the glare of the magic, its red eyes murderously bright.

Jonmarc hacked at the thing's leg, finally cutting through, freeing Clark. Clark moaned in pain as Jonmarc dragged him back from the fight. The creature gave one final howl of fury and collapsed. Madeg stabbed it once more through the skull, and the monster lay still.

The glow from Alyzza's staff faded. Jonmarc sprang back from the creature, alert for a trick, but the cat-thing slowly dissolved into dark tendrils of mist and disappeared.

From deep inside the black maw of the elder barrow, Jonmarc heard a new, angry growl.

He was breathing hard and bleeding fast. His entire body ached from the fight, and he was soaked in the monster's fetid ichor. Two of Jonmarc's companions had been destroyed and the third was in no condition to fight. One look at Alyzza told him all he needed to know about the toll the magic was taking on her. Madeg was bleeding and carried himself as if he might have broken ribs. They could not fight another creature.

"I am not finished!" Madeg roared. He strode toward the barrow, planting himself at the dark maw of the entrance, and raised his arms to the sky.

"*Lethyrashem!*" he shouted.

Madeg began to chant, a guttural, strange language unfamiliar to Jonmarc. As the stranger spoke, flashes of white light flared through the mist, moving between and over the immobilized caravan crew, driving back the malevolent fog and sending the blue orbs fleeing.

The thing in the barrow howled again in rage. Madeg brought his hands down and then together with a sharp movement, and the side of the elder barrow began to shudder and shake until rocks fell and the ground collapsed to fill the opening completely.

The fog vanished, and with it, the visions. The orbs winked out.

Jonmarc watched their rescuer warily. He had not sheathed his sword, though it no longer glowed its greenish hue. Alyzza left off chanting, and went to kneel beside Clark.

Madeg took several items from a pouch at his belt, then bent down and worked them into the dirt at the mouth of the barrow. To Jonmarc's eye, the items looked like charms and talismans, magical pieces that would bind whatever dwelled within, keeping it locked in its prison, at least a while longer.

Madeg spoke in low tones, still in the unfamiliar language. Jonmarc could not tell whether he was praying to the Lady or saying spells over the sealed barrow, or both.

Now that the fight was over, Jonmarc's anger flared.

"Two men and a child are dead. All those people have been trapped in torment. We nearly died!" Jonmarc snapped. "If you knew about the wights, why didn't you warn us? You rode this way earlier in the day." Anger and pain made him reckless, and he did not shy away from meeting the stranger's amber eyes.

"Your seer warned you, and no one listened," Madeg said, but how he knew that was a mystery to Jonmarc. "Would your people have listened to me, a stranger, when they would not heed one of their own?" As much as Jonmarc wanted someone to blame for the night's tragedy, he knew Madeg was right.

"I grieve your losses," Madeg said. "My people ride the barrows, up and down the length of the kingdom and beyond. There are few of us, and many barrows. My circuit is a long one. When you saw me earlier, I had just come from sealing another barrow, several candlemarks' ride away."

He paused. "I had to gather my strength to heal, because I feared there would be trouble." Up close, Jonmarc could see that in addition to the damage Madeg had taken in the night's work, he bore older wounds that were not yet fully healed. "It takes time to raise the kind of power needed to quiet the spirits."

"We have healers," Jonmarc said, trying to make up for his outburst. "You're hurt."

Madeg shook his head. "Thank you, but no. My people have their own ways." He looked behind Jonmarc. All across the meadow, the caravan was awakening, abuzz in confusion.

"You fought well," Madeg said. "Your people will be safe now. Avoid the barrows, and the road ahead is clear." With that, he headed off to the tree line, and disappeared into the darkness.

"Jonmarc!" Dugan and Kegan bounded up to him. The fog was gone, and the night air was cooler than usual. Both of his friends looked haggard, and Jonmarc could see the tracks of tears through the dust on their faces.

"Dark Lady take my soul!" Kegan exclaimed. "What happened to us?"

Dugan looked Jonmarc up and down, taking in his injuries, the torn clothing and bloodied sword, and the way Jonmarc stood, favoring his ankle. "We need to get you to the healers," Dugan said. "Here, lean on me." Dugan got under one of Jonmarc's arms and Kegan supported him on the other side.

"Clark needs it more than I do," Jonmarc said, trying to see past them to where Alyzza bent over the *vayash moru*.

"If he's still got his head and his heart, he'll heal up on his own," Dugan said. "You won't."

"Once we fix you up, I want to hear the story about how you ended up looking like you fought the Formless One," he said with a look that promised he wouldn't relent until he heard the tale.

Across the way, Jonmarc could hear Linton shouting and saw the caravan crew running to heed his orders. Near the elder barrow, the tinker and his wife keened in grief over their murdered child. Jonmarc shuddered, and hoped they would find her a more peaceful burial place.

"What's going on?" he asked, wincing as he put weight on his damaged ankle.

"Linton's made up his mind," Kegan said. "We pull up stakes and move out at dawn."

DEAD MAN'S BET

"IF YOU WANT to take up soldiering, you might as well practice by guarding the caravan when Trent can spare you." Karl Steen, caravan guard and one-time soldier leveled a challenging gaze at his sword-fighting pupil.

Jonmarc Vahanian splashed water on his face to wash away the sweat. Most nights after Jonmarc was finished with his tasks as apprentice to Trent, the caravan's blacksmith, he and Steen drilled with swords and knives. It was all part of Steen's attempt to make sure that if Jonmarc did carry through on his plan to join up with the mercenary groups in Principality, he was properly prepared to live through the experience.

"Fine by me. What did Trent have to say about it?" Jonmarc asked, shaking out water from his long, chestnut-brown hair like a wet dog. At eighteen, Jonmarc stood a little over six feet tall, with a body made strong by years working in the forge. He was good at blacksmithing, but he had a natural talent for fighting, and he hoped that making a fresh start in Principality might put distance between him and the losses of his past.

Steen shrugged. "Trent means well. He cares about you like a son, figures you've had enough raw deals in your life. And I don't think his own soldiering turned out like he expected. What do you think he said?"

Jonmarc shrugged, knowing that both Steen and Trent were trying to look out for him in their own ways. "I figure he still wants me to stay on with the caravan, helping him out." He sighed. "And I'm grateful for everything the caravan's done for me. It's just that I need to do this. Join up, I mean. I can't explain it. I just know."

Steen nodded. "Linton runs a great caravan. It's a place people come back to, when there's nowhere else to go. It's a place you end up. You're too young for that."

"Linton was fine with me helping out as a guard?" Jonmarc asked. Maynard Linton ran the most successful caravan in the Winter Kingdoms. His traveling road show of acrobats, animal trainers, artisans, performers and oddities crossed from one side of Margolan to the other, sometimes even into neighboring Principality and Dhasson.

"You're here, aren't you?" Steen replied. "Linton said you'd already proven your worth in a fight a few times over."

That much was true. It had been just a little more than a year since Jonmarc had begged Linton for sanctuary. Since then, he had seen more adventure than he had expected as the caravan's route took it on an unpredictable journey of the best and the worst that the kingdom had to offer. Danger went with a life on the road, and Jonmarc had helped to resolve more than one troublesome situation.

"With luck, we'll just have a nice ride out and back, nothing to worry about," Jonmarc said, and meant it. He never intended to go looking for danger, but it seemed to have a knack for finding him.

"With luck," Steen echoed.

The caravan was heading to one of its last stops before crossing the Nu River into Principality. It would take several more days to reach the small towns and villages where the caravan would set up its tents and wonders. Before then, provisions would be needed to help the cooks, healers, riggers, blacksmiths, and all the behind-the-scenes workers keep the caravan going. And since the wagons heading to market were likely to have money and those coming back from market had valuable items, guards were needed to protect them from highwaymen in an area where the king's guards were scarce.

"Tell me again why we couldn't just take the forest road?" Jonmarc asked as they rode. The two-wagon supply party was heading back laden with materials to keep the caravan eating and functioning. The cook's assistant and baker's helper had purchased barrels of flour and oil as well as baskets full of fresh produce and herbs for the healers. Casks of ale and a few small barrels of whiskey augured pleasant evenings. Boxes of wax, coils of wire and rope, lengths of canvas, a barrel of quicklime, and a box of nails rounded out the order, along with sundry odds and ends requested by the riggers, farriers, merchants, and others who kept the caravan in good working order. Large canvas tarpaulins were tied down over the cargo, since the hedge witches predicted storms on the horizon.

"You've really never heard of the Ruune Vidaya forest?" Steen asked, looking at Jonmarc in amazement.

Jonmarc shook his head. "Sorry, no. I grew up in the Borderlands, remember? We had hardly heard of the Nu River, or anything east of the palace city."

"The Ruune Vidaya forest is haunted," Steen said with a grin.

"Yeah, sure."

Steen nodded. "Truly. A couple of hundred years ago, a man named Jaq the Damned slaughtered peasants who dared to revolt. It's said that their spirits haunt the forest to this day, taking vengeance on oppressors. No one's exactly sure how the spirits figure out who they don't like, so everyone stays clear."

Jonmarc slid his gaze sideways. "And you believe that?"

Once again, Steen nodded. "I'm skeptical of a lot of things, but I believe in vengeful ghosts."

Just then, the party came to a halt. Jonmarc and Steen, who had been riding in the back, exchanged worried glances. "What's going on? Why are we stopping?" Jonmarc called out.

Two of the regular guards rode in front of the wagons. One of the guards gestured to where the road was blocked by a fallen tree. "Can't get past," he said. "We're going to have to go around."

Jonmarc sighed. Wild thunderstorms had raged earlier in the day, and they had seen many trees down along their journey. The storm had delayed their departure, keeping them in the village market several candlemarks past when they had hoped to begin the journey home. Now, they would have to backtrack and take an unfamiliar return route, nearly guaranteeing that they would still be traveling after dark.

"Let's see if we can move it," Steen suggested. "I'm not familiar with the roads around here."

Jonmarc and Steen dismounted, as did the guards. Kegan, one of the apprentice healers, and Dugan, a junior rigger, also jumped down from the wagons, and so did the baker and cook.

"Wait," the cook said, pointing. "Even if we move the tree, it won't make a difference. The bridge is out." Jonmarc followed his gesture. What the cook said was true. Just ahead, past the downed tree, the bridge they had crossed earlier in the day was badly damaged. It would be far too risky to take two heavily laden wagons across.

Steen swore under his breath. "All right. Turn around. There was a crossroads about a mile back. We'll use dead reckoning to figure out a way back to the caravan."

"Does this mean we can get dinner at a tavern?" Dugan asked expectantly.

Kegan elbowed him. "You just want to down a couple of pints before we get back to the caravan."

"We don't have time to drag your sorry asses back with us," Jonmarc jibed with a grin. Dugan and Kegan were close to his age, and the three young men had become fast friends.

"It would be best if we could return before dark," one of the guards said. "There've been reports of trouble in these parts. Highwaymen, and worse."

Worse? Jonmarc wondered. The village where they had gone to market seemed peaceable enough, and as he looked around them now, all he saw were well-tended fields and stone fences, hardly dangerous territory.

The road was narrow and muddy from the recent storm, but they managed to get the wagons turned without getting stuck. Though it was early afternoon, the sky was dark with rainclouds, and the fields around them were soaked and empty, too wet for farmers to work. It gave the area a desolate feel that made Jonmarc shiver.

Backtracking to the crossroads took most of a candlemark. The mud and ruts made the road slow for the wagons. Even the horses trod carefully, picking their way through the muck. Fields sprawled as far as the eye could see on three sides, and in the distance, the vast Ruune Vidaya forest stretched like thunderheads along the horizon.

"Not much choice about the way to go," Vitt, one of the guards said. He stood, hands on hips, in the middle of the crossroads. "We can go back to the village, which doesn't help. We can go south, but that's taking us farther from the caravan. Which leaves us one road."

"It looks to head in the right direction," Mort, the second guard agreed, peering through the drizzle. "But no way to tell if it bends off somewhere."

"It's farm country," Steen said. "That's why we're not set up and performing. Harvest was poor around here. Folks aren't feeling wealthy enough to spare coins for entertainment. So the roads will be few and far between so as not to cut up the fields." He swore under his breath. "Problem is, we could go miles out of our way before we hit another crossroads to take us back toward the caravan."

Jonmarc followed the run of the road. It took them north, into less traveled country, and veered closer to the forest. "Not likely to pass many travelers that way if we get stuck," Jonmarc observed. "Doesn't look like there's much in that direction."

Vitt nodded. "Less traffic might mean fewer ruts. Then again, with the main road out, there might be more of us than you'd expect going this way."

"I'd feel better with a few more travelers around," Steen muttered. "There was more traffic coming toward the village. Someone ought to be heading home besides us."

Mort shrugged. "Maybe the others had business that kept them longer, or decided to stay the night and avoid the rain." He gestured toward the wide-open fields. "It's not like anyone's going to sneak up on us."

"Can we move?" Betta, the cook's apprentice, yelled back to them. "We're getting soaked, and if that canvas doesn't keep the water out of the flour, Cook's going to serve your heads for dinner!"

They headed out, and for the first half-candlemark after the crossroads, the road was good. Jonmarc rode up alongside the wagon that Kegan drove, with Dugan alongside. Jonmarc and the other guards had worn their swords, but he was surprised to see that Dugan wore a long knife in a sheath on his belt.

"Did you expect to get into a fight at the market?" Jonmarc joked.

Dugan grimaced. "With you around, it's possible." Jonmarc had to agree that some of their past provisioning runs had ended in trouble.

"I heard the riggers talking," Dugan said quietly. "They heard some of the customers at our last stop mention that there've been highwaymen around these parts. Bandits, brigands, whatever you want to call them. People have gone missing."

"Murdered?" Jonmarc asked, raising an eyebrow. Throughout most of the kingdom, King Bricen's guards kept the roads well clear of cutpurse gangs. It was always folly to travel alone after dark for anyone but a skilled fighter, but the incidents that did occur usually were no worse than an unwary traveler relieved of his coins or possessions. Stealing a man's purse might earn a thief time in irons. Killing his mark was a sure way to a swift hanging.

"Who knows?" Dugan said, shrugging. "You know how rumors fly. People talk. *Dimmons*, rogue *vayash moru*, slavers, even blood mages—no idea seems too crazy when folks need something to do with their time."

"Maybe that's why Linton wanted extra guards on this run," Jonmarc said.

Kegan gave a harsh laugh. "Likely. He'd stand to lose good money if we got waylaid going in either direction."

Vitt and Mort rode in front, far enough ahead to scout the road. Betta and Jemman, helpers to the cook and the baker, drove the first wagon, while Dugan and Kegan drove the second. Jonmarc and Steen took up the rear.

If it came to a fight, Jonmarc knew Dugan and Steen could hold their own. Kegan wasn't much of a fighter, but he had nerve, and he could think on his feet. Jonmarc did not know Vitt and Mort other than to see them around the camp, but the guards were strong and their swords looked as if they had seen use. Betta had a temper, but Jonmarc doubted she had ever used a knife on anything more dangerous than a plucked chicken. Jemman was a little older than Jonmarc, and very shy. Kneading dough had given him strong hands and arms, but Jonmarc was not counting on help from him if things got rough.

"Thanks," Jonmarc said. "I'd better get back with Steen."

Dugan nodded. "I'd be just as happy if this errand stayed boring, if you know what I mean. We've had enough tales to tell."

"I brought my basic healing kit, but I'd rather not have reason to use it," Kegan added.

Jonmarc scowled. "You make it sound like I go looking for problems."

Dugan chuckled. "You don't have to. It finds you, like moths to flame."

"Very funny," Jonmarc remarked dryly and fell back to ride beside Steen. Dugan's comment bothered him far more than the other had intended. Jonmarc had never told Dugan—or any of the others—about the curse.

Three years ago, raiders had killed Jonmarc's family and his village. Jonmarc had fought with all his might, taking down several of the raiders before being badly wounded and left to die. One of the raiders had cursed him with his dying breath, damning him to lose all he loved to the flames. When a hedge witch and her daughter rescued Jonmarc and took him to their nearby village, he had discounted the curse, until a dangerous mage and magicked monsters brought the curse to his new home, destroying everything and leaving him alive to bear the pain.

Trent doesn't understand that I've overstayed my welcome with the caravan, Jonmarc thought. *Yes, I've helped them out of some tight spots, but maybe those misfortunes wouldn't have happened if I hadn't been part of the crew. I need to get out before more people I care about die. At least if I'm a soldier, dying is our business.*

"I don't like this." Steen's voice jarred Jonmarc out of his thoughts. Steen sat tall in his saddle, looking from side to side, on high alert.

"Not crazy about the rain myself," Jonmarc replied, slouching in his cloak against the drizzle.

Steen shook his head. "That's not what I mean. Even with the rain, even out here, we should have passed someone else. And look at this road," he said, gesturing. "It's getting worse the farther we go, without a crossroad in sight except a few farm lanes."

"You think we should have taken the southern road?" Jonmarc asked. "There's no guarantee it would have been the more traveled or better road."

"I'm thinking that we're being herded," Steen said. "What if that tree didn't fall by accident? Awfully convenient for the bridge to be out, too."

"Seems like a lot of work for someone to pick our pockets," Jonmarc replied.

"Maybe," Steen allowed. "But it might not be our pockets they're after."

Steen fell silent after that, and Jonmarc did not feel like talking. Whether it was Steen's worry or Dugan's rumors, something cast a pall over the afternoon, making Jonmarc ill at ease.

Up ahead, the ruins of an old barn hunkered on the right, and not far behind it, the dark fringe of the Ruune Vidaya forest. The sound of hoof beats made Jonmarc turn to see four men on horseback riding down one of the farm lanes. They turned onto the road behind the group.

In the distance, Jonmarc spotted more travelers, coming their way. "We're not the only ones traveling anymore," he said.

Steen looked worried. "No, we're not. Funny how that changed all of a sudden."

Vitt and Mort must have also concluded that something was amiss. Jonmarc saw both men flick their cloaks back to give them fast access to their swords. Dugan drew his knife and laid it across his lap. The drizzle gave way to rain, and in the distance, Jonmarc heard thunder.

Leaving the road to go around the newcomers would have been difficult on horseback. It was impossible for the wagons, even if the edges of the road had not been mud. The two wagons pulled to one side to let the oncoming rider pass. Behind Jonmarc and Steen, the second group of riders were closing quickly.

The oncoming riders moved to the other side. But once they drew level with the first wagon, two of the riders wheeled on Betta and Jemman, swords drawn, while the other two rode for Vitt and Mort.

Behind them, four more riders spurred their horses on, quickly closing the gap, swords raised. And rising from the tall, dead weeds on the side of the road, four additional men leapt from cover, armed with knives and swords.

Jonmarc drew his sword fast enough to block the downward swing of the nearest brigand. An odd triangle-shaped tattoo on the man's left hand caught Jonmarc's eye.

Steen was already battling an attacker of his own, while ahead, Dugan slashed at a man who tried to grab the reins. Kegan made boils rise on the arms of the man who tried to drag him from his seat. Betta was smacking one of the robbers with her walking stick. Jemman, for all his shyness, landed a solid roundhouse punch to the jaw of the man who grabbed at his leg.

"They're not robbers," Steen shouted, glancing at the odd tattoos. "They're slavers! Fight for your lives!"

Vitt was better with a blade than Jonmarc had expected. He got inside the slaver's guard and scored a cross-body slash that put the brigand on the ground, holding his slit gut. Mort used his bulk to his advantage, holding forth with a powerful onslaught of strikes that had his attacker backing up, barely holding his own.

Steen swung into a high Eastmark kick, planting his boot firmly in the slaver's chest, sending the man sprawling. Jonmarc fell into the moves he and Steen had practiced back at camp, and parried the strike from a second slaver who meant to come at Steen while he was regaining his balance. Then it was Jonmarc's turn to wheel into the high kick, and he smiled grimly as he heard a bone snap when his foot caught the slaver in the elbow, knocking him flat in the mud. Jonmarc and Steen dove forward, sinking their blades deep into the downed men's chests.

"Two down," Steen muttered.

Twelve slavers to eight caravaners wasn't a fair fight, but if Trent and some of the other men had been with them, Jonmarc had no doubt they could have easily evened the odds. Betta fought like a wildcat, poking, jabbing, and smashing with her solid walking cane. Jemman was better in a fist-fight than Jonmarc would have ever imagined, and the baker's strong hands and arms served well for grabbing a slaver in a choke hold and breaking his neck.

Steen and Jonmarc were holding their own, though two more of the slavers had appeared to take the place of the ones they had killed. Dugan was slashing at a slaver with his broad knife, while Kegan sent one slaver screaming in panic with seeping boils and another cursed and scratching himself bloody from red welts that sprang up all over the his body.

If we'd had Trent, Zane, and Corbin with us, this fight would be over by now, Jonmarc thought, gritting his teeth as he parried a wild swing by one of the slavers. But the blacksmith, the caravan's knife-thrower and the farrier had stayed back at camp, and all the wishing in the world would not change that.

Out of the corner of his eye, Jonmarc saw a slaver get inside Vitt's guard. The brigand sank his blade deep into Vitt's shoulder, and Vitt staggered backward, gasping, as he dropped his sword. He dropped to his knees, his shirt crimson with blood, and fell face-forward into the mud.

Jonmarc felt his anger rise, and he took it out on the slaver he fought. Behind him, he could hear Steen cursing in Common and in Margolense. Jonmarc was sweating even though a cold rain was falling, and his blood mingled with the rain from a score of gashes he had taken keeping his attacker at bay. Steen was bleeding from wounds on his chest, shoulders and arms, but he had felled a slaver and was rapidly gaining an advantage over another.

Lightning flashed overhead and thunder sounded loud enough to echo all around them. The late afternoon sky had grown dark, and rain fell in sheets. Jonmarc chanced a look at his fellow travelers. The caravaners were better armed than the slavers had expected, and less willing to surrender than the brigands might have predicted. But Jonmarc could see that the odds were against them even before five more slavers ran from the direction of the barn.

Betta and Jemman were not soldiers, and neither was Kegan. Vitt was down, and Mort was barely holding off a determined slaver. Dugan had gotten in several lucky slashes, but his experience was with rigging tents, not fencing. It was just a matter of time before the slavers won, but even so, Jonmarc was determined to make it an expensive victory.

The wind and rain made it difficult to see. A flash of lightning illuminated the scarred, angry face of the slaver who came at Jonmarc, sword raised. Steen closed with his attacker, driving his sword through the man's belly and out the other side. The slaver got in a final slash, opening a deep gash across Steen's chest. The two men fell together, rolling toward the rain-choked ditch, and neither rose.

"Throw down your weapons if you value your lives!" A dark-haired man with a crooked nose and pox-scarred face held his sword to Betta's throat. "Surrender, or I take her head."

Betta loosed a string of curses. "Keep fighting!" she shouted, until the blade bit into her neck, raising a scarlet line.

The fighting halted, and one by one, the caravaners threw down their weapons with muttered curses. Jonmarc glanced behind him, hoping Steen had crawled from the ditch, but in the darkness and rain, he couldn't see the man.

"Take the wagons to the barn, and tie up the prisoners. We'll get good money for them in Nargi," the pox-faced man said.

Jonmarc glowered at the slaver who bound his wrists. "Go to the Crone," he muttered.

The slaver cuffed him hard across the face. "It's going to take a while to break this one," he laughed. "I'm going to enjoy it." He grabbed Jonmarc's chin as he tried to clear his vision from the blow. "We have a long road ahead of us to Nargi, and by the time we reach there, I'll have taught you to lick my boots clean."

Jonmarc spat in his face, earning another blow that made his ears ring. The slaver would have struck him again, but the pox-faced man grabbed the slaver's wrist.

"Leave the merchandise alone," the leader said. "They'll pay less for damaged goods."

Whether or not the slavers intended to spend the night in the old barn, the storm made other plans impossible. They unhitched the horses from the wagons and tethered them in the barn, leaving the wagons under an overhang. The road was ankle-deep in thick mud, and the ditches ran full and swift. Wind howled across the fields and through the shadowed tree line. Thunder crashed overhead, and lightning touched down close enough Jonmarc could see the jagged streaks hit the ground.

His whole body ached from the fight. He was soaked through. Blood and rainwater made his sodden shirt cling to his skin. The slavers prodded them at swords' point toward the questionable shelter of the ruined barn, which was leaning badly enough that Jonmarc wondered if it would survive the storm.

Inside, three more slavers were waiting. Half the roof was missing, leaving only the space along one wall dryer than anywhere outside. Jonmarc tested his bonds, but the rough rope held fast. The slavers took their swords and Dugan's knife, even Betta's walking cane. Jonmarc had a small knife hidden against the small of his back, but his hands were bound in front of him, putting it out of reach.

Steen's dead. Vitt's badly wounded. That leaves sixteen of them to seven of us. The caravan won't have any idea where we are. If we're going to get out of this, it's up to us. He kept his head down, but watched his captors carefully as they moved about the rough camp. They rekindled a small fire that was sheltered from the wind. From the smell of the spices in their provisions, Jonmarc guessed the slavers were not Margolan-born. They spoke a language among themselves he had never heard before.

The slavers prodded their captives toward the posts that held up the second floor of the ruined barn, and tied them with their backs to the hard wood. Jonmarc was tied alone. Kegan and Vitt were lashed together against another pole, then Betta and Jemman. Dugan and Mort were tied separately.

"Show some respect, and we might feed you," one of the slavers taunted. He was a narrow-faced man with an eye-patch and he walked with a twisted foot. He kicked at Jonmarc's leg. "After all, they'll pay more if you're in good enough shape to work." He limped away, laughing at his own joke.

"We won't get much for the cargo," one of the slavers said. "Nothing much of value in the wagons. Might be able to sell the horses and the wagons themselves."

"Won't get top dollar for the slaves, either," his companion replied. "That one," he said with a nod toward Betta, "is too old to be worth much. The others might sell for some silver, though. Young enough to do some labor."

"Not a bad night's work," a third slaver replied. "And if we can't sell what's on the wagons, we might be able to eat some of it. Nothing wasted, that's what I say."

Jonmarc glanced down the row. Vitt still slumped against the pole, and from the look of his shirt, he had lost a lot of blood. But Kegan gave Jonmarc a nod, and managed to scoot close enough to touch Vitt, so that he could use his healing magic to repair the damage from the sword-strike.

The others were bruised and cut from the fight, but no one appeared to be likely to die. Yet.

Jonmarc worked at his bonds, but the ropes held tight. Perhaps tonight, once the slavers were asleep, he might be able to jostle the knife in his belt loose, but it would take some maneuvering. *And even if I get loose, what then? I can't fight the slavers by myself, and with the roads the way they are, we can't sneak out and get very far. They'd ride us down and capture us again before we got more than a few miles.*

He did his best to look as if he were dozing, keeping watch on their captors beneath half-closed eyes. The slavers drank the whiskey from the casks they took from the wagon and played cards as the storm raged outside, pausing briefly to give each of their captives a few crusts of bread and sips of ale.

Betta and Jemman looked defeated. Dugan and Mort appeared to be dozing, but Jonmarc was sure that Dugan, at least, was also watching for an opportunity. Kegan was intent on saving Vitt. Vitt still was not awake, but his color had improved.

By now, even without the storm, it would be dark outside, Jonmarc thought. When the storm cleared, the slavers would have them headed to Nargi. He had heard enough of Steen's horror stories about Nargi and its slaves. A cold deliberation settled over him. *I would rather die a free man than live as a slave. Even better if I can take down some of those slavers with me when I go.*

JONMARC ROUSED IN alarm out of a fitful sleep. The old barn was dark except for the slavers' banked fire. The slavers had settled into their cloaks for the night, which Jonmarc reckoned was already half-spent. A man's hand clamped down on his mouth, and a voice hissed in his ear.

"It's Steen. Don't make a noise. I'm going to cut your ropes, then we're going to give these bastards what they deserve."

With a wary glance toward the front of the barn where he had spotted a slaver on watch, Jonmarc silently melted into the shadows, scrambling out through a hole in the barn wall.

"I thought you were dead," Jonmarc hissed.

Steen grinned. "Would have been, without the chain mail under my shirt. I went down, and stayed down, figuring that one of us needed to be free." Steen drew him into the darkness of the overhang where the wagons were stored. "I've got an idea," he whispered.

"It had better be a good one."

Steen grimaced. "Not really. It's a dead man's bet, but it's all we've got."

"If it gets us out of here, I'm in."

"We create a distraction, delay the slavers, while we get the others into the forest and then hold the slavers off."

Jonmarc raised an eyebrow. "The haunted forest? With the angry ghosts?"

"You have a better idea?"

Jonmarc swore silently. "Anything's better than being slaved. Lead on."

One slaver stood watch near the barn door. Jonmarc pitched a handful of small stones as Steen moved in the brush just down from the door, a shadow the slaver was unlikely to miss.

The guard glanced at the other slavers who were sleeping off the whiskey, and then chanced one step and then another into the darkness, peering toward where the shadow had been.

Steen moved swiftly, coming up behind the slaver. With a hand over his mouth before he could cry out, Steen sliced his blade across the guard's neck, and then dragged him around the corner of the barn.

One down, Jonmarc thought grimly.

Together, Jonmarc and Steen dug under the tarpaulins that covered the caravan's wagons. Steen handed him several lengths of wire, as well as some rope. Together, they maneuvered a barrel of quicklime to the top of a small rise above the farm pond. Jonmarc and Steen pounded two sturdy sticks into the wet ground just far enough to hold the barrel, and attached rope to the sticks, which they led off into the darkness.

Next, they each took a length of wire and ran a maze of tripwires in front and in back of the barn, stringing the wire between hastily pounded sticks.

"That should slow them down," Steen said with satisfaction.

Finally, they grabbed a few more items from the wagon: a small cask of oil and a box of wax. These, Steen ran to the edge of the forest, then returned to the shadows where Jonmarc waited.

"You might as well swear Istra's Bargain right now," Jonmarc said. Soldiers in a no-win situation had been known to offer their souls to the Dark Lady in exchange for the life of their enemy.

"Not today," Steen murmured. "I think with luck, we might be able to make this work."

Not with my luck, Jonmarc thought, but said nothing.

"I'll go around front and pull the rope to send the quicklime into the pond," Steen said. "Should make quite an explosion, plus some nice flames. That should get their attention. With luck, we'll trip some of them up in the wires when they go to have a look." He jerked his head toward the barn.

"You get in there, cut the others loose, and lead them around the wire to the forest. Get a bucketful of hot coals from their fire and bring it with you. If they follow us, we'll make them wish they hadn't. I'll lead them on a merry chase to keep them away from you, and then double back to meet up. Got it?" Steen asked.

"Got it." The plan was the riskiest, craziest thing Jonmarc had heard in a long time, but since he couldn't come up with anything better, he did not argue. He doubted they would survive the night, but going down fighting sounded like a much better option than what the slavers had in mind for them.

"Get going," Steen said. "I'll count to thirty, then pull the rope. Stay hidden until you hear the explosion. Be quick, because I don't know how long I can hold them off." The look in his eyes said Steen knew just how risky the plan was, how impossible the odds. Then Steen flashed Jonmarc a grin. "If we pull this off, it'll be one for the legends."

Jonmarc headed toward the back of the barn in a crouching run. He had his hidden knife in his hand. With luck, the slavers were still sleeping and had not noticed their missing guard.

Luck didn't hold.

"Out for a stroll?" The voice sounded behind Jonmarc just as he neared the loose board at the back of the barn.

"Maybe I just needed to take a piss," Jonmarc replied. He felt the point of a blade in his back.

"Drop what you've got in your hand, and start walking," the slaver said. "See, I did need to take a piss, and I saw that we were one slave short."

Thirty. Jonmarc counted silently. He moved slowly, giving Steen time, praying to the Sacred Lady for the cask to do what Steen expected.

Just before they reached the barn door, an explosion shook the night and flames shot into the sky.

Jonmarc wheeled. He landed a high Eastmark kick just as Steen had taught him, going for the throat and chin so that the slaver could not cry out. Momentum carried him around, and he used it to bury the knife deep in the slaver's chest, and then slit his throat for good measure.

Jonmarc heard a commotion at the front of the barn as the slavers went to see what had happened. He slipped through the hole in the back, wary of another surprise like the man who had caught him outside, but saw none of the slavers.

The captives were awake, and he gestured to them for silence. He ran to grab their weapons, and scooped up hot coals from the fire in the bucket the slavers had used for water. Then he ran to where the others were tied, cutting their ropes.

"Come on! Get up. We've got to get to the forest."

"What's going on?" Betta asked. "That explosion—"

"I'll tell you later," Jonmarc cut her off. "Follow me, and stay close. We've trapped the path."

Vitt was still shaky, so Mort slung him over his shoulder. Betta's walking stick was not with the weapons, but Jemman offered her his arm. Jonmarc hastily distributed the knives and swords, just in case Steen's distraction did not fool the slavers. Then they headed along the safe path Jonmarc had left, twisting back and forth between the tripwires.

He froze as a shadow came sprinting up toward them. "Steen," the voice hissed.

Jonmarc did not relax until Steen was close enough for him to make out his features. "I don't know how long the slavers will take to investigate," Steen said. "We need to get into the forest and get ready."

"We're going into the haunted forest?" Mort stopped and gave Jonmarc a look of utter amazement.

"It's that or Nargi," Steen said.

Mort grimaced, and then shrugged. "Not much choice, when you put it that way."

They had nearly reached the forest when they heard the slavers shouting behind them. A dead run in a straight line would get the slavers to the forest in just a few minutes, but Jonmarc had wired the open paths as best he could to make it difficult for them. Steen veered off to pick up the two items they had stashed earlier.

As the captives cleared the trip-wired area, the slavers began to stumble and fall, cursing at the top of their lungs.

"Keep going!" Jonmarc shouted to the others, as he and Steen stopped at the tree line, ready to hold off the slavers if they closed the gap. He grabbed Dugan by the arm. "Get the others about thirty paces behind the edge of the forest, and off to the right, so we're not straight in front of them if the slavers make it this far."

"I'm coming back to fight beside you," Dugan said, gesturing for the others to follow him.

"Glad to have you," Jonmarc said sincerely. As the others disappeared, Jonmarc and Steen strung the last of the wire between the trees at neck level, a stretch of at least twenty feet. A few minutes later, Dugan returned, along with Mort.

"Watch where you walk," Steen cautioned, pointing out the wire.

Dugan and Mort nodded in acknowledgement. "Vitt's not on his feet yet," Mort said. "I left him with the healer."

Steen nodded. "Then let me get the second wave ready." He ducked into the shadows, taking the bucket of hot coals from Jonmarc.

"Do you think they'll find us here?" Dugan murmured.

"Probably, if they make it this far," Jonmarc replied. *But at least we die on Margolan soil.*

"What's Steen up to?"

Jonmarc shrugged. "No idea."

The slavers struggled through the wire, falling and stumbling as the snares caught their feet. *If we had archers, we could've picked them off while they're moving slowly,* Jonmarc thought. All they had were their knives.

"Take these," Steen said, suddenly reappearing. He handed Jonmarc and Dugan long sticks with a fork at the end, which had a rough pocket of cloth from Steen's cloak secured to the forks. Steen carried the bucket, but instead of hot coals, it had a strange-smelling mixture.

"What in the name of the Crone is that?" Mort asked.

"Fire from the Formless One," Steen said with a dangerous grin. "Mort, you stay alert with your sword. Jonmarc and Dugan, follow me."

Steen took the bucket and advanced to just inside the tree line. Jonmarc knew that with the sliver of a moon, they would be able to see the slavers better than the slavers could make out their shapes in the shadow of the trees.

The slavers were getting close. Steen motioned for them to hold off until three of the slavers were only a dozen feet from the trees. Then Steen dipped the pocket of his branch into the bucket and slammed the branch upright, catapulting the gloppy, steaming mixture toward the nearest slaver. Jonmarc and Dugan followed his example, hitting the three slavers in the face and shoulders.

Their attackers started to scream as the mixture of hot oil and wax hit and stuck. One of the slavers dug at his eyes, dropping to his knees. The others tore at their clothing, trying to rid themselves of the burning goo. Skin peeled from their faces and fluid, not tears, wept from their ruined eyes. They were out of the fight.

The rest of the slavers were closing, fast. Jonmarc and the others held their fire, waiting for the slavers to come into range. They got off another volley, stopping the new wave of attackers as the first group started forward again, angrier than before.

There was only enough of the oil and wax mixture for one more round of shots. "Make it count, boys," Steen muttered. Their aim held true, though this time the slavers were able to avoid catching the burning mixture in the face. Jonmarc and the others drew their weapons, and fell back behind the wire.

"Stay where they can see you," Jonmarc murmured. "Make them run at you."

A cold draft gusted around them from deep in the forest. Jonmarc shuddered, wondering whether the Ruune Vidaya's infamous ghosts knew they were there. The slavers spotted them among the trees and came at them at a dead run, swords raised. Eleven against four. Jonmarc and the others hesitated just long enough to make sure they were seen, then backed further into the shadows.

The first of the slavers hit the wire. It caught him on the throat, and he fell back, strangling, tearing at his crushed larynx with his hands. Two more crashed into the wire, dropping to their knees and gasping for breath as they gargled and spat blood.

The next group ducked underneath, and found Jonmarc and the others waiting for them.

"I don't care what the boss says," the pox-faced man said. "We're going to kill you right here, and leave you for the crows."

"You can try," Steen replied.

Ten slavers left. Anger fueled the slavers' swings, while Jonmarc and his companions were fighting for their lives. One of the slavers, a brawny, bald-headed man, came at Jonmarc, scything a wicked curved blade. Jonmarc held his sword two-handed against the force of the swing, and felt it reverberate up his arm, jarring his teeth.

"I'm going to kill you slowly," his opponent taunted. "I'm going to skin you alive, then hack you apart piece by piece, nice and slow. Cut out your tongue. Gouge out your eyes. Cut off your manhood. Even then, after all that, I can keep stabbing for quite a while before you finally die, drowning in your own blood."

After what Jonmarc had witnessed, between the raiders and the monsters, the slaver's words did not frighten him. He felt a familiar coldness settle over him. It distanced him from the fear, blocked out the pain, and made his attention snap into sharp focus.

Keep talking, Jonmarc thought. *I'm not listening, and if you're talking, you're not paying full attention.*

Jonmarc parried the slaver's blow, then blocked another swing that would have taken off his arm. A second slaver joined in the fight, as all around Jonmarc the rest of the slavers caught up.

"Think you can hold off all of us?" the newcomer asked.

Jonmarc had his knife in his left hand, his sword in his right. The new slaver thrust, and Jonmarc knocked the blow aside, and pivoted into a high kick, landing his strike on the first slaver's sword-wrist.

"I will slit you chin to nuts for that," the slaver howled, coming at him with a dagger in his left hand, poised for a downward slash.

"Dark Lady take your soul!" Jonmarc muttered, barely evading the death strike as the other slaver tried to get inside his guard, landing a deep gash on his left shoulder.

Howls like enraged wolves sounded from the forest. Betta and Jemman burst from among the trees, each swinging long, solid branches. Betta smashed one slaver in the head, and he dropped like a stone, bleeding from his ears, his scalp opened and his head crushed. Jemman rammed another slaver in the gut, driving him back against a tree and pinning him, hitting so hard that the branch severed his spine.

Jonmarc took advantage of the distraction to drop and roll, coming up behind the slaver who had been taunting him and running him through with his sword. The second slaver came at him with a snarl, and it was all Jonmarc could do to hold the man off. One powerful strike caught him on the hand, and his sword dropped from his numbed fingers. Jonmarc ducked a killing blow, slashing with the dagger in his left. He grabbed for a branch and swung hard, barely blocking another strike. His fallen sword lay just behind the slaver, but it might as well have been leagues away for all the good it did him.

Steen had felled another opponent, and Mort was holding his own. Jemman and Dugan had teamed up, a good thing since Dugan was fading fast. Betta's temper and the length of the branch she wielded was still keeping the slavers at bay, but the odds were in the attackers' favor.

Six slavers were still on their feet, and only five of the caravan crew were able to fight, though for how much longer, Jonmarc was not sure. He was growing lightheaded from hunger and blood loss. Steen looked like he was running on sheer willpower, bleeding from a score of wounds.

From deep in the forest came a moan like a dying man. The mournful sound came again, from elsewhere in the darkness. Jonmarc glimpsed a flash of foxfire, then another and another, bits of glowing green phosphorescence suspended against the blackness of the deep forest.

"Looks like the ghosts are waking up," Jonmarc said with a nasty grin. "They don't like slavers."

More moans sounded, as if from everywhere at once, and new glimpses of eerie green light danced in the darkness. The slaver looked rattled, and his momentary lapse was all Jonmarc needed to dive forward, slashing the attacker with his knife, opening up his belly and spilling out his guts onto the loam beneath their feet.

Jonmarc never saw the slaver behind him until the knife was in his side. He gasped, falling to his knees. The slaver withdrew the knife, and Jonmarc lunged for his sword, rolling to bring the blade up through the man's groin and into his body. The slaver screamed in pain, impaled on the blade, unable to move and unwilling to fall. Jonmarc brought up one foot and kicked as hard as he could, biting back a scream of his own from the pain. The slaver fell free from Jonmarc's sword, and Jonmarc collapsed, breathing hard, trying not to pass out.

"Let's get a look at your 'ghosts'," one of the slavers growled, dodging into the shadows and emerging with Kegan and Vitt. Both held bits of rotting log, alight with glowing fungus. Vitt was recovered enough to hurl his log toward the slaver's head, clipping him on the temple. The slaver punched Vitt in the shoulder, opening up his barely-healed wound. Kegan brought his free hand up, striking the slaver with his open palm full in the chest as he chanted a word of power. The slaver stiffened and clutched for his heart, his hold on Kegan forgotten, then collapsed.

Betta was caught, kicking and screaming. Dugan was down, bleeding from the mouth. Jemman swung his bloodied branch like a scythe, but he would not be able to hold off the slaver for long. Steen and Mort were fighting back to back to hold off their attacker.

A new sound came from deep in the forest's darkness. The moans had sounded human. The shrieks that carried from the depths of the Ruune Vidaya did not. Orbs of blue-white light careened from between the trees, dodging and weaving over their heads. Tendrils of cold fog seeped from the heart of the forest, cold and damp, gathering over the wet ground.

"Another trick, like your explosion?" the pox-faced slaver demanded.

"What was that?" A gray figure slid past the slaver who was trying to keep a hold on Betta. The cook's assistant got in a vicious bite to the slaver's arm, and scrambled backwards as the man dropped her.

"I'll get you for that," he muttered, coming at Betta with his sword.

The shrieking reached a crescendo, wailing so loudly that Jonmarc clapped his hands over his ears. Fog covered the ground as high as a man's knees, and Jonmarc dragged himself to stand, clinging to one of the trees, unwilling to be overtaken by the unnatural mist.

Just as the slaver lunged forward to strike Betta, the fog rose like a tide, no longer mist but figures with grasping hands and gaping maws. More of the nightmare figures coalesced from the mist. Jonmarc had seen ghosts and barrow wights, but he had never seen spirits like these. The ghosts that rose between Betta and the slaver had sharp teeth and bony fingers, their bodies twisted into hideous shapes with glowing eyes.

As Jonmarc watched in horror, the ghosts set on the slaver, raking him with their long fingers, opening up trails of blood on his skin. The slaver screamed, but the ghosts hemmed him in, slashing at his body, tearing out his hair, gouging at his eyes. Betta backed away, eyes wide with terror.

The howling was so loud that it was impossible to think. The orbs no longer danced in the air. Now, they took on a more sinister purpose, diving at the slavers from all sides, burning them with cold fire. Hands reached up from the mist along the ground, snatching at the slavers' clothing, tearing it from their bodies, rending their flesh.

"Come on." Betta helped Vitt get to his feet, while Kegan helped Jonmarc walk, one hand pressed against the deep cut in his side. "Let's get out of here while we can."

The pox-faced slaver was caught in the middle of a glowing whirlwind, screaming as the ghosts slashed at him with teeth and bone, until the whirlwind was crimson with the spray of blood. The forest was freezing cold, and their breath fogged in the air. The edge of the forest was no more than ten feet away.

Droplets of blood fell like rain, spattering them with gore. The slavers shrieked and cursed, begging for their lives, squealing like badly butchered sows. Jonmarc had no magic, but it did not require a mage to sense the hunger for revenge, the anger and the long-denied vengeance of the spirits.

The revenants ignored the prisoners as they hobbled their way toward the tree line. Jemman slung Dugan over one shoulder, while Mort and Steen managed to stumble forward on their own. All the caravaners were covered in blood, some of it from the slavers, much of it their own. Vitt looked the worst. His skin had a grayish pallor, and his lips were turning blue. He leaned heavily on Betta, barely able to move.

Just a few steps separated them from the edge of the forest when one of the slavers dove toward Jonmarc, grabbing him from behind. Jonmarc glimpsed the slaver's face, skin torn in strips down to muscle and bone, hands a bloody mass of sinew. The ghosts of the forest surged forward to drag the slaver back with them, and the slaver grappled to hold onto Jonmarc, screaming incoherently.

Instinct took over. Jonmarc plunged his dagger deep into the slaver's gut, jerking it upward, cutting off the slaver's scream with a gasp. Dugan pulled Jonmarc back, tearing him free of the slaver's grip as the spirits swarmed around the slaver and drew him back into the darkness.

Jonmarc was leaning hard on Dugan. He stumbled, struggling to breathe, trying not to lose consciousness until they were free of the forest and its sentinel spirits. The last thing he remembered, as they left the trees behind, was the sight of a dozen silhouettes striding toward them, and the certainty that they had lost.

"YOU'RE A HARD man to kill." The voice was Trent's, and Jonmarc opened his eyes to see the blacksmith leaning over him with a concerned look beneath the jovial tone.

"I'm dead—aren't I?" Jonmarc managed through dry lips.

"No, but it's not for lack of trying." Anger warred with worry in Trent's voice. "By the Dark Lady, Jonmarc! What did you think you were doing going into the Ruune Vidaya forest?"

"Trying to get free of the slavers. Seemed like a good idea at the time." Talking took far too much energy, but if he wasn't dead, Jonmarc had questions. "How did you—"

"Alyzza came thundering into Linton's tent shouting about omens and portents. You were all overdue by that time, so it wasn't a stretch to figure something had gone wrong, but we thought it was just the storms that held you up." Trent shook his head.

"There's always talk about slavers when you get closer to the Nu River, but most of the time, it's just brigands," he added. "King Bricen's soldiers make short work of slavers when they catch them. Hang them from the trees, leave the bodies to rot as a warning to others." He cursed again under his breath. "Linton would never have sent you out if he'd really thought there were slaver gangs nearby."

"There aren't, anymore."

JONMARC RECOGNIZED THE healers' tent back at the caravan, but how he got from the edge of the forest to here, he did not remember. Kegan walked by, then stopped when he saw Jonmarc was awake, and stood behind Trent who was seated next to Jonmarc's cot.

"Good to see you awake," Kegan said. "With luck, you've got most of the blood back that you lost, and the gashes are mostly healed, though I can't say you won't have scars." He grinned. "Thank Ada and the senior healers. You gave them a run for their money."

Kegan moved on, but Trent regarded Jonmarc darkly. "He means you almost died," the blacksmith said curtly. "We found all of you outside the forest—thank Alyzza for that— but we weren't sure you'd make it back. Vitt didn't. You were too close for comfort."

"Steen?"

Trent grimaced, and Jonmarc knew he and Steen had words about Jonmarc's future soldiering. "He'll live, but he's cut up in more places than you are, just not as deep. Betta and Jemman got away with some bruises, so they'll be limping for a few days, but nothing serious. Dugan was banged up pretty badly, but he's coming around. Mort managed to get out of it with some broken ribs and a few cuts, but nothing that won't heal."

"What about the slavers?"

Trent looked away. "No one came out of the forest. We found their things in the barn. No doubt that they were working for the Nargi, given the coins and bounty warrants they were carrying." He paused. "We heard them," he said quietly. "Heard them screaming in the forest, and we heard the howling of the ghosts. Not a man among us was going to set foot in there, and no one doubts the legends about the Ruune Vidaya, if they ever did."

"You didn't see them die." Jonmarc's voice was just above a whisper.

Trent met his gaze, and saw the horror there. "No. I didn't. The others won't talk about it at all. It must have been bad."

"Bad" did not begin to cover it, but Jonmarc could not find words to explain. "Yeah. It was bad. Real bad."

"Steen said you held your own, that you fought well," Trent said, straightening. "Maybe you're right about going with the mercs, once we get to Principality. Sweet Mother and Childe, it's not like we've kept you safe here."

"Thank you," Jonmarc said quietly.

Trent laid a hand on his shoulder. "You say that now. I don't know that you'll feel the same way a year from now." He stood. "I'll see you back in the forge once you're ready."

Jonmarc closed his eyes and laid back. *The sooner I'm gone, the safer they'll be,* he thought. *And once I'm gone, I'll take the curse with me. There's nothing else I can do. Dark Lady take my soul.*

DARK PASSAGE

"HE'S BEEN POISONED." Ada, the caravan healer, said. She knelt next to the dead man and shook her head. "Looks like he ate something that didn't agree with him." She nodded toward a basket partly filled with crisp green stalks.

The corpse at her feet was all the warning anyone needed to resist the appeal of the crunchy treat. Petran, one of the tent riggers, lay in his own vomit, his body contorted from convulsions. Spittle flecked his lips. The pupils in his staring eyes were so wide that the irises were just thin rims.

Ada sighed and rose to her feet, straightening her robes. "Who found him?"

Dugan, a young man with straight, dark hair stepped forward from the small crowd that had gathered near the dead man's tent. "I did. He was late for work, and I was sent to get him when he didn't show up." He shrugged. "Sometimes he drinks too much and forgets."

"Was this how you found him?" Ada asked, still staring at the corpse as if gazing at the body might shed some light on the circumstances of his death.

Dugan gulped and nodded nervously. "Yes, ma'am. I yelled for him at the tent flap, and when he didn't curse me—like he usually does—I poked my head inside, expecting a cuff on the ear. He was just lyin' there, splayed-like, and not moving."

Ada nodded. "Do you know any reason why he might have decided to go off eating strange plants?"

Dugan swallowed and nodded again. "Petran always complained of stomach problems. He went on and on about how certain foods didn't set well, how he couldn't sleep for the burn in his throat, that kind of thing. To shut him up, people were always giving him things to try. Sometimes they worked; usually they didn't."

"I see," Ada replied drily. "He didn't come to the healers for help?"

Dugan looked uncomfortable. "Aye, ma'am. Too often. I heard him complaining loudly to his mates that the healers had run him off for bothering them."

Ada's cheeks flushed. "I'll look into that." She drew a deep breath and looked up at the crew gathered around the tent flap. "Time to get back to work," she said tiredly. "Nothing more to see here."

Jonmarc Vahanian was waiting outside the tent for Dugan. "You all right?" Jonmarc asked, taking in Dugan's pallor.

Dugan nodded. "Not like I haven't seen dead men before," he said with uncertain bravado. "It's just, twisted up like that, Petran didn't look like himself." He shivered although it was warm in the sun. "I couldn't shake the feeling that a ghost might stick around when a man ends that way."

"We've seen worse." At eighteen, Jonmarc stood a little taller than Dugan, and his work in the forge as the blacksmith's apprentice had broadened his shoulders and thickened his arms. Dugan was wiry and strong, quick at climbing up the poles that supported the caravan's large tents and fearless about heights. In the year Jonmarc had been with Maynard Linton's caravan of wonders, he and

Dugan had seen plenty of dead men when they had helped defend the traveling company. They had killed some of those men themselves.

Jonmarc pushed a length of chestnut brown hair behind one ear. It almost covered the jagged scar that ran from his ear to below his collar bone, a reminder, as if he needed one, of the night his family was killed. "Karov won't be happy to lose another rigger."

Dugan swore under his breath. "Petran was a grouchy bastard, but he knew how to rig and he was fast. I won't miss him cursing me, but we'll all have more work to do without him."

They fell into step as they headed back across the field that the caravan had temporarily claimed as its own. Maynard Linton ran one of the biggest, best traveling shows in the kingdom of Margolan, complete with artisans, acrobats, exotic animals, musicians, and oddities. Behind the scenes, a crew of cooks, riggers, healers, blacksmiths, farriers, and others kept the caravan moving and functioning.

"Seems we've had nothing but trouble since we've come east," Dugan muttered. "I hope Linton changes his mind about crossing the river." When the current performance wrapped up, Linton had announced plans to take the show across the Nu River into neighboring Principality. The wealthy kingdom might make for a prosperous tour, but many among the caravan's crew grumbled their nervousness about leaving Margolan.

"I'm crossing one way or the other," Jonmarc said with a shrug.

Dugan gave him a sidelong glance. "Still planning to join up with a merc group?"

Jonmarc nodded. "Steen thinks I'm ready." Karl Steen, one of the caravan guards and a former soldier, had agreed to train Jonmarc in sword fighting and hand-to-hand combat.

"And what does Trent think?" Dugan asked with a knowing look.

Jonmarc looked away. "He's not pleased with the idea, but he's stopped fighting me on it."

"I'd try to tell you that it was safer here than with the mercs, but the way the last few months have gone, that would be a lie," Dugan said dryly. "I guess if you change your mind, you know how to find us."

Jonmarc nodded. "I'm not leaving for a while, so let's talk about something else, huh?"

"Do you think Petran's death has anything to do with the other man who died?" Dugan asked, obligingly switching topics.

"The animal trainer's assistant?" Jonmarc asked.

Dugan nodded. "Aye. He was pretty young to just fall over dead. They said that he clutched his heart a moment before he died, and his body went all a-tremble."

"Bad heart," Jonmarc replied. "It happens." He glanced at Dugan. "Why? You think they're connected?"

Dugan shrugged. "Just seems odd, that's all." He looked over his shoulder to make sure no one was listening. "There's a rumor he might have gotten a bottle of bad wine."

"Oh?"

"Just telling you what I've heard," Dugan said, raising a hand to forestall protest. "I wasn't there, thank the goddess. But I heard a couple of the men talking, and one of them was friends with the man who found the body. He said that there was an open bottle and a glass of wine spilled on the ground, like it had been dropped when the man fell over."

"Could be a coincidence," Jonmarc replied. "People fall over dead in the middle of all kinds of things."

Dugan chuckled. "True enough. Remember when that one fellow died on top of one of the whores, in the midst of the action? I think you could have heard her screaming all the way to Trevath!"

Jonmarc rolled his eyes. "I wasn't going to bring that up, but you just made my point. And there was the cook's assistant who died using the latrine and fell in."

Dugan wrinkled his nose. "Of the two of them, at least the fellow with the whore went out with a smile on his face."

"My point is, people fall over dead doing all kinds of things without anything being amiss," Jonmarc pointed out with labored patience.

"You're probably right," Dugan admitted, "but that won't stop people from talking, and the tales get larger with the retelling."

Jonmarc and Dugan parted company at the big tent, and Jonmarc headed on toward the forge. Karl Steen met him midway. "I heard you were there when Dugan found the body," Steen said. Steen was a former soldier who had signed on as a caravan guard. He had rapidly earned the trust of Linton and his inner circle. When Jonmarc wasn't working in the forge with Trent, the caravan's blacksmith, he was usually helping Steen and serving as an extra guard.

"Not exactly, but soon after," Jonmarc replied. "Word travels fast." He paused. "Does Linton know?"

"If he doesn't yet, he will soon," Steen said, nodding toward the open area between the tents. Maynard Linton was striding toward them, jaw set and brow creased in a frown. Linton was short and stocky, with a coppery tan from a life lived outdoors. He was a skilled impresario, a shrewd businessman, and when times got tough, a savvy smuggler. Linton's temper was as quick as his wit, and his usual bombast disguised the fact that he would face down the Crone herself for his people.

"Steen. Glad I found you. I've been robbed."

Jonmarc and Steen exchanged glances. That was not what either of them had expected. "What's missing?" Steen asked.

Linton scowled. "A basket of vegetables and a bottle of wine."

Steen gave Linton a wary look. "What kind of vegetables? Where did the basket and wine come from?"

The expression on Linton's face suggested that he thought the guard had taken leave of his senses. "Why does it matter what kind of vegetables they were?" Linton roared. "They're missing."

"The thief might have saved your life," Jonmarc said. "There's a good chance the items were poisoned."

That brought Linton up short, and his bluster disappeared. "Poisoned? What in the name of the Dark Lady are you talking about?"

"Come on," Steen said, gesturing for Linton to follow. "We'll show you."

Linton trudged after them as Jonmarc retraced his steps to the tent where the dead man had been found. Ada and the healers were still there, and Jonmarc spotted Kegan, one of the apprentice healers, standing near the back.

"Linton. Glad you're here. I was just about to send someone." Ada walked over to where Linton and Steen were standing. Petran's body lay where he had fallen, with ashen-skin and blue-tinged lips.

Linton was staring in horror at the basket and its half-eaten bounty of green stalks. "What happened?" he asked, his voice oddly subdued.

Ada sighed. "Petran might have thought the stalks were celery, but they are water hemlock. Nasty poison—awful way to die, and no antidote. Even if we'd have found him sooner, we couldn't have done anything except put him out of his misery. At least, not unless we had a mage of some power, and I'm not sure even that would have helped."

She noticed that Linton had paled. "What's the matter?"

"That's my basket," Linton said, pointing at the deadly bounty. "Whatever was in it was meant for me."

TWO CANDLEMARKS LATER, a small group convened in Linton's tent. Steen was there, along with Trent, Corbin the farrier and Zane, the caravan's knife-thrower, plus Jonmarc, Ada, and Linton himself.

"We hadn't thought much about the animal handler's assistant until Petran's death," Ada said. "But after we were able to confirm Petran was poisoned, we went back and dug up the other poor man." She looked grim. "He was also poisoned. Something in the wine. We think it might have been yew. It's a sneaky poison: sometimes there aren't any symptoms at all and the person just falls down, dead. And if there are signs, it's easy to mistake for a bad heart: trembling, weak pulse, that sort of thing.

"There was wine in his stomach," Ada continued, with a pointed look at Linton. "And the man the animal handler's assistant shared a tent with said he remembered seeing a bottle right before the man died and wondering where it came from."

"It came from my tent," Linton said soberly. "And if those items hadn't been stolen, that would have been me lying in my puke, curled up in a ball."

Trent sighed. "Normally, I'd ask if you had any enemies, but we already know the answer to that one, and that leaves a lot of suspects."

Jonmarc said nothing, but he knew Trent was right. Just in the time Jonmarc had been with the caravan, they had faced bounty hunters and vengeful *vayash moru*, murderous ghosts and treacherous slavers, bandit gangs and corrupt town officials. Those were just the people Jonmarc knew about.

"Can you think of anyone who might have a recent grudge, or someone with an old grudge who's near where we've pitched camp?" Corbin asked.

Linton thought for a moment and shook his head. "There are always business rivals, local merchants who don't like the competition from the caravan even though we're only around for a week or two."

"Have you dismissed anyone from the caravan recently?" Zane asked. "Disciplined someone? Or, maybe, run into an old lover?"

Linton gave a snort. "No, no and most definitely not. Since that run-in with the slavers, it's been quiet. I should have known that meant trouble was coming."

"Where did you get the basket?" Ada asked.

"I sent a messenger into town to do some shopping for me," Linton said. "I was hungry for a meat pie recipe that I'm quite fond of, and cook told me he didn't have some of the ingredients on hand, but that he'd bake one for me if I could supply what he needed. Since the messenger was going into town, I had him pick up a couple of bottles of wine for me as well."

"Did you see the messenger when he returned?" Corbin asked, frowning.

Linton shook his head. "No. But that didn't surprise me. I had asked him to leave the basket by my tent. I saw it was there when I walked past on my way to talk with the merchants, but I didn't stop to put it inside. When I came back, it was gone."

He paused. "I looked inside my tent, thinking someone had set it on the other side of the flap, but it wasn't there, so I went to see if cook had picked it up. When he hadn't seen it, I figured someone had stolen it, which is when I ran into Jonmarc and Steen." The attempted poisoning had dented Linton's usual bravado. Tonight, he seemed uncharacteristically sober.

"Has there been anything else unusual?" Ada pressed. "Anything at all?"

Linton thought for a moment. "I had a bad night a few days ago—felt like my heart was going to beat right out of my chest. Thought maybe I'd just been working too hard. I was terribly thirsty—nothing seemed to satisfy me. And that night, my dreams were disturbing, and so real I doubted my senses."

Ada raised an eyebrow. "If I had to guess, I'd say someone put some belladonna in something you ate. Lucky for you, that's what they picked."

"Lucky?" Trent challenged. "I know that weed. Some call it Widow's Heart. Mussa poison. It's a witch's tool. What's lucky about that?"

Linton managed a dry chuckle. "What Ada means is I've managed to build up a tolerance for that particular weed, since I take a bit of it every day for a bad stomach. So I can handle a dose that might harm someone who wasn't used to it."

"You didn't think about belladonna when you had the bad night?" Corbin asked.

Linton shrugged. "If you mean, was I on the lookout for someone trying to poison me, the answer is no. I just wasn't thinking that way. Getting a bad bit of rabbit from the stew or just having a touch of ill humours seemed likely at the time." He frowned. "Although I'll admit looking back on it, all the signs were there."

"The attacks seem to have happened since we've pitched camp here," Zane said. "Can't we just strike the tents and go? Maybe if we put some distance between us and this place, whoever's behind this won't bother to follow."

Linton shook his head. "We need the money," he replied. "It's been a couple of weeks since our last set of performances, and it's expensive to keep this show on the road. Food alone goes through quite a bit of coin, not counting what we need for the animals, supplies, repairs... Whether we go on to Principality or double back across Margolan, we need money to go anywhere."

"We need to summon the messenger who brought you the basket and find out where he bought your provisions," Trent said.

Linton and Ada exchanged glances. "We already thought of that," Ada replied. "It seems that the messenger has gone missing. No one's seen him since he left on his errand for Linton."

"Someone had to deliver the basket," Trent pointed out.

"But not necessarily the man I sent," Linton answered. "It would be easy enough for someone dressed as a messenger to find my tent. All he'd need to do is ask around." He shook his head. "It's likely that whoever sent the basket eliminated my man and substituted his own man in his place."

"We need Alyzza," Corbin said. "Perhaps she can read something from the omens to figure out who's behind this."

"I'll get her," Jonmarc said, and headed out of the tent.

Nighttime was deceptively quiet in the caravan. After the hectic activity of the day, the campgrounds seemed relatively deserted, the activity less manic. Yet behind the scenes, dozens of people labored to keep the caravan and its crew functioning. Cooks and bakers prepared for the next meal. Animal trainers fed and cared for their charges, as did the other members of the crew who kept chickens, horses, goats, or sheep. Riggers mended tents, seamstresses and tailors made garments to sell or mended costumes for performances, craftsmen created more wares and parents put children to bed. The small number of *vayash moru* caravaners went out to hunt, then set about their evening chores, while the *vyrkin* shapeshifters spotted game to help stretch the caravan's resources.

Campfires dotted the night. People sat and talked as they worked around the fire, or shared their ale or wine and told tales. Over to one side, the caravan's musicians played together, either for practice or for the sheer joy of it. Smoke hung on the night air, mingled with the scent of horses and livestock, pine trees and dinner. Jonmarc took a deep breath. This was one of his favorite things about Linton's caravan, one of the many things he knew he would miss.

It didn't surprise him that Alyzza seemed to be waiting for him. The old woman was much more powerful than most members of the caravan believed, and not as crazy as she liked to appear. She made it easy to underestimate her, and Jonmarc guessed that was intentional.

"I expected you sooner," Alyzza chided. Her long gray hair fell unkempt to her shoulders, greasy and tangled. It was impossible to guess her age. Her face was lined but her eyes were clear, though sometimes, Jonmarc had seen madness dancing in them. The air around her tent smelled of candle smoke and incense.

Jonmarc knew better than to smudge the salt circle that surrounded Alyzza's tent. A willow staff topped with feathers and animal skulls had been plunged into the ground next to the tent's opening. "We've had a couple of murders, and we think someone was trying to kill Linton," Jonmarc said. "Linton and Ada sent me to ask you to come."

Alyzza chuckled to herself. "Did they now? Ahh. Late. Things already set in motion are difficult to stop." It did not seem to matter to Alyzza whether anyone else could make sense of her musing.

Without hurrying, Alyzza got to her feet. She wore a mismatched array of faded and torn garments that had seen better days. Around her neck hung several charms and amulets, and while Jonmarc had no magic of his own, he had seen the power Alyzza took pains to hide. Like so many of the caravan's members, the old woman was more than she appeared.

"Hurrying won't make a difference; not now," Alyzza murmured, as if answering Jonmarc's unspoken comment. "The enemy is planning. We have time to think."

Jonmarc waited as Alyzza gathered some items and placed them in a canvas bag. "All right," she said. "Let's go."

The others looked up expectantly when they entered Linton's tent. While Jonmarc had been gone, someone had retrieved the basket of green stalks and the poisoned bottle of wine. They sat in the middle of the tent floor, set off by themselves.

"Hello, Alyzza." Linton's voice sounded tired. "I figure Jonmarc told you what happened. I'm hoping you can give us a clue to who's behind all this before more people die."

Alyzza nodded and turned her attention to the basket and bottle. Everyone scooted back from where they sat to give her room to work. Alyzza chanted under her breath, her voice rising and falling. She let her hands hover just above the items, careful not to touch them. Then she used a knife from her belt to mark a circle on the ground around the two objects, and before she closed the circle, she added a candle from a pouch on her belt. She lit the candle, and sprinkled the flames with herbs from the satchel she carried,

"Show me," she murmured, and said more in a language Jonmarc did not understand. "Show me."

The thin veil of candle smoke shimmered, and Jonmarc glimpsed a man's face, a stranger. He saw the back of another man's head, and two more people he recognized immediately.

"Chessis and Vakkis," Trent muttered as if the names were a curse. "Why are they back on your trail?" The two bounty hunters had caused plenty of problems for the caravan in the past, but they usually had a patron for any mayhem they caused, no matter how much they disliked someone.

"If they're involved, someone's paying them," Corbin said. "They don't work for free."

Linton swore. "I thought we were rid of those two."

"Apparently not," Trent replied. "And from what they've done, it seems more likely that someone put a death mark on your head than a bounty. Who have you pissed off lately?"

Linton shrugged, palms up. "No one, at least not enough to warrant something like this."

"Can you pick up anything else from the objects?" Ada asked, looking to Alyzza.

Alyzza frowned, then concentrated on the smoke once more. Jonmarc strained to see the face of the fourth man, but the person did not turn. Alyzza stopped chanting, and the smoke dissipated.

"Whoever hired the two men you recognized also hired a third—the one who stole your goods and poisoned them," Alyzza said, dispelling the circle and extinguishing the candle. "He has means. There will be others sent until he achieves his goal."

"Killing Linton?" Corbin asked.

Alyzza nodded. "It is not an issue of recompense," she said. "It's a matter of pride."

"How long has it been since the caravan last passed this way?" Jonmarc asked.

"More than a year," Linton answered. "The last time we crossed into Principality, we went north and took the bridge. We weren't carrying cargo that the king's soldiers might dispute."

"Could it be someone nursing a grudge from the last time you came through these parts?" Ada asked. "I was new with the caravan back then, so I probably didn't hear all the inside gossip. Did something happen that might have stung someone enough to remember it this long?"

Linton shook his head, looking mystified. "I can't think of anyone on this side of Margolan who would have reason to see me dead," he replied. "One or two might recall a few gambling debts, a hard negotiation over terms on a shipment perhaps, but nothing to warrant more than a thorough beating."

Linton was a shrewd businessman, but keeping the caravan solvent often meant deals with smugglers or other shadowy folks whose approach to commerce was bare-knuckled. Jonmarc and the others had helped the caravan master out of more than one tight situation, but poison and assassins seemed extreme, even for Linton's dissatisfied customers.

"Until we figure this out, I think we need to make sure you've got a bodyguard at all times," Steen said. "Guards around your tent would be a good idea, too. And let's make certain that the caravan guards are on the lookout for outsiders near the camp."

Trent and Corbin nodded. "We've tangled with Chessis and Vakkis before," Trent said. "I'm betting that some of our *vayash moru* and *vyrkin* remember their scent. We can alert them."

"I don't think they'll show up in person," Ada added. "They probably know people here might recognize their faces or their scent. That's why they used the messenger to deliver the poisoned items. Odds are, whoever the man was, he's probably dead in a ditch somewhere. They can always get another."

"It just doesn't make any sense," Linton fretted. "I'd always gotten on tolerably well with Duke Ostenhas."

"Who?" Steen asked.

"The man who controls most of the area between that last creek we crossed and the Nu River," Linton replied. "Duke Horgan Ostenhas. He's a small fish when it comes to Margolan politics. No one very important, although I think his wife might be the sister of someone with money. A rather portly and boring sort, without a mind for much else than his ledgers."

"You didn't happen to have a bit of fun with his wife the last time the caravan passed this way, did you?" Trent asked, raising an eyebrow.

Linton stared at him with a horrified expression. "By the goddess, no! His wife has the looks and temperament of an addled goat. I'm not a celibate man, but I assure you, that's one case where I was not tempted in the least."

"Well, we can rule that out," Trent said. "Unless you somehow offended the Duke—or Duchess—by not attempting a seduction? You know, maybe he took it as a slight that you didn't find his wife worthy of a dalliance?"

Linton shuddered. "By the Crone! I hope not."

A man cleared his throat loudly at the tent entrance. Ada rose and pulled back the flap to reveal Elian and Gil. Elian was blond and slim, a *vayash moru* who helped with patrols and did chores at night. Gil was a *vyrkin*, a shapeshifter who had taken refuge with the caravan and helped out where he could. At any time, several *vayash moru* and *vyrkin* traveled with the group, and Linton's people did their best to hide them from those who would do them harm.

"Thank you for coming," Ada said. It was crowded in Linton's tent, but everyone moved aside to allow the newcomers to enter.

"I asked Elian and Gil here because their senses are keener than ours," Ada continued. "I was hoping that one of them might pick something up from the basket and bottle, and that would allow us to track the poisoner."

Ada gestured toward where the items sat, and the group parted to allow Elian and Gil to approach the pieces. Jonmarc knew that Gil had a wolf's sharp senses of smell and hearing, and Elian's *vayash moru* senses and reflexes would be many times sharper than those of mortals. The two stood silently, eyes closed, moving around the bottle and basket, bending near and breathing deeply, careful not to touch the items.

Finally, they stood. Elian looked at Gil, and the two men nodded. "I think we've got something," Elian said.

"Hard to get much from the bottle, but the basket definitely has a scent, and it matches what I can pick up from the bottle," Gil agreed.

"It's only been a few candlemarks," Steen said. "Can you track the scent?"

Gil nodded. "I think so. How far do you want us to go?"

Steen's eyes glinted. "If you can find the person to whom the scent belongs, we can question him and figure out who he's working for."

"We can do that," Gil said. "Do you want us to capture him?"

They looked at Steen, who thought for a moment, then shook his head. "No. We might learn something from his location. Just find out where he is, and we'll take it from there."

The two men nodded and left silently. Linton sighed, and stared at the basket and bottle. "So now what?" he asked.

"We wait," Trent replied.

THE NEXT EVENING, Steen, Zane, and Jonmarc slipped quietly into the city of Dobarton. Despite being the home of Duke Horgan Ostenhas, the city itself was unremarkable. It appeared to be middling prosperous, though not wealthy. Its location near the main trade route of the Nu River likely afforded it many opportunities for commerce, both legal and not. Having grown up in a coastal town, Jonmarc was quite aware of how many upstanding merchants skirted the king's taxes whenever the opportunity presented itself.

"All in all, not much to look at," Steen muttered as the three men moved in the shadows. They had managed to get by the guards at the gate without remark. Jonmarc only hoped that their return journey would be as uneventful.

"Stay sharp," Zane said. "Just because the city looks sleepy, doesn't mean it is. We already know we've got enemies."

And we know that Chessis and Vakkis are out there, somewhere, Jonmarc added silently. He was quite certain that both of the bounty hunters would gladly slit his throat for his role in thwarting their plans.

They quickly left the better parts of city behind them, and wound their way through Dobarton's narrow, twisting streets to a section of seedy inns and run-down rooming houses. Laundry hung out to dry, still stained and torn despite its washing. Dirty children and filthy stray dogs watched them pass with a baleful eye.

"There it is," Steen murmured, with a nod toward one of the buildings. It was difficult to tell color in the darkness, but the place might have been painted blue once upon a time. Faded by the sun, stained by water and soot, the whole building seemed to hunch against its neighbor as if its supporting beams had sagged under the weight of desperation.

"It could be a trap," Zane warned.

Jonmarc shook his head. "Elian and Gil checked it out. They didn't see anything that made them worry—more than usual."

More than any sane person—mortal or immortal—should worry about confronting a poisoner who likely worked for the highest bidder.

"I'll watch the door," Zane said. He had throwing knives hidden all over his body, tucked away discreetly so as not to alarm the guards, accessible in a second if needed. "You know the signal."

Steen nodded. "Come on," he said to Jonmarc.

No one paid them any notice as they made their way up the rickety steps to the second floor. Steen and Jonmarc paused at the door to the room Elian had indicated, and Jonmarc noticed a small smudge of soot just above the lintel, the mark Elian had told them he had left so that they would know they were in the right place.

Steen listened at the door, then nodded. "No voices," he mouthed. That meant Steen heard someone inside, but not multiple people.

One sharp kick broke the latch.

Jonmarc and Steen were inside with the door closed behind them before the poisoner had time to turn.

"I told you I'd pay you tomorrow!" The speaker was a scrawny man with a complexion the color of raw dough. Lank red hair fell in his eyes that looked bleary; Jonmarc suspected that the man sampled some of the herbs that produced wild dreams.

"We're not here about your debts," Steen growled. Both he and Jonmarc had their swords in hand, and Steen gestured for the poisoner to step away from his table and hold his hands where they could be seen.

"Who are you? Why are you here?" Fear made the poisoner bold.

"Sit," Steen ordered, and Jonmarc kicked a wooden chair toward the man. From beneath his cloak, Jonmarc produced a length of rope. Steen held the point of his sword against the poisoner's throat as Jonmarc bound the man firmly to the chair by the arms and legs.

"Now," Steen said. "Let's start with your name."

In response, the captive spat at Steen.

Steen sighed and looked at Jonmarc with exaggerated disappointment. "Ah, well. We'll just have to call you 'Bastard' then." He gave a predatory smile. "So, Bastard, why did you try to poison the caravan master?"

The prisoner glared at Steen and said nothing. Steen put on a pair of heavy leather gloves and began to poke around at the wares on a sturdy wooden table in the back of the room. "Let's see here. There's belladonna, some nasty mushrooms, water hemlock, yew, nightshade, and wolf's bane," he said, casually identifying the plants and leaves in bottles strewn around the table.

"If I didn't know better, I might think that you were a poisoner," Steen said.

"Go to the Crone."

Steen chuckled. "Oh, I'm sure you have plenty of ways to send me there, but I don't think I'll go just yet." He nodded, and Jonmarc pulled on a pair of gloves as well.

"Let's play a game," Steen suggested. "I'll feed you a leaf, and we'll see what it does to you. If you survive, you get to tell us some information. If the information is good, you get to tell us some more. If it's not interesting…" He shrugged. "We'll feed you another leaf, or berry, or seed, and watch what happens."

Jonmarc knew something about plants. His late wife's mother had been a hedge witch, and Jonmarc and Shanna had often helped harvest plants for healing mixtures. Shanna and her mother had told him which plants were deadly poisons, and which could be used—with caution—as medicine. A glance at the leaves and berries on the table told him that their unnamed captive had little interest in the medicinal uses of the plants.

"Pick something," Steen said, waving a gloved hand at the table.

Jonmarc pretended to take a moment to decide. "Let's try some wolf's bane," he said finally. "It won't kill him right away—if we're careful. And if he's helpful, we just might reverse it… depending on how things go."

He picked up one of the fresh leaves with his gloved hand and walked over to the bound captive. "Last chance," he said. "Why did you try to poison the caravan master?"

The poisoner muttered something in a language Jonmarc did not recognize, but the intent was clear. Jonmarc glanced to Steen, who shrugged.

"Ah well. Your funeral." Jonmarc placed the fresh leaf on the captive's bare arm and began to rub it back and forth along the skin. "Funny thing about wolf's bane. Just touching it lets the poison in."

"All right!" the captive shouted. "My name is Matvei. And I don't even know your caravan master. It was a job. That's all."

"Is your arm tingling?" Jonmarc asked. "That's how it starts." The terrified look on the poisoner's face confirmed his guess. "But you know that, don't you? I bet you've tried your wares out on animals, people, just to watch what happens."

He ground the leaf against the man's arm again. "A healer can reverse a light dose. But the longer it goes on, the bigger the dose, the less likely anyone can save you."

"What do you want to know?" Matvei asked, his voice reedy with fear.

"Now we're getting somewhere," Steen said. "Who hired you for the job?"

"A couple of guys," Matvei replied. Jonmarc ground the leaf another time.

"All right! Two bounty hunters. Chessis and Vakkis."

Steen nodded. "That's better. What did they tell you?"

Matvei watched Jonmarc warily. "They said they needed some poison that was hard to detect. Something that could be slipped into food without someone noticing. Said that they wanted to use a couple of kinds, just to make sure."

"What did you put it in?" Jonmarc asked. Matvei paused.

Jonmarc poked a finger into the flesh of Matvei's arm. "Is it numb yet? The poison goes up the arm to the chest, then into the heart. Once it gets that far... well, you'd need a really good healer."

"I poisoned some wine, and I switched out the vegetables in a basket for some poisonous plants that are look-alikes," Matvei replied, clearly nervous. "Before that, I slipped some belladonna in his stew. Pretty basic."

"What else?" The wide variety of poisons on the work table gave Jonmarc a gnawing suspicion that the poisoner might have done more.

"Nothing," Matvei said. But his gaze slid to the side as he spoke, and Jonmarc was certain the man was lying.

Jonmarc walked back to the table and found a small jar of salve. "How about you tell us the whole truth, and I don't try this ointment on you to see what it does?"

Matvei's fear of the poison wavered, and Jonmarc guessed that the poisoner was even more afraid of Chessis and Vakkis.

"Who hired Chessis and Vakkis?" Steen asked. "They don't work for free. Someone was behind this. Who?"

"I tell you that, and I'm a dead man," Matvei said.

"You're already a dead man," Jonmarc replied. "You don't think Chessis and Vakkis won't come around to finish you off? They aren't the kind to leave loose ends."

Matvei took several shallow breaths. By now, Jonmarc was certain that the plant's poison had reached his shoulder and the muscles of his chest.

"Tell us what we want to know, and I swear we'll get you to a healer," Jonmarc said. He was queasy about using Matvei's poisons against him, but his concern for Linton's safety and the safety of the caravan pushed him on.

"A healer can't do me no good!" Matvei said, his voice pitched high with fear. "You don't know who you're messing with."

"Tell us," Steen urged. "We can get you out of here, give you safe passage across the river."

"You really don't understand," Matvei said. "But since it's too late to change anything, I'll tell you. Duke Ostenhas hired the assassins, and the assassins hired me."

Jonmarc's eyes widened, and he and Steen exchanged astonished glances. "Duke Ostenhas?" Steen replied incredulously. "Why would the Duke hire assassins to kill a caravan master?"

Matvei was laughing; a high-pitched, nervous laugh tinged with madness. "You don't know, do you? But I do!"

"Tell us," Jonmarc growled, removing the lid from the salve jar. "What in the name of the Crone is going on?"

Matvei giggled, a disquieting hysterical sound. "It's the Duke's wife. She's behind it."

"Does Linton know the Duchess?" Steen asked, and Jonmarc swore under his breath, hoping that they were not all paying a high price for one of Linton's indiscretions.

"No, no, no." Delirium was beginning to set in, and Matvei sounded as if he had drunk too much wine. "The Duchess is Lord Guarov's sister. Lord Guarov doesn't like your caravan master. Don't ask me why."

Jonmarc growled a curse and thumped his head with his fist. "Sweet Mother and Childe!"

"This makes sense to you?" Steen asked. "Lord Guarov's lands aren't even on this side of Margolan. How in the name of the Formless One is he involved, and why in the world should he care about a caravan master?"

Jonmarc signaled that he would explain everything, and returned his attention to the prisoner. "Were there any other poisoned items, besides the wine and the vegetables and the stew?"

Matvei's pupils were dilated. He began to heave, and retched up his dinner down the front of his shirt. "One more," he said, his voice trembling. "He's dying and he doesn't even know it."

Steen pressed his sword against Matvei's neck. "Tell us!"

Matvei looked to Jonmarc. "I'll tell you, but then I want the salve."

"You want it?" Jonmarc echoed incredulously. "It's not too late. We can get you a healer."

Matvei's laughter verged on madness. "Do you know what the Lord will do to me if he finds out I've told his secret? Chessis and Vakkis will cut me to ribbons, while I'm still alive." His mad, wide eyes turned beseechingly to Jonmarc. "Promise me you'll use the salve on me—and I'll tell you everything."

It could be a trick, Jonmarc thought. *But it's the only chance we've got.*

"We'll use it," Steen said before Jonmarc could find his voice. "Tell us what you know."

"I paid a man who worked for the cook to slip deadly mushrooms into Linton's stew," Matvei said. "They're slow poison, but sure. That's why people call them 'Destroying Angel'. He won't feel anything at first, then when it hits, he'll suffer for a while and die. Just a few candlemarks—no more than a day."

Steen snarled a curse under his breath. "Give me that!" he said, snatching the jar of ointment out of Jonmarc's gloved hands. Using his own heavy leather gloves, he began to spread the salve on Matvei's face, arms and chest. Then he shoved a bit of cloth into Matvei's mouth, to stifle his screams.

"What is that stuff?" Jonmarc asked, horrified and fascinated.

"Witch ointment," Steen replied. "Or so it's called. It's a mix of poisons that cause waking dreams—usually quite intense and often very nasty dreams. Legend says it's how witches fly."

"Does it kill?"

Steen met his gaze. "Often. But it's a kinder death than he's doled out for Linton."

They left Matvei to his dreams, and headed back toward the caravan, dodging the guards. Steen kept his poisoned gloves on, careful not to touch his own skin. Jonmarc kept his sword sheathed, but his hand was close to the pommel.

Just as they rounded the corner, two guardsmen spotted them. "You there! Halt!"

The guardsmen blocked the path to where Jonmarc and Steen had left the horses. Jonmarc gave a shout and brandished his sword, going straight for the two men. Steen appeared to be unarmed, though he brandished the tainted gloves like a lethal weapon.

One of the guards went for Jonmarc, while the other attacked Steen. Jonmarc parried, blocking the guard's sword, then pivoted into a perfect Eastmark kick, as Steen had taught him, slamming his foot into the guard's sword arm. Angered, the guard came at him again, but Jonmarc was ready, and drove him back, channeling his anger at the bounty hunters and his fear for Linton's safety.

Steen dodged and wove, evading the second guard's blade. The soldier regarded him with derision. "Why won't you draw your blade? Is it smaller than mine?" he challenged.

Steen's silence, and his manic smile, unnerved the guard. "Stand still, and I'll make this easy on you," the guard taunted.

In answer, Steen dropped and rolled, coming up behind the soldier. Before the man could turn, Steen grabbed the guard's face with his gloved hands, covering the soldier's eyes, nose and mouth with the ointment, pushing the man's lips apart to expose the potent salve to the tender membranes.

The guard's sword clattered to the ground, and he fell to his knees, clawing at his face in terror.

"I've got the same poison on my sword," Jonmarc lied. "Want a taste of it?"

The second guardsman glanced between Jonmarc's blade and his fallen companion, who was writhing on the ground and scratching long bloody cuts into his face. With a muttered oath, the second guard ran.

Steen gingerly discarded his leather gloves into an ash can. "Let's get out of here," he said. They made it back to their horses without further incident and rode for a while in silence, until they were both certain they had not been followed.

"Why would Lord Guarov care about Maynard Linton?" Steen asked.

Jonmarc swore under his breath. "It happened a while ago, before you joined up with the caravan. We had some *vyrkin* with us, not causing any harm. Lord Guarov hates shapeshifters. He heard a rumor that the caravan was harboring some, and sent bounty hunters after them. It turned into a full-on battle, between the caravan and the Lord's troops, until the king's guards intervened. By then, Conall was dead. We got his wife and child to safety."

He shook his head. "I imagine Guarov is still plenty sore about taking a drubbing. I never thought he'd be after us this far from his lands, but the connection through his sister makes sense."

"I don't know what we can do to help Linton, if what the poisoner said is true," Steen replied. "I've heard of that kind of mushroom. It kills."

"Maybe Ada will have an idea," Jonmarc said. "Maybe if she knows what poisoned him, she can do something about it."

Steen's expression gave Jonmarc to know that hope was slim, but the former soldier said nothing.

"What do you think will happen when someone finds Matvei?" Jonmarc asked.

"I think the bounty hunters will know straight off that the caravan's onto them. We'd best get the troupe on the road,"

Steen said. "I don't think this area is likely to be friendly much longer."

THEY RODE HARD for the caravan, fearing that they would hear soldiers behind them at any moment. The caravan's guards closed ranks as they heard the hoof beats pounding toward them, then parted as they recognized the riders. Both men jumped down from their horses and Steen sent one of the guards running for Ada and the healers, and others heading for the cook's tent to find the traitor.

"Tell the rest of the guards we're likely to be attacked," Steen warned. "Bounty hunters, or the whole Ducal guard."

Jonmarc was already sprinting toward Linton's tent.

"Maynard!" he called at the tent door, but there was no answer, though lamps glowed inside the tent.

Jonmarc pushed the tent flap back. Linton lay on the ground, clutching his belly, rolling back and forth in pain.

"Jonmarc," Linton said in a weak voice. "Get Ada."

"She'll be here in a minute," Jonmarc promised, crossing to kneel next to Linton. Steen took up a watchful position at the tent doorway, though the damage had already been done.

"Damn sons of the Crone got me," Linton murmured.

"We found the poisoner," Jonmarc reported. "He's dead."

"Did you happen to find out what he used?" Ada stood in the doorway. Her face was flushed from running, and her hair fanned out behind her on the night wind. Alyzza was with her. Kegan, an apprentice healer and a friend of Jonmarc's, was close behind.

"Destroying Angel. Poisonous mushrooms," Steen answered.

Ada cursed under her breath. "How long ago?"

"Several hours, at least," Jonmarc replied. "The poisoner

paid one of the cook's assistants to slip the mushrooms into Linton's stew."

"I assigned a *vyrkin* to sniff the food," Ada said. "He didn't find anything amiss. A *vayash moru* could have even tasted the food with no harm done. Linton wouldn't wait until sundown."

"Even a *vayash moru* might not have caught it," Steen said. "I've heard that type of mushroom tastes sweet—and its poison is delayed."

"Can you heal him?" Jonmarc asked.

Linton moaned in pain. Ada used her healing magic to check him over, then sat back on her heels. She and Alyzza conferred quietly, and Alyzza planted her willow staff at the head of Linton's bed. This time, Alyzza chanted and raised a yellow mist around Linton that sparkled and glowed. Ada placed both hands on Linton's abdomen, closed her eyes, and together, the two called on their magic. As the attempt to heal Linton stretched on, Ada beckoned for Kegan to join them, and she drew from his strength as well.

Trent, Corbin, and Zane stood silently near the tent doorway, awaiting an outcome. Steen moved to talk quietly with them, filling them in.

Finally, the glowing mist faded, and Ada dismissed Kegan. She and Alyzza looked spent and haggard.

"Did you heal him?" Trent asked.

"We can slow the absorption of the poison in his gut," Ada said finally. "That will protect his organs—for a little while. But it's beyond my healing to rid him of the poison. It's too far through his system."

"And healing is not my magic," Alyzza admitted. "My magics are better suited to war and defense. I don't have the gift for this."

"Throwing up won't get rid of the poison—he'll be retching soon enough," Ada said. "The body will void, trying to purge, but the poison is already moving through his blood."

"Surely there's something you can do?" Jonmarc pressed.

Ada looked up. "There's a mage who might be able to help. Sister Birna. Last I knew, she was in the Floating City. She used to be one of the Sisterhood, but she left them several years ago—I don't know why. She's one of the finest healers I've ever met—and a damn strong mage as well. She's our best bet."

"I can get us to the Floating City. Where would we find Sister Birna?" Steen asked.

"Ask Mama. She'll know," Ada replied.

"Let's get a wagon," Steen said. "And get him bundled up. I'll take him through to the Floating City."

"Count me in," Jonmarc said. Steen opened his mouth to protest, but Jonmarc shook his head. "We were going to the river anyhow, to take me across to Principality. And I want to see this through."

"We're coming, too." Trent stood with his hands on his hips. "If the Duke does send his men after you, you'll need reinforcements."

Before Steen could argue, Elian and Gil pushed to the fore. "We've got your traitor," Elian said. He held a chubby young man by the scruff of his neck and threw him face down on the ground just outside the tent.

Trent did not spare a second glance. "We already know who he's working with. Tie him up and put him under guard," he said. "If Linton dies, hang him." The cook's assistant blubbered apologies and begged for mercy, but with Linton sprawled on the floor and moaning in pain, the man's appeals fell on deaf ears.

"Take this," Ada said, pressing a pouch into Jonmarc's hands. "It's milk thistle. I've already given Maynard one dose. Sometimes, it can help with poisoning." She sighed. "But not always."

"Thank you," Jonmarc said, and paused as Kegan and Dugan stepped closer.

"If you go to the river, you're not coming back, are you?" Dugan asked.

Jonmarc shook his head. "Not now. Not for a while."

Dugan punched him in the shoulder, and Kegan clapped him on the arm. "Goddess go with you," Dugan said. "I hope you find what you're looking for."

"Let's get moving," Steen interrupted. "We don't have much time." He glanced down at Linton. "The Duke's sure to send his men after us when he finds out what happened to the poisoner. We need to get the caravan moving, get out of his lands as quick as possible."

Ada nodded. "Leave that to me. We'll meet you in the Floating City." She made the sign of the Lady in blessing. "Mother and Childe go with you."

They loaded Linton into the back of a wagon, and Jonmarc climbed in to ride with him. He carried a canvas bag with all of his possessions, and around his neck, he had a pouch with the coin he had saved from his months of working for Trent. On his belt he wore the two swords his father had forged, along with a long knife Trent had made for him, and a dagger he'd forged for himself. Steen handed him a crossbow and quiver. "You know how to use one of these?"

Jonmarc nodded. "Yeah. But I'm better with a sword."

Steen's expression was grim. "We'll try not to get close enough for you to use your sword. But I figure the duke already has men on the road, coming for us. Your job is to keep them off the wagon."

Steen swung up to the driver's bench. Trent, Corbin, and Zane rode separately. Zane had a bandolier of daggers, the throwing knives that had earned him fame in his act with the caravan. Trent had a large hammer, and Corbin carried a wide hatchet in addition to their swords.

"How far to the Floating City?' Jonmarc asked as Steen flicked the reins. He drove the horses as fast as they dared on the dark, rutted roads.

"A man riding full-out might make it in two candlemarks," Steen said. "With the wagon, a little longer. But you see the roads. If we go any faster, we could lame the horses, or break an axle."

Jonmarc nodded, and tried to rein in his impatience. Linton groaned quietly, moaning louder whenever the wagon jostled. At times, he raved incoherently, caught in delirium. Violent cramps seized his gut, making him curl into a ball and rock back and forth, tears running down his cheeks.

"Hang on, Maynard," Jonmarc murmured, patting the caravan master's shoulder. "Just hang on."

The road was empty at this hour, and all Jonmarc could hear was the sound of the horses' hooves and the creak of the wagon. Trent, Corbin and Zane rode three abreast behind them, their faces nearly lost in the shadows.

A dozen of the duke's soldiers poured out of the darkness on both sides of the road. They were sorely mistaken if they expected the wagon to stop. Steen let out a battle cry and snapped the reins, driving the wagon straight ahead, faster than before. Soldiers cursed and shouted, but they got out of his way.

Guards were riding up on either side of the wagon. Jonmarc leveled his crossbow at the man on the right, squeezing off a shot that threw Jonmarc backwards in the bed of the wagon, but caught the guard in the chest, knocking him from his horse.

The second guard rode up on Steen's left, hoping to knock him from the driver's bench or snatch the reins from his hands. Steen was ready, with a sword in his left hand and the reins in his right. He might have left his work as a mercenary, but his skills stood him in good stead.

Jonmarc heard the clang of steel as Steen and the guard clashed. Steen edged the wagon over, hoping to run the rider off the road. Jonmarc reloaded, and caught the soldier in the back, high on his right shoulder as Steen brought down a hard strike that severed the man's hand at the wrist.

Another soldier leaped from his horse and landed in the back of the wagon. Jonmarc kicked him hard in the face and then sent a quarrel between his eyes.

Half of the duke's soldiers were down, but the remaining guards fought on. But now, Trent, Corbin, and Zane had maneuvered their horses to block the road, keeping the guards from following the wagon.

"We'll hold them!" Trent shouted. "Go!"

"Trent—" Jonmarc had not been looking forward to saying good-bye to his mentor, but riding off into the darkness without a word wasn't what he had in mind.

"Save it! We'll meet you there."

Trent wheeled his horse and went on the attack, bringing his sword down in a powerful stroke. Zane hung back, lobbing knives with deadly precision. Corbin scythed his hatchet in one hand.

Jonmarc stayed low, and got in one last shot. The quarrel struck one of the duke's soldiers square in the chest, and the man cried out in shock and pain before he toppled from his horse. With a shout of victory, Steen took the wagon around a bend, and they left the fight behind them, though the sound of it carried for some distance.

"How's Linton?" Steen asked when he dared slow the wagon.

Jonmarc glanced at their passenger. Linton's skin was sallow and his breathing was ragged. He had long ago retched up the contents of his stomach and voided what was in his system, but the dry heaves wracked him, and from time to time, tremors seized his whole form.

"We need to get him to the healer," Jonmarc replied, unwilling to voice his worry where Linton might hear. Steen dared a glance backward, and nodded worriedly.

"Hang on. I'll get us there," Steen promised.

To Jonmarc's relief, no more guards appeared from the darkened byways. He wondered how Trent and the others had fared, and whether Ada had gotten the caravan on the move before the duke could make reprisal. Worrying about them kept him from worrying about Linton, who seemed to be fading before his eyes.

At this hour, the road was empty, so no one took note of the wagon rumbling along at top speed. Gradually, the land grew flatter as they neared the Nu River. Fraught as their errand was, Jonmarc could not avoid a streak of curiosity. The Nu River was the eastern border of the kingdom of Margolan, something he had never dreamed to see, let alone cross. On the other side lay four of the seven Winter Kingdoms: Eastmark, Principality, Dhasson, and Nargi. He had heard about the other kingdoms, but they had always been like something out of a storybook, not places he might ever actually see. Now that his goal of joining up with the mercenaries in Principality was nearly within reach, Jonmarc felt a jolt of nervousness and anticipation that was both unsettling and exciting.

"There's the Nu." Steen pointed ahead of them, into the darkness. Jonmarc listened, and he could hear the rush of water, and the distant sound of voices. Squinting, he could make out the shadows of the river banks from torches all along its edge.

"And there's the Floating City," Steen added. Jonmarc strained to see, but at this distance, it looked like a hodgepodge of shacks in the dim torchlight.

Up close, the Floating City was still a hodgepodge, but the buildings were houseboats, fishing vessels, and rafts, not shacks. Lashed together and bobbing with the current in an inlet, the Floating City glowed against the night, and Jonmarc could hear music and voices, and smell spiced fish and baked leeks.

"Is it always here?" Jonmarc asked.

Steen chuckled. "Except when it isn't. The boats can cut their ties and float away if there's a bad storm, or a large garrison heading this way. When things calm down, they tie back up again. Means that nothing in the city is ever in the same place twice."

"Is it really a city? Or just a bunch of boats?"

Steen swept his arm to indicate the lights and boats. "Oh, it's a city, all right. Think of each of those boats as a shop or business. Markets, pubs, inns, whorehouses, merchants, fish mongers, and grocers, bakeries and weapon-dealers—it's all there."

He glanced over his shoulder at Jonmarc. "The folks who spend much time here have reason to keep one eye out for trouble. The regulars are tight, and they're wary of strangers. Let me do the talking."

Steen slowed the wagon as a man approached from the darkness. The sentry was a large man, tall and broad, and torchlight glinted on the steel of the man's sword. He spoke to Steen in words Jonmarc did not recognize, a languid, accented language that seemed as drawn out as the river itself.

To Jonmarc's surprise, Steen replied fluently, gesturing to indicate Linton and Jonmarc. Linton's name and his own were the only part of the conversation Jonmarc understood. The sentry looked into the back of the wagon, peered intently at Linton, then nodded curtly and took the reins from Steen, saying something that Jonmarc guessed was an offer to stable the horses, which Steen accepted.

"Come on," Steen said, switching back to Common, the language spoken by most of the people of Margolan. "He says we can find Mama on her boat. He told me where it is. Let's go."

Between the two of them, they hefted Linton out of the wagon and carried him by the shoulders and ankles down the gangplank and onto the deck of the first boat in the jumble of ships. No one seemed to think it odd that they were carrying an unconscious man covered in vomit, which gave Jonmarc an idea of what passed for normal in these parts.

"That language you were speaking back there—"

"That's the river patois," Steen replied. "It's the language of smugglers, whores, and blackgards of every manner—quite handy to know. It's a bit of a mashup of the different languages spoken along the riverbanks, plus thieves' slang and some words all of its own."

"You speak it like a native," Jonmarc commented.

Steen shrugged. "I've been around. You pick things up."

Considering that the Floating City changed every time its denizens cut loose and tied back up, Steen navigated the rising and falling decks and the general confusion with aplomb. It looked like chaos to Jonmarc. Dozens of ships that hardly looked like they could stay afloat each bearing painted signs proclaiming the services or wares within, its narrow gangplanks crowded with ambling drunks, tired strumpets, and fast-talking shopkeepers anxious to make a sale.

Steen bantered his way through the crowd, calling out to people he recognized, and nodding to those who shouted to him. Jonmarc smelled fish and river water, cooked cabbage and onions, unwashed bodies and wet dogs, pipe smoke and dreamweed.

Abruptly, Steen turned up a small ramp leading up to an old houseboat. The paint was peeling and the hull looked as if it had veered close to some rocks, but it was afloat, and larger than many of the other boats. The smell of stew and whiskey reached Jonmarc, and his stomach rumbled, despite his worry for Linton.

"Hey, Mama!" Steen shouted. He called out something else in the patois.

A large woman dressed in flamboyant colors ambled into view. She was very tall, and quite wide, with a broad, pleasant face and dark hair caught back into a knot. At first, her eyes narrowed, and then she recognized Steen and let loose a barrage of patois.

Steen bantered back, then grew serious, nodding toward Linton. When Mama recognized the caravan master, she let out an exclamation of dismay, and gestured for them to hurry up into the main section of the houseboat.

She led them through the front two rooms, which were set out like a tavern with a bar and a few tables, and into the back, where the boat held a couple of very small rooms. They laid Linton on a bed, and Mama leaned out of the room and shouted to someone.

A young man who looked a few years younger than

Jonmarc came from around the corner, pushing his lank blond hair out of his eyes. Mama rattled off a string of commands, pointing and gesturing, and the young man nodded, then took off at a sprint.

"She sent for the Sister," Steen translated.

Mama fussed over Linton like he was a sick child, pulling his soiled clothing off him and finding him a fresh tunic, then covering him with blankets when he began to shiver. When she had settled him the best she could, she strode back to where Steen and Jonmarc waited.

"Tell me," she said in heavily accented Common. "Tell me what happened to him."

Steen gave a colorful version of the tale, and to Jonmarc's surprise, did not omit the details of their confrontation with the poisoner, or the fight with the duke's guards.

"You bested Duke Ostenhas's guards?" Mama said, and chortled in approval. "Damn. I wish I had seen it."

Mama turned her attention to Jonmarc, as if she had only now noticed his presence. Again, she and Steen exchanged conversation in the patois, and Jonmarc was uncomfortably aware that whatever they were saying was about him. Finally, Mama nodded.

"Steen vouches for you," she said, regarding Jonmarc as if taking his measure. "He says you fight well. Says you're a good friend of Linton's."

"I do my best when it comes to a fight," Jonmarc said. "And I owe Linton. He took me in when I had nowhere else to go."

"Humph," Mama said. "He says you do very well with a sword. Says you intend to join up with the mercenaries across the river."

"If they'll have me," Jonmarc replied.

Mama snorted. "Oh, they'll have you. Question is, how long will you last?"

Linton lay still, except when a convulsion jerked and trembled his frame. They waited for the mage-healer, and to Jonmarc it seemed like forever, though only minutes had passed. Minutes Linton did not have to waste.

Finally, the blond boy returned, leading a woman Jonmarc guessed was Sister Birna. She was thin as the reeds along the riverbank, with dark hair cut short like the cat-tails in the shallows. She wore the brown robes of one of the Sisterhood, a fabled community of female mages whose powers were so legendary that whispers of them had even reached the Borderlands where Jonmarc had grown up.

"Where is he?" Sister Birna asked, dispensing with pleasantries. She had intelligent eyes and a serious, but not severe expression. Mama motioned for Sister Birna to follow her, and led the way to where Linton lay.

"Sweet Chenne," Sister Birna murmured. "How long ago was he poisoned?"

Steen filled her in with what they knew, and Jonmarc noticed that he and the Sister both spoke Common and not the river patois.

"Can you heal him?" Steen challenged. "Ada said that you had strong magic, as well as the healing gift."

Sister Birna set her jaw. "If the poison has not destroyed too much, it may be possible." She paused. "What can you offer me in payment?"

Steen's expression hardened. "Name your price."

"Passage with your traveling caravan to the Palace City," the Sister said. "And a handful of silver when I get there."

"Done," Steen said.

Sister Birna nodded, and accepted the chair Mama pulled

up near Linton's bedside. "Then let's get to work," she said. "There isn't time for me to be gentle."

Jonmarc had watched Alyzza's magic, and he knew that despite her protests to the contrary, she was a powerful mage, at least when her madness did not block her power. He knew the ways of hedge witches, like his late wife's mother, workers who had a bit of magic, not strong enough to be a true mage. He had seen healers like Ada in action, pulling badly wounded men back from the brink of death. But he had little experience with real mages, and he was as curious about Sister Birna's power as he was anxious to see her results.

Birna shooed everyone but Jonmarc from the small room. She placed her hands on Linton's belly, and closed her eyes, chanting under her breath. Linton moaned and twitched, breathing shallowly. After a moment, Birna opened her eyes.

"The work that your healer and mage did have kept him alive this long and slowed the poison, but not removed it," Birna said. "They did well, but not enough. Give me what you have left of the milk thistle."

Jonmarc removed the small amount he had left after dosing Linton several times on the journey. Birna took it, and produced a bowl from the bag she carried. "I will need charcoal, turmeric, tea, and anise, and four large smooth, black stones."

The blond boy nodded, then ran to fetch what she required. Birna collected the items in her bowl, then produced a small mortar and pestle from her bag and ground the items together, except for the tea, which she bade Mama steep for her. The four stones, each the size of a small fruit, she set out on the four points of the compass around Linton's bed. When the tea was hot, Birna made a slurry of the ingredients and poured it into a cup.

Birna used a piece of charcoal to mark a circle around Linton's bed. She drew the warding so that the four stones were on the inside. Then she walked widdershins around the circle, chanting as she moved, raising a curtain of power that sealed her in with Linton. The lambent curtain pulsed with golden light, glowing and dimming with Birna's chant.

First, Birna took the tea slurry and lifted Linton's head to help him swallow the mixture. Linton gave a weak moan, and Birna stroked his throat to help him swallow a few drops at a time. She reserved some of the mixture, and poured the last few drops onto her hands, then smeared it onto Linton's belly in a slow, circular movement that mirrored the direction she had walked to close the circle.

Next, Birna rose and took up a smooth willow stick from her bag to use as an athame. Four times, once for each of the light faces of the Goddess, Birna circled the bed to the right, calling on the Sacred Lady for healing. And four times, once for each of the dark aspects of the eight-faced goddess, Birna circled widdershins, asking for death to be averted.

Finally, Birna squared her shoulders and pointed the athame at Linton's belly. She drew in a deep breath, then spoke the words of power. Linton began to shout and convulse. Jonmarc started forward, but Steen grabbed him by the shoulder.

"Let her work," he said. "There's nothing to lose at this point."

Violent convulsions seized Linton, and his body shook and writhed. Birna shoved a wad of blanket between his teeth so that his clenching jaws did not break his teeth. The cords on Linton's neck stood out with the strain, and he sweated profusely, soaking the sheets. Birna was also sweating, and her face grew flushed with the effort.

Birna cried out in a strange language, a shout of command and magic and ancient power. Dark tendrils of smoke unwound from around Linton's body and snaked into the four waiting stones. Linton convulsed once more, then lay pale and still.

Birna walked the path around the circle one last time. She let the golden curtain of power drop. The others started to surge forward, but she held out a warning hand.

"Bring me a sturdy bag and a wooden box," Birna ordered. "One big enough for the stones." Once again, the blond boy ran to fetch what she required, and returned in a few moments. Careful not to touch the rocks, Birna used a piece of wood to roll the stones into the canvas bag, then dropped the wood in on top when all four stones were contained. She tied off the top with rope, and spoke quietly as her hands ran above the bag's surface, careful not to touch it. Then she used another piece of wood to push the bag into the box, sealed it closed with magic, and stood.

"Take the box into one of the caves along the river, as deep inside as you dare to go. Bury it there. Mark it with the plague symbol, and forget where you left it. There is death in the box for any who open it."

The young man gave the box a wary look, but did as he was bid. Birna smudged the circle, and stood back, allowing the others into the crowded sickroom.

Linton's color had already improved, and his breathing was regular. He was covered with sweat, and Jonmarc was certain that Linton would have pulled muscles from the violence of his convulsions, but he was alive and looking well.

"He'll live," Birna said. "He'll be weak for a while. Let him sleep. It was very close. He was nearly beyond my reach."

"Thank you," Steen said. Mama and Jonmarc echoed his

gratitude. "I'll make sure we keep our bargain," Steen said.

Jonmarc moved closer to where Linton lay. "I'll sit with him," he offered.

Steen nodded. "I'll come by and spell you after a bit."

Jonmarc dozed in a chair while Linton slept. Several candlemarks later, a noise outside the room woke him, and he jumped to his feet, sword ready to guard the door. He sighed in relief when he saw Steen with Trent and Corbin.

"It took us a while to get rid of the duke's guards," Trent said. "Zane went back to help get the caravan moving. But we wanted to make sure you made it all right."

"Glad to see you," Jonmarc replied.

A groan from behind him made them all turn toward Linton. "By the Crone!" Linton muttered. "I feel awful."

"You were poisoned—again," Jonmarc replied. "Mushrooms. Nasty stuff. You're in the Floating City. Sister Birna healed you."

"Damn," Linton replied. "Last time I eat vegetables, that's for sure."

"The caravan is safe," Trent said, moving into the small room. "They'll catch up with us sometime tomorrow. Do you still intend to cross the river?"

Linton shook his head. "Not this time. Maybe next year. We'll head back toward the Isencroft border."

"Just as long as we stay well to the South of Duke Ostenhas's lands," Trent replied.

"Fine by me."

"I'll make sure the caravan knows," Trent said. "We'll provision here, then head out when you're ready."

The others filed out of the room, but Linton called out to Jonmarc to stay. "You still intend to join the mercs?" he asked.

"It's something I need to do."

Linton regarded him for a moment, then nodded. "Then go with my blessing, for what it's worth. And if you ever need a place to go, the caravan will always take you in."

"Thank you," Jonmarc replied.

THE NEXT MORNING, Trent and Corbin accompanied Jonmarc to the riverbank, where Steen had hired a man named Nyall and his boat to take them across into Principality.

"You've got a job with the forge, if you decide soldiering isn't for you," Trent said, shaking Jonmarc's hand.

Corbin clapped him on the shoulder. "Between the forge and the farriers, there's always work for you. The blessing of the Lady go with you," he said.

Jonmarc managed not to look back as the boat pulled away from shore. Neither he nor Steen spoke. Before long, Steen instructed Nyall to guide the boat to shore at a rundown dock that made the Floating City look plush by comparison.

"Are you sure we're in the right place?" Jonmarc asked. He grabbed his bag, felt for the sack of coins that hung around his neck beneath his tunic, and assured himself that his swords were secure at his belt.

"No point complicating things by coming in at one of the main ports," Steen said. "We're closer to where the mercs camp this way. Let's just hope that my friend isn't out on a mission."

Steen paid Nyall. The boat master muttered a benediction against harm, giving Jonmarc to know that they were heading into territory that was as dangerous as it looked. Jonmarc followed Steen up the worn stairs that led to a path through the woods. Near the far side of the forest, a burly guard stepped out from the shadows to block their path.

Steen and the guard traded words in the river patois, and then the guard waved them on. "What was that about?' Jonmarc asked when they were well past the man.

"Just making sure we had good reason to be here," Steen said. "Mercs don't win popularity contests. They aren't fond of being knifed in their sleep. I mentioned a few names. Good to know my contacts are still held in high regard."

Jonmarc let Steen do the talking as they emerged in a campground many times the size of what Linton's caravan required. Tents, wagons, and campfires filled the flatland for as far as the eye could see. No one moved to stop them, but Jonmarc could feel the weight of the stares that followed them as they made their way through the crowded encampment.

A tip from one of Steen's contacts led them to The Wobbly Goat, an inn of dubious reputation at the edge of a dilapidated town. Jonmarc stayed close as he followed Steen into the run down tavern. The sign hung only by a chain on one side, making it more wobbly than its namesake, and the inn smelled of burnt bread, overcooked venison and bitter ale.

"Steen! By the Crone's tits! What brings you to Principality?" The man who hailed them was barrel-chested, with a dark, full beard.

"Harrtuck, you old dog! I've got a favor to ask."

Harrtuck gave Steen a sidelong glance. "It doesn't involve money, does it? Because except for some ale coins, I'm broke as a fat whore's bedsprings."

Steen shook his head. "I don't need a loan. I need a tutor."

Harrtuck slammed his tankard down on the rickety bar, and the entire counter shook. "Then you've come to the wrong place, mate, unless you'd like to learn to curse in four languages."

Steen chuckled. "I can already do that," he said. He motioned for Jonmarc to step forward. "Tov Harrtuck, I'd like you to meet a friend of mine, Jonmarc Vahanian. Jonmarc's been a guard and an apprentice blacksmith with Maynard Linton's caravan, and he's pretty good at fighting."

He looked to Jonmarc. "Harrtuck here has soldiered with the king's troops and several of the merc groups. He knows his way around."

Steen returned his attention to Harrtuck. "Jonmarc aims to join up with one of the merc groups. I told him you might be able to steer him toward a good fit."

Harrtuck nodded. "I just might." He looked Jonmarc up and down. "Too bad you weren't a week earlier. Gregor's mercs just shipped out. By the Lover and Whore! He's a son of the Bitch, but he runs a tight company, and most of his men come back alive."

Steen shook hands with Jonmarc. "Well then, you're in good hands," he said. "Take care, Jonmarc. I hope our paths cross again."

"Thank you," Jonmarc said. "For everything."

Steen turned away and disappeared into the crowd. Harrtuck clapped Jonmarc on the shoulder. "If Steen vouches for you, that's enough for me." He pushed a tankard of ale toward Jonmarc. "You're going to make a fine mercenary."

Fresh Blood

"A MERCENARY, HUH?" Tov Harrtuck looked at Jonmarc Vahanian and raised an eyebrow. "How did you decide that's what you want to be?"

Jonmarc looked back at him with a level gaze. "Because I'm good with a sword. I'm good in a fight. And I can't go home."

They sat in a rough bar, a place called The Wobbly Goat. The tavern was busy with traders and soldiers, along with weary, wary travelers. The tavern's walls were splintered and dented in places where old fights had gotten out of hand. The floorboards were sticky with ale and dirt, and the air was stale with pipe smoke and the smell of too many bodies gone too long without a proper bath. Jonmarc hoped he looked seasoned and tough. He had never been out of Margolan before, never this far away from home. And while he told himself he was ready, that decision would not be his to make.

Harrtuck regarded him in silence for a moment before speaking. "You could have stayed with Linton's caravan. I'm betting they didn't want to see you go. I'd also bet coin I don't have that Steen tried to talk you out of this."

Jonmarc's lips tightened and he gave a curt nod. "That's true. I'm grateful to Maynard, and to the caravan. But I've been enough trouble to them. Trouble seems to follow me. So I might as well get paid to get into it and out of it."

Again, Harrtuck studied him, sizing him up. The mercenary was probably ten years older than Jonmarc, in his late twenties. Harrtuck was short and barrel-chested, strong and scarred. Steen had made a point to introduce them, going out of his way to make sure that if Jonmarc was going to join up with a mercenary group, he at least got a chance to pitch his services to Harrtuck and, if he passed muster, to the War Dogs.

"What kind of trouble?" Harrtuck asked. "If your idea of what mercenaries do is drink and carouse and bust up towns, then the War Dogs aren't your troop."

Jonmarc shook his head. "No. That isn't what I meant. It's just that, fights seem to find me. Raiders burned my home village. Then different kinds of raiders destroyed the village that took me in." In truth, they had been monsters, but he didn't think Harrtuck would believe him if he said that.

"When there were attacks on the caravan, I did a good job helping fight off brigands," he continued. "Well enough that Linton brought me along as a guard many times, although I was officially the blacksmith's apprentice."

Harrtuck nodded. "Brigands are one thing," he said. "But here in Principality, the mercs fight more than raiders, although that's some of what we do."

Jonmarc's gaze was unyielding. "I've gone up against mages, *vayash moru*, *vyrkin*, and monsters. And trained soldiers too. I've fought with a team, and on my own."

"Can you fight under orders?" Harrtuck asked. "Not just brawl, but fight like soldiers do, together for a cause, one you might not even care about, aside from the money?"

Jonmarc had been asking himself that same question for days. *I think so. But how can I know, until I'm in the thick of it?* In the three years since his father died, Jonmarc had never missed his counsel so much as he did now. Principality was a foreign place, filled with people who spoke strange languages and who kept unfamiliar customs. And while he had fought and killed and faced down fearsome creatures, Jonmarc felt completely out of his depth.

"Yes," he replied, with as much conviction as he could muster.

Harrtuck's eyes narrowed. "The fights you've fought, why did you get involved?"

Jonmarc looked at him as if he were crazy. "Because someone was hurting my family, my friends, or threatening the caravan. Because I didn't want to die—or let them die."

Harrtuck nodded. "Fair enough. But what about a fight you could avoid? One that isn't any of your business— except that you've been paid to make it your business?"

That was a question Steen had asked him, before agreeing to bring Jonmarc to Principality. *You're a good man in a fight, Jonmarc,* Steen had said. *And you pick your fights pretty well. You have your friends' backs. But mercs don't fight for loyalty, or friendship. They fight for coin. What will you do, when you find yourself on the side of a fight you wouldn't have picked? Mercs do a job. It's not about right and wrong.*

Steen had done everything he could to warn Jonmarc away from selling his sword. Like others among the caravan, Steen had been a merc and left it behind him. Jonmarc heeded Steen's warning. But what drove him on was something he could not have explained, to Steen or Trent or Corbin, or even to Maynard Linton himself.

I have to leave because the caravan has become family, Jonmarc thought. *Because the curse will follow me. Eventually, it will catch up with me. I don't want it to destroy them, like it's destroyed everyone else. Soldiers can take care of themselves.*

"I'll do what I have to do," Jonmarc replied, hoping he sounded resolute. Steen had told him that the War Dogs were choosy about the jobs they accepted. Choosier than most, anyhow. From what Steen said, the War Dogs stayed away from hiring on with the worst of the nobility or the brigands wealthy enough to pass themselves off as aristocrats, interested only in their petty squabbles for territory. King Staden himself had turned to the War Dogs on more than one occasion, Steen told him, to guard the royal family or to settle a dispute. And Steen had spoken of their Captain Valjan with respect and admiration, something the former soldier did not grant easily to anyone.

Finally, Harrtuck nodded. "All right," he said. "I'll speak to Valjan about you."

"When? Where?" Jonmarc pressed. "I've got nowhere to go."

Harrtuck shrugged. "Stay here tonight. You'll be safe enough; safe as anywhere in this part of the city. I'll arrange a meeting, and we'll let the others have a proper look at you."

Jonmarc swallowed down his fear with the rest of his ale. Most of his food had gone cold on his plate. Harrtuck, on the other hand, had finished off his meal, talking with his mouth full. *Maybe I'm not as tough as I think I am. If I were tougher, I'd still have an appetite.*

No one in the bar gave much notice to Jonmarc, but he saw that they cleared a path for Harrtuck when he rose from the table and headed for the door. The tavern's customers looked as hard worn and seedy as the bar itself, and much more dangerous. Harrtuck regarded the tavern's occupants with a cold gaze, and they soon went back to their business. Jonmarc's hand was near the hilt of his sword, but Harrtuck never moved for his weapon. His reputation—or perhaps the reputation of the War Dogs—was defense enough here.

The door closed behind Harrtuck, and the Goat's patrons went back to their drinks and conversations. Jonmarc sat with his back to the wall, nursing a tankard of ale. Harrtuck's assurances notwithstanding, he did not feel safe. Then again, until he knew his way around Principality, he doubted he would feel safe anywhere, even among the War Dogs.

He sipped his ale and glanced around the smoky room. Two minstrels played in the far corner, music from their drum and pennywhistle nearly lost in the rumble of conversation. Three strumpets in faded and smudged dresses made half-hearted rounds of the room, offering their companionship. A dice game to one side drew a crowd, and the loud wagering, plus the shouts of the winners and groans of the losers drew a harsh glare from the barkeeper. Most of the tavern's patrons looked like they had seen their share of fights, whether or not fighting was their business or a side-effect of too much ale. A few might have been traders or travelers, but Jonmarc guessed the majority were, or had been, soldiers.

Jonmarc saw two men at a table toward the rear of the tavern conclude their conversation and rise to leave. One of the men ducked his head, but Jonmarc got a glimpse of his face as he walked to the door. He was missing the tip of his nose, and the scar from the blade that took that tip had left a furrow across the man's cheek and chin. To Jonmarc's surprise, the man's table companion walked over to where he sat.

"Mind if I join you?" the stranger asked.

Jonmarc shrugged. "There's a chair. Suit yourself." He kept his voice neutral. His right hand stayed on his tankard, while his left went to the pommel of his sword, just in case

"Saw you talking with Tov Harrtuck," the stranger said. "Thinking of joining up with the War Dogs?"

"I'm thinking that the ale is watered down," Jonmarc replied. "What's it to you?"

"I used to be with the War Dogs. Thought I might spare you that mistake."

Jonmarc's eyes narrowed. "How, exactly, is any of this your business?"

It was the stranger's turn to shrug. "It isn't. But I've seen too many young men come to town looking for adventure and get tangled up with the wrong sort. Happened to me. Figured you might want to know a little more about the Dogs, if you're thinking of joining up."

"I'm listening," Jonmarc replied, his voice flat. "Doesn't mean I'll believe what you have to say, but I'm listening."

The stranger gave a curt nod. "Fair enough. All right then. Name's Hagen. I did a few years in the Margolan army, and came over to Principality looking for a little more money in exchange for risking my neck. Heard that the War Dogs were the best bunch of mercs in the kingdom. So I signed on with them. Found out the hard way they weren't what I was led to believe."

Jonmarc raised an eyebrow, indicating for Hagen to go on. He studied the newcomer. Like many of the other men in the tavern, Hagen had the fit, muscular build of a career soldier. His dark blond hair was cut short, and he carried himself like a fighter. He wore a tunic and cloak that could easily hide a cuirass. He carried both a broadsword and a short sword, though Jonmarc was sure that Hagen, and everyone else in the inn, had more weapons hidden about themselves.

Hagen was probably seven or eight years older, Jonmarc guessed, a bit younger than he judged Harrtuck to be, old enough to have been around a bit, and perhaps close to

Steen's age. From the bruises and cuts on Hagen's hands and forearms, Jonmarc guessed his new 'friend' was no stranger to fights, or had extremely bad luck. Hagen's looks were passable but nothing special, except for his eyes, which were mismatched: one blue and one brown.

"Everyone says Valjan's such a hero," Hagen said. "He's nothing special. No less greedy than the rest of the merc commanders. That's why I got out. Got tired of fighting for whoever had the money, no matter what kind of a sorry bastard they were."

"That's what mercs do," Jonmarc replied. "No surprise there."

Hagen leaned across the table. "You don't think so? Wait until you're in the pay of one of those murdering sons of bitches. Wait until you're part of an army marching in to put down an uprising, and you see what kind of animal is paying your wage."

"So far, I've heard a lot of opinion, and nothing solid," Jonmarc said, eyes narrowing. "If you've got a point, make it."

"My point," Hagen said with emphasis, "is that I hate to see a young man make the same mistake I made. Especially with the War Dogs. Seeing how I don't think Valjan and his crew will be around much longer."

Jonmarc did his best to appear disinterested. "Oh? Why's that?"

Hagen gave a nasty smile. "Just rumors. It's on the street that some of the other merc troops might be looking to shuffle the deck a bit. If Valjan wants to keep his place at the top, he's going to have to fight for it."

"Talk is cheap," Jonmarc drawled in his Borderlands accent. "Thanks for the warning. See you around." He picked up his ale and took a sip, clearly looking away from Hagen.

After a moment, Hagen stood. "All right. Don't say I didn't do you a good turn with a warning. Guess you need to learn your lessons the hard way."

Jonmarc did not speak, but he turned so that the lantern's light fell on the old scar that ran from his left ear and jaw down below his collar. "Already have," he said, letting Hagen hear the steel in his tone.

That night, Jonmarc dozed sitting up against the wall in the crowded, shared sleeping quarters. He stayed awaked until the others were asleep, or at least snoring like bears, before he let himself drift off, his knife in his right hand, and his coin purse well-secured beneath the laces and straps of his clothing. A few times he startled awake, only to find that one of the men in the room was lurching downstairs to the latrine, or thrashing from bad dreams.

Morning came, and Jonmarc was pleasantly surprised to find that his throat had not been slit nor had he been relieved of his possessions. From the outcry from one man on the opposite side of the room—and the suspiciously notable absence of a trader who had disappeared in the night—not everyone had been so lucky.

Not long after daybreak, the others left the tavern, and Jonmarc managed a candlemark or two of sleep before being roused by the tavernmaster and shooed downstairs. Although it was still early morning, a couple of florid-faced, rough-looking men were already happily drinking their ale at a table beside the fireplace. Jonmarc took a seat as far away as he could and spent a few more coins on a breakfast of cheese and sausage, a hard roll, and a cup of hot, bitter *kerif*.

Harrtuck returned a little after noon. "Things have been busy," he said abruptly. "Some trouble brewing. I told Valjan it couldn't wait, but he's likely to be plenty distracted, so expect that."

Jonmarc could see a difference in Harrtuck's manner. The mercenary was wary and on edge, and while Jonmarc did not press him for information, given Hagen's comments the night before, he was not completely surprised.

"All right," Harrtuck said. "Changed your mind?" When Jonmarc shook his head, Harrtuck rolled his eyes. "Gave you a chance. Remember that. Come with me."

Jonmarc debated whether or not to mention Hagen, and finally decided to see what Harrtuck would make of the conversation. "Ever heard of a man named Hagen?" Jonmarc asked, trying to sound off-handed.

Harrtuck made a rude noise followed by a few obscene and descriptive curses. He stopped in his tracks. "Best tell me how you know that name right now," he said, and his expression had grown unfriendly.

Jonmarc shrugged. "He came over to my table after you left, invited himself to sit down, and tried to warn me off of joining the War Dogs."

"Did you tell him that's what you meant to do?" Harrtuck asked sharply.

Jonmarc rolled his eyes. "I'm not stupid. I told him nothing, but I tried to get him to talk. Lot of garbage, nothing substantial." He looked at Harrtuck. "So what's he got against Valjan? And are the War Dogs in danger from other merc groups?"

This time, Harrtuck's outburst was loud and lengthy, and inventively crude enough to draw a censorious glare from one of the king's guards. Harrtuck and Jonmarc hurried on their way, and Harrtuck waited until they were out of the guard's hearing to reply.

"Hagen was trouble. That's why he doesn't like Valjan. Valjan doesn't put up with lying, double-crossing scum. He stole from his bunkmate, lied about it, tried to pin it on someone else, and showed up drunk for night watch. Valjan threw him out on his ear."

Sounded fair enough to Jonmarc. "Linton wouldn't have put up with that either, and we were just a caravan," he said.

"Damn right!" Harrtuck replied. "You join the Dogs, you are family. Now there are all kinds of families," he said with a note of distaste, "but Valjan runs a good one. We have to be able to trust each other. Don't like all the Dogs, and they don't all like me, but I trust them with my life."

The narrow walkways beside the rutted, muddy streets were cheek and jowl. Elbows and shoulders cleared a path through the press of bodies, shoving their way through to wherever they were going. Jonmarc had been enough places with the caravan to keep his small purse of coins hidden beneath his shirt, and his hands close to his swords, not only to draw them if necessary, but to keep someone from trying to make off with them.

He tried not to look around himself, not to give away that he was a newcomer, but Principality City was much bigger than anywhere he had been before. Far larger than his home village of Lunsbetter, or any of the towns where Linton's caravan had put on their show. He heard a babble of languages from the strangers in the street. From the way they were dressed, he guessed they came from nearly all of the seven lands of the Winter Kingdoms. A few of the people around him spoke Margolense, but many spoke the Common tongue here in a kingdom that cautiously welcomed merchants and mercenaries within its boundaries. He even glimpsed a few ebony-skinned men he guessed to be from Eastmark, Principality's neighboring kingdom, a place that had once seemed too far distant to be real.

"King Staden's ancestor invited the mercenaries to winter here to keep the peace," Harrtuck said as they walked. "Because of the gem mines, to keep all the other kingdoms from trying to invade. So the mercs can shelter here on neutral territory, so long as they swear never to raise their swords against Staden or his kin."

"What about the nobles?" Jonmarc asked.

Harrtuck gave a cold smile. "They're fair game, as long as their squabbles are with each other and don't threaten the king's power. Actually, I imagine it's to the king's benefit if his nobles spend their blood and gold fighting each other. Weakens them all, and keeps them from getting any dangerous ideas."

Jonmarc kept his wits about him as they took several turns away from the main road. Steen had said he could trust Harrtuck, but much as Jonmarc trusted Steen, he had no history yet to extend that faith to Harrtuck. Traffic thinned out as they left the bustle of the city's thoroughfare behind them. A glance down the alleys made it clear that seedy as The Wobbly Goat had been, Principality City had worse to show.

He quickened his step to keep up with Harrtuck, who strode down the narrow alley as if he owned it. Rats skittered away from garbage heaps, and beggars cursed them or begged for alms as they passed. Pedestrians of a worse sort hustled past them, more numerous here than on the main road. Some of them had the look of men who had been soldiers and left when it scarred them too much to do anything but kill. Others had a thin, hungry look that told Jonmarc they had one foot over the abyss and would do anything to keep from sliding the rest of the way. If this was the path to the War Dogs' headquarters, than the mercenaries had done nothing to secure the area. And if their way was not leading them to the

War Dogs, then Jonmarc readied himself for the possibility that his trust—and Steen's—might have been betrayed.

We're being watched. Jonmarc knew in his bones that their presence had attracted attention, although there was nothing he could call to Harrtuck's attention. Just the gut instinct that had served him well for so long. The alley was narrow enough that it would be folly to draw his swords if there was trouble, so Jonmarc made certain that his two long knives were handy, just in case. He had a shiv in his boot and a few dirks in his belt as well. With luck, he would not need them. *That all depends,* he thought wryly, *on whether it's my luck or somebody else's.*

Smoke rose from a building up ahead. Harrtuck's pace quickened. "Look sharp," he cautioned. "Something's wrong."

They rounded a corner at just under a dead run, only to find the smoking ruins of a building, burned nearly to the ground. Its blackened chimneys still stood, leaning precariously without the walls that supported them. In some places, the roughhewn stones of the foundation could be seen, and darkness gaped where floorboards had fallen into a cellar beneath. Smoke was heavy on the air, stinging Jonmarc's eyes and making him choke.

Harrtuck let out a string of curses.

"Where are the others?" Jonmarc asked, drawing his knives. He saw a splatter of blood on the paving stones near where the burned house's doorway had been, and a pool of blood a little farther on.

"Not here, Dark Lady take my soul!" Harrtuck replied, drawing his sword as well. "We were supposed to meet in that house. It was standing just a candlemark ago." He muttered a curse. "There aren't many who would dare make a move like this against us." Harrtuck looked at Jonmarc.

"Go back to the inn. This isn't your affair."

Jonmarc shook his head. "No. I came to be a War Dog. Well, it looks like you could use a spare." He had taken a fighting stance, and scanned the alley for threats. *I'm hardly going to turn tail and run to shelter, if there's work to be done,* he thought. *And frankly, I feel safer in a fight beside Harrtuck than back at the tavern by myself in a strange kingdom.*

"Suit yourself," Harrtuck said with a shrug. "But don't expect me to protect you, if it comes to a fight."

"I can take care of myself," Jonmarc replied. "So—you got enemies that might have done this?"

Harrtuck barked a harsh laugh. "Yeah, the War Dogs have enemies. Can't help it. But torching one of our buildings is asking for retribution. We don't start those kinds of fights, but we finish them. Have to. Bad for business. I want to know what happened to Valjan and the others."

"I think we're likely to find out," Jonmarc murmured. He caught a glimpse of motion, and saw something else move off to the side. A dozen armed men ran toward them, shouting and hollering war cries and threats.

Jonmarc fell into a defensive crouch, as two of the attackers came right at him. He shouted an oath as he beat back a flurry of knife strokes, and one of the blades skidded down the vambrace on his arm. He was glad Steen had insisted that he wear a padded leather breastplate beneath his clothing, and leather cuffs on both wrists. *Can't be too careful in a strange place, Steen said. Guess he knew better than I did what to expect.*

Harrtuck waded into battle cursing and shouting. Three men ran at him, but Jonmarc was too busy fighting off his own assailants to keep a careful eye on Harrtuck's battle. Jonmarc's second attacker made a vicious swipe at his midsection. Jonmarc dodged, then dove forward to score a gash on the man's shoulder, drawing blood. The first fighter ran at him, but this time, Jonmarc swung into a high Eastmark kick, sending the man hurtling backward to slam against a stone wall and slide to the ground.

Whoever the attackers were, they came well-armored. Jonmarc managed to land blows at the weak points of their protections, but their vambraces and cuirasses deflected the worst of his strikes, and helmets hid their faces.

More fighters swarmed into the street. Harrtuck downed two of his three opponents, but others ran forward to take their places. Jonmarc had never fought beside Harrtuck before, but they had both seen enough of battle to fall into a rhythm, and after taking out two more opponents each, they found themselves fighting back to back.

A shrill whistle sounded in a distinctive pattern, and all at once, the attack ceased. The fighters stopped where they were, but did not lower their weapons. Jonmarc and Harrtuck remained poised.

"We only want the mercenary," a voice called from the shadows of the alley nearest the burned out building. "Our business is with the War Dogs. This is none of your concern, stranger. Go your way, before you have reason to regret staying."

"Screw that," Jonmarc muttered.

"Don't be a fool," Harrtuck said. "This isn't your fight. Get out while you can."

Jonmarc knew that Harrtuck was probably right. Still, there was no way he was going to walk out on the fight, not when the odds were so terribly skewed, or when the fate of the rest of the War Dogs was uncertain. "Shut up," he said. "I'm staying."

"You're mad," Harrtuck said. "This is not about proving yourself."

"No, it's not," Jonmarc replied, "I don't break my word." In the next breath he let out a feral cry and launched himself at the two closest attackers.

Long ago, the night his family died, Jonmarc had learned to close out his fear and pain and feel nothing in a fight, nothing at all except clear, cold purpose. It seemed to him that time slowed down, everything came into a sharp focus, and he moved with deadly confidence. Live or die, there was a rough joy in fighting, in the way his body and blades moved together, in the satisfaction of seeing his enemies fall to his strikes. Jonmarc's high kicks struck his opponents down and broke bone. His knives slashed their chests and arms, scoring hits that would have killed had it not been for the enemy's protections. Harrtuck muttered a curse at Jonmarc's headstrong refusal to give up, and then bellowed as he attacked, wading into a group of four men who were stouter and taller than he was.

Together they felled half of their attackers before the others crowded in on them, swarming around them so thickly that there was no more room to fight. Trapped in the press of bodies, Jonmarc could not pivot to kick or do more than jab with his knives. One of the soldiers brought the baton down on Harrtuck's head, and the beefy mercenary dropped to his knees. Jonmarc continued to struggle until men pinned his arms and legs and wrested his knives from his grip.

"We gave you a chance," their leader said, regarding Jonmarc as he still fought against his captors.

"Go to the Formless One," Jonmarc spat.

The leader chuckled nastily. "That's very likely," he replied. "But not any time soon." Jonmarc met his gaze, looking right into their attacker's mismatched eyes. A sharp pain exploded in Jonmarc's head as he was struck from behind. His vision darkened, his knees gave out on him, and he fell to the ground.

Jonmarc awoke with a groan. His head throbbed, his mouth was dry and tasted of blood, and one attempt at moving let him know he was bound at the wrists and ankles.

What a wonderful mercenary I make. Didn't last a day in Principality. Not even long enough to get hired on by the War Dogs. How could I have been so wrong?

A groan nearby ended his recriminations. He struggled to roll onto his side, and saw Harrtuck lying not far from him. The back of Harrtuck's head was bloody, and his dark hair was matted around where he had been hit. Jonmarc suspected he did not look any better himself. "Harrtuck," Jonmarc hissed. "Are you awake?"

He forced himself to ignore the headache, and looked around the room that was their prison. For now, they were alone. Jonmarc tried to sit up, to see if he could work at the knots that held his ankles, but the effort nearly made him pass out as the pain in his head flared with the movement. He grunted as he eased back, willing himself to remain conscious.

"Aye," Harrtuck managed groggily. "And a pox on the one who hit me. Damn, that hurts!"

"They've left us alone for now," Jonmarc whispered.

"Probably because we didn't seem like much of a threat," Harrtuck muttered.

"Pretty sure one of them was Hagen," Jonmarc said. "The one giving orders. Had the same eyes."

Harrtuck's tirade this time managed to include phrases in Markian and Crofter, for good measure. "Son of a bitch," he said. "Well, then he was either the one who torched the building or he knows who did it. We'll get him. He'll pay." He tried to move and gave a grunt as he struggled against the ropes.

"I've got an idea," Jonmarc said quietly. He could feel the shiv in his boot pressing against his calf. Their captors had obviously not taken the time to search them thoroughly. It took him a few tries before he could manage the stretch required to reach his boot. He swore as he twisted, but he managed to get his fingertips to nudge the knife out of its scabbard and it fell into his hand.

"Stay where you are," Jonmarc added, grasping the knife with his numb fingers and sawing at the ropes. "I'll have you out as soon as I'm free."

A few minutes later, he had cut their ropes, and they sat rubbing at their wrists and ankles to restore the circulation. "We've got trouble," Harrtuck said.

Jonmarc glared at him. "Did you only just figure that out?"

Harrtuck swore and shook his head. "No. Someone from the War Dogs should have been with the burning building, protecting the ruins, in case we could retrieve valuables. Since there was no one around, I've got to figure there are bigger problems—and that no one is going to notice I'm missing for a while." He regarded Jonmarc. "You fought like a *dimonn*. I hadn't believed Steen when he said you were a natural fighter, but he was right."

"So who attacked us?" Jonmarc said, moving cautiously around the small room. "And why did they pick now to go after the War Dogs?"

"We've been having some trouble with the Black Wolves, another merc company," Harrtuck replied. "There's been talk that some of the Wolves think we get too many of the plum contracts." He snorted. "'Course, there's a reason for that—we're damn good at what we do."

"We need to get out of here before someone comes back," Jonmarc said. He had regained the feeling in his hands, and his legs were steady enough to walk without stumbling.

"It's not your fight."

"It is now."

After a moment, Harrtuck swore and turned away. "Suit yourself." He eased the door open to the next room, with a knife in his hand that had appeared from somewhere in his clothing. Jonmarc held his shiv at the ready. The room where they had been held was mostly empty except for a washstand and a small bed. Jonmarc managed to pick the lock on the door. Beyond it was an outer room that held a table and two chairs, a chest, and a fireplace.

Harrtuck looked around the room, went to the chest, and gave a grim smile as he opened it. "Our weapons, at least," he said, bending to retrieve their blades. Jonmarc nodded his thanks as he returned his swords to their scabbards, and once he had his long knives back, he returned the shiv to his boot.

Harrtuck headed for the door. "This is your last chance to turn away," he warned.

"Get moving," Jonmarc said. "We've got to find your people."

Principality City's dodgier quarters were a warren of narrow alleys and tight ginnels, but Harrtuck moved through them like a native. Only a few blocks over, the sound of fighting carried on the air, down near the waterfront in a section of the city that looked like it had seen far better days.

The open area might once have been a grand square, but its beauty had been sullied long ago. A cracked, broken fountain sat dry and filled with refuse along one side of the space. The large stone buildings that flanked the square were covered in soot, their columns scarred and covered with vandals' messages, their steps smelling of urine. Any vagrants that had made their lodgings there were smart enough to scatter at the first sign of trouble

Two small armed gangs fought their way back and forth across the soiled paving stones, swords clanging, blades flashing in the sun. Given the neighborhood, Jonmarc doubted the king's guards would care what happened down here, so long as it did not burn down the city. The two warring sides pushed each other back and forth through the open courtyard, and to Jonmarc's eyes, they appeared evenly matched.

He nearly asked Harrtuck how to tell one group from the other before he spotted a man who fit Steen's description of Captain Valjan. Valjan was a tall man with a patch over one eye, tanned from years outdoors and scarred from decades of soldiering. He was laying-to with a broadsword in one hand and a shorter blade in the other, driving his opponent back with pounding blows that sounded as if they might shatter steel. Like the rest of his men, Valjan wore a black armband emblazoned with the face of a snarling dog.

"Let's go!" Harrtuck shouted, as he and Jonmarc waded into the fray.

There could easily have been a hundred men in the fight, more or less evenly split between the two warring sides. Harrtuck wore a War Dogs arm band, but Jonmarc did not, and realized the lack as soon as he followed Harrtuck into the fight. He glanced around, spotted a fallen mercenary, and stripped off his arm band, doing the best he could to secure it around his own arm before one of the enemy mercs closed on him.

"Fresh meat," Jonmarc's attacker said with a toothy grin as he came at Jonmarc, sword raised.

Jonmarc dropped low, bringing his own blade across the man's knees, then swung up, knocking aside the attacker's sword, planting his boot squarely in the man's chest. "Your mistake," Jonmarc muttered as he drove forward, slipping his sword into the downed man's gut before the astonished merc had time to react. Hot blood spattered across Jonmarc's face and arms.

So much was going on that everything seemed a blur. Yet as Jonmarc watched and waited for another opening in the fight, his eyes widened as he spotted a familiar face: the man with the cut nose from The Wobbly Goat. Jonmarc gave a cry and tried to head toward the man, sure he was one of the enemy fighters, but the battle surged and a sea of bodies cut Jonmarc off from his quarry. By the time he had fought his way clear, the man had disappeared.

The whistle of a blade nearby made Jonmarc duck, barely missing the sword that nearly took off one ear, he spun to meet the challenge. A big man cursed his mistake, and his two-handed swing came at Jonmarc hard enough to slice through bone. Jonmarc deflected the blow, having no desire for the powerful swing to break his wrist, and then slashed with the short sword in his left hand, scoring a slice across the big man's tunic. The enemy mercenary's cuirass kept the blow from doing damage, but the man's face reddened at the insult and he came at Jonmarc with a bellow like a wounded bull.

Jonmarc dropped and rolled, barely managing not to be kicked or stepped on in the crowded plaza, and came up in a squat just behind the giant, slashing through the merc's boots and across his hamstrings. The huge man gave a shout of pain and let loose with a torrent of obscenities, then staggered and fell to his knees. He growled like a feral beast and took a last, desperate swing at Jonmarc, managing to get in a deep gash on Jonmarc's left arm before he could run him through from behind.

The battle gave him no leeway to bind up his wound. A few steps away, Jonmarc saw Harrtuck fighting not far from where Valjan had cleared a path for others of the War Dogs to follow. While Jonmarc had been busy with his opponents, it looked as if the fighting had turned in the favor the Dogs, though their enemies were far from ceding defeat.

The knife slid into Jonmarc's side before he saw it coming, and he gasped with pain but kept his feet, even as hot blood trickled down his skin. Anger fueled him as much as courage, and perhaps a dose of fear. Maybe his attacker expected Jonmarc to go down quickly, but one thing was certain: he was not prepared for Jonmarc's crashing blow that slid along his blade to the hilt, or for the tip of a short sword ripping into his ribs.

The enemy merc's face twisted into an ugly mask as he raised his sword for a death blow. But before he could bring down his strike, the merc's body jerked and he stiffened, as a bloody blade poked through his belly. The big man fell to his knees with a garbled cry, and Harrtuck pulled his blade loose.

"By the Dark Lady! You look hard used," he observed. "Can you walk?"

Jonmarc nodded, following on sheer willpower, ignoring the sharp pain in his side although it threatened to black him out. By now, the square was definitely less crowded with fighters, though bodies littered the paving stones and the ground was red with blood. He staggered, fixing his gaze on where the War Dogs rallied near the center of the plaza. Most of the fighting had moved off to the edges of the square, and it looked like the War Dogs were running off the last of their enemies.

Valjan and Harrtuck were bloodied, as were the other Dogs, but there looked to be more of them standing than fallen. Jonmarc gritted his teeth, determined he would not give in to the blackness that edged his vision. He sheathed his sword and clapped his hand to his side. His shirt was soaked, and warm, wet blood covered his hand.

Valjan shouted orders to the War Dogs giving chase to the quickly retreating attackers. Harrtuck was just off to one side, already shouting for soldiers to gather the wounded and dispatch the dying. A handful of other War Dogs were nearby, but their attention was on the square's perimeter, alert for another attack. That was when Jonmarc spotted the man behind Valjan, and saw the glint of a knife raised behind the Captain's back.

"Stop!" Jonmarc shouted, still a few steps too far away to reach the attacker in time. The man glanced his way, just enough for Jonmarc to see that he was missing the end of his nose.

Jonmarc's reaction came before he had time to think. He threw his short sword at the man with all his remaining might, a move he had often practiced but never perfected. His aim went wide, but the blade caught the noseless man in the shoulder instead of the chest and he staggered backward with a grunt, enough of a warning for Valjan to turn. His sword batted away the assassin's knife, then drove forward into the man's chest. Only then did Jonmarc realize that the man with the cut nose wore the armband of a War Dog.

Valjan's sword sank hilt-deep between the assassin's ribs.

The man gave a choked cry, blood leaked from his open mouth, and then his body jerked and sagged, sliding down the crimson length of Valjan's blade.

Jonmarc felt the world tilt around him and sank to his knees. Everyone was shouting, and two War Dogs grabbed Jonmarc by the shoulders as Valjan strode over.

"This is the man! He tried to kill you with his short sword!" one of the mercs said, giving Jonmarc a hard shake

"You idiot!" Harrtuck barreled through the fray. "Ekstan was the traitor. He was about to knife the Captain from behind. Jonmarc threw his sword to stop him. I saw it all—I was just too far away to do anything about it," he said, glowering at the men who held Jonmarc.

"Who are you? And how did you suspect Ekstan?" Valjan snapped, turning his attention to Jonmarc, who was sure that only the guards holding him upright were keeping him from collapsing onto the bloodied paving stones.

"I saw him... in the tavern. He was with Hagen."

"He told me earlier about spotting Hagen," Harrtuck said, after a few creative curses. "This is Jonmarc Vahanian. Steen recommended him. Came from Linton's caravan."

"I want to be a War Dog," Jonmarc managed. His mouth was dry, and his sight was dimming. Valjan might have said something in reply, and Harrtuck was yelling at the guards, but Jonmarc could not make out the words, and all around him, the bloody square faded to black.

"You CERTAINLY TOOK your time about waking up." Harrtuck's voice was a growl, but Jonmarc thought he heard a hint of relief in the words. He tried to move, grimaced at the tenderness in his side, and lay still.

"Yeah, it'll be sore for a while," Harrtuck said. "You were lucky the one who knifed you wasn't a few inches to the side, or you'd have been even harder for the healer to fix. As it was, you gave them a hard go of it."

"How long was I out?" Jonmarc managed.

"Most of a day," Harrtuck replied, and it sounded as if he had a mouthful of food. Jonmarc opened his eyes, and saw that Harrtuck was chewing on a biscuit. "Don't worry," He said with a chuckle. "There's enough for both of us—and a flask of whiskey beside the bed, if your side still pains you." He grinned. "Or even if it doesn't."

"Valjan—"

"The Captain sends his regards," Harrtuck said, spraying crumbs as he talked. "Made me go over the story three times of who you were and why you were there, but in the end he agreed to take you on."

"I'm in?" Despite his weariness and the discomfort of his healing wound, Jonmarc felt relieved.

"Conditionally," Harrtuck said, raising a hand as if to slow him down. "You have a month to prove yourself. Although I think you've done some of that already."

"Hagen?"

"The whore-spawned son of a bitch ran off," Harrtuck replied. "We'll find him. My bet is he was behind the attack on the house, and you saw him with the men who jumped us in the alley. Good observation, spotting those eyes of his." He sighed. "Ah well. Valjan's a patient hunter. He'll find Hagen, and make him pay." Harrtuck raised an eyebrow. "Another point for you, since you're the one who tipped us off to him."

"What now?" Jonmarc asked. Despite the healer's magic, he felt awful, and he suspected it would be several days before he was ready for another fight. But he was alive, healing, and at least conditionally a War Dog. It was a good day.

"Now, we regroup, get people patched up, and line up more work, like we always do," Harrtuck replied. "We put a dent into the Black Wolves they won't forget, so I don't think we'll have anything to worry about from them for a while."

Harrtuck tore off another hunk of bread and washed it down with ale. "So for the moment, get some sleep. Heal up. Rest while you can. There'll be new trouble, soon enough. There always is."

If you want to see more stories about Jonmarc Vahanian, check out The Chronicles of the Necromancer series and The Fallen Kings Cycle books, as well as the Jonmarc Vahanian Adventures on ebook.

ABOUT THE AUTHOR

GAIL Z. MARTIN writes epic fantasy, urban fantasy, and steampunk. She is the author of The Chronicles of The Necromancer series (*The Summoner, The Blood King, Dark Haven, Dark Lady's Chosen*) from Solaris and The Fallen Kings Cycle (*The Sworn, The Dread*) from Orbit. The Ascendant Kingdoms Saga is her post-apocalyptic medieval epic fantasy series, with *Ice Forged, Reign of Ash, War of Shadows, and Shadow and Flame* from Orbit.

Iron and Blood: The Jake Desmet Adventures a new steampunk series (Solaris) was co-authored with Larry N. Martin. *Deadly Curiosities* and *Vendetta: A Deadly Curiosities Novel* are her urban fantasy series set in Charleston, SC; and Gail writes four series of ebook short stories/novellas: *The Jonmarc Vahanian Adventures, The Deadly Curiosities Adventures, The Blaine McFadden Adventures* and *The Storm and Fury Adventures* (co-authored with Larry N. Martin). Her work has appeared in over 20 US/UK anthologies. Newest anthologies include: *The Big Bad 2, Athena's Daughters, Heroes, Space, Contact Light, With Great Power, The Weird Wild West, The Side of Good/The Side of Evil, Alien Artifacts, The Shadowed Path, Realms of Imagination, Clockwork Universe: Steampunk vs. Aliens.*

Find her at www.ChroniclesOfTheNecromancer.com, on Twitter @GailZMartin, on Facebook.com/WinterKingdoms, at DisquietingVisions.com blog and MagicalWords.net blogs, on GhostInTheMachinePodcast.com, on Goodreads https://www.goodreads.com/GailZMartin and free excerpts on Wattpad http://wattpad.com/GailZMartin. Join Gail's street team, The Shadow Alliance, on Facebook for exclusive sneak peek excerpts and more!

CHRONICLES OF THE NECROMANCER
THE SUMMONER

The world of Prince Martris Drayke is thrown into sudden chaos when his brother murders their father and seizes the throne. Forced to flee, with only a handful of loyal colleagues to support him, Martris must seek retribution and restore his father's honor. But if the living are arrayed against him, Martris must learn to harness his burgeoning magical powers to call on a different set of allies: the ranks of the dead.

The Summoner is an epic, engrossing tale of loss and revenge, of life and afterlife – and the thin line between them.

The Summoner *marks the debut of a stunning new talent in the fantasy firmament, and the beginning of an epic story that will leave readers gasping for more.*

"Adventure with whole-hearted passion." – *SFX*

UK/US ISBN: 978-1-84416-468-4

Book Two of the
CHRONICLES OF THE NECROMANCER
THE BLOOD KING

Having narrowly escaped being murdered by his evil brother, Jared, Prince Martris Drayke must take control of his magical abilities to summon the dead, and gather an army big enough to claim back the throne of his dead father. But it isn't merely Jared that Tris must combat. The dark mage, Foor Arontala, has schemes to cause an inbalance in the currents of magic and raise the Obsidian King...

Gail Z. Martin returns with the second thrilling installment in the Chronicles of the Necromancer series.

> **"A rich, evocative story with vivid, believable characters moving through a beautifully realized world with all the quirks, depths and levels of a real place. A terrific read!"**
> – *A.J. Hartley, author, The Mask of Atreus*

UK/US ISBN: 978-1-84416-531-5

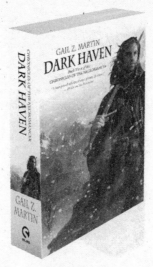

Book Three of the
CHRONICLES OF THE NECROMANCER
DARK HAVEN

The kingdom of Margolan lies in ruin. Martris Drayke, the new king, must rebuild his country in the aftermath of battle, while a new war looms on the horizon. Meanwhile Jonmarc Vahanian is now the Lord of Dark Haven, and there is defiance from the vampires of the Vayash Moru at the prospect of a mortal leader. But can he earn their trust, and at what cost?

Dark Haven continues the thrilling adventures of the Chronicles of the Necromancer series.

"Attractive characters and an imaginative setting combine in an excellent, fast-moving quest novel." – *David Drake, author of the* Lord of the Isles *series on* The Summoner

UK ISBN: 978-1-84416-708-1 / US ISBN: 978-1-84416-598-8

Book Four of the
CHRONICLES OF THE NECROMANCER
DARK LADY'S CHOSEN

Treachery and blood magic threaten King Martris Drayke's hold
on the throne he risked everything to win. As the battle against a
traitor lord comes to its final days, war, plague and betrayal bring
Margolan to the brink of destruction. Civil war looms in Isencroft.
Finally, in Dark Haven, Lord Jonmarc Vahanian has bargained his
soul for vengeance as he leads the vayash moru against a dangerous
rogue who would usher in a future drenched in blood.

**"Every time I start to get bored with epic fantasy, a writer
like Gail Z. Martin comes along and makes me fall in love
with the genre all over again."** *– J. F. Lewis,*
author of Staked, Revamped

UK ISBN: 978-1-84416-830-9 / US ISBN: 978-1-84416-831-6